MURDER
at the MILL

A picture hides a thousand lies . . .
And only Iris Grey can uncover the truth

M.B. SHAW

TRAPEZE

First published in Great Britain in 2017 by Trapeze
an imprint of The Orion Publishing Group Ltd
Carmelite House, 50 Victoria Embankment
London EC4Y 0DZ

An Hachette UK company

1 3 5 7 9 10 8 6 4 2

A CIP catalogue record for this book
is available from the British Library.

ISBN 978 1 4091 7123 2

Typeset by Born Group

Printed and bound in Great Britain by Clays Ltd, St Ives plc

www.orionbooks.co.uk

To Fred Kahane
Who keeps me sane.

PROLOGUE

Christmas Day 2017

The sound of the water was deafening. This stretch of the River Itchen was narrow, little more than a stream in places, but it was deep, and the current was fast, causing the ancient waterwheel to churn and splash and creak with unexpected ferocity, like a battlefield's roar. Somewhere in the distance, church bells were pealing, fighting their way through the din. *Five o'clock. As good a time to die as any.*

Tying on the stone was easy, despite the darkness and the noise and the cold that numbed one's fingers. Everything had been easy, in fact. All that fear, the stomach-souring anticipation of the act, had been for nothing in the end. Everything had gone exactly according to plan. So far, anyway. There was a symmetry to that, at least, the satisfaction of a job well done. One could even call it a pleasure of sorts.

Across the bitterly cold water, the lights of Mill House glowed warm and inviting. Through the sash windows of the Wetherbys' grand drawing room, a Christmas tree twinkled. Gaudy and colourful, rising out of a shiny sea of discarded wrapping paper, torn from joyously opened gifts, it had clearly been decorated by children, as all Christmas trees should be. Few things in life were sadder than an 'adult' Christmas tree, tastefully decked out in themed colours. Where was the magic in that?

Not that it mattered anymore.

Nothing mattered anymore.

The water was as cold as stone, cold enough to make one flinch. But only momentarily. It was time to let go. The river opened up eagerly to receive its Christmas gift, pulling it down into the familiar black depths with the cloying, greedy embrace of a lover.

Feet first. Then legs. Torso. Head.

Gone.

On the opposite bank of the river, a torchlight danced.

Lorcan Wetherby, youngest son of the celebrated author Dom Wetherby and his wife, Ariadne, had ventured outside to play with his Christmas presents: a *Scooby-Doo* flashlight and a motorised toy boat, his pride and joy. Lorcan could still feel the excitement of the afternoon, when his oldest brother Marcus had pulled the big parcel wrapped in holly-sprigged paper out from under the tree. Handing out Christmas presents one by one under the tree after lunch was a family tradition, prolonging both the agony and the ecstasy for generations of Wetherby children.

'"To Lorcan",' Marcus read aloud. '"Merry Christmas and all our love, Mummy and Daddy."'

Lorcan had torn at the paper like a puppy, emitting a squeal of pure delight when he saw it. Exactly like the one on TV.

'Remoke control!' he beamed at his mother. 'It's remoke control!'

Ariadne beamed back. She adored her son. 'That's right, darling.'

Waiting for his father to put the batteries in and set the boat up had been torture. But after inhaling two slices of Ariadne's homemade Christmas cake so quickly Marcus could have sworn he saw marzipan chunks coming out of his little brother's nose, the boat was finally ready and Lorcan had raced down the sloping lawn to the banks of the Itchen to play with it.

Dark had long since fallen. Recently Lorcan had felt afraid of the dark, and particularly of 'ghosts', which he saw constantly, hovering around every tree or lichen-covered wall. His father, Dom, blamed it on *Scooby-Doo*, a new obsession. His mother wasn't so sure.

'I wouldn't be too quick to dismiss it. Maybe he's really seeing something.'

'Like what?' Dom Wetherby frowned. 'Things that go "bump" in the night?'

Ariadne smiled patiently. For a writer, Dominic could be terribly unimaginative at times. 'This house is over four hundred years old, darling,' she reminded him. 'There may well be ghosts here. Children like Lorcan often see things other people don't, or can't. Maybe he's just more attuned to the supernatural than we are.'

Attuned or not, Lorcan wasn't afraid tonight. He *had* seen a ghost as it happened, less than an hour ago, moving through the woods, white and tall and looming. But the ghost hadn't seen him. He was too busy with whatever he had in his hands. Besides, Lorcan had his *Scooby-Doo* torch, it was Christmas, and he was at home at the Mill with Mummy and Daddy. He was safe. Cocooned. It was like Mummy said: 'Ghosts are only people, Lorcan. Ordinary people. It's just that you're seeing them in an extraordinary way.' Lorcan wasn't sure what that meant exactly, but it made him feel better.

Ghosts were people.

People, in Lorcan's experience, were nice.

He played with his boat till his hands were so cold they hurt. The church bells rang. He counted them. *One, two, three, four, five . . . six.* Time to go in.

Crossing at the bridge safely, where his father had shown him, he reached down gingerly to pull his boat out of the reeds. Behind him, he could hear the waterwheel turning, the familiar sound of rushing water that was the soundtrack to his life. Lorcan Wetherby loved the river. He loved it like a person. He loved the waterwheel and the Mill. He loved his home. His family.

The boat was stuck. The spiky part at the bottom – the 'keel', Marcus had called it – had become entangled in something, some part of the cold, watery underworld of the Itchen. Lorcan tugged harder, but still it wouldn't budge. Carefully setting down the remote-control handset next to him on the bridge to get a better grip, he tried again, with both hands this time, plunging his arms into the frigid water right up to the elbows. Leaning back, he pulled as hard as he could, his muscles burning with exertion as he yanked and twisted the precious boat, willing it to break free.

Beneath the surface, something snapped.

A small movement at first, then a bigger one, then in one great rush up came the boat, rising out of the water like the kraken. It was still heavy, still caught up in something, but Lorcan had hold of it now, the whole, beautiful vessel safe in his two strong hands. He sat back triumphant and exhausted. After a few deep breaths, he began to try to unwind the slimy strands still coiled round the boat's bottom.

And then he saw it.

It wasn't reeds that had wrapped themselves, vice-like, round the keel.

It was hair.

Human hair.

Lorcan stared down in horror into the face of the corpse, its skin stretched tight and ghoulish from being pulled by the scalp. White, sightless eyes stared back at him.

Not even the sound of the river could drown out Lorcan's screams.

PART ONE

CHAPTER ONE

Two months earlier

Iris Grey set down her brush and blew on the tips of her frozen fingers.

It was a bitterly cold morning in Hazelford, leaden and drear, with a stinging October wind that presaged the end of autumn and the onset of winter in earnest. But despite the cold, there was something about the heavy darkness of the morning sky, with its clouds purple and swollen like bruises, that made Iris want to get outside and paint. That and the fact that she'd been awake since four, staring at the ceiling in Mill Cottage, fighting back her own dark clouds of depression, running over everything in her mind until she could stand it no longer. She had to *do* something.

Picking up her brush again, she dipped the tip into the bright white oil paint she used to recreate the tiny, glancing flashes of light reflected off the river. *At least I'm here and not in London*, she thought. *Not stuck in that miserable flat with Ian.*

Ian McBride, Iris's husband of almost eighteen years, was back at their place in Clapham, no doubt still fast asleep. Nothing stopped Ian from sleeping. Not earthquakes or hurricanes or bombs, and certainly not the trivial matter of a disintegrating marriage. *He's my estranged husband now*, Iris thought. Then she laughed, because 'estranged' was a stupid word that nobody except newspaper columnists ever used, the same way that railway announcers said 'alight' when they meant 'get off the train' or 'beverage' instead of drink.

Still, 'estranged' was what Iris and Ian were, given that Iris had rented Mill Cottage on her own and often spent weeks here at a time without so much as a phone call home. Then again, whenever she did go home, she and Ian barely spoke to one another, making it hard to know what the point of a phone call might be.

Five foot two and naturally slim, people generally considered Iris to be pretty in a petite, elfin, slightly bird-like way. At forty-one, she could easily have passed for five years younger, with her dark hair, shiny like a raven's feathers, pale, clear skin and sad chocolate-brown eyes that were too big for her face and lent her an almost cartoonish look. On the other hand, she was not a woman who 'took care of herself', as the women's magazines liked to say. She rarely wore make-up, and had never in her life indulged in a pedicure or a facial or any of the other countless rituals that most of her girlfriends seemed to devote so much time to. And although she did like clothes, her art agent had once defined Iris's style as 'deranged jackdaw' – picking out the brightest, shiniest, most colourful garments available and throwing them onto her body in as random and thoughtless a manner as possible. From time to time, for special occasions, Iris would tone it down and, when elegantly dressed, was a strikingly beautiful woman. But today she was wearing a more typical ensemble of oversized dungarees tucked into wellington boots, a rainbow-striped polo-neck sweater, fingerless gloves made to look like sheep, a charity-shop duffel coat two sizes too big for her and a knitted Peruvian hat.

Staring intently at the swirling waters of the Itchen, Iris considered her next brush stroke, pushing thoughts of her husband out of her mind. God, it was hard to paint water. An accomplished portrait painter, Iris was an expert at capturing human expression and emotion, boiling her subjects down to their essence and recording that essence on canvas. Stupidly, she'd always imagined landscape painting as being more static. Less challenging, perhaps, because it was less alive. How wrong could you be?

If nothing else, standing on a cold Hampshire riverbank since the crack of arse had taught Iris that everything was alive. Everything was moving, evolving, changing constantly. The river swirled and danced and rushed; the clouds drifted and morphed their way across the sky; the spindly tree branches swayed and shivered pathetically in the wind like the starved limbs of concentration-camp prisoners, pleading for escape. Even the mellow gold stone of the Mill itself seemed to have a life of its own, glowing with light and warmth at one moment and retreating into gloomy shadow the next.

It really was a beautiful house. The perfect size – large enough to feel stately and grand, yet small enough to remain romantic and charming – the Mill at Hazelford was Iris's idea of the quintessential English country idyll. Both the house and Iris's rented cottage in the grounds belonged to Dom Wetherby, author of the wildly popular Grimshaw books, a series of crime novels featuring an ageing, cantankerous detective of the same name. Iris had started reading one of the books a few years ago, but then lost it halfway through and never got around to finishing it. It was some story involving a Swiss bank and Nazi gold. There might have been a Russian prostitute in it. In all honesty, Iris wasn't really a fan. In her view, the real world was already more than sufficiently populated with grumpy middle-aged men without the need to add to their number in fiction. But she admired Dom Wetherby's larger-than-life personality and had always coveted his stunning house, which she'd driven past numerous times, en route to various repertory theatres with Ian.

Iris's husband was a playwright, at one time very successful, although these days a medium run in provincial rep, otherwise known as crumbling, half-empty small-town theatres, was the best Ian McBride could realistically hope for. One dreary weekend at the end of the summer, Iris had just happened to see an advertisement in the *Sunday Times* 'Property' section that felt like fate.

It was headed: 'The Mill at Hazelford'.

I know that house, Iris thought. *That's my dream house.*

'Two-bedroom cottage to let,' ran the copy, 'on idyllic private Hampshire estate. Would suit artist or writer.'

Before she had time to talk herself out of it, Iris rang the number on the ad and rented Mill Cottage for six months. *It will be my artistic escape,* she lied to herself. *A place to go and paint in peace.*

She waited for the inevitable explosion from Ian – they couldn't afford it, not after all the money they'd blown on IVF. It was an indulgence. How dare Iris commit to something like that without discussing it with him first, et cetera, et cetera . . . But in the event, he merely shrugged and went back upstairs to write. Iris tried not to admit to herself how bad a sign this was for the state of their marriage.

Originally the idea was that she would go to the cottage to paint at weekends, but weekends soon became weeks. Fast-forward a month and a half and here Iris was, effectively living in Hazelford full-time. Alone. Like a mad cat lady, only without the cats.

In their place Iris had her doll's house, a beautifully made antique Dutch model, hand-turned in elm and complete with working sash windows and miniature louvred shutters. It had been Iris's most prized possession since childhood, a gift from her grandmother Violet, and she had always treasured it. Obviously she knew a forty-one-year-old woman 'playing' with doll's houses had more than a touch of the pathetic about it. No doubt she should have grown out of it years ago. But admiring and re-arranging the miniature rooms, adding over the decades to her collection of tiny, perfectly formed objects, had brought Iris immense pleasure and peace, and it was such a harmless hobby, in the end, she couldn't bring herself to give it up.

Pulling her thick duffel coat more tightly around her against the cold, she glanced up and smiled broadly. A swan had unexpectedly appeared round the river bend, followed by four cygnets. Pristine white and regal, the mother bird extended her elegant neck and dramatically spread her wings just for a moment, shaking them out like a Brazilian carnival dancer showing off her bejewelled costume. Then she re-folded them neatly onto her back, all the while gliding towards Iris. Behind her, her four adorable brown chicks bobbed along awkwardly, as ungainly as their mother was graceful.

'Oh, how lovely!' Iris said aloud, watching the little family pass. But as soon as they'd disappeared from sight, the sadness hit her like a bowling ball in the stomach.

You're being ridiculous, Iris told herself firmly. *You're an educated, rational woman. You will not feel envious of a bloody bird!*

Time for a cup of tea. Putting down her brushes, cold to the bone, Iris held the still-wet canvas at arm's length and was heading towards the cottage when raised voices made her turn round.

'Stop! What are you *doing*?'

Ariadne Wetherby, Dom's wife and Iris's landlady, sounded frightened. Iris had barely met the family since she took the cottage. The Wetherbys kept themselves to themselves,. But on the rare occasions their paths had crossed, Dom Wetherby's wife had always come across as a gentle, floaty, hippyish, softly spoken sort of person. It made the alarm in her voice now doubly disconcerting.

'What? D'you think I'm going to drown you?'

The other voice was a man's, a young man's. Also loud, but there was no fear in his tone. Only malice.

'Push you in and hold you down? Like the witch that you are?' He laughed, a horrible, throaty sound that broke into a smoker's cough at the end. 'God knows you deserve it.'

'Stop it! Billy . . . no!'

A scream, loud and shrill, made Iris drop her brushes and canvas and scramble up the bank. Slipping on the wet ground, mud splattering onto coat and face, she saw them within seconds, just a few yards further along the bank. A slim, dark-haired young man had grabbed hold of Ariadne Wetherby's outstretched arms and was forcing her backwards towards the rushing river. From where she was, Iris could only see Ariadne's back, but the man's face was clearly visible: handsome, yet made ugly by the contorted, sadistic expression, the narrowed eyes and the cruel, mocking curve of his lips.

'Is everything all right?' Iris shouted over the roar of the river. Clearly everything wasn't, but this seemed the best way to get their attention, to make the man realise he'd been seen at least.

It worked. He looked up, startled, and instantly released Ariadne.

'Everything's fine,' he shouted back coolly.

Ignoring him, Iris moved closer to where they were, addressing herself solely to Ariadne. 'Mrs Wetherby? Are you OK? Do you need help?'

'No, no, thank you. I'm fine.' Ariadne straightened her wind-swept hair, the imprint of her earlier panic still visible in her strained expression. But then she smiled, relieved, and the tension evaporated. Slipping her hand around the young man's waist, she leaned into him, as if the two of them were the best of friends. 'And please, you must call me Ariadne. Sorry if we disturbed you. This is my middle son, Billy. He'll be living with us at the Mill for a while.'

The young man raised an unenthusiastic hand in greeting. 'Hello.'

Iris didn't wave back, or move any closer. She'd seen the cruelty in Billy's smile and eyes earlier, the way he'd revelled in his mother's terror until Iris came along and surprised them.

'Billy, this is Iris Grey, our tenant at the cottage,' Ariadne Wetherby continued briskly, doing her best to normalise the situation. 'Iris is an artist.'

'So I see,' said Billy, taking in Iris's eclectic outfit with a sardonic, disdainful look. 'I took an art class last year,' he added, more convivially, mirroring his mother's cheerful manner.

Ariadne looked pained. 'Iris doesn't need to hear about that, darling.'

Billy shrugged. 'Doesn't she? Oh well. If you say so, Mother dear. Doesn't matter, anyway. Turns out I was shit at it.' He winked at Iris.

An awkward silence descended. How exactly was Iris supposed to respond to a comment like that? Had she warmed to Billy at all, she might have offered some words of encouragement. As it was, she couldn't remember the last time that she'd taken such an instant dislike to a person.

'You're sure you're all right?' she asked Ariadne, pointedly ignoring Billy.

'Quite sure, thank you.'

Iris turned away. Making her way back down the slippery bank towards her cottage, one thought played and replayed in her head.

I wonder what would have happened if I hadn't interrupted them? Would he really have hurt her? Pushed her in?

After a disappointing morning's sketching, and still haunted by her earlier encounter on the riverbank, at three o'clock Iris decided to walk into the village for a restorative brew at Hambly's Tea Shop and to buy some food for supper. Ian had once described her as being as skilled in the kitchen as an octopus on a mountain bike. Unkind, perhaps, but undeniably true. Iris couldn't make toast without setting off the smoke alarm, and sometimes had fantasies about the horrible deaths she would like to inflict on Deliciously Ella. Thankfully, Hazelford was posh enough to have a village shop that stocked excellent organic ready meals (not Ella's) and homemade deli salads, so she was in no immediate danger of starvation.

Hazelford Stores was at the very top of the High Street, a charming, steeply cobbled lane leading from Jessop's Rise at the top of the village all the way down to St Anne's Church and the river at the bottom. Widely regarded as the prettiest village in Hampshire, Hazelford had been used as the setting for numerous Jane Austen adaptations and ITV period dramas, and since taking the cottage, Iris couldn't shake the feeling that she was living on a film set. Not that that made her love the place any less. On a clear day, standing outside Hazelford Stores, you could make out the spires of Winchester Cathedral in the distance, although today's miserable weather made it hard even to see across the road to Tannenheim's bookshop, another of Iris's favourite haunts.

A little bell rang as she opened the shop door, but nobody heard it. They were all too busy arguing.

'It's a bloody disgrace is what it is. Skipping the meeting is one thing, but not to send apologies? It's so rude, Jean. It's insulting. He's supposed to be the sodding chairman!'

Harry Masters, a retired piano teacher in his early seventies and a devoted, life-long Hazelford resident, had worked himself up into a fury. The usually mild-mannered old man was red in the face, with strands of grey hair sticking up at oddly wild angles from where he'd run his hands through them. The artist in Iris would have loved to sketch him.

'All Dom Wetherby cared about was stopping the planners from developing those fields. Now his beloved view is safe, he can't even be bothered to *pretend* to do his job. He's probably sat at home, sending out invitations to his precious Christmas Eve party. Wondering which D-list celebrities he's forgotten to ask this year.'

'Come on, Harry,' Jean Chivers, Hazelford Stores' proprietress said reasonably. 'We're all happy enough to go to the Christmas Eve party and drink his champagne, you included. And we all voted against the development. Nobody liked that smarmy Russian. It wasn't just Wetherby.'

'Yes, but *why*, Jean? *Why* were we against the development?'

'Because it was bad for the village.'

'Exactly!' The piano teacher warmed to his theme. 'We cared about the village. But do you honestly think Wetherby gives a rat's arse about Hazelford? Course he doesn't. All Dom Wetherby cares about is Dom Wetherby. He only asks us to his party every year so he can look like the lord of the manor, throwing a few scraps to the village peasants.' Harry Masters folded his arms with furious finality.

'Look, Harry, we all know you was upset when Wetherby got elected chairman,' Alan Chivers, Jean's husband, observed good-naturedly, loading the old man's groceries into an eco-friendly paper bag. 'But at the end of the day, he *was* elected. He put his name in the hat and people voted for him. Lots of people.'

'Blinded by celebrity,' Harry muttered darkly, handing over a twenty-pound note and pocketing his change. 'More fool them. Well, now they're reaping what they sow, aren't they? They've got a chairman who's too important, too famous, to turn up to meetings. I call it bloody outrageous.'

Grabbing his groceries, he stormed out, brushing past Iris and a couple of other customers in his blind anger.

Jean Chivers looked up and rolled her eyes at Iris. 'Don't mind Harry. He's got his knickers in a twist about Dom Wetherby again.'

'Oh,' said Iris, still feeling shaken from her earlier run-in with Dom Wetherby's wife and son, and not quite sure what she could add to the conversation.

She came into Hazelford Stores most days for something or other, but had never spoken to Jean or her husband, or to any of the locals really, barring the usual 'good morning's and 'thank you's. She couldn't say why that was, exactly, as she'd never considered herself shy. As a younger woman, she'd been very sociable, happy to talk to strangers or to meet new people. But in the past few years, as things became worse and worse with Ian, and no baby arrived to miraculously fix everything, Iris had retreated. She'd continued working, trying to laugh off her dying marriage and failed fertility treatments, pretending to herself that nothing had changed. But the reality was, her world had shrunk, imperceptibly at first, and then irrevocably, until one day she woke up to find the only things left in it were a husband she no longer loved, a pair of clapped-out ovaries and her painting.

'Harry used to be chairman, you see,' Jean Chivers prattled on. 'Before Wetherby. He ran this village for a long time.'

'Nine years,' another customer piped up, a young woman pushing a snotty, whining toddler in a buggy.

'Nine years, was it?' Jean nodded sagely, turning back to Iris. 'But then last year, out of the blue, Dom Wetherby stood against him. Turned up to a meeting one night in the hall and gave a speech about stopping the developers, some Russian group, and how important it was to have a "strong voice" for the village, someone people would really listen to. And of course everybody voted for him, because we all love them Grimshaw books, and Dom Wetherby's famous and you know . . .'

'Influential!' her husband shouted helpfully from the stockroom.

'Exactly,' said Jean. 'Influential. But poor old Harry took it personal. He lived for that job, you see.'

'Yes, I can see that,' said Iris uselessly. She was woefully out of the habit of making small talk.

'Of course, it won't stop him turning up to the Mill on Christmas Eve and stuffing his face at Wetherby's expense. Eyeballing all the famous people, like the rest of us do,' said Alan Chivers, emerging from the stockroom and cracking his knuckles as he put forth his opinion. 'Personally, I reckon he's got a bit of a thing for Wetherby's wife.'

Iris rallied, slightly. This sort of gossip was much more her forte. She enjoyed a good love-triangle scandal, and hadn't spent years of her life glued to *Coronation Street* and *EastEnders* for nothing.

'I can see why, too,' the shopkeeper continued, getting into his stride. 'Harry's lonely. Never been married. And Mrs Wetherby's a wonderful woman. Great-looking, too. For an older lady, obviously,' he added, glancing nervously at his wife. 'She's not a patch on my Jean. But for someone like Harry . . .'

'Oh, Mrs Wetherby's lovely,' Jean Chivers agreed magnanimously. 'She really is. The way she cares for that poor boy.'

Iris took 'that poor boy' to be Lorcan, Dom and Ariadne's fifteen-year-old son. Lorcan had been born with Down's syndrome and had the mental capacity of a five-year-old. He also had a relentlessly sunny, happy nature, no doubt thanks in part to having a mother who doted on him.

'And then that awful business with the other son.' Shaking her head ruefully, Jean dropped her voice to a stage whisper. '*Going to prison.*'

'Do you mean Billy?' Iris piped up. Nothing could have surprised her less than learning that the bullying, spiteful young man she'd witnessed terrorising his mother at the riverbank this morning had been in trouble with the law.

'That's right.' Jean peered at Iris more closely. 'Do you know him, then?'

'Me? Oh no,' Iris explained hastily. 'I ran into him with his mother this morning, that's all.'

Jean's eyes widened. 'He's never back home already! So soon? You ran into him, you say?' The shopkeeper suddenly pointed at Iris, as if she'd just remembered something. 'You live down there, don't you? Aren't you that artist who rented Mill Cottage?'

Iris's heart sank again. Now she was going to get the third degree from these well-meaning people. She should have just bought her sodding ready meal and run. 'That's right,' she said briskly, hoping to end the conversation there. Fumbling in her handbag for her purse, she plonked her chicken risotto and cheap bottle of Rioja down on the counter with an air of finality.

'What's your name again?' Jean asked.

'Iris. Iris Grey.' She sighed, wondering how long it would be before she could escape back to her sofa and box set of *The Affair* and get quietly drunk on her own.

'And you actually met Billy Wetherby? Today?' Apparently Jean wasn't giving up.

'When'd he get out?' asked Alan.

'I didn't meet him, exactly,' Iris explained. Clearly the only way out of this conversation was going to be through it. 'I saw him and his mother down by the river when I was painting.'

'What's he like?' the young mother asked. She'd been waiting to pay, and listening all this time, glued to the drama.

He's creepy, thought Iris. *Creepy and cruel and vile and unsettling.*

'I really don't know. It was freezing and wet. We said hello and then I went back inside.'

'You must know them a bit, though? The family? Living there and all . . .'

'I really don't.'

Jean and Alan exchanged glances. Clearly Iris was disappointing her audience. She was the 'Belgium' of village gossip, having scored the proverbial *nul points*. Stuffing her shopping into a bag, she blurted out an awkward 'goodbye' and bolted out of the door.

Outside on the cobbled street, Iris actually ran down the hill all the way to the churchyard and the entrance to Mill Lane, desperate suddenly to be alone. Rounding the corner, she stopped at last, doubling over against the flint wall to catch her breath. Setting her groceries down on the pavement, she felt a complete fool.

What on earth is wrong me? Since when can't I handle a little village gossip?

Perhaps the threat of violence that had hung around Billy Wetherby at the river earlier had unnerved her more than she'd realised. Whatever the reason, she found herself reluctant to talk about him, or any of the Wetherbys for that matter.

Iris trudged home, depressed. But as she approached Mill Cottage, her spirits suddenly lifted. Someone had left something on her doorstep, a beautifully wrapped package in classic striped red-and-green paper, with a large red silk bow on the top. *How adorable!* Things like that never happened in London.

Setting her shopping on the ground, Iris picked it up and unlocked the door.

Carrying the present inside, she placed it on the table, taking off her coat and putting her food to one side before turning her attention back to its gaudy loveliness. The ribbon was so shiny and thick it seemed wrong to cut it, so instead she carefully untied the bow, peeling off all the tiny strips of sticky tape gently and one by one, so as to keep the paper intact while she unwrapped the box. Inside, carefully nestled on a soft bed of cotton wool, was a tiny Victorian lamp for her doll's house. Rare and perfect, just looking at it made Iris feel instantly happy. She searched around in the box for a card or note, but there was nothing.

How extraordinary.

Pottering around the kitchen, Iris pondered the mystery of her secret gift. Only her family and very closest friends knew about her doll's-house fetish. But the lamp had clearly been hand-delivered, by someone local. None of Iris's friends or family lived near Hazelford. There was Ian, of course, but he was in London and, as far as Iris knew, not in a gift-giving frame of mind, at least not where she was concerned.

Baffled, and suddenly exhausted after her eventful day, Iris put the lamp aside and went upstairs for a bath. Afterwards she changed into an old, stretched man's T-shirt she wore as a nightie and settled down to ogle Dominic West's naked bum while eating her chicken supper, washed down with almost an entire bottle of Rioja. *Bliss.* Since living alone, Iris had noticed she'd started drinking more. It was on her list of 'things I need to deal with', just not terribly close to the top. Once the episode was over, she finally returned her attention to the lamp, taking it with her as she climbed up the rickety attic stairs to the room under the eaves where her doll's house had been stored since she moved in.

Lovingly blowing dust off the tiny dining-room table, and placing the lamp inside, Iris realised Freud would have had a field day with her 'hobby': she was holding on to her inner child. Acting out an impulse to control. All those little flights of stairs probably meant something wildly sexual and depraved. In recent years Ian, who'd once considered her love of doll's houses an endearing quirk, had begun mocking her mercilessly for her 'obsession', more or less implying the tiny wooden dolls were substitute children.

Perhaps they are, thought Iris, still woozy from the Rioja. *But who cares?*

Increasingly, since turning forty, Iris found that she didn't.

Gazing into the small, glowingly lit dining room, its table laid with a miniature, unchanging feast of fruit and cheese, and tiny loaves of bread, she felt herself calm at once. A familiar, warm feeling of contentment flooded through her, better and deeper than the one from the wine.

This was a perfect house, a perfect world, ordered and beautiful. So what if it wasn't real? In Iris's view, reality was seriously overrated.

Later, in bed, Iris pushed aside her usual dark thoughts about Ian and her own future, and instead focused on Billy Wetherby. When she closed her eyes, she could still hear the fear in his mother's voice on the riverbank this morning. *'Stop it! Billy . . . no!'*

Would Billy have stopped if Iris hadn't come along? Would he really have hurt Ariadne, as he threatened, or was he all talk and bluster, like so many of the bullies Iris had known, even before her husband? More importantly, where did his hatred of his mother spring from? And why was Ariadne at such pains to conceal it?

What was Billy sent to prison for? Iris wondered, cursing herself for fleeing the village store like a lunatic earlier, before she'd established this vital piece of information.

She must find out. Just as she must find out who had sent her the thoughtful, exquisitely wrapped present.

Coming to Hazelford to paint and hide and lick her wounds was all very well, but Iris's natural curiosity would not be so easily silenced, or subdued. Something was amiss in the house of Wetherby. Iris couldn't rest, not properly, until she knew what it was.

Lying in her creaky cottage bed, unanswered questions pirouetted through her brain in a manic ballet, denying her the sleep that the wine had promised. And so her day ended as it began, staring up at the ceiling.

CHAPTER TWO

Ariadne Wetherby looked at her reflection in the antique walnut mirror and smiled.

Not bad for fifty-seven.

Ariadne wasn't a vain woman. It was more that she was grateful, at this age, to still look like herself. Her face was lined, of course, and there were liberal streaks of grey in her long blonde hair. But she hadn't thickened in the middle like so many of her friends, or worse, succumbed to the temptation of Botox and fillers that seemed to have become the curse of her generation, turning countless fifty-something women into plump-cheeked, waxen aliens.

Dom would hate it if she did that.

Ariadne's husband was forever telling her how beautiful she was, in that deep, mellow, sensual voice of his, begging her to 'never change'. Women had always swooned over Dom Wetherby's voice. Ariadne used to joke that he was Hazelford's answer to Richard Burton.

She felt lucky to have him. Theirs was a genuine love marriage. Of course, Dom's success as an author and the lovely lifestyle they enjoyed as a result was an added benefit. It meant that Ariadne could sculpt to her heart's content, with no pressure to sell her work or take commercial commissions – quite a luxury. But it was love that had brought her and Dom together, and love that had kept them together, through all the ups and downs of the last three-plus decades.

And there had *been* ups and downs. Big ones. Dominic could be selfish, as most artistic people could. Ariadne had brought up their three sons almost single-handedly while he pursued his career, obsessively at times and blind to his wife's sacrifices. This house, the Mill, had been a constant joy and comfort to Ariadne through those difficult times, especially after Lorcan's birth, when they'd come to realise the full extent of his disabilities. And then later, with Billy. All his problems. Prison.

Ariadne shuddered at the memories, but quickly regained her composure. Things were better now. Billy was home again. He would change. Improve.

The Mill had brought Ariadne strength, but like her children, all of whom had been born here, it was a labour of love, constantly needing repair and care and attention. And of course, Dom never lifted a finger around the house. The exquisite gardens, the welcoming, tastefully decorated rooms and the leak-free roof were all down to Ariadne. Sculpture was her passion, but in a very real sense the Mill had become her life's work and greatest triumph.

Everybody who knew Ariadne Wetherby marvelled at her patience, that gentle, softly spoken perseverance that made her such a good mother and wife and hostess, and the antithesis of her husband's loud, charismatic, look-at-me persona. In the Wetherbys' case at any rate, it seemed opposites really did attract.

Slipping a row of brightly coloured wooden bangles onto her wrist, to cover the scar left by a long-removed tattoo (the things we do when we're young!), Ariadne drifted down to the kitchen and began making coffee on the Aga. Outside, dawn was breaking over the kitchen garden. The grey-green leaves of the sage bushes glistened and glinted with frost. Gazing through the window, Ariadne was marvelling at how peaceful and magical it all was when Billy shuffled in. Silent and sullen as usual, he sat down at the table and began rolling a cigarette at lightning speed.

'Morning, darling. Would you like some coffee?'

Ariadne cringed at the nervousness in her own voice. Recently, talking to her second son had started to feel like sticking one's head into a bear's mouth. He'd really scared her yesterday, by the river. God knows what might have happened if their tenant – 'our artist in residence', as Dom called Iris – hadn't turned up.

'No,' Billy growled. Pushing a mass of unruly black curls back from his face, he shoved the cigarette in his mouth and lit it, inhaling deeply and angrily. The flame tip flared red, lighting up a face that was clearly sleep-deprived. His skin looked sickly and wan, and the shadows under his eyes were almost black. Handsome despite all of this, he looked a lot older than his twenty-seven years.

'It looks like it's going to be a beautiful day,' Ariadne ploughed on, determinedly cheerful.

'I'm sure the TV people will be thrilled,' Billy replied bitterly. Producers were coming up from London today, supposedly to scout out some possible locations for filming scenes from *Grimshaw's Goodbye*, Dom's televisual swansong, to be screened on New Year's Day. Billy winced at the prospect of his father puffing out his chest like a smug cockerel while being fawned over by London media types, who all just *adored* Grimshaw and were *soooo sad* this was the end! '*Can't you write another one, Dom? Just one more?*'

'Do you want to come down to the chickens with me to get the eggs?' asked Ariadne, trying vainly to change the subject. 'Do you remember when you were little, we used to—'

'No,' Billy said, more loudly. 'I don't.' Glancing up at his mother with loathing, he added, 'Just stop it, would you?'

Ariadne was hurt. 'What do you mean? Stop what?'

'For fuck's sake!' Billy yelled, pushing back his chair and getting up. '*Stop*. You're not fooling anyone, you stupid bitch. Least of all me.'

At that moment Dom appeared in the doorway. He'd been up since five, writing and planning for the TV crew's arrival, but the smell of coffee had drawn him downstairs like a snake charmer's song.

'How dare you speak to your mother like that!' He rounded furiously on Billy. 'Who the hell do you think you are?'

Billy stood his ground, glaring back at his father.

'I know who I am. I'm the fallen son, remember? The one you're fattening the Christmas calf for. Because you're so fucking happy I'm home.'

Taking another deep drag of his cigarette, he blew smoke contemptuously into Dom's face. Dom froze. For an awful moment Ariadne thought he was going to hit Billy. Not that Billy wouldn't have deserved it. Still, she couldn't bear the idea of such a beautiful morning being sullied with violence. In the end, however, Dom restrained himself. Billy elbowed past his father and stalked out into the garden, heading for the river.

Dom looked at his shaken wife. 'What was that all about?'

Ariadne shrugged, tears welling in her eyes despite herself. She hadn't told Dom about yesterday, and Billy's earlier outburst towards her.

'It was my fault. I asked him if he wanted to come and get the eggs . . .'

Walking over, Dom pulled her to him.

'It wasn't your fault. None of this is your fault.'

They were still hugging when Lorcan burst in, all smiles as usual in his favourite *Scooby-Doo* pyjamas and a pair of fur-lined wellington boots he'd taken to wearing as slippers. 'Can I do the eggs, Mama? Can I?'

Extracting herself from Dom's embrace, Ariadne clasped Lorcan's lovely, round, eager face, the antithesis of Billy's, in both her hands, gazing at him lovingly.

'Of course you can, darling,' she said. 'Let's have some breakfast first and then we can go together.'

'I'm heading out myself,' said Dom, grabbing a slice of toast from the stack on top of the Aga on his way to the back door. 'I've got a bunch of things to do this morning.'

'Don't you want a coffee first, darling?' Ariadne asked.

Dom shook his head. *Not anymore.* The truth was that Billy's poisonous temper had woken him up far more effectively than any shot of caffeine could hope to.

Awful, angry boy.

Billy Wetherby strode down the sloping lawn, scrunching up his eyes to protect them from the bright morning sun. Not that the blue sky or crisp air did much to lift Billy's spirits.

He was glad to be out of prison, although returning to the Mill had been hard in different ways. More like transferring to a larger, more luxurious jail than the euphoria of freedom. Besides, actual prison had not been so terrible, not like they made it out to be on TV. No one had threatened him or abused him inside. The worst thing was the boredom. That and the insomnia. Angry thoughts about Susan, the bitch who'd got him sent down in the first place, made it hard for Billy to switch off at night. Sometimes he had fantasies about hurting her. About getting his own back, being in control, punishing her the way that he had been punished. These fantasies were familiar, variations on the ones he'd had since his teens about his mother. And occasionally his father, too. And his blinkered, stupid older brother, Marcus, who couldn't see the truth when it was right in front of him. Forced to spend his life surrounded by a family who had consistently failed him, because he was reliant on them for money and – even now – scraps of affection, Billy seethed with a lava-hot resentment. It burned a lot of people, but none as badly as Billy himself.

Crossing the footbridge closest to the waterwheel, he spotted the first of the TV people arriving. The sleek silver Mercedes he knew belonged to Rachel Truebridge, a pretty girl and senior producer at ITV who'd worked with Billy's father, Dom, on the last two Grimshaw adaptations. Rachel wasn't as bad as some of them. She admired Dom – everyone loved Dom Wetherby – but she wasn't as loathsomely sycophantic as the rest of them.

'*Oh, Dom, you're a genius!*'

'*I think this might be your best book yet.*'

'*How do you* do *it?*'

'*Where do you get your inspiration?*'

None of them knows the real Dom Wetherby, thought Billy. Not even a little bit. After ten, or in some cases almost twenty years of working together, not one person at ITV had ever got past the bullshit stage.

Turning left towards the footpath, Billy was about to head into the village – the King's Arms didn't open till eleven, but he could hang out in the coffee shop until then, anything to avoid staying home watching his father getting his ego massaged – when he saw the lights go on suddenly in the kitchen at Mill Cottage. Iris Grey, the artist, was inside in her dressing gown making coffee. Her dark hair was pulled back in a messy bun with bits escaping, and she yawned and stretched out her slender arms like a just-awakened cat. Billy watched, enjoying the sensation that he was witnessing something private, something he wasn't supposed to see.

Iris was an attractive woman. Older, obviously, but poised, despite her penchant for flamboyant dressing, and . . . how would he put it? Delicate. *Fragile.* Billy appreciated vulnerability in a woman. It made him feel strong. Iris clearly hadn't liked him when they met yesterday. Thanks to his bitch of a mother, she'd got the wrong impression. Perhaps now was the moment to rectify that. To show his parents' attractive new tenant just how charming he could be.

Making his way gingerly up the bank towards the cottage, Billy suddenly froze. Standing at the back door, knocking loudly, was his father, with a bunch of flowers clutched in his hand. 'Anybody in?'

His father had been in the kitchen moments ago. *How had he got to Mill Cottage so fast? He must have been in one hell of a hurry. And what was he doing here?*

Slinking back into the shadows, Billy watched as Iris opened the door.

'Sorry to bother you so early.' Dom Wetherby's smooth, mellifluous voice carried on the still morning air. 'I just wanted to apologise in advance for the disturbance. I'm afraid we're going to have cameramen and sound guys traipsing all over the shop today. I brought these as a pre-emptive peace offering.'

Billy watched his father hand over the flowers, smiling broadly. He saw Iris take them, returning the smile, charmed. All women were charmed by Dom.

'How thoughtful of you. They're lovely. Would you like to come in?'

Billy's chest tightened as he watched his father step into the kitchen, laughing and joking with the beautiful artist, helping himself to her coffee. Just like that Dom had infiltrated the scene and become one with it. He had inserted himself into Billy's private moment and stolen it.

Like a wounded fox, Billy turned and slunk away.

Ariadne rested one hand on the rabbit's soft, warm body and the other on her cool slab of clay. Closing her eyes, she allowed herself to feel the animal's slow, drugged breathing. It was an almost transcendental moment, a prayer before the sacred act of creation, the creature's life force passing through Ariadne's body in some mystical way and into the clay.

Stepping back to the other side of her workbench, Ariadne began to sculpt, her eyes still fixed to the chloroformed creature as she attempted to capture its essence, moulding the soft clay with her fingers into a rabbit-like form, vague at first but quickly becoming more defined and detailed. Most sculptors preferred to work with dead animals, but Ariadne loved the calm slumber she could achieve with chloroform. It didn't hurt the creatures at all, and it enabled her to combine stillness with life – the perfect still life – in a way she felt sure added a deeper dimension to her work.

The only problem was timing. The local vet had told her that it wasn't wise to keep small mammals deeply anaesthetised for more than forty minutes at a time, which meant Ariadne had to work swiftly and deftly, pushing all other thoughts out of her mind as she produced each piece. She enjoyed the discipline and the focus, turning each session in her sculpting shed on the edge of the woods into a sort of hands-on meditation.

Irritatingly, she'd barely been working for ten minutes this morning when the interruptions started. First it was the revving engines. Then the relentlessly ringing mobile phones just outside the shed window. Finally, two of the producers, a man and a woman, had started arguing loudly about the set-up for a pivotal scene.

'If he has the heart attack there, under those trees, the whole thing's going to be in shadow,' the man was saying. Ariadne recognised the voice as belonging to John Pilcher, a dreadful little man in her opinion, but evidently an up-and-comer at ITV. John wore his trousers too tight and frequently presaged his observations with 'TBH', a habit Dom found hilarious but that set Ariadne's teeth on edge. 'We want an open field with a clear skyline behind.'

'The script clearly specifies woodland,' a frustrated Rachel Truebridge shot back. Curious, Ariadne set down her clay and moved to the window so she could hear their conversation more clearly.

'Viewers haven't read the script, love,' said John patronisingly. 'Nobody cares.'

'*I* care,' insisted Rachel. She was wearing tight dark green jodhpurs tucked into boots and a chocolate-brown polo-neck sweater that clung to her gym-honed body in all the right places. Her honey-blonde hair had been tousled by the wind, and her cheeks were flushed, whether from cold or anger it was hard to tell. She was, Ariadne observed with her cool artist's eye, a very beautiful young woman.

'Yeah, well, as of next week what you care about won't matter, will it?' John Pilcher sneered viciously. 'They're moving you to

32

children's, aren't they? That's what I heard. CBeebies! Everyone knows Dom wants you out.'

Rachel laughed, but it was a forced, strained, unnatural attempt. 'You wish, John. This is *my* show, and we're filming the heart attack *right here*, whether you like it or not.'

Now it was John's turn to laugh. 'Oh dear, oh dear. Hell hath no fury, eh?' he scoffed.

'You don't know what you're talking about,' said Rachel, through clenched teeth.

'Don't I?' her rival sneered. 'How about I go and find Dom right now and ask him?'

'Be my guest,' Rachel snapped.

Ariadne watched as Pilcher scuttled back towards the house like a malicious rat. Rachel Truebridge watched too, standing stock-still, apparently trying to calm herself down. Ariadne couldn't see her face from this angle, but Rachel's body language suggested she was distressed, possibly close to tears.

A familiar tension crept back into Ariadne's own chest.

'*Hell hath no fury . . .*'

Who had scorned Rachel Truebridge? she wondered. Not Dom? He wouldn't be physically unfaithful, not at this stage in their lives. They were long past all that nonsense. But he'd always been a terrible flirt, and was more than capable of ruffling female feathers, even at fifty-nine *Please let him not have done something stupid. Not like last time.*

The rabbit had started to stir, its ears and nose twitching, as if in the midst of a dream. She had ten minutes left at most. Hurrying back to her work, Ariadne said a silent prayer that there wasn't going to be any more drama at home today. The sooner they really did say goodbye to Grimshaw, the better.

*

'Well, I don't know. I mean, I'm flattered obviously. It's just . . .'

Just what? thought Iris. *Why am I even hesitating?*

It was a few days after the Grimshaw shoot, and Iris was sitting at her kitchen table opposite Ariadne Wetherby, who'd 'dropped in' for a cup of tea with her adorable son Lorcan and promptly offered Iris a commission. Would Iris consider painting Dom's portrait, as a celebration of his retirement? He'd agreed to hang up his pen for good after the last Grimshaw aired, a date that was fast approaching.

'I hope you don't mind, but I googled you,' Ariadne confided in that soft, half-whisper voice of hers. 'I see you've done all sorts of wonderful work. My eldest son, Marcus, told me your painting of a Moroccan boy was exhibited in the Tate last year. Is that true?'

'Well, yes. For five minutes,' Iris admitted coyly. It was the first she'd heard about this third, older son.

'Nonsense. That's an incredible achievement,' Ariadne insisted. 'Marcus said it was one of the most haunting portraits he'd ever seen.'

'Well, that's very kind of him. Is Marcus an artist?' Iris asked.

'No. Marcus is the sensible one, bless him. Two hopelessly artistic parents and our firstborn becomes a lawyer.' Ariadne laughed, as if still not quite able to believe it. 'He works for a big London firm. You'll meet him at Christmas, and his wife, Jenna, and the children.'

'Lovely,' said Iris, who felt she ought to say something, but hadn't even thought about Christmas yet, or where she'd be, and certainly hadn't counted on cosy nights at home with the Wetherbys. Everything was still so up in the air with her and Ian, it was impossible to plan.

'Marcus does *appreciate* art, though,' Ariadne continued. 'He sort of had to, growing up in this family. Oh, please say you'll do Dom's portrait. I know he'd love it more than anything. You can name your price.'

Iris liked the idea of naming her price. Part of her liked the idea of painting Dom Wetherby, too. He'd already struck her as a complex character: charming, charismatic and warm on the one hand, yet oddly steely and determined beneath. It would be fascinating to see how all that complexity emerged on canvas.

The problem wasn't Dom. It was Iris.

Painting somebody's portrait was always an intense, intimate experience. In her current fragile emotional state, Iris wasn't sure she was ready for that intensity. The whole purpose of renting Mill Cottage had been to de-stress, to paint rivers and trees, and eat apple crumble and fiddle about with her doll's house without Ian glaring hatefully at her from across the room. Taking this commission might change all that.

'How long would it take you to finish, do you think? If you agreed to paint him?' Ariadne asked. 'I'm vaguely thinking of throwing him a surprise retirement party, you see. It might be nice to unveil it then.'

Dom Wetherby's wife looked radiant as usual this afternoon in a floaty cream-coloured dress and long cashmere cardigan, like some sort of angel or medieval saint. *The patron saint of motherhood*, Iris thought, watching Ariadne smile beatifically at Lorcan, playing with the pieces of Iris's ivory chess set. 'He won't break it,' Ariadne said, catching Iris looking. 'He knows to be careful.'

'Oh, I'm not worried. He's fine,' said Iris, waving a hand. 'It's not valuable anyway.'

Iris was fond of Lorcan. Although they'd never been formally introduced, the teenager always waved cheerfully to Iris when he saw her out painting. Despite his problems, Iris didn't think she'd ever seen him looking glum. Unlike his brother Billy, the snarler.

'It's really hard to say how long a portrait might take,' she told Ariadne, belatedly answering her question. 'Some come more easily than others. I suppose about four months is typical.'

'Oh.' Ariadne looked momentarily disappointed. 'That might be a bit late for his retirement. Still,I suppose I could always give it to him afterwards. It doesn't really matter, does it?'

'It does also depend on how many sittings the subject can do,' Iris clarified. 'I imagine your husband's very busy, especially with the TV special coming up.'

'Oh, Dom's never too busy to have an attractive woman focusing solely on him.' Ariadne rolled her eyes indulgently. 'He'll adore the attention, believe me. Just as long as you don't go all Lucian Freud and make him look ninety. I'm afraid my husband's terribly vain.'

It must be tough being married to a man like that, thought Iris, and even tougher when the man was a 'star', accustomed to having his every whim indulged. Constantly having to subjugate one's own ego. Then again, having witnessed Ariadne's patience with both Lorcan and Billy, the woman seemed to positively thrive on abnegation and sacrifice.

'Can I think about it?' asked Iris, getting up to refill Ariadne's tea and offering a delighted Lorcan another Jaffa cake, his fourth. 'I'm very flattered by the offer, but I'm on a sort of hiatus at the moment. The timing might not be ideal, for either of us.'

'Of course.' Ariadne rose too, smoothing down her skirt and picking a tiny piece of lint off the sleeve of her cardigan. 'No pressure at all. But I do hope you will think about it. Because, honestly, I think it might be fun. And it seems silly to have you living in the cottage and not take advantage of your amazing talents.'

My amazing talents, thought Iris, watching mother and son walk back up to the big house, arm in arm, sweetly devoted. She hadn't thought about her art in those terms for a long while.

Maybe it *was* time to start another portrait. Dom Wetherby would certainly be a prestigious commission, not to mention a fascinating man to get to know. The author, his family and their idyllic house all intrigued Iris. And Ariadne Wetherby had said she could 'name her price'.

'I'll think about it,' Iris said aloud to herself.

But in her heart, she already knew her answer.

Somewhere above her, a cloud had started lifting.

CHAPTER THREE

The first thing Ian McBride was aware of was the pain in his head. As if a miniature army of malicious dwarves were now bashing away from the inside with countless tiny pickaxes.

Then he sat up in bed, realised immediately that he was going to be sick, and staggered into the bathroom, only just making it to the loo in time.

Christ, he felt dreadful. *Dreadful.* He was too old for this.

Dropping two Alka-Seltzers into a toothmug and filling it up with water, he forced himself to drink the frothing liquid, only narrowly avoiding throwing up again. Then he shuffled along the corridor into the kitchen, leaning on the walls for support. He managed to put some coffee on to brew before slumping down at the table, still strewn with the detritus of last night's epic drinking session, resting his throbbing head in his hands.

What had happened yesterday exactly?

His latest play, *Dreamers*, had been cancelled. Ian got the call from his agent, Mike Rogers, just before lunch.

'I'm sorry, Ian, I really am. But the ticket sales were just so poor. Small theatres like Pickering barely break even in a good year. They can't afford to take risks, however good the production.'

Poor Mike, Ian thought, remembering guiltily how he'd torn a strip off the agent on the phone. It wasn't Mike's fault that North Yorkshire's theatre-going public had all the critical discernment of a heap of slurry, or that they'd only ever part with their money for bloody Alan Ayckbourn. Still, Ian had lashed out like a wounded animal, then proceeded to the bar at the Butcher's Arms in Battersea, drinking solidly through the afternoon so that by the time Iris called – was it around six? – he'd been in a dark, belligerent mood.

Only fragments of their conversation came back to him this morning. Iris had told him excitedly about her commission to paint Dominic Wetherby. Coming on the back of his own cancelled play, his wife's small success had felt like a well-timed kick in the ribs. Ian had been jealous, and his jealousy had made him angry and scathing: Dom Wetherby was a giftless bastard, on the pages of whose novels Ian would be reluctant to so much as wipe his arse. If Iris wanted to cheapen her own modest talent fawning over smug tossers like Wetherby, that was up to her. But she needn't call Ian expecting a round of applause.

He knew he was being a dick. Even at the time, he knew it. It was like that proverb they used to trot out at AA meetings about resentment: 'It's like swallowing poison and then wondering why the other person doesn't die.' But how were you supposed to stop? How could you *not* feel resentment when everything you'd worked for, everything you deserved, was crumbling around you like the bloody Parthenon?

After that, the conversation was a bit of a blur. The commission meant Iris would have to stay on at the Mill through Christmas and possibly New Year too, working. She'd asked Ian if he wanted to join her at the cottage for Christmas, an offer he'd dismissed instantly and unkindly, and then been hurt by the relief he detected in her voice after he said no.

He'd hung up on her then and, to his intense shame now, had gone home to their Clapham flat, rushed straight into Iris's home office, emptied her precious drawers full of doll's-house furniture onto the floor, all the stuff she'd left behind, and stamped on the miniature chairs and tables and beds in a jealous rage, listening to the satisfying *crack* as they shattered beyond repair under his feet, like the bones of tiny mice.

What the hell is wrong with me?

The whistling coffee pot interrupted his miserable retrospective, slicing into his throbbing skull like a Gamma Knife. Grimly Ian shuffled back to the stove, poured himself a strong and bitter mug of Colombia's finest, and headed into the sitting room.

Sinking into his favourite armchair, Ian looked around the room. The small but light-filled space was the nicest room in the flat by far and was dominated by Iris's portraits, which hung from every wall, a constant reminder of her absence. The only spot not taken up by Iris's work was directly over the fireplace, where a heavy gilt mirror had been hung, to make the room look bigger. Ian caught his reflection in it now and grimaced. He'd been a handsome man once, for a long time in fact, but in the last few miserable years, age had caught up with him, swiftly and brutally. His once-thick head of dark hair was now distinctly wispy and grey, and his grey eyes, though still soulful and intense, were now ringed with an ugly latticework of lines and grooves, liked the cracked bed of a dried-out river. His jowls drooped; his shoulders sagged. He looked like a once-proud sailing ship, now sodden and cracked from the relentless pounding of the waves. Waves of disappointment and humiliation, of unfulfilled promise.

Iris's portrait of him, a miniature she'd painted in the early years of their marriage, hung just to the left of the mirror, and was almost unbearable to look at now. Where had that person gone? Not just the good looks but the hope, the confidence, the *joy*? It took all of Ian's remaining self-restraint not to destroy that too.

Things hadn't always been like they were now. When Ian first met Iris at Oxford, the attraction had been instant and profound, on both sides. Ian had been Iris's tutor, sixteen years her senior and on the brink of his first major professional success. His play *Broken* was about to be given a West End run. He'd been full of joy back then, full of confidence and creative energy, proud of his own work but also generous about the work of others, including Iris's.

'Her writing's good,' Ian used to tell people, 'but you should see her paint. She's incredible.'

Ian didn't think Iris was incredible anymore. There had been too many fights for that, too much water under the bridge. Unable to live up to his own early promise as a playwright, Ian's confidence and creativity had been replaced by anger and bitterness to the point where he no longer made any attempt to hide his naked loathing of any writer more successful than he was. Increasingly, he began taking his frustration and disappointment out on his wife.

Not that he'd ever hurt Iris physically. She wouldn't have stood for that. But in other, more subtle ways, he had worn away at her over the years, just as her artistic success had worn away at him. Iris had run through a list of his marital misdemeanours in one of their last, most vicious rows: his barbed 'jokes' about everything from her appearance, especially her clothes, which for some reason had begun to embarrass him lately, to her taste in music, to her friends. He'd come to particularly dislike Iris's friend Annie Proctor and her boyfriend, Joe. Annie taught yoga and reiki healing. Iris had met her on one of the alternative fertility treatment courses she dabbled in, and the two women connected at once. Joe owned the Love Organic health-food café on Clapham High Road.

'I mean, what on earth is there to resent about Annie and Joe?' Iris challenged him. 'Their kindness?'

'How about the fact that they're a pair of grubby, ignorant hippies without a brain cell between them?' Ian shot back. 'I always expect to find a dirty toenail clipping in my lentil soup at Love Organic, and that Annie should be ashamed of herself, peddling false hope to desperate childless women at eighty quid an hour. She's a charlatan.'

His relentless negativity rankled. Although perhaps worst of all was his constant criticism of Iris's paintings, dressed up as praise: 'Thank God Iris produces such commercial stuff. If it weren't for her paint-to-order portraits, we'd have starved long ago. I don't know how she does it.'

Ian knew there was truth to some of Iris's accusations, but he'd reached a point where any criticism, justified or not, was unbearable. So instead he'd hit back, turning the tables on Iris about the IVF, round after failed round, the endless rollercoaster of hope and despair, longing and loss that had taken its toll on both of them, emotionally and financially. Was it any wonder he'd grown fed up with a wife who cried all the time? Whose hormonal depressions meant that she frequently struggled to get out of bed, never mind put dinner on the table?

'Jesus, Iris,' Ian had finally snapped. 'I never even wanted kids! You knew that when we met. I've wasted a hundred grand on this shit, five fucking cycles, and now you want to do another one? When's it going to end? Listen to the doctors! Get it through your head. YOU. CAN'T. HAVE. CHILDREN.'

Weirdly, it was the '*I've* wasted a hundred grand' that seemed to rankle with Iris the most. Scathingly, she'd reminded him that it was *her* paintings that had produced the money for their fertility treatments, *her* 'commercial paint-to-order' portraits that had paid for IVF, just as they paid for everything else, from the mortgage to Ian's beloved bespoke Savile Row suits. 'My wardrobe may make me "look like a clown", as you so sweetly put it, but at least they don't cost us the bloody earth!'

Again, in his more rational moments, Ian was intelligent enough to recognise the truth of his wife's arguments. But his deep shame made it impossible for him to admit his own failure, as a provider as well as a writer. Iris had waited in vain for days for an apology, or even a kind word from him, but none was forthcoming. A few days later she'd answered the ad in the *Sunday Times* and buggered off to Hampshire. The rest, as they say, was history.

Flicking on the TV, Ian let the self-justification begin. He reminded himself that he wasn't the only one to blame for the breakdown in his and Iris's marriage, or for last night's row. Iris had long ago stopped supporting him, stopped believing in his writing, stopped caring about anything at all except her longed-for baby, an imaginary infant that Ian had grown to hate over the years. How ironic that a person who had never even existed should have robbed him, robbed both of them, of so much.

And then of course it was Iris who'd left, buggering off to Hampshire and abandoning him. Although they both knew that, emotionally, she'd jumped ship long before she ever rented Mill Cottage.

He'd been wrong to break her doll's-house things last night, he admitted to himself, sipping the bitter coffee as he channel-surfed, looking for something distracting to watch on television. It was spiteful and childish and he regretted it.

But then hadn't Iris done the same thing to his heart? Stamped on it till it cracked, till it was as broken and ruined as the rest of him? And wasn't that worse, in the end?

If Iris cared more about painting the portrait of some two-bit fiction writer than she did about coming home and repairing their marriage, she could go to hell.

A few miles across London in Wandsworth, four-year-old Lottie Wetherby twirled proudly round her kitchen.

'Look, Daddy! Look how sparkly I am! Do you think I'll be the sparkliest out of all the snowflakes?'

Marcus Wetherby looked up from the *Sunday Telegraph Magazine*. 'The sparkliest? Oh, no question. Definitely.'

Marcus grinned at his wife, Jenna, who was busy wiping porridge out of their son's hair with one hand and trying to clear away the breakfast things with the other. Poor Jenna had been up till midnight painstakingly gluing pieces of glitter-covered polystyrene together and sewing them into specially made 'pouches' on Lottie's leotard for her school Christmas concert. And it wasn't even December yet! Miss Quinley, Lottie's sadist of a teacher, had decided that all the reception girls were to be snowflakes this year and that parents were responsible for costume-making.

'*Parents!*' Jenna had scoffed when the letter came home. 'Mothers, you mean. Why not call a spade a spade? I don't think any of the dads will be rushing home and racing for their sewing boxes, do you? It's bad enough that she sends Lottie home singing that *dreadful* song twenty-four seven.'

Marcus agreed, on both counts. He was the first to admit that his wife did everything with the children. Jenna was a devoted mother, just like his own mum, Ariadne, had been with him and his brothers. As for Lottie's singing of 'I'm a little snowflake, white and soft' to the tune of 'I'm a Little Teapot' tunelessly and incessantly for the last three weeks straight, this was more than even Marcus's highly developed doting-father gene could tolerate.

Putting down the paper, Marcus took the dirty plates from his wife and kissed her.

'The costume's a triumph.'

Jenna kissed him back. 'A very fragile triumph. See if you can persuade her to take it off before something snaps,' she said, thinking how handsome and English Marcus looked, with his tortoiseshell glasses and polished brogues. An American herself, from Kansas City, Jenna Franklin had met Marcus Wetherby when she was an exchange student in London, the year before she qualified as a child psychologist. The attraction was instant, on both sides. Jenna was a classically beautiful girl, tall and blonde and athletic. And Marcus was so gloriously different to all the boys she knew from back home, bookish and funny and intensely charming. A less selfish version of his father, in fact, as Jenna would later learn.

While Marcus dutifully scooped Lottie up and carried her upstairs to extricate her from her costume, Jenna distracted their three-year-old, Oscar, with a *Thomas the Tank Engine* DVD and was about to start loading the dishwasher when the phone rang.

'Oh, good morning, Jenna darling. Is Marcus about?'

Ariadne's voice drifted gently over the line like thistledown on a soft breeze. Jenna felt herself tensing. It wasn't that she disliked her mother-in-law. Ariadne had never been anything other than kind towards her. But Jenna did resent the degree to which Ariadne relied on Marcus, ringing him up constantly and asking his advice on everything from financial decisions to what dress Marcus thought she should wear to Dom's latest book launch. Now, with Christmas and the all-important cocktail party fast approaching, she was being more intrusive than ever.

Christmas was a big deal in the Wetherby family. And it always 'officially' began with Dom and Ariadne's Christmas Eve cocktails at the Mill, an event so star-studded and fabulous that it always made the pages of *Tatler* and *Vogue*. This lavish and very public Yuletide celebration was followed by an equally perfect but strictly private family Christmas Day, the order of which was always the same: stockings, breakfast, church, family quiz, late lunch and present opening around the tree, followed by a long walk with the dog along Hazelford Meadows. Ariadne's elderly father, Clive, was always invited, getting deafer and more demanding by the year, but even his waspish asides were indulged and appreciated as 'part of the fun'. Nothing about Christmas at the Mill could be anything less than wonderful.

Except that of course none of it was *really* wonderful. To Jenna's eyes, the entire holiday felt like a performance. Like one long, rigidly scripted play, designed to conceal all the resentments and enmities and jealousies bubbling beneath the Wetherby family's glamorous surface. There was a pervasive dishonesty to Christmas at the Mill that bothered Jenna more with each passing year. The fact that Marcus either couldn't or wouldn't see it only made matters worse.

Right now it was the Christmas Eve party that was consuming Ariadne the most. Just last night she'd kept Marcus on the phone for well over an hour, rabbiting on about Billy, Marcus's black sheep of a brother, how hard things were with him at home, and how worried she was that he might be going to spoil the event or embarrass Dom in front of their famous friends, not to mention everyone in the village.

Once she'd finally exhausted the subject of the party, she switched into a monologue about some artist they had staying in Mill Cottage who might be going to paint Dom's portrait, Iris somebody or other. And of course Marcus had listened, patiently, as he always did, while the supper Jenna had prepared for him grew cold. Marcus was incapable of saying no to his mother, whom he seemed to regard as some sort of paragon. It was bad enough that they had to go to the Mill for Christmas every single year, but the daily calls about canapé menus and guest lists and God knows what else, starting in November? That, in Jenna's view, was too much.

'He's busy just now, Ariadne,' she said, quietly but firmly, cupping her hand over the receiver so that Marcus wouldn't hear it was his mother and demand the phone. 'Can I help?'

'Oh . . . no, thank you, dear.' Ariadne let out a disappointed sigh. 'If you'd just let him know, I forgot to mention yesterday, but we've invited Graham Feeney down for the party this year.'

Jenna bit her tongue in irritation. Had that insignificant nugget of information really warranted yet another phone call?

'Right. And do you want Marcus to *do* something about that, Ariadne?'

'Do something? Oh no. I just thought he'd want to know. He and Billy both adored Graham when they were small boys, you see. I remember once—'

'Ariadne, sorry, I don't mean to be rude, but I'm actually just in the middle of something here.'

'All right, dear.' Ariadne sounded chastened. 'I'll let you go.'

'I'll let Marcus know you called.'

Jenna hung up, annoyed with herself for feeling guilty.

'Who was that?' Marcus came back downstairs with a grumpy-looking Lottie, now wearing one of her myriad Princess Elsa outfits teamed with a pair of pink bunny slippers.

Jenna contemplated lying, but bottled it. 'Your mother,' she said brusquely. 'She wanted me to let you know that Graham Feeney's coming to the party this year.'

'Oh great!' Marcus beamed, reaching for the phone. 'I'll ring her back.'

'*No*,' Jenna said, more loudly and crossly than she'd intended. Marcus looked taken aback.

'I'm sorry,' said Jenna, through gritted teeth and sounding anything but sorry. 'But we're late as it is.'

'Late?' Marcus frowned.

'The Philmores' dinner? Don't tell me you've forgotten.' *You're more interested in your bloody mother's social arrangements than you are in ours.*

'Of course not,' muttered Marcus, who had. He wished things weren't so tense between his wife and his mother, the two women he loved most in the world and whom he considered to have a huge amount in common. Both were intelligent, thoughtful and kind. Both were utterly devoted mothers.

And yet, increasingly, Jenna seemed to despise Ariadne, or at the very least to resent his relationship with her.

'You need to change,' she told him tersely now, focusing on putting a bow into Lottie's hair and refusing to meet his eyes.

It struck Marcus that perhaps she didn't just mean his clothes.

Stepping out of the warm fug of the high court into the cold air of Edinburgh's Parliament Square, Graham Feeney buttoned his cashmere overcoat and allowed himself a small smile.

Today's case had gone remarkably well for Graham, the younger brother of Dom's childhood best friend, Marcus Feeney. It wasn't a done deal yet, but it looked as if Graham's client, a hardened fraudster and inveterate liar named Donny Truro, with considerably more money than scruples, was going to get off this time. Graham Feeney was no fan of Truro's. A slum landlord with a sideline in loan-sharking and extortion, Donny was a thoroughly unpleasant piece of work. But everybody, even the toerags, deserved a decent defence, and the Crown Prosecution had been unforgivably sloppy with their handling of the evidence, exposing multiple chinks in their armour, which Graham had exploited mercilessly all afternoon.

It wasn't only the satisfaction of a job well done that was lifting Graham's spirits. It had snowed last night, the first really deep snow of the winter, and Edinburgh looked magical beneath its blanket of sparkling white, covering the city from the iconic castle all the way down Princes Street.

A successful barrister, Graham Feeney divided his time between his elegant flat on Northumberland Street and his townhouse in London, on the edge of Holland Park. Graham was fond of London, but his heart had always belonged to Scotland, and the imposing grey-stoned city of his birth. He felt more real here, more himself, in ways that were hard to put into words.

Picking up a smoked sausage supper from a street vendor on the corner, warming his fingers on the steaming vinegar-soaked chips, he decided on a whim to take the bus back to his flat, instead of his usual taxi. In his early fifties, tall and slim, with close-cropped grey hair and a likable if not exactly handsome face, Graham Feeney looked like what he was: a wealthy, educated, successful man. And yet despite the six-figure flat, the expensive watch and the sharply tailored suits, he had never lost touch entirely with his roots. A grammar-school boy from Niddrie, distinctly on the wrong side of the Edinburgh tracks, Graham Feeney was every bit the self-made man. Education and hard work had rescued him, just as they had once rescued his elder brother, Marcus.

Marcus. After all these years, it was surprising how often Graham still thought of him. Although not so surprising today, with the invitation arriving.

That was the real reason for Graham Feeney's good mood. The stiff, formal card that landed on his doormat yesterday morning, inviting him to the Wetherby family's annual Christmas Eve party, his first invitation to the Mill in well over a year.

Not that Graham could blame the Wetherbys for that. *He* was the one who'd initiated the distance between them. The one who'd pulled away. And only he knew why. But the time had come to change that, to move back into the fold. Just as Graham had been pondering how he might achieve this, the invitation had arrived. Talk about serendipity!

Every year enormous thought and effort went into the design of the invitation, the unveiling of which had become an event in itself, eagerly awaited by society-pages editors across London. This year the Wetherbys had decided to go kitsch. The card consisted of a picture of a bright green glittery Christmas tree bedecked with baubles, inside each of which was a photo of Dom and Ariadne from the early 1980s to today. There were plenty of dodgy perms and wing-tipped collars in evidence, and underneath the picture, in embossed italic script, was the message '*Step back in time and say, "Goodbye to Grimshaw", this Christmas Eve at the Mill!*' with the letters arranged to look like a Christmas garland.

'It's been far too long.' Dom Wetherby's distinctive looped handwriting sprawled over the back of the card. 'Please come!' And more neatly, underneath, in Ariadne's rounder hand, 'We all miss you.'

They miss me, Graham thought, smiling.

His relationship with the family went back a long, long way. Most of his life.

Dom Wetherby had been best friends at school and university with Graham's older brother, Marcus. When Graham was growing up, Dom had been almost like family. As an adult, Dom had even named his first child after Graham's brother. (And what a great kid Marcus Wetherby had turned out to be, kind and steady, brilliant but unassuming, just like his namesake.)

These days, the Wetherbys were effectively Graham Feeney's last link to his dead brother. The Feeney parents were long deceased, there were no other siblings or cousins, and none of Marcus's other friends had bothered to keep in touch with his younger brother. For this reason alone, Graham's relationship with Dom Wetherby and his family had grown very precious to him over the years.

Settling down into his seat on the bus, his newspaper-wrapped supper in his lap, Graham pulled Dom Wetherby's latest and last Grimshaw novel, *Grimshaw's Goodbye*, out of his briefcase and removed the invitation, which he'd used as an impromptu bookmark earlier. He'd already replied, of course, accepting immediately and with thanks.

'I miss you all too! Can't wait. G.'

So what did he feel now? Excitement. Anticipation. Perhaps even a touch of adrenaline. But only a touch. Graham Feeney was a calm man, calm and measured and thoughtful.

Yes, it had been too long. A return to the Mill meant many things, all to be pondered and savoured between now and Christmas Eve.

What a deeply satisfying Christmas it was going to be.

CHAPTER FOUR

'So how does this work? Should I sit at the desk? Or on the sofa? I'm entirely in your hands.'

Dom Wetherby led Iris into his study, a warm, oak-panelled room with lush wine-red velvet curtains and bookshelves crammed mostly with Grimshaw novels. Here or there, other books had managed to work their way in. Iris clocked a couple of volumes of Renaissance poetry, as well as a complete Shakespeare and a recent Scandi noir thriller. But the bulk of the room was clearly a shrine to Dom Wetherby's ego.

To be fair, it was Iris who'd selected the study as the best setting for the portrait, partly because it was where Dom wrote his books and spent the majority of his time, but also because the room itself was vibrant and rich, full of texture and meaning.

'I'd say the sofa,' she said, hitching up the deep purple kaftan she'd chosen to work in (teamed with Ugg boots and cheerful red-and-white snowflake scarf) and drawing back the curtains to assess the light. 'But it's up to you. Wherever you're most comfortable really. Remember, wherever you choose, you're going to have to sit still there for hours on end.'

Dom grimaced. 'Never my strong suit.'

In contrast to Iris's typically eclectic ensemble, Dom had kept things classic in a maroon cashmere sweater over an open-necked white shirt and corduroy trousers in a very dark blue. The colours suited him, bringing out his eyes and accentuating his lightly tanned skin, and although the outfit was casual, Iris suspected a lot of thought had gone into choosing it. She'd been struck by his vanity as soon as they met. It permeated everything about Dom, his voice, his manner, his physical movements, the way he carried himself.

He's successful and rich and famous and handsome, and he knows it. More than that, he needs everybody else to know it, Iris thought *Especially women.* Dom's 'I'm entirely in your hands' comment earlier had been as loaded with flirtatious undertones as everything else he said to Iris. She might have been flattered, if she weren't so sure he was like this with every female with whom he came into contact. It was a role he played: the charmer. One of many roles, Iris suspected. This was only their first sitting, so she mustn't expect too much. Eventually, Dom would start to shed his outer skin and reveal more of the man beneath. These things took time.

In this regard, Dom Wetherby was no different to the other people Iris had painted over the years. Every subject was a mystery, and every portrait an unravelling. Setting up her sketchpad and pencils – she always began with sketches – Iris felt the familiar tingle of excitement and anticipation of a new commission, a new adventure. Who would Dom Wetherby turn out to be?

'How about this?' Dom asked, lounging back with his arm stretched casually along the back of the Chesterfield. Iris loved the way the battered old sofa creaked and cracked as he shifted his weight on it, the faded lines in the leather like cracks in a dry riverbed, a sharp contrast to Dom's own glossiness and polish. 'Too relaxed?'

'No, no,' Iris assured him. 'I love it. Is that a pose you feel comfortable holding?'

'Sure.' He smiled wolfishly, clearly enjoying the attention. 'Ready when you are, Maestro.'

Iris was already at work, her pencil dancing over the paper in big freewheeling arcs, taking in both Dom and the bookshelves behind him. To the right of his head and just above, one gold photograph frame caught the light and seemed to glow, star-like, creating a sort of halo. Iris smiled, thinking how undeserved that was, but also that the room, with its layered light and different textures, was going to provide a perfect backdrop for the portrait. Although she might leave out the television that someone had incongruously stuffed in one corner, ruining the olde-worlde effect, and the blown-up version of this year's Christmas Eve party invitation, a green sparkly monstrosity plastered with old photos of Dom and Ariadne, like cheesy ghosts of Christmases past.

Iris had received her own invitation a couple of days ago and was still pondering the best way to decline. Noisy cocktail parties full of self-important people she didn't know were the closest thing to hell on earth she could imagine.

'Is talking allowed,' Dom asked, 'or does my face need to be still?'

'Talking's allowed. Encouraged, in fact.' Iris smiled. 'The better I get to know you, the better I'll be able to paint you.'

'Is that so?' Dom arched an eyebrow. 'In that case, I suppose we ought to get to know one another much better.'

He was *so* flirty, it almost seemed rude not to respond in kind. But after two decades with Ian, Iris was so much out of the habit of flirting that she wasn't sure she had it in her.

'Let's talk about you.' Dom's eyes locked with hers and Iris could feel her cheeks burning.

He's playing with me, she realised. *He can tell I'm no good at this.* No doubt it was his way of trying to get the upper hand, to dominate the relationship between them so that he could control the image Iris ultimately produced on canvas. As a portrait painter, she was familiar with this tactic. Subjects usually gave it up in the end.

'How about something more interesting?' she replied. 'How's the last Grimshaw TV show coming on? Have you seen it yet?'

'I've seen some footage,' said Dom, apparently quite happy to turn the subject back to himself. 'They're behind schedule, so filming isn't finished yet. But what I've seen so far I like.'

'Is it strange, seeing your characters up on screen?'

'Not really,' he preened. 'Not anymore. I've been at this game a long time, you know.'

'I know. Almost forty years,' said Iris, sticking the pencil between her teeth as she stood back and frowned critically at something on her sketch.

'God, don't say that,' said Dom. 'That makes me sound ancient.'

'You're not happy about turning sixty?'

'No!' Dom forced a laugh. 'I'm not. Is anyone?'

Iris thought about Ian, and what a hard time he had accepting the ageing process. It had always struck her as odd how women were supposed to be the youth-obsessed sex. In Iris's experience, men often struggled far more with the indignities of getting older than their wives did, although at least Dom Wetherby was able to laugh about it. Unlike Ian.

'Still, I reckon I look all right for an old buffer, don't you?' Dom asked Iris coyly. 'Not quite ready for my pipe and slippers yet, am I?'

My goodness, thought Iris. *For such a successful man, he needs an awful lot of reassurance.* She wondered how Ariadne coped with that. It was almost endearing, the way Dom wore his insecurity on his sleeve, all the more so for being unexpected. But at the same time Iris could imagine the exhaustion involved in having to constantly prop up someone's ego to that degree.

'You're looking good from here,' she assured him. 'Just sit up slightly, would you?'

Dom did as he was asked, but then a buzzing from the desk distracted him and he turned his head, just as Iris was working on the shape of his skull.

'Aaagh. Don't move!' she said, but it was too late. Dom had already stood up and reached for his mobile phone, vibrating like an angry bee beside an expensive box of Cuban cigars. Grabbing it sheepishly, he resumed his former position on the sofa.

'Sorry,' he mumbled. 'Force of habit.'

He was looking down at the text he'd just received – or perhaps it was an email. Iris never could tell one buzz from another. Iris watched him change. Not just the scowl on his face but the tensing of his shoulders and jaw and the anxious, irritated *tap-tapping* of his foot all indicated a marked degree of agitation.

He's angry, thought Iris. *Angry and frightened.*

What of? I wonder.

'Bad news?' she asked, lightly.

Dom looked up, smiling, as if the reaction Iris had just witnessed had never happened. Iris shivered. Right before her eyes, he had picked up a mask and slipped it on. And yet he wore it so well, so convincingly. It was deeply disconcerting.

'Not at all,' he replied smoothly. 'Quite the opposite, in fact. We just got a terrific offer from a new American publisher for the Grimshaw backlist. Ha!'

His eyes danced, daring Iris to call him on what she knew with a hundred per cent certainty to be a lie.

Instead, Iris played along. 'Congratulations. You must be thrilled.'

The transformation she'd just seen was horribly, stomach-lurchingly familiar. As a teenager, Iris's sister, Thea, used to don a 'mask' all the time. Thea could slip on a fake emotion the way that other girls slipped on a new dress. The change was instant, and seamless. Meanwhile Iris could do nothing but stand there and watch, horrified and helpless, *willing* her parents to see through it.

She's not upset! She's not hurt! She's not scared!

She doesn't give a shit. She's fooling you!

But it never worked. Iris, it seemed, was the only one who saw through her bipolar sister's bullshit. Yet Iris was never believed. Instead, *she* was accused of jealousy, of resenting the attention lavished on her sister, day after day after day.

Which of course she did.

'*I know it's hard, Iris.*' She could hear her mum now, her tone kind but also pleading and loaded with reproach. '*But Thea's ill. You have to understand that.*'

'Iris?' Dom Wetherby's deep, mellifluous voice brought her back to the present with a jolt. 'Are you all right?'

'Hmm? Oh yes. I'm fine,' Iris said numbly. Picking up her sketchpad, she snapped it shut. 'We're done for today.'

'Are you sure?' Dom sounded disappointed. 'I'm sorry I moved. Did I throw you off?'

'No, no,' said Iris with a calm she didn't feel, putting on her own mask. 'It's not that. I have what I need for now, that's all.'

Getting up, Dom unsettled her further by wrapping a kind, apparently paternal arm around her shoulder. 'Sorry,' he purred. 'I'll get into the swing of it, I promise. I'll be a model sitter next time. No more phone calls.'

'Really, I'm used to it,' said Iris, gathering up her things and leaving before he could say anything else. She knew she was over-reacting. But anything that reminded her of Thea and that time in her life left her feeling wounded and raw. Sittings were supposed to be about the *subject* revealing themselves to the artist, not the other way around.

She would have to do better next time.

CHAPTER FIVE

Rachel Truebridge felt a muscle in her jaw start to twitch.

She could not believe this. This couldn't be happening. It was a bad dream, and any moment now she would wake up, relieved and laughing. Several weeks had passed since the Grimshaw shoot out in Hampshire, and the whole of England was now deep in pre-Christmas cheer, putting up decorations and skiving off work early for drinks parties and mince pies. Rachel had been too – until today.

'Try not to take it personally, Rachel. As I said before, this is not a demotion.' Tony Dymoke, the head of drama, was still talking, but Rachel was barely listening as his Brummie voice bounced off the white office walls.

She was thinking about a different voice. A voice that had made her promises. A voice that had lied and lied.

'We have two really exciting projects we want you to spear-head. It's just that Grimshaw really only needs one producer, and John Pilcher—'

'Is a visionless moron,' Rachel jumped in caustically. In a fitted Victoria Beckham suit and ruffled blouse, she'd made sure she looked her absolute best for today's meeting. *Sexy but powerful* was the message. *In control.* And yet the truth was that with each passing second, Rachel Truebridge's 'control' was being prised out of her hands by grasping, unworthy, backstabbing men. 'Pilcher's a pen-pusher, Tony, and you know it as well as I do. Grimshaw is *my* series.'

'It's an ITV series,' Tony Dymoke said pompously. 'We're a team, Rachel.'

'Some team,' Rachel scoffed. 'John Pilcher's stabbing me in the back and you're letting it happen. I'll go to court, Tony. I mean it. And to the press. This is classic sex discrimination. I won't just roll over.'

Her mind wandered back to the lawyer who'd left her messages a few days ago. '*I'd like to talk to you about Dom Wetherby. I believe you may have information about his past that might be relevant to a case of mine. Perhaps we can help each other?*'

She'd dismissed the guy as a crank at the time, but now she found herself wondering whether she'd saved his number.

'Oh, give me a break.' Tony Dymoke pushed back his chair in exasperation and ran a hand through his thinning hair. 'You're getting a pay rise and two series instead of one. You'd be laughed out of court.'

'I don't care!' To her fury, Rachel found herself fighting back tears. 'I've given eight years of my life to Grimshaw. If John Pilcher thinks I'm going to sit back and—'

Her boss cut her off. 'Are you really that blind, Rachel? It wasn't *John* who wanted you off the series. Even if he did, do you really think he has that kind of influence? Think about it.'

Rachel opened her mouth to respond, then closed it again. Her mind was racing. John Pilcher was a slimy snake of a man and he'd long been gunning for her job; that much she knew. But Dymoke was right. John *didn't* have the clout to depose her. Not on his own. Her mind drifted back to last month's shoot at Hazelford. Pilcher's spiteful words rang in her ear: '*Everyone knows Dom wants you out.*'

'Dom told the network flat out he won't work with you anymore. Now, I don't know what went on between the two of you, and I don't want to know. All I know is Wetherby had lunch with the CEO, OK? This is as far over my head as it is yours. And for what it's worth, I'm sorry.'

Afterwards, Rachel couldn't remember leaving Tony Dymoke's office. She couldn't remember getting her coat, or walking to the Tube, past all the glittering Christmas lights, or getting off at Angel and navigating the short maze of streets from the station to her flat off Upper Street. All she was aware of was the bitter, burning sensation in her chest and the refrain pounding in her head, like a song on repeat.

He's trying to ruin me!

The bastard's trying to destroy my career.

Well, he won't get away with it.

Not this time.

This time, Rachel was going to do something. Hit back. Hurt Dom, the way he'd hurt her.

What the hell had she done with that lawyer's number?

When the doorbell rang, it was late, after eleven, and Rachel was drunk. A string of gin and tonics had deadened the shock, but not her anger, or her resolve.

There was only one person who paid her house calls at the flat after eleven. Wrenching open the front door, her defiant glare morphed into an expression of genuine surprise when she looked into her visitor's eyes.

'What the hell do *you* want?'

Iris hurried down the High Street and round the corner into Mill Lane, anxious to get home. Hazelford was Christmas-card perfect this evening, cold and crisp and with a light snow falling, flakes drifting lazily down through the woodsmoke-filled air. How Iris loved that smell! Fires burning in the cottage hearths seemed to symbolise all that was kind and joyous and good about the season, and about this magical, idyllic place. Combined with the pealing church bells, the brightly coloured lights of the village Christmas tree at the top of the hill and the displays of toys and chocolates and glistening marzipan fruits in the shop windows, Hazelford seemed almost to be daring Iris *not* to get into the festive spirit.

Sadly, it wasn't that easy. The bitter cold outside echoed a lingering chill in Iris's heart that not even Hampshire's most beautiful village could completely shake. For some reason, the sittings with Dom Wetherby seemed to be making it worse. There was that time a few weeks ago, when he'd brought back difficult memories of Thea. But it was more than that. Something about the author's warmth, his happiness and light, seemed to throw Iris's own inner darkness into painfully sharp relief.

She'd also had a horrible, vicious row with Ian yesterday. She'd gone up to London just for the day to see him. After his mean, drunken phone call when she got the commission to paint Dom, he'd apologised – an event in itself – and then invited her to lunch.

'So we can talk through everything calmly, face to face. I don't think the phone's helping.'

He'd even proposed marriage counselling in the new year, and suggested a couple of names to Iris, which was an astonishing turnaround.

But it didn't take long for the old Ian to make an unwelcome reappearance.

'What on earth is that?' he'd asked, laughing belittlingly at the bright patchwork coat Iris was wearing when she walked in.

She'd chosen it deliberately for its cheerful colours, hoping they might inject some joy into today's encounter. They didn't. 'You look like a court jester!'

'Thanks,' Iris said stiffly. 'Nice to see you too.'

'Oh, come on,' Ian frowned. 'I'm joking with you. You can take a joke, can't you?'

From that inauspicious start, the meal had deteriorated quickly. When Iris raised the subject of going to see one of the counsellors Ian had proposed, he backtracked instantly. 'Oh yeah, I called them both, but the rates are ridiculous. A hundred quid an hour! We don't need that.'

Iris looked incredulous. 'How do we not need it?'

'Because,' Ian said blithely, 'it's a racket. Once you move back home, things'll get better.'

'How? How will they get better?'

'We can set aside a time each week to talk about things ourselves,' said Ian, reaching for the wine list. 'I mean, it's not rocket science. I'll try harder. You'll try harder. Red or white?'

'Neither.' Every muscle in Iris's body seemed to have tensed up. 'I don't want to drink.'

'Since when?' Ian laughed, beckoning the waiter over and ordering an expensive bottle of Burgundy, as if Iris hadn't spoken. Belatedly noticing her stony face, he frowned. 'Do you have to be so bloody miserable all the time?'

'I told you. I'm not drinking.'

'Well, why the fuck not?' Ian snapped. 'We're here to try and enjoy ourselves, Iris. Remember that? Enjoying yourself?'

Not really, thought Iris, wishing she were anywhere else but here. Did he really not see how serious their problems were, or was he doing this on purpose?

'At least not being pregnant means you can drink at lunchtime, eh?' he winked, grinning as the waiter returned with the bottle. 'I believe that's what's known as a silver lining.'

Iris pushed back her chair and stood up. She was so angry it was an effort not to start shaking. 'This was a mistake,' she said. 'I'm leaving.'

'What?' Ian looked genuinely amazed. 'No, you're not. Don't be silly! Sit down.'

Iris put on her coat.

'For God's sake, this is ridiculous.' Ian's voice started rising. 'I'll drink the sodding wine if it means that much to you. Sit down and order some food.'

'While you get drunk and insult me? No, thanks,' Iris hissed back.

After that things became a bit of a blur. Iris walked out onto the street and Ian followed her and an ugly public screaming match ensued. Both of them had accused the other of being insincere and hypocritical, of not making a real effort to try and fix the marriage.

'We can't talk if you're not here!' Ian yelled at one point. To which Iris had yelled back, 'Well, we can't talk if I *am* here either, can we? Look at us!'

Not until she was alone in the back of a black cab, heading to Waterloo Station, did Iris give way to tears. Ian, she suspected, had gone back to their table and drowned his own sorrows in the expensive wine, no doubt downing the entire bottle. His drinking was definitely part of the problem. Although recently, Iris knew she'd been hitting the bottle increasingly herself.

Maybe he's right. Maybe I am a hypocrite.

I know the marriage is dead, but I'm still going through the motions.

After her sitting with Dom today, Iris had dashed into the village to pick up some cheap Mr Kipling's mince pies, her favourite, and (guiltily) a small bottle of sloe gin to go with them. She'd planned to cheer herself up with a long, indulgent evening at the cottage, rearranging the furniture in her doll's house from top to bottom and installing the new standard lamps she'd bought from her favourite American supplier online.

Ian had once called her doll's-house obsession 'playing God'. Iris had been offended at the time, but perhaps he was right about that, too. Then again, wasn't that the same thing he did, creating characters in his plays whose lives he got to control? And didn't Dom Wetherby do the same with his books, and Ariadne with her sculpture? Wasn't all art, at least in part, 'playing God'? An acted-out impulse to control?

Quickening her pace, Iris chided herself for brooding again about Ian. After yesterday it was clear that she couldn't go home for Christmas – if their flat in Clapham could even be called 'home' anymore. At some stage, she would have to ring him and agree some sort of official 'plan', not just for the holidays but for next year and the rest of their lives. But it didn't have to be done today. Today she could be alone and happy. *Focus on the present.* That was what all the self-help books said. That and stop drinking yourself into oblivion.

A clatter behind her made her jump. Iris had reached the far end of Mill Lane now, the part where the last of the cottages petered out and gave way to a few hundred yards of empty road before the imposing walls of Mill House suddenly appeared and she took the left-hand turn down to the river and along the track that led to her cottage. The noise sounded like someone bumping into an old-fashioned metal dustbin. Except there were no dustbins here, only fields to either side of the lane, with a few wiry goats their sole occupants.

'Hello?' Iris called into the darkness.

Silence.

The sound of her voice, isolated and querulous on the night air, made her feel more frightened.

You're being ridiculous, she told herself firmly. *It was probably a goat knocking over a water trough or something.*

Even so, she quickened her pace. The feeling that someone, or something, was following her intensified. She heard cracking twigs – *footsteps?* – followed by a whining sigh or groan that could have been the wind but could also have been something else, something human. By the time she finally reached Mill Cottage, her cold fingers fumbling with the key as she tried to turn the lock to the side door, her heart was pounding so violently it was difficult to breathe. She was so isolated, so totally alone. No one would hear her if she screamed.

Stop catastrophising, she tried to tell herself. *If someone was there, he'd have jumped you by now.* But terror trumped her logical thoughts. Bursting into the kitchen as the door finally swung open to receive her, Iris whipped round and slammed the door shut behind her, sliding in the deadbolt and dropping her shopping on the floor, weak with relief.

For a moment she contemplated ringing her friend Annie Proctor. They hadn't spoken in a while, but the urge to hear a reassuring human voice was suddenly very powerful. But Annie was miles away, and wouldn't be able to do anything to help if Iris really *were* being followed. Maybe she should call Ariadne instead, up at Mill House, just to let her know what had happened? But she quickly realised how stupid she would sound if she did that.

What *had* happened? Nothing, that's what. She'd heard a few, normal country noises after dark and got herself spooked. Safe now in the warm, bright normality of her kitchen, Iris's fears began to recede like evening shadows. Her heart rate slowed, and her breathing returned to its usual rhythm. Even so, she decided she would work on her doll's house down here tonight, close to the Aga and the woodburner.

She pushed away the unconscious thought that the kitchen was also closer to the door, and escape, should she need it, and unwrapped two mince pies, sticking them in the microwave to warm. Then, lighting a comforting clove and cinnamon candle, she poured a generous three fingers of sloe gin into a Hello Kitty mug and took a long, slow sip before climbing the stairs to fetch down her doll's house.

Walking past the open bedroom door, she froze.

There, neatly positioned on Iris's pillow, was a perfectly carved doll's-house-sized grandfather clock.

Iris walked over to it slowly, cold fear gripping her like the hand of a ghost on her neck.

Tick, tick, tick, went the clock, like a tiny whispering bomb. Her home, her sanctuary, was no longer safe, no longer private. She felt violated.

Shaking, Iris grabbed the phone by her bedside and dialled 999.

'Police,' she rasped, her throat dry as dust. 'I want to report a break-in.'

CHAPTER SIX

'You see – I told you. It's starting to move now.'

Marcus Wetherby smiled across at his wife, Jenna, as their Volvo inched forwards. It was five days before Christmas and they, like everybody else, it seemed, were on the road, trying to make their way to the Mill for the holidays. Marcus's parents had been expecting them over an hour ago, but the M3 had other plans.

Ignoring him, Jenna turned to gaze out at the motorway traffic. Anything was better than looking at Marcus's face, and the scratch that still ran livid down his cheek, from his left eye almost to the top of his lip. A little over two weeks ago Marcus had come home late – very late – and clearly the worse for wear. It was so utterly out of character that Jenna had struggled to process his behaviour, but the facts spoke for themselves. His breath smelled of alcohol, his shirt was rumpled, and his face was bleeding. As if all that weren't bad enough, he'd then lied, right to Jenna's face, making up some utter nonsense about a late meeting at a client's country house and an accidental stumble into a rose bush – *a rose bush!* – a story that, ludicrously, he had stuck to rigidly the morning after, and the next day, and every day since, refusing to discuss the matter further other than to insist, with increasing irritation, that 'There's nothing to tell, Jenna. Nothing happened!'

And so the scratch incident had been shelved, unresolved. And now they were on their way to the Mill, where God forbid anybody should have problems of any kind, never mind a problem as big and toxic as suspecting one's husband of having an affair, or at least a one-night stand, and lying about it through his straight, white, smiling teeth, and where the children and Marcus's family would be around them every minute of every day, constantly, ruining any chance of them having a meaningful conversation.

Marcus reached out, resting a hand on his wife's leg. 'Please don't be angry all through Christmas,' he begged, grateful at least that Lottie and Oscar had both fallen asleep before the Winchester turn-off. 'Please try.'

'I am trying,' Jenna said stiffly.

'I love you.'

She heard the break in Marcus's voice. Instinctively, she slipped her hand over his.

'I love you too, Marcus.'

And she did. She really did. She just didn't know if she could trust him anymore. He insisted he wasn't having an affair, and maybe he wasn't. After all, throughout their long years together, he'd never once given her reason to doubt him. And yet Jenna knew there was something he wasn't telling her about the other night. She just knew it.

They relapsed into silence. Miraculously, the traffic did clear, and less than half an hour later they were exiting the roundabout at the top of Hazelford Hill and chugging down the High Street towards the church and the river.

'We'll talk more when we get back to London,' Marcus said suddenly. 'I promise. But please can we leave it for now?'

In the back seat, Lottie started to stir.

'I swear to you on the kids' lives that I am not having an affair.'

'OK,' said Jenna. It wasn't ideal, but it would have to do for now.

'Are we there yet?' Lottie asked groggily.

'Almost!' Marcus's voice had already taken on the happy, magical, everything's-absolutely-perfect tone he always adopted when visiting his childhood home. 'We're in the village. Look at the tree!'

'Oh! It's *lovely*!' Lottie gasped.

And it was. Even Jenna had to admit that Hazelford looked enchanting. And the Mill, when they arrived, was even more so, decked out in holly and berries and hundreds of lit candles in preparation for the big party, a Victorian Yuletide fantasy. Ariadne had outdone herself as usual.

'My darlings! You're here! Come in, come in. Oh, how gorgeous you all look!' Ariadne emerged from the house in a thick and rather marvellous woven woollen poncho, a riot of colour and pattern that made her look like Hampshire's answer to an Inca queen, sweeping first Lottie and then a deliriously groggy Oscar into her arms for a hug. 'Lorcan's inside. He's been waiting all afternoon to give you both one of his Bethlehem star biscuits. You can bake some more together in the morning if you like.'

Jenna and Marcus heaved buggies and suitcases out of the boot as their children ran squealing into the house, as excited as two piglets on speed.

'You must both be exhausted,' said Ariadne, hugging Marcus warmly and beaming at Jenna. 'Come and have some mulled wine. Billy can help unload the car later.'

'Oh, I can, can I?'

Right on cue, Billy emerged behind his mother, lounging against the front door like a dissolute lizard. *God, he looks thin*, thought Jenna. *Gaunt.* She wondered whether that was prison food or the stress of being back home under his parents' roof at the age of twenty-seven, and with his life in ruins. He'd had to sell his flat to cover his legal costs, after Dom point-blank refused to fund his defence, snorting robustly that Billy was guilty as sin and must face the consequences of his own actions 'for once'. Jenna knew from Ariadne's daily calls to Marcus that things with Billy had been tense. But Billy's sunken eyes and curling upper lip suggested the reality went far beyond that innocuous word.

'Do I look like a fucking porter?' he snarled. 'Let Saint Marcus carry his own bloody bags.'

'Don't be silly, darling.' Ariadne tried and failed to keep her tone light. 'Poor Marcus and Jenna have been on the road since three. Everyone's got to muck in.'

Billy glided towards Marcus's car. Opening his arms, somewhat to Marcus's surprise after his earlier spiteful outburst, he enveloped his older brother in a hug. Marcus tentatively hugged him back.

'Good to see you.'

'You too,' said Billy.

The words were warm, but over Marcus's shoulder, Jenna shuddered at the rage she saw glinting in Billy's eyes. Was he angry at Marcus, specifically, or just life in general? Jenna wasn't sure, but either way his skinny arms wrapped around Marcus's broad back suddenly put her in mind of a boa constrictor, choking its prey. Their problems momentarily forgotten, she found herself feeling overwhelmingly protective of Marcus. *Get your hands off him, you bastard.*

'Billy, would you help me with this?' she asked, pulling vainly at the heaviest suitcase.

'Of course,' said Billy, releasing Marcus to Jenna's relief. 'Anything for my favourite sister-in-law.' It was uncanny how every word out of his mouth managed to sound like a curse.

'Thank you.' Jenna watched him swing the case out of the car one-handed as easily as if it were empty before setting it down softly on the gravel. Thin or not, Billy was incredibly strong.

'You're welcome.'

'Yes, darling. Thank you,' Ariadne echoed, touching a hand lightly on Billy's back.

Billy spun round as if he'd been branded with a hot poker. 'Don't touch me!' Snarling at his mother like an animal, he stalked back into the house, all pretence at civility gone.

Jenna watched slack-jawed as the blood drained from her mother-in-law's face. Meanwhile, astonishingly, Marcus pretended not to notice, slipping an arm around his mother's waist and leading her inside, full of chatter and smiles and merry Christmases, as if the horrifying exchange they'd all just witnessed had never happened.

Another Christmas at the Mill, Jenna thought bitterly. *Let the denial begin.*

'So you heard some strange noises on your way home. You got back to your cottage all right. And when you went upstairs, you found the toy clock on your pillow. Is that right, Ms Grey?'

Iris looked at the police sergeant's doughy face and realised that, in the nicest possible way, he was dismissing her.

He thinks I'm an hysterical woman. That I'm hearing things. Seeing things.

She'd driven all the way into Winchester to file a formal incident report about what happened last night, but from the moment she sat down, the irritating man on duty had made her feel like a fool.

'Or to put it another way, Sergeant . . .' *Damn it. Why am I so awful with names?*

'Trotter,' he reminded her patronisingly.

'To put it another way, Sergeant Trotter,' Iris continued, annoyed, 'someone *broke into* my house. Came into my bedroom, without permission or invitation. Invaded my private space with a deeply intimate gift.'

'The little clock, you mean?' The policeman raised an eyebrow. Clearly this wasn't his definition of 'intimate'.

'Yes, the clock.' Iris's exasperation was getting the better of her. 'Surely you can see that only somebody who knows me well, or who's been watching me closely, would know about my interest in doll's-house furniture? And it's not the first time it's happened either.'

Sergeant Trotter rubbed his eyes wearily. 'You're referring to the present you found on the doorstep a couple of weeks ago?'

'The lamp,' said Iris. 'Yes.'

Sergeant Trotter leaned back in his chair. He'd been taught in training how to deal with all sorts of people. The great British public came in many different shapes and sizes. He'd already pegged this Grey woman as falling under the categories of 'posh' and 'arty-farty'. Clearly she was making a mountain out of a molehill about the toys that some overzealous admirer had been leaving her. She was a pretty woman – badly dressed but pretty. Short of major mental illness, there was really no excuse for the cardigan with the pink appliquéd horses on it, or for the striped leggings underneath. But despite this, it wasn't hard to imagine that someone in Hazelford had taken a shine to Iris Grey. Clearly her nervous disposition had misconstrued her admirer's efforts at playing Secret Santa.

Luckily, Sergeant Trotter was here to offer reassurance and put the situation right.

'If I might make a couple of observations, Ms Grey,' he began, pleased with how intelligent and professional he sounded. 'It's coming up to Christmas. That's a time when people like to leave presents, as you know. I daresay some people also think it's romantic to surprise a lady at Christmas. To "go the extra mile", as they say.'

'By breaking and entering?' Iris's brown eyes widened.

'Ah, but that's the thing,' said the sergeant. 'You yourself said there were no signs of forced entry. The main door to the kitchen was locked, but the little door round the back was left open. Isn't that right?'

'Well, yes, but only because no one ever uses that door. You have to fight your way through brambles to get to it, and it's practically wedged shut it's so stiff.'

Sergeant Trotter spread his hands wide over the desk and smiled at Iris almost pityingly. 'All I'm saying is, the door *was* unlocked. Isn't it possible that some friend or admirer snuck in while you were out for a walk and left you the clock as a nice surprise?'

'It's not a "nice surprise" to have a strange man invade your *bedroom*!' Iris shouted, getting furiously to her feet. 'Never mind,' she snapped. 'I can see I'm wasting my time.'

'That's not true, Ms Grey. You're welcome to lodge a report if you'd like to,' said the sergeant calmly.

'That you'll file away under "Ignore completely"?' Iris shot back witheringly. 'No, thank you, Sergeant. I have better things to do with my time.'

74

For once this was true. She had a sitting scheduled with Dom Wetherby at five o'clock, and a mountain of emails and admin to do before that, stupid things that she'd been putting off for ever but needed to be finished before Christmas.

Outside the police station, Iris drew her heavy duffel coat more tightly around her and stalked angrily to her car. *Useless bloody police.* Heaven forbid that a really serious crime should happen out in Hazelford. The idea that, if it did, Sergeant Trotter and his colleagues would be the men on the case was deeply, deeply disturbing. Like having Chief Wiggum from *The Simpsons* in charge.

God help us all.

'Sorry, sorry, sorry!' Dom blustered into the study at five fifteen to meet Iris. 'How awful of me to be late. These bloody parish council meetings are the bane of my life, I tell you. You can never get away. Has anyone offered you a drink?'

Iris smiled. She was used to Dom's lateness by now, as well as the bonhomie that followed it, like being engulfed in a warm cloud of charm and attention and light. That was her overwhelming impression of her subject so far. *Light.* When Dom Wetherby walked into a room, any room, he lit it up at once, a veritable meteor of charisma. It could be hard to resist.

'I'm fine, thanks, very comfortable,' she said. Her earlier fury at the inept police sergeant who'd taken her statement had dissipated, now that she'd successfully finished all the forms for her driver's licence renewal (joy!), taken a shower and changed, and made a heroic start at tidying the cluttered cottage kitchen, mess that had been getting her down for days. 'Besides, I never drink and paint.'

'Don't you?' Dom raised a mischievous eyebrow, pouring himself a dry sherry before assuming his usual spot on the

Chesterfield. 'I often drink and write. Nothing like a decent amontillado to get the old creative juices flowing, I find.'

Iris smiled again. She highly doubted this was true. For all his good humour and easy, flirtatious manner, she suspected Dom was rigidly disciplined about his work. It was his eyes that gave him away. Beneath the generosity and the teasing smiles, there was a steeliness that was almost frightening at times. It was still early days in their sessions together, but Iris was coming to know a man with two distinct sides. A man who was both kind and ferociously ambitious. A man who loved people yet could also be deeply selfish. Get on the wrong side of Dominic Wetherby and his light could burn you, like a too-bright sun.

'So tell me about the meeting,' said Iris as she started to paint. She found it easier to work when her subjects were talking. Animation was always better than forced stillness, which looked unnatural.

'Oh God, it's so awful. *Awful.*' Dom groaned. 'I know I sound like a terrible snob, but these dreadful Little Englanders with their dreary lives and petty grievances. "*My neighbour* this" and "*The bin men* that." I don't know how anyone can stand it. Sometimes I think they should all be rounded up and shot.'

Iris laughed. 'That's the Christmas spirit! Spoken like a true chairman of the parish council.'

'I know, I know.' Dom grinned ruefully. 'I should never have taken the job.'

'Why did you?'

He took another long sip of sherry. 'To see off the developers, mostly.'

'Developers?' Iris asked, remembering the conversation she'd overheard in Hazelford Stores and interested to hear Dom's side of the story.

'They were a Russian company with operations in Oxford,' said Dom. 'I'm not keen on the Russians, as a rule. They're bullies. Although if I'm honest, I also took the job to irritate that tit Harry Masters. Seriously, if the chip on that man's shoulder got any bigger, you could build a bloody wardrobe out of it. And the way he leers after Ariadne. It's pathetic.'

'You're jealous?' Iris looked at him archly. She'd have thought Dom Wetherby far too arrogant to be threatened by the likes of a retired village piano teacher, but apparently not.

'Don't be silly,' Dom purred, fixing her with his most direct, flirtatious stare in return. 'I know my wife only has eyes for me.'

I highly doubt she can say the same, thought Iris, feeling more and more like a gazelle being eyed up by a lion.

'You're looking particularly gorgeous today, by the way,' said Dom, reading her mind. Or perhaps just playing to the gallery; Iris wasn't sure which. 'New sweater?'

'Yes, actually.'

She hoped she wasn't blushing. The tight green scooped-neck cashmere she'd changed into after her Winchester trip had been an impulse buy, a cheer-herself-up present after another painful phone call with Ian. It was a lot more muted than her usual attire and it suited her, accentuating her slender arms and drawing attention to her small but buoyant apple breasts. Suddenly, ridiculously, Iris felt as if wearing it might have looked like some sort of come-on to Dom, and wished she were wearing something brighter and baggier, like she usually did.

She quickly changed the subject.

'I saw Lorcan out in the village yesterday. He was admiring the Christmas tree. Is he getting excited?'

Dom's face lit up with love. Whatever else he might be, there was no doubt he was a devoted father.

'"Excited" doesn't begin to cover it. He's like a puppy with a new chew toy. Lorcan *loooooves* Christmas. I think he keeps the magic going for all of us. And, you know, he's a great comfort to his mother,' he added, thoughtfully. 'Especially this year, with Billy back home.'

The mere mention of Billy's name was enough to drag a cloud into the room. It was obvious to everyone, even Iris, that it was Ariadne who bore the brunt of her son's anger. But no one at the Mill was immune to Billy's dark energy, which hung around him like a rotten, sulphurous smell.

'He hasn't been bothering you, has he?' Dom asked Iris, out of the blue.

Iris frowned. 'Bothering *me*? No. Why do you ask?'

'Oh, no reason,' muttered Dom, unconvincingly.

'I've hardly seen him,' said Iris.

This was a lie. The truth was, she often glimpsed Billy, watching her from one of the upstairs windows in Mill House or hanging around in the shadow of the kitchen wall, shivering and hateful in the bitter winter air, sometimes dressed in little more than a T-shirt. Billy seemed to relish the cold, venturing out into the December weather half dressed, as if seeking out the punishment of a wind-whipped face and frostbitten fingers.

'It's a strange thing, having children,' Dom mused, opening up as the sherry warmed his blood. 'You give them everything: life, love, a home. And then they grow up and hurt you.'

'Not always, surely?' said Iris, her eyes still focused on her canvas.

'Always,' said Dom, deadly serious all of a sudden. 'Some hurt by leaving. Others by staying. Either way, growing up's a great betrayal.'

Iris kept painting, her brush capturing the fluid curve of Dom's upper lip as he spoke. *What a strange thing to say*, she thought.

'That's the wonderful thing about Lorcan,' Dom added, the light rushing back in as quickly as it had been extinguished. 'He'll never grow up. He's our Peter Pan.'

'Who's our Peter Pan?'

Ariadne appeared in the study doorway in an apron with bright red cherries printed on it, her hands and forearms and face dusted with flour.

She looks like a poster for domesticity, thought Iris, as Dom beckoned her over and made a great show of pulling her into his lap and kissing her. *The Angel in the House.*

'Lorcan,' said Dom. 'I was just telling Iris how he'll never grow up.'

'Nor will you, apparently,' Ariadne teased, kissing him indulgently on the top of his head. 'The chap from the Bentley dealership called earlier to confirm a delivery date. *Another* new car, Dom?'

'It's a Christmas present. From me to me.'

'It's two hundred thousand pounds!'

'I've done well at the card table lately.' Dom shrugged sheepishly. He knew Ariadne disapproved of his poker habit, even if he won. 'I'll take you for a spin up Hazelford Hill as soon as it arrives. Rev the engine outside old Harry Masters' house. See if I can *really* piss him off. He fancies you something rotten, you know.'

'Oh, please. You are ridiculous!' Ariadne blushed. 'I'm almost sixty years old.'

Dom gazed into her eyes. 'You're beautiful.'

Ariadne swatted him away, but Iris could see her positively basking in the warmth of his affection.

Dom Wetherby did that to people, Iris had noticed, to men as well as women. He made them feel special, like the most important person in the world. With a shock, Iris recognised the unpleasant feeling building in her own chest as envy. Not because she wanted an old roué like Dom Wetherby to love her, but because she wanted somebody to. Ian used to, once. But that was so long ago it no longer felt real. More like a story she half remembered, that had happened to somebody else.

In that moment, watching Dom and Ariadne Wetherby canoodling playfully on the sofa, Iris wished she had what they had. And yet at the same time, she couldn't completely shake the feeling that she was watching some sort of show. That their entire interaction, ever since Ariadne walked in on the sitting, had been somehow choreographed. Edited for her benefit. She remembered the mask Dom had slipped on at their last sitting, after he'd looked at the text on his phone, and felt her disquiet deepen.

'I won't disturb you,' Ariadne said, getting up and wandering round to Iris's side of the room to take a peek at her canvas. 'I was just curious to see how it's coming along.'

As she bent down, Iris noticed for the first time a faded scar round Ariadne's left wrist. The flour on her hands made the pinkish-red lines and raised skin stand out, and Iris found herself wondering how Dom's wife could have come about such a mark. If it were anyone else, she would have suspected youthful cutting or self-harm, but it was impossible to imagine the cool, capable Ariadne Wetherby as the suicidal type, even in a past life.

'And how *is* it coming along?' asked Dom. 'I promised Iris I wouldn't look till it's done. But is she capturing my devilish good looks?'

He's only half joking, Iris thought, hastily looking away from Ariadne's scar and refocusing her attention on her subject. Iris liked Dom, but Ariadne had been spot on about his vanity. Iris couldn't remember the last time she'd met a more self-absorbed man. Which, considering that she was married to Ian McBride, was really saying something.

'Oh, I'd say she's more than doing you justice, darling,' Ariadne assured her husband. 'Supper will be ready at eight. I'm up to my eyes in baking till then.' And with that she drifted back to the kitchen, as silently as she had come in.

'She's a vision, isn't she?' sighed Dom, watching his wife go. 'Hard to believe it's been more than thirty-five years since we first met at Oxford. My old don at Christ Church, Professor Nevers, introduced us.'

'Ian and I met at Oxford,' said Iris without thinking, instantly regretting having shared such a personal detail with Dom. This was just the sort of nugget he might use to try to control their sittings, to get the upper hand over her psychologically. In reality, she needn't have worried. Dom didn't even acknowledge the comment. He was still obsessing over Ariadne.

'You noticed the scar on her wrist just now.' He looked at Iris, not quite accusingly, more letting her know that he knew.

'Yes,' said Iris, astonished that he'd noticed. Clearly he was more observant than she'd given him credit for.

'You're wondering if she tried to kill herself. End it all, thanks to the misery of being married to me.' He said it so deadpan, it took Iris a moment to realise he was joking.

'Your face!' Dom laughed loudly. 'Ah, that was priceless. Don't worry, it was nothing like that. She had a tattoo when we first met – hideous, naff thing it was, a sort of bracelet of roses. Got it removed years ago, thank God.'

'For you?' asked Iris.

Dom looked briefly taken aback by the question, as if he'd never considered this possibility before. 'I don't know. Maybe. She knew

I wasn't a fan, that's for sure. Ariadne's the real hero of this family, you know,' he added, his voice once again full of affection. 'She's the real star. It's her you should be painting, not me.'

And yet it's you who's sitting here, getting all the attention, thought Iris. *As usual.*

She wondered whether professional jealousy had played any part in the Wetherbys' marriage, as it had so destructively in her own. If so, they'd obviously ridden out the storm.

Increasingly, Iris feared there would be no such happy ending for her and Ian.

At this point, she wasn't even sure she wanted one.

CHAPTER SEVEN

The next morning, courtesy of another cheap bottle of Hazelford Stores' finest Argentine plonk, Iris woke with a pounding headache to a bright but frozen day. Stepping outside to take the rubbish out in a pair of Snoopy pyjamas tucked into wellies, both the cold air and the dazzling winter sun made her wince. Squinting as she staggered back from the bins to the cottage, she jumped a mile when Billy Wetherby suddenly materialised from behind the hedge, practically leaping onto her doorstep.

'Jesus!' Iris gasped, clutching her chest.

'Sorry.' Billy looked genuinely apologetic. 'Did I startle you?'

'A bit,' Iris admitted.

There was something different about Billy today, she noticed. Something less angry. It struck Iris again how handsome he was, albeit in a sunken, watchful way. She also noticed that he was holding a wrapped box in his hand, and that he smelled of after-shave and toothpaste.

'I brought a peace offering,' he said, holding up the box with an unexpected shyness that was rather endearing.

'A peace offering?' said Iris, opening the door to let them both in to the warmth of the kitchen. 'Were we at war?'

'Well, not war exactly. But I felt as if we got off on the wrong foot when I first got back,' Billy explained. 'That day by the river.'

'I see,' said Iris.

On the one hand, it was nice of Billy to make this effort. On the other, Iris couldn't just forget the fact that the 'wrong foot' they'd got off on was her witnessing him trying to physically assault his mother. It would take more than a nicely wrapped box of chocolates to erase that first impression.

Still, Iris was a firm believer that any kind gesture should be met with kindness, even if all she really wanted was for Billy to go away. He still made her nervous; plus his presence was preventing her from going back to bed with the bacon sandwich and Alka-Seltzer she so sorely needed.

'Would you like a cup of tea?' she asked him.

'Thanks.' Billy sounded genuinely grateful. 'That would be lovely.'

Watching him take off his coat and sit down at the table, Iris clocked his dilated pupils for the first time and began to regret her decision to ask him in. Was he high? If so, he was holding it together remarkably well, so far. But the thought that he might melt down at any minute added another layer of tension to an already awkward situation.

After some stilted small talk about Dom's portrait and the art world in general, Iris brought the pot of tea over to the table and poured them both a cup in matching Emma Bridgewater cockerel mugs. As if there were some magic by which a wholesome, middle-class china tea set could make this a wholesome, middle-class encounter. Instead, a painful silence descended. Not sure what else to say or do, Iris opened Billy's present: not a box of chocolates, as it turned out, but a polished and rather beautiful ammonite.

'I love fossils,' Billy announced, watching Iris turn the ancient creature over in her delicate painter's hands. 'Don't you?'

'I don't think I've ever really thought about them much,' Iris admitted. 'Although it's certainly a beautiful object.'

'I find there's something so calming and peaceful about them,' Billy mused, sounding more stoned by the minute.

'Hmm,' said Iris, who was struggling to muster up any similarly profound feelings for a long-dead snail, but not wanting to seem ungrateful.

'When I'm rich, once I get my inheritance money from Dad, I'm going to start a serious collection,' said Billy, warming to his theme. 'I saw a beautiful set of trilobites on eBay the other day, but they're not cheap. Thirty thousand pounds. I'd get ten of those if I could. I'd never waste money on stupid things like cars and clothes the way my parents do. They're so shallow sometimes. It makes me sick.'

Iris listened silently. His entitlement was breathtaking. He simply assumed he would inherit a large sum from Dom one day, despite their strained relationship and the fact that he'd done nothing whatsoever to deserve it. He also seemed to see no irony in criticising his father's career and spending habits, while at the same time planning how he, Billy, would spend his share in the fortune that Dom had made.

Unable to think of any polite response to this, Iris changed the subject. 'How are the preparations going? Up at the house?' she asked. 'Your mother's done an incredible job decorating the place. It looks like a film set.'

'Fake, you mean?' Billy couldn't help himself. 'Yes. She's good at that, my mother: the art of artifice.'

His eyes had become even bigger and he'd started to tap his leg in a distinctly manic fashion.

He's definitely taken something, thought Iris. *Why did I let him in?*

'Have you always had a difficult relationship?' she heard herself asking, opening up the very can of worms that she'd hoped to avoid, but finding her curiosity was suddenly overwhelming

Billy gave a snort. 'You could say that.' He picked at a hanging thread on Iris's tablecloth, winding it round his finger till the tip turned red, then purple and finally almost blue. 'Let's just say that my mother is not who she pretends to be,' he said cryptically, avoiding Iris's gaze.

'No? Who is she, then?' Iris asked.

Billy's head jerked up. 'A witch!' he shouted, banging his fist on the table. Iris couldn't tell if he was joking or not. 'She's a wicked, wicked witch. And I hope she rots in hell.'

OK. Not joking.

Despite her growing anxiety, Iris remained fascinated. 'If you hate her so much, why did you move back home?'

Billy shrugged. 'To punish her? I don't know. The truth is, Iris . . .' He rolled her name around his tongue in a way that made the hairs on Iris's forearms stand on end. 'I didn't have too many other options. I'm flat broke, thanks to my tight-fisted father. And, you know, it's a nice house.'

'It's an incredible house,' Iris agreed.

'And all the better now *you're* here.'

Before Iris could stop him, Billy lunged across the table and kissed her. Strong, sinewy hands gripped the back of her head as his lips found hers, grinding against her in a violent, unwanted rhythm.

'What the hell are you *doing*?' After the initial shock, Iris found her voice and strength at last. Ducking out of his grip, she scraped her chair back and jumped up from the table as if she'd been stung.

'What does it look like?' Billy said angrily, also standing. 'Don't pretend you haven't thought about it.'

'Excuse me?' Iris looked at him, incredulous.

'Stuck here alone, day after day. No husband. No boyfriend. I mean, you must miss it.'

'Miss what? Being lunged at?' Iris said furiously. 'Not really.'

'Sex,' Billy said bluntly. Clearly whatever he'd taken had made him wildly disinhibited. 'You're not *that* old.'

If she were less shocked, Iris might have laughed. Clearly Dom Wetherby's charm gene had not been passed to his son. Not this son, anyway.

'I think you'd better leave.'

'Fine.' Billy picked up his coat, his face assuming its familiar aspect of victimhood and bitterness. 'No doubt I'll see you around.'

He feels wronged, Iris thought, in disbelief. *He actually blames me for rejecting him.*

Storming out of Iris's cottage, the first person Billy saw was his father, trudging over the frost-hardened ground, apparently on his way there himself.

'Good luck,' Billy barked at Dom.

'What do you mean?' asked Dom.

'Only that you've no chance of thawing the ice maiden,' Billy grunted, stomping off.

'Thawing the what? What are you talking about? Billy? Billy!' Dom called after him, but Billy kept walking, oblivious.

Walking into Mill Cottage's kitchen through the still-open door a few moments later, Dom saw Iris leaning over the sink with her back to him. 'Knock, knock,' he said cheerfully. 'I just popped over to let you know I can't make our sitting tomorrow. Something's come up in London and I . . . Are you all right?'

He noticed Iris's shoulders were shaking.

'I'm fine,' she sniffed, unconvincingly.

Dom frowned. 'I passed Billy on my way here,' he said. 'He seemed agitated. Did he do anything to upset you? Iris?'

He didn't get any further. Turning round, sobbing uncontrollably, Iris launched herself into his arms. Suddenly it was all too much – the hostility from Ian, the recurrent feeling that someone was following her, the break-in, being dismissed by the police, and now Billy with his unexpected 'peace offering' followed by unwanted sexual advances and Jekyll-and-Hyde rage. It wasn't that Iris needed Dom's comfort particularly. Chances are she would have hurled herself into the arms of whomever had been next to walk through her door. And yet there was something especially comforting about Dom. His broad chest and deep voice, like distant rolling thunder, combined with his warmth and the fact he was almost twenty years Iris's senior made him feel both paternal and safe. She found herself clinging to him embarrassingly tightly, like a flightless baby bird to its nest.

'Sorry,' she sniffed, once she'd cried herself out. 'I'm not sure where that came from.'

'It's quite all right,' said Dom, with a calmness he didn't feel. 'Iris, you must tell me the truth. Did Billy hurt you? Just now?'

'No.' Iris shook her head vehemently. 'It was nothing like that. He made a pass at me, that's all.'

'What?!' Dom went white.

'It wasn't anything terrible. It was more the fact that it sort of came out of nowhere. That was what threw me.'

'Oh God,' Dom groaned. 'I'm so sorry. I'm afraid my son's got a problem with women.' He rubbed his eyes wearily. 'A huge problem. It's what got him sent away.'

Wiping her eyes on a tea towel, Iris sat down, gesturing for Dom to do the same. 'Tell me. What happened?'

Dom didn't need to be asked twice. Assuming the seat that Billy had just vacated, he poured out the story. To Iris's surprise, he seemed to want to talk about it.

'About three years ago Billy became obsessed with a young woman who lived in the flat below him in London. Susan Frey. She was a legal secretary. I think they'd had a drink together once or twice at the pub on the corner, but that was it. Anyway, somehow Billy got it into his head that this girl wanted to be with him. That her boyfriend was controlling her, holding her against her will or some such nonsense.'

'Did he have any reason to think that?' Iris asked, calm again now and eager to hear as much of the story as Dom was willing to tell.

Dom shook his head, visibly pained at the memory. 'None whatsoever. It was all in his head. I think he knew that really; he just couldn't admit it to himself. Anyway, it started with emails and phone calls. But I mean literally hundreds and hundreds of phone calls. The poor girl was terrified. The boyfriend tried to reason with Billy, and when that didn't work, the police got involved and Susan took out a restraining order against him. That was when things really went tits up.'

Iris waited for him to elaborate.

'Ever since his early teens Billy's had a problem with anger, mostly directed at his mother.'

'Do you know why that is?'

Dom gave a joyless laugh. '"Why that is" . . . As far as I know, there is no "why". It just happened. He woke up one day and decided to start hating her. Accusing her of God knows what.

Mistreating him. Lying. Turning the family against him. He was incredibly paranoid.'

'Do you think it was drug-related?'

'Maybe.' Dom shrugged. 'He smoked a good bit of weed as a teenager, but then who didn't? No one ever diagnosed him as addicted to anything. After the restraining order, he became furious with this poor Frey girl for rejecting him and started stalking and harassing her, slashing the tyres on her bike and leaving threatening messages in the middle of the night. Showing up at her work, yelling obscenities one minute and asking her to marry him the next.'

'It sounds like he needed psychiatric care, not prison,' said Iris.

She sensed a lot of anger in Dom's tone and not much compassion for his troubled son, although she tried not to judge. Perhaps Billy had simply exhausted his family's reserves of patience. That could happen. Iris's own sister, Thea, had had bipolar disorder throughout her teens, so Iris knew from bitter experience what a fine line it could be between mental illness and straightforwardly selfish behaviour.

'Well, he ended up getting both,' Dom told her. 'After he tried to set fire to her car, he was arrested and charged. A psychiatrist assessed him as fit to stand trial. I would have helped him if he'd admitted it, but some moronic friend of his persuaded him to plead innocent to harassment and criminal damage. The stupid sod didn't show a shred of remorse.'

'They found him guilty,' said Iris.

'Yup.' Dom smiled wryly. 'Right after they found the Pope Catholic. The judge gave him two years, with mandatory therapy three times a week. He got released on parole in the autumn after just over a year and moved back home. At first he seemed better.

Calmer, and more aware of what he'd done and that it was wrong. But the more time he spends around his mother, the angrier he gets.'

'Do you think it's a good idea to have him living here?' Iris asked tentatively. She was hesitant to pry too deeply into another family's private turmoil, although it was obvious that Dom wanted to talk about it. 'I mean, if Ariadne's some sort of trigger, wouldn't it be better for him to live independently?'

'It would, yes,' Dom said bluntly. 'A lot better. But his saint of a mother won't hear of it. She refuses to kick him out. We do love him,' he added, rather touchingly, Iris thought. 'But it's been bloody hard. Anyway, I'm so sorry that he scared you.'

Reaching across the table, Dom took Iris's hand in his. She'd seen a flirtatious side to him before, during their sittings, but this wasn't like that. It was a gesture of genuine kindness and care.

'I'm fine. I overreacted.'

Releasing her hand, Dom suddenly noticed some pieces of doll's-house furniture, tucked away behind the sugar bowl at the far end of the table. Iris had started repainting one of the bedroom 'suites' last night, and the less-than-impressive results were still drying on a sticky piece of newspaper.

'What are these? Christmas presents?' His tone had changed completely, back to his usual charming, engaging self. 'Do you make them yourself?'

'Oh, no.' Iris blushed. 'I just . . .' The words trailed off lamely.

For some reason, Iris found that she really, *really* didn't want Dom Wetherby to know about her private passion. Her doll's house was a sacrosanct fantasy, not to be invaded by outsiders, and especially not by a relative stranger. Although it occurred to her that, after everything he'd just shared about Billy, perhaps Dom no longer saw her in that light.

'Who's it for? I wonder. Let me guess. Goddaughter?'

Iris shook her head. 'I should really take a shower and get dressed . . .'

'Niece?' Dom tried again.

'All right, look, actually it's mine,' Iris blurted, wondering why on earth she hadn't grabbed at the 'goddaughter' lifeline and run with it.

Dom looked amused. 'Yours?'

'Yes.' Iris cleared her throat. 'I'm a collector. It's a hobby of mine.'

There was an awful moment's silence. Then Dom suddenly burst into laughter, a deep, full-throated guffaw loud enough to make the tiny kitchen shake.

'Oh, that's priceless!' He wiped away tears of mirth.

'Why? What's so funny about it?' Iris demanded primly.

'Nothing! I mean, it wouldn't be funny if you weren't so defensive about it. And so adorably pompous!'

Iris's colour deepened to an ugly beetroot. Really, it was infuriating to have someone see through her like this, to be stripped bare. As a portrait painter, Iris was usually the one doing the stripping. She found the shift in the power dynamic between her and Dom deeply unsettling.

'I'm sorry,' said Dom, still chuckling but sensing he might have gone too far. 'I'm surprised, that's all. You always seemed so *poised*.'

Iris was flattered. Did she seem 'poised'? It wasn't a word she'd ever associated with herself before.

'But now it turns out you're like one of those old buffers who keep dog-eared copies of *Train Lovers* magazine in the garden shed instead of porn and spend every Sunday up in the attic with their Hornby train set!' Dom added with a grin.

'I am *not* like an old buffer,' Iris protested, painfully aware that she was once again sounding pompous. Drawing herself up to her full five foot two, she attempted to look as 'poised' as a person could hope to look while wearing a pair of Snoopy pyjamas and wellington boots and with last night's mascara smeared, panda-like, round their eyes.

'Don't get your knickers in a twist,' said Dom, nudging her good-naturedly in the ribs. 'I'm only teasing you.'

'Ugh. Sorry,' said Iris, forcing a smile. 'It's been a rough few days.'

'Has it?'

He was being kind, but again Iris had the uncomfortable sensation that Dom Wetherby was seeing through her. That he knew, or wanted to know, more than Iris wanted to tell him.

'What are you doing for Christmas?' he asked, out of the blue.

'I . . . well, I . . . I'm not sure,' Iris stammered. Actually, she was sure. She'd finally summoned up the courage to call Ian yesterday and tell him she wouldn't be coming home for the holidays.

'I figured,' was all Ian had said in response. 'Thanks for letting me know.'

Neither of them had had the energy to bring up the subject of what might happen after Christmas. Instead, they'd exchanged a few polite words and hung up as quickly as possible. It was all terribly muted and depressing.

'I only ask because you mentioned you and your husband were separated,' said Dom.

Did I mention that? thought Iris.

'So I assumed there was a good chance you'd be staying here on your own.'

Iris opened her mouth to speak, but Dom cut her off.

'And if that's the case, then you must come to us.'

Iris paused for a moment. She was touched by the invitation. He was so sincere and sweet, underneath all the bombast, she found herself warming to him yet again. *He doesn't want me to be lonely at Christmas. For all his vanity, Dom Wetherby's a kind man.* But at the same time she really didn't think she could face sitting through Christmas lunch with the Wetherbys *en famille.* She could picture it now: Billy's sniping, Ariadne's all-round saintliness, Dom three sheets to the wind on expensive Burgundy and Iris struggling to make small talk with Lorcan, or the grown-up son she hadn't yet met. As kind as Dom's offer was, this wasn't Iris's idea of festive fun.

'It's terribly nice of you to offer,' she began, 'but I couldn't possibly intrude.'

'Bollocks! No intrusion,' Dom said robustly, his tone firm almost to the point of bullying.

'Really, I can't,' said Iris. 'I've already made plans here at the cottage.'

'What plans?' Dom challenged her. 'Are you having friends over?'

'Well, no, but—'

'I'm sorry, Iris,' Dom interrupted, 'but I can't have you sitting here on your tod, carving up toy turkeys with your dolly friends while we're all enjoying ourselves up at Mill House, eating Ariadne's world-class Christmas lunch. I simply can't do it.'

'I do *not* carve up toy turkeys!' Iris protested vehemently. 'I'm a collector!'

'Whatever you say.' Dom winked at her. 'But you're spending the day with us and that's final. I refuse to take no for an answer.'

'Over my dead body!' Undoing the clasp on her pearls, Ariadne threw them down angrily onto her dressing table. 'What were you *thinking*, Dom?'

Dom Wetherby watched, distressed, as his wife continued undressing, each gesture and movement angrier than the last. Pulling on one of the old-fashioned white linen nighties she always wore and that Dom secretly hated (deeply unsexy and they made her look like a ghost), Ariadne began brushing her hair in swift, violent strokes.

After a long and difficult dinner, with Billy being his typical prickly self and obvious, unspoken tension between Marcus and Jenna, Dom and Ariadne had retired to bed. Only then, in passing, had Dom mentioned his invitation to Iris Grey this morning, to join the family for Christmas lunch. Ariadne had hit the roof.

'I wasn't thinking anything,' Dom protested. 'I felt sorry for her, that's all. She's on the outs with her husband. I was trying to be nice.'

'Nice to whom?' Ariadne snapped, her usually soft voice shearing sharply upwards into a staccato bark. 'Not to me, that's for sure.'

'Billy had just harassed her! I had to do something. Anyway, I thought you liked Iris.'

'I do!' Ariadne yelled. 'That has nothing to do with it.'

'Doesn't it?' Dom's confusion was genuine. He would never understand women.

Ariadne spun round to face him, quivering with rage and frustration. 'No. It bloody doesn't! Don't you realise that I spend my life, my entire life, playing the hostess *for you*? Throwing parties and dinners and drinks and shooting weekends for *your* friends, *your* business associates, to further *your* all-bloody-important career. The Christmas Eve party alone is weeks of work, Dom.'

'I know. And I'm very grateful,' said Dom. 'You do an incredible job, my darling.' He put a hand on her shoulder, but she shrugged it off furiously.

'Yes. I do,' she snapped. 'And in return I have one day – *one day* – that is family only. *One day* when I get to relax, and not play hostess, running around at your beck and call. Christmas Day is sacrosanct, Dom, and you know it is. I see so little of Marcus . . .'

'Marcus,' Dom muttered darkly. 'Is that what this is about? You know you call the poor boy every damn day?'

'Yes, I do know,' Ariadne seethed. 'And I don't suppose it's occurred to you that I talk to Marcus because he actually listens to me?'

Dom turned away, stung.

I listen, he thought. *I'm forever bloody listening. But it's never enough. You're never happy.*

'I can't un-invite Iris,' he said grumpily. 'I'd look like a total fool.'

'And we can't have that, can we?' Ariadne shot back snidely. 'Don't worry. I'll talk to her tomorrow. I'll explain that you took leave of your senses. I'm sure she'll understand.'

'Oh really? And how are you "sure" of that?' Dom asked, angry himself now. It was true that family Christmases were something of a rule. But then they'd never had a tenant staying at the cottage before. He didn't understand why Ariadne insisted on blowing this whole thing up.

'Because Iris is an understanding person,' Ariadne announced confidently, fastening her long hair up into a tight, unforgiving bun. 'As you said before, I like her.'

Through the wall, Marcus and Jenna heard the raised voices as they prepared for bed.

'What d'you think they're arguing about?' asked Jenna. 'I bet it's Billy. Wasn't he vile at supper, the way he cut your mother down all the time?'

'I don't think they're arguing,' said Marcus, pulling back the covers and sliding wearily into bed. 'They never really argue.'

Jenna laughed loudly. 'Are you mad? Your mom's screaming like a banshee in there. Listen!'

'I don't want to listen,' Marcus said, more curtly than he intended. 'She's animated, that's all.'

Climbing in beside him, Jenna propped herself up on one elbow and raised a languid eyebrow. 'Animated?'

'I hate it when you do this, you know,' grumbled Marcus.

'Do what?' Jenna asked.

'Psychoanalyse. Go all American on me. Next you'll be telling me I have unresolved abandonment issues.'

'Everyone has those,' Jenna smiled.

'You see?' said Marcus.

'What I see, again, is your absolutely pathological need to keep pretending your family is perfect,' said Jenna, not unkindly. 'It is beyond you to admit that your parents are fighting. Or that your brother is a class-A dick.'

Marcus rolled over uncomfortably. Jenna was right, of course, especially about Billy. His behaviour at dinner tonight had shocked Marcus, as had his appearance when they first arrived. He looked thin and ill and utterly changed, somehow. Strong feelings of both compassion and revulsion churned in Marcus's chest every time he spoke to his brother. And yet he didn't want to admit that things with Billy were as bad as they were. Unlike Jenna, Marcus remembered Billy as a small boy, so funny and charming and full of life. So profoundly, painfully different to his adult self. Something had gone catastrophically wrong between then and now. And whatever it was, Marcus had missed it. Admitting the extent of Billy's problems would mean admitting his own guilt. At the same time it felt like a betrayal of the old Billy, the brother Marcus had known and loved, the brother he still missed desperately.

He kissed Jenna's bare shoulder. 'Let's go to sleep. I'm wiped out.'

'OK,' said Jenna, stiffening.

They lay in silence as the shouts from the other side of the wall peaked and then subsided.

One storm had passed. But their own was still brewing.

Deciding to strike while the iron was hot, Ariadne set off straight after breakfast the next morning in search of Iris. She saw her out in the lane before she reached the cottage, clipping sprigs of holly berries from the hedge and putting them into a wicker trug at her feet.

Ariadne called to her.

'You're out early. Decorating?'

'Oh, yes!' Iris turned round, red-cheeked from the cold. 'Belatedly. Your house looks so fabulous I thought the least I should do was hang a bit of holly and put some fairy lights up.'

Helping her remove a recalcitrant stem of prickly leaves and blood-red berries, Ariadne got straight to the point.

'Listen, I'm terribly sorry, and I do hope you won't be offended, but I'm afraid Dom made a mistake yesterday. You see, we have a strict rule, a sort of long-standing agreement between us, that Christmas Day is supposed to be family only. The party is such an enormous effort every year, you see, and I desperately need to decompress afterwards. I know Dom invited you up to the house for Christmas lunch, but—'

Iris interrupted her, holding up a hand half covered by a pair of tatty fingerless gloves. 'Please, don't worry at all. I completely understand.'

'It's nothing personal,' Ariadne explained.

'Honestly,' said Iris, 'I get it. To be perfectly frank with you, I'm relieved. It was so kind of Dom to ask me, and he was so . . .' she searched around for the right word, 'so forceful about it, I didn't have the heart to say no.'

'Yes. He does that,' Ariadne said, through pursed lips.

'The truth is, I'd actually much prefer to be by myself this year. I'm not sure I could face a long lunch making polite, festive conversation over the turkey. Is that awful?'

'Not at all,' said Ariadne, delighted that they seemed genuinely to be on the same page. 'Besides, you'll probably be festive-conversationed out after our party. I know I always am. It's great fun, but there are so many people coming, especially this year. It's what my children would call "full on".'

'Right,' Iris said awkwardly.

This was her moment to tell Ariadne she wasn't coming on Christmas Eve either. She'd been putting it off for ever, but now the party was a mere two days away. It didn't help that the entire village was abuzz with gossip and anticipation about the annual Wetherby Christmas shindig. For weeks now Iris had been hearing about the paparazzi descending on Hazelford and the slew of famous folk who'd be wending their way to Hampshire.

The very idea of spending Christmas Eve mingling with an army of preening celebrities and self-important media types brought Iris out in hives. She'd come to Mill Cottage to escape London and all its artifice and pretence. Her idea of Christmas Eve in the country was carol singers and candlelight and church bells. Cattle a-lowing. Peace. Clearly with the catering vans and florists and lighting people already starting to arrive, there would be little chance of that.

Say something! a voice in Iris's head screamed. *Tell her you can't make it.*

But the only audible voice was Ariadne's as the two women walked up the lane and crossed the stile leading to the river and Iris's cottage.

'Dom's great friend Graham Feeney is coming this year. You'll like Graham,' Ariadne told Iris. 'Everybody does. He's a barrister, very successful and terrific fun.'

With a jolt, Iris realised that Ariadne was trying to set her up. Had Dom told her she was single? Or implied it? Or perhaps Ariadne had just assumed, what with Iris spending so much time at Mill Cottage alone, and now staying on for Christmas.

'I'm sure he is. But I'm actually still married. Technically,' Iris said, fingering her wedding ring uncomfortably.

Ariadne looked embarrassed. 'Of course you are. How crass of me.'

'No, no, it's fine,' Iris said quickly. 'It was a kind thought.'

'It's just that Dom mentioned things were difficult for you at the moment, with your husband,' Ariadne went on carefully. 'Marriages can be tricky things.'

'They can,' Iris agreed.

'Well, if nothing else, hopefully our party will be a distraction. And who knows, you may even get some new commissions out of it. I have a long line of friends simply dying to meet you. I've told them all about you doing Dom's portrait.'

Oh God, thought Iris. *She's being so kind. There's no way I can say no now, not without sounding churlish.*

She thought back to Billy's angry words about his mother yesterday.

'*My mother is not who she pretends to be. She's a wicked, wicked witch.*'

It seemed to Iris that Ariadne Wetherby was in fact the exact opposite of a witch. She was more like a Good Fairy, floating around on an aura of kindness and peace and goodwill.

If anyone was wicked in the Wetherby family, and not what they seemed to be, it was Billy. Having to see him again was another reason Iris dreaded Christmas Eve. But her fate was sealed.

'We'll see you at the party, then?' Ariadne hugged Iris warmly as they parted ways.

'See you then,' said Iris.

'And sorry again about the misunderstanding with Dom.'

Walking back to Mill House, Ariadne felt pleased with herself.

The conversation with Iris had gone well. Dom had caused a problem and Ariadne had solved it. And so the time-honoured rhythm of their marriage continued, the long ebb and flow of wrong and right, disaster and repair. It was tiring sometimes, being the one whose job it was to fix everything. But Ariadne was used to it. It was the life she had chosen, in the end.

Walking back into the warm cinnamon fug of the kitchen, it struck her forcefully how very much easier her life would be if Dom weren't in it. More boring, certainly. And perhaps less happy. But oh, how easy! How calm!

For a second she allowed herself to fantasise about the Mill without Dom. About a life that was truly her own. But only for a second. Soon Lorcan came in needing help with his present-wrapping, and Oscar started whingeing, looking for Jenna, and the vortex of family life sucked Ariadne back into its bloody, warm, throbbing heart.

CHAPTER EIGHT

Iris watched from her tiny bedroom window as the local TV news team clambered out of their van, looking for a suitable spot to set up their cameras. In less than an hour the first guests should start arriving for Dom and Ariadne Wetherby's long-awaited Christmas Eve bash, and space along Mill Lane was already scarce. TV crews and print reporters competed for parking spots along the verge with wine merchants, caterers and the DJ for tonight's event, a spotty boy of about nineteen, who seemed to have brought an army of 'technicians' with him, for reasons Iris couldn't fathom, especially since Ariadne had told her that the playlist was to be carols and American Christmas music, which hardly warranted Moby or Fatboy Slim.

Word in Hazelford village was that tonight's party was expected to be an altogether more spectacular event than last year's, although the increased media presence probably had more to do with the fact that Dom Wetherby's beloved Grimshaw series was coming to an end, and the entire nation was bracing itself for a tearful goodbye to its favourite detective on New Year's Day.

In reality, it was the Grimshaw novels rather than the television series that had made Dom his fortune. The bulk of his net worth, estimated at around fifteen million pounds, had come from book sales. But it was the TV series that had turned Grimshaw's creator into a celebrity in his own right, something close to a national treasure. Thanks to the power of television, everyone in England knew that Dom Wetherby was turning sixty next year and officially about to retire, just as they knew the ins and outs of Carl Rendcombe's colourful love life. (Carl played the epony-mous detective in the ITV series and was a regular in the gossip magazines and the *Daily Mail* Online. He would be at tonight's party, along with the rest of the cast.)

If tonight's event turned out to be Dom Wetherby's last hurrah as a literary and TV powerhouse, then that made it newsworthy, not just in Hazelford but everywhere.

Pouring herself a second small shot of Laphroaig (Iris wasn't typically a whisky drinker, but her nerves tonight went way beyond Rioja, and needs must), she stood in front of the mirror and tried to see her reflection with her own artist's eye. She'd chosen an unusually understated outfit for tonight's party, a simple grey sheath dress and shiny black boots. There was a possibility she looked a little bit like an elf – her shorter, feathered haircut might be making that worse, amping up the whole 'pantomime boy' thing. But at least no one could accuse her of looking like a jester, or a clown, or a lunatic, or a 'drug-addled art teacher', or one of the many choice insults that Ian had come up with over the years to describe Iris's off-the-wall dress sense.

She recognised with some irritation that it was partly due to Ian's barbed remarks about her appearance at their ill-fated lunch that she had also attempted make-up tonight, carefully following the instructions on a YouTube video for how to do a 'smoky eye'.

'We all know the basic smoky eye,' the appallingly over-made-up girl on the video had announced cheerfully at the beginning of her spiel.

'I don't!' Iris had yelled back at her.

Having followed the girl's advice to the letter, she now either looked sultry and mysterious or like a sleep-deprived raccoon, depending on one's point of view. Thanks to the whisky, Iris was leaning towards the former assessment. She was going to a fancy party and she looked good.

Well, she looked normal.

She looked OK.

Not terrible.

Oh God, oh God, oh God! Why on earth did I ever accept?

A commotion outside jolted her out of her self-pity and sent her rushing back to the window. Billy, looking even angrier than usual, if that were possible, in a long black overcoat and dragging a battered-looking suitcase behind him, had slammed the front door of Mill House and was heading down the side path towards the gravelled area beside the river where his filthy Citroën C3 was parked.

A taller, lighter-haired man in a dark blue suit followed him out, looking exasperated. Man two was yelling loudly enough that Iris could hear him, which certainly meant that the reporters could too, although the high wall surrounding the garden ensured that neither he nor Billy could be seen from the lane.

'For fuck's sake, Billy. Grow up! You're not twelve.'

The voice was very like Dom's. Almost identical, in fact.

That must be the other son, thought Iris. *Marcus. The oldest.*

'Tonight isn't about you!' he boomed.

A slammed car door and the start of an engine were the only response from Billy. Moments later Iris saw his car emerge onto

Mill Lane and tear off to the left, away from the village, buzzing along the side of the valley like an angry bee till it disappeared from sight.

Iris watched Marcus Wetherby run both hands through his hair and bend double. Then he stood up tall and seemed to be taking a deep breath, collecting himself, before going back into the house.

Despite her nerves, Iris was fascinated by this little exchange. What had prompted Billy to storm off like that? She found herself wondering what Marcus Wetherby was like, and whether his relationship with his younger brother had always been so fraught. She was also cheered by the fact that apparently Billy Wetherby would not now be coming to tonight's party. Knowing she wouldn't be lunged at, or cornered by Dom and Ariadne's manic, erratic middle son certainly took some of the pressure off.

Who knew? She might even have fun.

Two hours later, squeezed into the drawing room of a packed Mill House like an overdressed sardine, Jenna Wetherby helped herself to another glass of mulled wine and began swaying, only slightly drunkenly, to Nat King Cole's Christmas song. The music, at least, reminded her of America and home, of happy, tacky childhood Christmases, where the only show being put on was the neighbourhood Christmas lights, and the only competition was whose snowman was the biggest and fanciest.

Christmas at the Mill was the exact opposite: a fevered spectacle of competitiveness and one-upmanship, but all beautifully wrapped in the sort of traditionalism that only the British could do really well.

Everything from Ariadne's divine country-house décor to the roaring log fires and vast mismatched vases of holly berries screamed, 'England.' And not just England but the sort of smug, self-satisfied, upper-middle-class Englishness that wanted everything to appear homemade and rough around the edges – so the caterers' mince pies were delicious but deliberately stodgy, with burnt crusts, and the mulled wine was served in jam jars rather than glasses – when in fact it had been meticulously planned and contrived down to the very last detail, with no expense spared.

'Any news on where Billy's got to?' Jenna asked Marcus, sliding over in what she thought was rather a sexy red dress and slipping an arm around his waist. It was the first time she'd seen him alone all evening. From the moment the party started, Ariadne had appropriated him, dragging him round from guest to guest like a prize pig she wanted to show off.

'If there were, don't you think I'd tell you?' Marcus snapped back, bad-temperedly.

'I don't know. Would you?' Jenna's anger was quiet and controlled. 'I guess that might have been hard as you've been glued to your mother's side like a limpet for the last two hours.'

'For God's sake, give it a rest,' hissed Marcus. 'This is Mum's night, not yours. It's bad enough with Billy behaving like a teenager.'

Jenna opened her mouth to speak, then closed it again. White with fury, she turned on her heel and stalked off.

'Jenna!' Marcus called after her, to no avail.

Fuck.

Things had been so lovely earlier today, despite the mayhem of party planners and press. Jenna had finally stopped with the questions about his scratched face, thank God, and they'd had such a sweet session of carol singing round the nursery piano. He'd got properly carried away during 'The Twelve Days of Christmas', giving it the full Pavarotti, and Lorcan and Lottie had both collapsed into fits of giggles changing the lyrics of 'most highly favoured lady' in Mary's song to 'most highly flavoured gravy'.

But of course that was before Billy had spoiled everything.

Again.

Why did it always have to be like this?

While Jenna and Marcus bickered, Iris had nabbed herself a coveted spot by the fire, perched on the edge of the club fender. It was the perfect position from which to observe goings-on without being dragged into conversation herself, or worse, dragged off by Dom to be introduced to yet another 'brilliant' producer/actor/writer/journalist who was 'absolutely passionate' about art. He meant well, and Iris was grateful for the effort, but the last thing she wanted to talk about tonight was work.

In fact, thanks to the pretty, posh and very young waitresses who seemed to be constantly refilling her champagne flute, Iris was rapidly reaching the point where talking at all would be beyond her. The pre-game whisky shots had been a mistake. Then again, who cared? No one here knew her, except for Dom Wetherby, who was clearly hammered. And it was nice to let herself go for once. Back in her 'real' life, Ian was the one who always got drunk at parties, forcing Iris into the unenviable role of designated driver/caretaker. Here at the Mill, she could forget all that and let her hair down doing three of her favourite things: eating, drinking and people-watching.

Alan and Jean Chivers from Hazelford Stores, who'd recently 'adopted' Iris as a friend and taken it upon themselves to baptise her in the fire of village gossip, had already provided an exhaustive list of stars expected to attend tonight, presumably so that Iris could tick them off in her book like a birdwatcher. Unfortunately, most of the names meant nothing to Iris.

'I don't really watch TV, except *EastEnders* and *Corrie*,' she told Jean apologetically. 'Everyone I know would be too lowbrow for this crowd. And all the pop stars I've heard of are dead.'

'They don't call 'em "pop stars" no more,' Alan Chivers had informed her kindly. 'It's "recording artists" these days. They'll be the ones with next to no clothes on,' he explained helpfully.

'And they'll probably be black,' added Jean, with no hint of irony.

So far Iris had only spotted one black, half-naked girl, talking to a gaggle of Grimshaw actors. But according to Carl Rendcombe, one of the few celebs Iris *did* recognise, the girl was in fact the presenter of a literary quiz on Radio 4 and boasted a first-class degree in classics from Cambridge, information that would no doubt have disappointed Alan and Jean Chivers enormously.

Far more compelling than the celebrities, for Iris anyway, were the Wetherby family themselves. All sorts of complicated dynamics were playing out there, as gripping as any of Iris's beloved soap operas. Through her semi-drunken haze, Iris scanned the room for Ariadne, who wasn't hard to find, gliding between groups of guests like a slightly stoned Christmas angel, basking in the ceaseless praise of her skills as a hostess. Which, to be fair, were impressive. Short of providing snow, which was beyond even her skills, Ariadne had created a veritable Christmas carol of cheer and warmth and Yuletide magic at the Mill. Everybody, villagers and celebrities alike, looked happy. Well, almost everybody.

Iris recognised Marcus Wetherby as the shouty man she'd seen in the garden earlier. He still looked tense, rigid-jawed in conversation with some of his parents' friends. He'd also clearly just had a blazing row with the gorgeous girl in red, whom Iris assumed must be his wife.

And then there was Dom Wetherby, grinning from ear to ear, utterly in his element as the evening's centre of attention. In a dark suit with a blue Turnbull & Asser shirt and a deep purple Italian silk tie, Dom looked unusually formal tonight and about as handsome as a man could at his age. Right now he was chatting with a rotund giant of a man who would have made a perfect office-party Father Christmas and whom Iris eventually recognised as the legendary literary agent Chris Wheeler. They were joined by Raymond Beatty, whom Ariadne had introduced Iris to earlier, Dom's elderly but still great fun publisher at Bell & Mason. Despite looking as if he were a sneeze away from the morgue, Raymond had immediately regaled Iris with a hilariously blue joke that somehow seemed even ruder, and funnier, coming from such a frail and sweet old man. All three men were talking animatedly, apparently about the latest and last Grimshaw, if the snatched fragments of conversation floating across to Iris were anything to go by. But Iris noticed that Dom was only half listening, and that his gaze was repeatedly drawn to both the door – *he's waiting for somebody. Billy?* – and his wife, who'd just been drawn aside by the former parish council chairman Harry Masters.

Harry and Ariadne were huddled on a window seat in the back corner of the room. Iris surreptitiously edged closer, hoping to overhear their conversation, but it was difficult. Harry was speaking quickly and in hushed, urgent tones. At one point he placed his hand on Ariadne's forearm and gripped it tightly, making her look up. Whether she was shocked or angry or just surprised, Iris couldn't tell.

'. . . won't come back. Not tonight,' Iris heard Harry whisper.

'What if he does?' There was an unmistakable note of fear in Ariadne's voice.

Infuriatingly, Harry's reply was muffled. Iris heard the word 'smile' and two emphatic 'listen's. Then he stood up, his joints visibly stiff and arthritic with age, aware of Dom watching them. He made a point of kissing Ariadne on the cheek, presumably to irritate Dom, and Iris noticed his stubby pianist's fingers lightly stroke the back of her head before he shuffled off into the throng.

A firm tap on the back of Iris's shoulder made her jump. She spun round guiltily to find herself face to face with a man she'd never met before. He was older, in his mid-fifties, Iris guessed, and handsome in a distinguished, nerdy way. Like a newsreader.

'You must be Iris.'

His grey eyes danced when he smiled, and a deeply grooved fan of lines spread out from each corner, making him look simultaneously older and more attractive. Combined with his thin lips, strong jaw and nose and slightly crooked teeth, he reminded Iris of a more everyday version of Liam Neeson.

'Ariadne described you perfectly. I'm Graham Feeney, an old friend of the family.'

He extended a hand that was more like a bear's paw. Iris shook it, her own hand looking like a child's in his.

'Hello.' Her voice sounded croaky. This must be the friend of Dom's Ariadne had mentioned to her, the day she came over to un-invite Iris to Christmas lunch. Of course Ariadne had failed to mention quite how good-looking he was.

'I gather you're doing Dom's portrait,' said Graham. 'He's a fascinating man.'

'He is,' agreed Iris, wishing she could remember any salient detail about Graham Feeney's life with which to prolong the conversation, before deciding that Ariadne probably hadn't told her any.

'Charming but complicated,' said Graham.

'I agree,' Iris croaked. 'Although I'm curious as to why you think so.'

'Ah well. We go back a long way, Dom and me. He was terrific friends with my older brother, back in the day. So I suppose you could say I've seen him evolve.' Graham smiled again and Iris was embarrassed to feel herself blushing. *For heaven's sake, woman, get a grip. You're not fifteen.*

'I'd love to see it. Your painting,' Graham added. 'I don't suppose it's here, is it?'

'Oh . . . no.' Iris shook her head, her blush deepening. 'It's at home. No one's seen it yet. It's very much a work in progress.'

'Like Dom,' Graham observed.

'Like all of us,' Iris countered, horrified by how much she was enjoying talking to this man she didn't know from Adam. Without noticing, she'd started twisting her wedding ring round her finger, like a talisman to ward off wicked spirits. *Wickedly attractive spirits.*

'Can I get you another drink?' Graham asked, his gaze lingering just a little too long on Iris's slender legs, before slowly moving back upwards to her smoky eyes.

'Why not?' She handed him her glass.

Perhaps tonight's party was not going to be such an ordeal after all.

After a walk outside to let the freezing air help clear her head, Jenna Wetherby made her way over to the 'puddings station' and helped herself to a shot-glass-sized mini Christmas pudding, topped with a sinful smudge of brandy butter. A few feet away from her, lounging against the impressive Bechstein grand piano that Dom had bought at auction at Christie's at great expense for Mill House's drawing room but then never allowed anyone to play, were Dom and Ariadne's artist tenant, Iris Grey, and Graham Feeney, flirting heavily.

Graham was Marcus's unofficial godfather, and Jenna had grown familiar with his 'story' over the years, although she'd only met him in person a handful of times. A successful barrister from Edinburgh, Graham was the younger brother of Dom's best friend from college, Marcus Feeney. Marcus had been a depressive who'd tragically taken his own life the year after he and Dom left Oxford. Jenna's Marcus had been named after him.

Graham Feeney had remained close to the Wetherby family after his brother's death and for many years afterwards, although recently that relationship seemed to have started to drift, for reasons no one in the family quite understood. There had been no argument, no falling-out that any of the Wetherbys could think of. And yet something had clearly shifted in Graham, prompting him to stop calling and visiting the way that he used to.

Jenna remembered how delighted Ariadne had been when, out of the blue, Graham accepted the invitation to this year's Christmas party. Marcus also seemed pleased. He was fond of Graham, and felt sad about the distance that had inexplicably grown between his godfather and his parents. Marcus's own theory was that it might have had something to do with Billy's conviction. Graham had attended the court case, but it was shortly after that that his visits and calls began petering out. Whatever his reasons, Marcus was happy he'd had a change of heart, more so than Jenna, who'd always found Graham Feeney to be rather a cold fish. He seemed to have warmed up tonight, however, and looked positively animated chatting with Iris Grey. If Iris's body language was anything to go by, the feeling appeared to be mutual. Jenna noticed lots of arm-touching and leaning in, no doubt fuelled by Dom's champagne and Ariadne's positively lethal mulled wine.

Iris was very short, and looked tiny standing next to Graham, who was well over six foot tall, like a pantomime Jack to Graham's giant. She was extremely pretty, with enormous striking eyes, high cheekbones and a lithe figure that Jenna knew from experience was irresistible to a certain type of man. Ariadne had told Jenna that Iris was in her forties, but she looked much younger, as small and vulnerable as a child.

Jenna thought back to the other night's argument and the raised voices she and Marcus had heard drifting through Ariadne and Dom's bedroom wall. Iris's name had been mentioned more than once.

Was it possible that Dom was smitten with his new portrait artist? Jenna wondered. If so, he clearly had some competition in Graham Feeney. Although Graham only had tonight to woo the fair lady, whereas Dom had the advantage of repeated exposure: all those long, intimate sessions on the study couch. All that uninterrupted gazing at one another.

I'm being silly, thought Jenna, although her father-in-law was certainly capable of an affair. Then again, the psychologist in her knew that that applied to pretty much everyone. Including Marcus.

Marcus. All at once the dark thoughts came flooding back. His unkindness to her tonight. The scratch on his face. The lies.

A dark shadow at the window suddenly caught Jenna's eye, distracting her for a moment from her brooding thoughts.

Was that a man's face, pressed against the glass?

'*Billy?*' Jenna mouthed, setting down her pudding glass and moving towards the shadow, walking at first but then quickening her pace to a run. But by the time she got to the window, whoever it was had gone.

Graham sipped his drink and watched Iris's sexily retreating back in those adorable black boots as she nipped to the loo.

Talk about unexpected! To meet someone, fall for someone, tonight of all nights. The irony wasn't lost on Graham, although perhaps it was dulled a little by the copious amounts of alcohol roaring through his veins.

Dom had prepped him about Iris when he arrived in Hazelford last night. 'Got an artist coming to the party, Iris Grey. She's been living in the cottage, doing my portrait. She's bloody good.'

'OK,' said Graham. 'And you're telling me this because . . .?'

'She's a lovely girl,' Dom shrugged. 'Great-looking, a bit hippy-dippy, but clever, and her marriage is in the shitter.'

'I see,' said Graham. He'd forgotten Dom's legendary tactlessness. Or perhaps just blocked it out.

'You should have a crack at her,' said Dom.

'You make her sound like a nut,' Graham replied dryly.

'Well, if she is, she's not a tough one,' said Dom, either ignoring or simply not hearing the disapproval in Graham's tone. 'All she needs is a bit of love and attention and she'll be putty in your hands, believe me. I know women.'

Graham wasn't sure if he was joking or if he really meant it. Dom could certainly be breathtakingly arrogant when he tried. But this was a bit OTT even for him.

'I'm not sure I'm looking for putty in my hands,' Graham replied calmly. 'Especially not married putty.'

He meant it at the time. But then Iris had walked in wearing those fantastic kinky boots and all Graham's sensible thoughts had deserted him like rats from a sinking ship.

Of course, he couldn't act on it. Not with things the way they were. But still . . .

Iris disappeared from view and Graham turned his attention to a conversation going on behind him. Two middle-aged men and an exquisite-looking young girl were sitting together on one of the sofas. The men were speaking Russian, and although the girl didn't contribute, she seemed to understand them. In an alternate, better universe, Graham would have taken the girl to be the daughter of one of the men. In reality, however, she was probably a high-class hooker.

Graham's Russian wasn't brilliant these days, but it was good enough.

'He's acting like it's over with,' the taller, uglier man was saying, bitterly picking at a dried spot on his face. 'He doesn't care.'

'Oh, he cares. It's an act. He knows what he owes.'

'You think so? Did you see his new car?' the first man snorted. 'He hasn't paid up, but he thinks he's entitled to drop two hundred grand on a Bentley?'

The shorter man shook his head. 'You're wrong. It's all part of the act. Keeping up appearances. Playing the rich, successful author.'

His friend grunted. 'I hope you're right. For his sake.'

At this point Iris emerged from the loo and started weaving her way through the heaving mass of partygoers towards Graham. She'd reapplied her make-up, which had to be a good sign, and was smiling at him warmly.

Pushing the Russians' disconcerting conversation out of his mind for now, Graham turned his attention back to Iris Grey.

'Is that for me?' Iris asked, swiping the champagne flute out of his hands.

'It is now.' Graham beamed down at her, stepping out of the darkness and back into the light.

Ariadne touched Dom lightly on the elbow as he finished regaling a group of journalists with a very risqué story about the last BBC director general.

'Can I borrow him for a sec?' she interrupted softly, steering him away. Guiding Dom into the corridor, she waited till they were alone before letting her emotions show, the anxiety etched on her white face revealing itself like an ancient carving chiselled into chalk.

'He hasn't come back yet.' She twisted the fabric of her sleeves in anguish. 'Where *is* he, Dom?'

'He's just letting off steam somewhere,' Dom tried to reassure her. 'You know Billy.'

'I don't!' It was almost a shout. 'That's the whole point. I don't know him anymore. Neither of us do. I never know what he's going to do next.'

'He'll be back when he needs us, darling.' Dom's voice was soothing and rich, like warm molasses. 'How's Marcus doing?' He tried to change the subject. 'Is he enjoying himself?'

'He would be,' Ariadne said crossly, 'if Jenna would stop giving him such a hard time. Have you seen them tonight, squabbling?'

'I'd stay out of it if I were you, love,' said Dom.

'Poor Marcus. He works so hard, but that woman's never happy.'

'Not like you, my angel,' Dom purred, pulling her close, enveloping her in the strength and warmth of his embrace, his smell and the slow, regular beat of his heart lulling her into a deep, calm trance. 'You're always happy.'

'No one's always happy, Dom,' Ariadne sighed. But she let herself be held and comforted. She'd seen that the Russians were here, but she didn't have the heart to bring them up, not now. 'I do love you, though.'

'I know you do,' he told her. 'And I know you're worried about Billy. But I promise you, everything's going to work out all right.'

'But . . .?'

'Nobody knows,' Dom whispered softly in her ear. 'That's the bottom line, darling. Nobody knows.'

'Do you really believe that?' Ariadne looked up at him pleadingly. She so desperately wanted this to be true.

'I do,' said Dom. 'I really do. You must try to relax.'

'Isn't it uplifting?' The vicar, a nice but ineffectual young man from Sutton Coldfield, helped himself to another mince pie as he watched the Wetherbys embrace. 'Especially at Christmastime, to see a long-married couple so deeply in love? So committed to each other, and to their family and their community. It warms one's heart, don't you agree?'

Reverend Brian Glazier had only recently arrived in Hazelford and wasn't yet fully up to speed on the rivalries and jealousies that ran through his parish like mould through cheese. As a result, he'd made the mistake of addressing this remark to Harry Masters. Harry occasionally obliged the vicar by playing the organ at church, so the Reverend Glazier considered him an ally at least, if not quite a friend.

The piano teacher grunted something noncommittal as he watched the hateful Wetherby disengage from his wife and return to his cronies, grabbing a canapé from a passing silver tray and stuffing it greedily into his open, wet, rapacious mouth.

I hate you, Harry thought. *I hate you more than I've ever hated anyone in my life. I hope you die in a fucking fire.*

A waitress shimmied past. Declining the offer of a glass of mulled wine or champagne, Harry helped himself to another elder-flower fizz instead and took a long, cooling gulp, as if the flavoured Perrier stood a chance of cooling the roiling volcano of rage that boiled within. Harry wasn't about to risk getting tipsy and letting that bastard Wetherby and his fancy, too-clever-by-half London friends make him look foolish. Only last week at the reconvened council meeting, Dom had tried to patronise him, talking down to Harry as if he were a child, or one of Dom's underlings at the publishing house that printed his Grimshaw rubbish. Of course, Harry had stood up for himself, giving as good as he got. At least, that's what he'd thought at the time. Afterwards he'd worried that he might have overreacted. Allowed Wetherby to goad him into saying more than he should, or adopting positions more extreme than his own, real views. The idea that he had been manipulated, that Dom Wetherby had outsmarted him, burned in Harry Masters' throat like battery acid.

I know things about your wife that you'll never know, Harry reminded himself gleefully. Dom Wetherby wasn't the only one with secrets.

'Is everything all right, Harry?' Reverend Glazier asked.

'I'm fine, thank you, Vicar.' Harry's gaze followed Ariadne, who'd moved back into the drawing room now to join her oldest son, Marcus. Ariadne's father, Clive Hinchley, a slight, stooped, wizened little man with a face like a pickled walnut and the conversational skills to match, was also part of the group, leaning heavily on his wicker walking frame. On Ariadne's other side, Lorcan hovered with a silver tray of caviar blinis, adorably proud as one of the 'waiting staff' in his church suit and tie.

Harry tried to catch Ariadne's eye, but to no avail. Once she was in 'mother mode', she had eyes for no one else. It was one of the things Harry most admired about her.

'My goodness.' Reverent Glazier tapped Harry on the shoulder again, determined to get his attention. This time, however, it was for something interesting. 'Who is *that*?'

Harry turned round. A very attractive, and apparently very drunk blonde had just walked in. In killer heels and a skintight gold dress that made the most of her figure, she staggered towards the bar, ricocheting off people and furniture like a glamorous gold bullet.

'Merry Chrishmash to all, and to all a good night!' the girl slurred loudly, before dissolving into fits of giggles. 'Ishn't anyone going to offer me a drink? Johnny, darling, how about you? Or you, Dom – there you are! The man of the hour!'

She clattered noisily over to join Dom Wetherby and his cronies. Dom greeted her arrival with a smile so stiff it looked like the onset of rigor mortis.

From their cosy window seat, Iris and Graham Feeney were also glued to the unfolding drama. It wasn't just Dom who seemed upset by the young lady's arrival. Marcus Wetherby looked like he'd seen a ghost. On the far side of the bar, Marcus's wife, Jenna, put down her drink and stared at her husband intently, the frown she'd been wearing all night deepening as the woman in gold made more and more of a spectacle of herself.

'Aye aye. That looks like trouble,' observed Graham. 'Who's she?'

'No idea,' said Iris. 'A colleague of Dom's, I assume.'

They both watched as Dom's agent, Chris Wheeler, extracted himself from his conversation with Raymond Beatty and marched up to the drunken blonde.

'Come along, Rachel. Why don't the two of us get some air?'

'I *do* know her,' Graham suddenly blurted to Iris. 'It's Rachel Truebridge. She's the ITV producer who works on the Grimshaw series. Or she used to, anyway. Christ, I didn't even recognise her.'

'Do you know her well?' Iris heard herself asking, a preposterous feeling of jealousy sweeping over her.

'No,' said Graham. 'I met her once or twice at things of Dom's in London. She was very professional, very together. Nothing like this.'

They both winced as Rachel staggered backwards, moving away from Dom's fat agent, and lost her footing, almost landing flat on her back before one of the waiters stepped in to catch her.

'Fuck off, Chris!' Rachel snarled, loudly enough to bring conversations around the room to a shuddering halt. Everyone was watching now. 'I don't need babysitting. I need a damn drink.'

'Who is that?' Ariadne's father, Clive, asked Marcus loudly, cupping his hearing aid.

'She's nobody,' said Marcus. He started walking towards her, but Dom stepped in and put a hand on his arm. 'I'll do it.'

Marcus began to protest, but Dom insisted. 'Go to Jenna. I'll handle this.'

Gliding smoothly forwards, Dom placed a warm hand on the small of Rachel's back and steered her gently but firmly towards the smaller champagne bar, near the garden doors. 'Let me get us both a drink. Then we can get some air together, hmm? Walk and talk.'

Looking confused, Rachel eventually acquiesced, and the party chatter naturally resumed as Dom helped her outside.

'The poor thing's had a few too many,' Ariadne observed, smiling indulgently, as she drifted past Iris and Graham. 'There's always one, isn't there? How are you two doing?'

'Fine, thanks,' Graham grinned. 'Couldn't be happier.'

Iris smiled thinly. There was something jarring about Ariadne's reaction. Something false. Worse than false. Something sinister.

'Are you OK, Iris?' Graham leaned forward, concerned.

'Sorry. Yes.' She pulled herself together. 'I felt a bit woozy suddenly.'

'I'll get us some food,' said Graham. 'Don't move.'

Outside, a figure watched through the sash window as a tall man appeared with a plate of bread and canapés, and began chatting to Iris.

Her face through the glass looked like one of her own portraits, a picture in a frame. In profile, her head thrown back, she was laughing at the tall man's jokes, like a giddy schoolgirl.

Bitch. Heartless bitch. A little attention and she's anybody's.

The figure shifted his weight from one foot to the other in the undergrowth, cold and uncomfortable in his hiding place. Raised voices made him turn. They were coming from the kitchen garden, or just beyond. Dom Wetherby and a woman, arguing.

Emerging from the shrubbery, creeping along the shadow of the high wall to the very end, where the kitchen garden met the edge of Mill Woods, the figure saw them head into the trees together. Thinking quickly, he slipped into the wooden shed Ariadne Wetherby used for sculpting and bolted the door behind him, crouching below the window. It was the perfect vantage point, sheltered and silent, deep in the wooded gloom.

'You think you're God!' the woman hissed at Dom. 'But you're not. And you won't get away with it.'

'I'm not *getting away* with anything,' Dom snapped back. 'For God's sake, Rachel. You always knew this was going to end.'

'Oh, it's ended all right! It. Haszh. Ended. But on *my* terms, not yours, you bastard.'

The woman was blind drunk. Staggering around like a newborn fawn at the edge of the wood, she could hardly stand.

'I know your secrets, Dominic,' she slurred.

'Stop being so melodramatic. This isn't a television show, Rachel.'

'I can bring you *down*.' Jabbing a finger wildly in the air, she lost her balance, falling to the hard ground with an audible thud.

The figure waited for Dom to help her, to pick her up or at least see if she were hurt. Instead he just stood there, his voice dripping with derision.

'Look what you've sunk to, Rachel. You're an embarrassment.' He started to walk away.

'I know 'bout the Russians!' she sobbed.

Dom stopped in his tracks, but didn't turn to look at her.

'Go home,' he told her sternly. 'Before you say something you'll regret.'

'Is that a threat?' She tried to sound defiant, but all the fight had gone out of her like air from a popped balloon.

'Goodbye, Rachel,' said Dom.

The figure watched from the shed as the famous author strode away, back to his party, to the bright lights and noise of his beautiful house with all his beautiful friends inside, while the girl lay alone in the darkness, sobbing quietly. Eventually she heaved herself up off the frozen ground and slunk away, fumbling with her mobile phone.

He'd seen enough.

Tracing a line round Ariadne's cold potter's wheel with one finger, he began to whistle.

We wish you a merry Christmas.

We wish you a merry Christmas.

He formed an imaginary gun with his fingers and with each 'wish' fired a pretend shot towards the house.

We wish you a merry Christmas

And a happy New Year.

By the time Dom returned from his walk outside, minus the drunken producer, whom he'd presumably managed to usher into a cab, Iris was feeling less sick, but still far from sober. She found her attention swinging, pendulum-like, between Graham, who was still being charming and funny and whose hand seemed to have taken up permanent position just above her knee, and Dom, who seemed oddly rejuvenated after his walk outside and could be heard throughout the party boasting loudly and animatedly to his daughter-in-law, and the vicar, and anyone else who would listen about how proud he was of the Grimshaw finale, to be aired on ITV 1 on New Year's Day.

'You'll all be in shock, believe me,' he announced, self-importantly and sounding more than a little drunk himself by this point. 'There's gonna be quite a twist.'

Everyone clamoured at him for hints and spoilers, apparently quite willing to forget the embarrassing incident with the drunk woman. Only Clive, Dom's elderly father-in-law, refused to let the Rachel incident go so easily, continuing to demand noisily why the producer had been allowed in in the first place, if she wasn't invited, and 'what her problem was' with Dom.

'I don't understand. Where is she now?' Clive yelled, to no one in particular.

'Grandpa, let it go,' Marcus Wetherby snapped. 'Perhaps you should go to bed? It's getting late.'

'I'm not tired.'

'Even so,' Marcus insisted, taking the frail old man by the shoulders with a firmness that unsettled Iris. Meanwhile, Dom raised his own voice to drown out the old man's protests.

'We wanted to give the TV finale a different ending to the book,' he explained to his enraptured audience. 'If we've done our jobs right, and I think we have, people's jaws should hit the floor. Don't you agree, darling?'

He turned to Ariadne, who nodded dutifully. Something had changed since Dom's little trip outside with Rachel. When he left, Ariadne had been acting as if nothing was the matter. As if Rachel Truebridge's embarrassing behaviour hadn't offended or affected her in any way. Now she looked as if she might be about to burst into tears at any minute.

It couldn't have been Dom who'd upset her. He wasn't even in the room.

Was it the sinister-looking Russian men Iris had seen hovering around Ariadne earlier? Or Harry Masters, who'd cornered her briefly after Dom went out and been shooed off? Or her father, Clive, with his loud, unwanted questions? Iris had been too focused on Graham Feeney to know what had happened. But something clearly had.

'Look at Ariadne's face,' Iris whispered to Graham. 'She looks fit to explode.'

Graham laughed. 'She's just a bit tired, I expect. You're always watching people, aren't you? Always thinking.'

'Not always,' said Iris, embarrassed. She didn't want him to think she was some sort of weird stalker type.

'What are you thinking about me?'

His voice had thickened and his face, suddenly, was just inches from hers. There could be no mistaking his intent. Iris felt a wave of desire, quickly followed by a second, bigger wave of panic. But before she could get the words 'I can't' or 'I'm married' out of her mouth, Graham's lips were already on it, kissing her just once, unbearably quickly, on the lips. It was all over in a second, and all so *chaste*! She wanted more! Much more. Or less. Or nothing, because she was still married, and very drunk, and the whole thing was ridiculous and—

'What on earth?' There was a clattering of glass. Dom's horrified voice rang out like a clanging bell.

Ariadne was standing, as if in a trance, with blood dripping profusely from her hand. The champagne flute she'd been holding seemed to have inexplicably broken, slicing her palm and fingers in multiple places.

'Darling! What happened?'

'I . . . I don't know. Someone bumped into me. It was an accident,' she muttered.

Accident my arse, thought Iris. *You squeezed that glass so tightly it shattered.*

'Mummy!' Lorcan took one look at the blood and burst into noisy tears.

'Is Doc Ingalls still here?' Dom barked at one of the staff. 'Someone go and fetch him. And turn off that damned music.'

After that everything blurred a bit. The party wound down rapidly, with the last of the trendy London limpets prising themselves reluctantly off the Wetherby sofas and armchairs, like barnacles off the keel of a booze-soaked boat. Graham retrieved Iris's coat and helped her into it before fetching his own. Then before

Iris knew it, they were outside in the freezing cold, watching everybody pile into their cars.

Graham unlocked his Audi and turned on the ignition to warm it up before saying goodbye to Iris.

'Are you sure you don't want me to walk you over to the cottage?'

No! the voice in Iris's head screamed. *I'm not sure. I'm not sure of anything anymore!*

'Quite sure,' she said aloud. 'If you're driving all the way back to London tonight, you need to get going.'

'OK. Well, thank you for a lovely evening, Iris. And merry Christmas.'

'Merry Christmas,' said Iris.

They didn't kiss again, or mention the kiss inside. No one said anything. Instead, after an awkward few moments, Graham hugged Iris briefly, got into his car and drove away.

Deflated, Iris walked alone back to Mill Cottage. By the time she'd undressed, found her pyjamas in the messy pile that was her bedroom floor and flopped into bed, it was well past midnight. Gazing upwards, the ceiling and walls with their quaint rose-print paper began spinning around her at a dizzying rate.

You're drunk, Iris told herself.

You kissed another man.

She examined her heart for traces of guilt, but couldn't find any. Her conscience had taken the night off, apparently. It was Christmas, after all.

Reaching out to turn off her bedside lamp, she suddenly caught sight of Dom Wetherby's half-finished portrait staring at her from the chair where she'd propped it earlier. Something struck her. The way the light shifted over Dom's pupils, it was as if he were deliberately avoiding the artist's gaze. *Her* gaze.

Iris hadn't intended to paint him that way, and indeed had never noticed the expression before. Not consciously, anyway.

It seemed important. In her hazy, drunken state, she cast around in her mind for a link between that look of Dom's, guilty and avoiding, and the things she'd witnessed tonight: the drunk producer. Harry Masters' rage. Marcus Wetherby's fear. Dom's boasting. Ariadne's bloody hand. And before all of that, Billy Wetherby, driving angrily off into the night.

Was there a connection, or was it all a concoction of Iris's alcohol-addled mind?

Too tired to care, she switched off the light, plunging Dom's portrait back into darkness. Her mind turned wistfully to Graham Feeney's face, and the fleeting thrill of his lips against her own. Then Iris sank into a deep and dreamless sleep.

CHAPTER NINE

The first thing Iris was aware of was church bells ringing. That beautiful, ancient, cascading melody of pealing bells that signalled Christmas morning.

Groaning, she pulled the pillow over her head and fell back asleep.

The next time she woke, it was noon. Her mouth was dry as dust and smelled as if a small rodent had died in it. Her head hurt when she moved, and her stomach growled so loudly she wondered if she might have swallowed the small rodent and was now having trouble digesting it. In short, Iris felt less than festive. But her need to pee overrode her deep longing to stay very, very still indeed. After making her way unsteadily to the bathroom, coffee began to feel like the next attainable goal. *To the kitchen and beyond!*

Well, perhaps not beyond. Pulling back the curtains and opening the kitchen window, she was immediately assaulted by a blast of cold air and the sort of crisp, blue, perfect Christmas Day that seemed to demand she pull her socks up and get into the spirit of things *at once*. She was about to redraw the curtains and beat a hasty retreat when she suddenly saw Lorcan, who saw her too and waved back enthusiastically, racing down the hill towards the cottage.

'Merry Christmas, Iris!' he boomed in that strange, deep voice of his, incongruously adult given his childlike nature. Seconds later he was standing outside the open window, panting like a puppy. 'Did Father Christmas came?'

'I'm not sure,' Iris grinned. 'I haven't checked yet, but I'm not sure he comes to grown-ups.'

'He comed to me and Lottie and Oscar!' Lorcan announced delightedly. He often got his tenses muddled up, possibly because he lived so much in the present. 'All my whole stocking was *full*.'

'What was your favourite thing?' Iris asked, forgetting her sore head for a moment in the face of Lorcan's utter, unadulterated Christmas joy.

'Chocolate coins.' He pulled a half-melted one out of his trouser pocket and offered it to Iris through the open glass. 'You can eat it. But save room for Mummy's special lunch!' He patted his belly, repeating the line he'd no doubt heard from Ariadne scores of times this morning. Iris could just imagine the feast she would have prepared today up at the house – organic turkey dripping with juices, pigs in blankets, truffle mashed potatoes, Brussels sprouts with pecorino cheese. Ariadne was an incredible cook, and not a woman to do things by halves. Iris wondered idly where her landlady's perfectionist streak had come from. It was hard to picture her father, the diminutive and wizened Clive, as the pushy, demanding parent. Although perhaps he'd been different when he was younger.

Iris's own parents had been poster children for 1970s liberalism, no more capable of 'pushing' their children than they were of holding down a job. Which probably partially explained why Iris's Christmas feast would consist of a Pot Noodle and mince pies in front of the telly. Not that she was complaining. If she'd had to go up to the Mill now and sit through a polite gourmet lunch party, she'd have put a gun to her head.

'Well, give Mummy my love. And merry Christmas.' Iris leaned further out of the window and kissed Lorcan on the cheek.

'After lunch it's presents,' he informed Iris merrily, by way of goodbye, before turning abruptly and scampering back up the hill the way he came.

'Not for me it isn't,' Iris murmured contentedly, pouring herself a coffee and tearing a large hunk off the Marks & Spencer's panettone that her mother sent her every year as a treat. 'After lunch it's back to bed.'

The answerphone was flashing. In a moment of madness, thinking it might be Graham Feeney, Iris hit 'play'.

'I suppose I should wish you a happy Christmas.' Ian's voice was so heavy with bitterness, each word sounded like it was choking him. 'You'll be out having fun with your new friends, I daresay. Ah, well. Take care, Iris. Have a good one.'

Take care. It was what you said to a stranger.

And was that sadness Iris heard, beneath the anger?

Incredible how a few short words from the man she was married to could turn Iris's mood from happiness to something approaching despair. Like a click of the fingers, or a flick of a switch, he brought her down, back into the darkness. Back into the trap.

Forget lunch. She might as well go back to bed now.

"'To Dom and Ariadne. With love, Graham.'"

Marcus handed the simply wrapped red package to his father. Dom smiled as he opened it, revealing an exquisitely bound early edition of Wordsworth.

'Bloody hell, that's generous of him,' he said, examining the book briefly before passing it to Jenna to give to Ariadne. 'Must have cost a small fortune.'

The whole family were in the drawing room, gathered round the magnificent Christmas tree for the annual present-giving ritual. When the boys were little, Dom had acted as master of ceremonies, but for the last few years Marcus had taken over the role, doling out gifts one by one while somebody else (Jenna, today) made notes of who had given what, for thank-you-letter purposes.

The room itself could have been a scene from a Christmas card. The tree was hung with three decades' worth of decorations, some now desperately tatty but of sentimental value to generations of Wetherby children. The most dog-eared of them all, a crudely sewn Father Christmas made by Billy in his last year of primary school, before his teenage anger and paranoia had taken hold, was now so rotted and horrifying it had been nicknamed 'Death's Head Santa' by Jenna and the name had stuck. This year Lorcan and Lottie had stuck cloves in oranges with Ariadne and tied them on with ribbons, adding another layer of sweet scent to the pine and woodsmoke. Cards from the family's countless friends littered every available surface, after which more had been hung from strings over the door and mantelpiece. On the Egton chest was a wooden nativity set from the 1970s that had become a family joke, thanks to the donkey's disproportionately enormous penis.

Along with these and other kitsch touches – Dom's American publisher had sent him a singing Rudolph one year that glowed and shuddered when you pressed its nose – there were more traditional adornments. A large sprig of mistletoe hung over the doorway, and each of the sash windows was decorated with simple but beautiful holly wreaths. Little silver trays of sugared almonds and Carlsbad Plums from Fortnum & Mason had been placed on all the coffee and side tables, and in the background 'Jesus Christ the Apple Tree' provided a soothing, spiritual soundtrack to this most soulless and commercial of Christmas rituals – and everybody's favourite – presents.

'What's that? What have you got there?' Clive bellowed from the corner, watching Graham's gift doing the rounds. Ariadne's tiny father was sinking into the soft cushions of a small velvet loveseat that was threatening to swallow him whole.

'It's a book, Dad. A poetry book,' Ariadne explained patiently.

'*What?*' the old man barked, his deafness making him bad-tempered.

'It's *poetry*, Clive!' Dom yelled back, momentarily bad-tempered himself. Dom's father-in-law only ever came to stay at Christmas, but his visits were always a trial, not least for the strain they put on Ariadne, who wound herself up like a toy mouse whenever she was around him. God knows Clive Hinchley had been pompous and dull enough when he was middle-aged and a senior partner at Hinchley Crewe, the dreary mid-level accounting firm his father had founded. But age and its accompanying loss of faculties, most recently hearing, had made Clive's company borderline intolerable. Dom had long held a private belief that Ariadne's mother, Elise, must have died of boredom and not the brain haemorrhage so lazily cited by her doctors. Marriage to Clive was surely enough to explain the world's worst headache.

Turning Graham's book over in her hands – how strange that Marcus Feeney's brother should be back in their lives, now of all times – Ariadne pressed the soft leather against her sore palm. The cuts from last night's shattered glass were still livid and red, but the pain was a welcome distraction. Outwardly Ariadne had regained her composure, cooking up a storm all morning and laughing contentedly with her grandchildren and Lorcan as they played with their stocking fillers. But inside she was stretched taut like an over-tuned violin. Her father. Her husband. Her son. Each one of them slowly but painfully turning their respective screws. If life had afforded her the luxury, Ariadne Wetherby could happily have snapped at any minute. As it was, however, family life went on. Resting the poetry book calmly in her lap, Ariadne assumed an expression of peace and love and went on with it.

Billy, *curse his wicked heart*, had not come home last night, or this morning. Dom was typically dismissive, confident that their troubled son had holed up with a friend somewhere, that the whole episode was a master class in attention-seeking and that Billy would slink back home in a day or two with his tail between his legs.

'He's trying to ruin your Christmas,' Dom told Ariadne, almost angrily, as he dressed for church, admiring his handsome reflection in their bedroom mirror. 'Just don't let him.'

Apparently it hadn't occurred to Dom that his own behaviour last night, fawning over that producer girl, had already ruined Ariadne's Christmas, or at least cast a long shadow over it. Afterwards, dear, sweet Harry Masters had helped her to dress her cut hand, while Dom had as good as ignored her, yucking it up with their remaining guests as if nothing had happened. Damage control had always been one of his specialities.

Looking at him now, ensconced in his favourite Victorian armchair beside the Christmas tree, gorged on the pitch-perfect Christmas lunch she'd just prepared, washed down with far too much Domaine Leroy Burgundy, Ariadne marvelled again at

Dom's ability to see only what he wanted to see and blot out the rest. As if life were a script that he could compose and edit to suit his own needs, a story he got to write and control. In his Grimshaw books, he managed to convey his hero's selfishness as an almost endearing quirk. Gerry Grimshaw and Dom Wetherby were not the same person, but Ariadne sometimes felt they had more in common than Dom cared to admit. Both were possessed of a well-developed sexist gene, as well as the typical firstborn's sense of entitlement; Detective Grimshaw and his creator both viewed themselves as the sun, around which other, more minor characters orbited like planets.

Ariadne loved Dom, of course. She had to. It was too late for anything else. Their lives were as intimately entwined as the roots of a tree: twisted but unbreakable. And yet, on some levels, Dom didn't understand her at all.

Couldn't he see that if anything had happened to Billy, it would be her fault?

Dom didn't understand guilt because he never felt it himself. He considered it a waste of emotion. Perhaps it was.

Closing her eyes, Ariadne imagined herself walking into her sculpting shed, pulling the chloroform mask over her nose and mouth, and allowing herself to slip peacefully away. To forget. To escape. How blissful that would be!

Marcus was still talking, announcing the presents as quickly as he could, but still not quickly enough for the children. *He, at least, looks happy*, Ariadne consoled herself, although the tension between him and Jenna remained palpable. When Jenna had opened Marcus's present to her, a simple silver locket in the shape of a heart, she'd looked as if she might burst into tears, and was clearly only holding it together for the children.

Putting aside all Billy's presents in a silent, reproachful little pile, Marcus finally reached under the tree and dragged out the biggest, and final box.

'"To Lorcan",' he read aloud, grinning as his little brother literally jumped up and down with excitement. '"Merry Christmas and all our love, Mummy and Daddy."'

Everybody watched indulgently as Lorcan tore at the wrapping on his gift like a starving child clawing at a bag of rice. Inside were two boxes, one containing an enormous bright red toy speedboat and the other a *Scooby-Doo* mystery-maker torch.

'Remoke control!' he exclaimed joyously. 'It's remoke control!' Putting the boat down on the floor carefully, he flung himself into his mother's arms and hugged her so tightly Marcus half expected to hear a rib crack. 'Thank you! I love you, Mummy!'

Watching the two of them, Jenna found herself torn. Lorcan's love was touching in its innocence. But she couldn't shake the bitter, uncomfortable feeling that Ariadne didn't deserve it. What *was* it that Lorcan and Marcus so worshipped in their mother?

'Hey! What about Daddy?' Dom asked, mock reproachfully. Lorcan bounced over to hug him, too. 'Come on,' said Dom, heaving himself up out of his chair with an effort. 'I'll put the batteries in for you and you can take it down to the river for a spin. After that I'm going to go for a walk, I think. Clear the old head. D'you want to come, Marcus?'

Marcus, who was busy extricating Lottie's Barbie from its Fort Knox-like packaging, looked up, surprised.

'OK,' he said, stealing a sidelong glance at Jenna. 'Sure. I could do with stretching my legs. Mum?'

'Me? Oh no, thank you, darling,' Ariadne said, distractedly. 'I'll be in the kitchen, washing up. There's so much to do.'

'Who's making a to-do?' piped up Clive. 'Have we missed the Queen's speech?'

'I'll put it on for him,' Jenna said kindly, offering the old man her arm. 'Come along, Clive. There's a television in the study. Come with me.'

When Iris woke again, the daylight was already fading. To her shame, she saw that her bedside clock said 3.15 p.m. Had she really slept away almost all of Christmas Day? How awful.

She spent the next twenty minutes in a flurry of activity, dressing quickly and then proceeding to tidy up the cottage, hoovering the downstairs room, cleaning the kitchen and bagging up the rubbish. Feeling virtuous, she carried two groaning bin bags out to the dustbins. At the top of the field, she saw a pair of figures walking together. In the failing light, it took a moment for her to recognise them as Dom and Marcus, no doubt walking off the excesses of lunch up at the Mill.

Wedging both bags as deep into the plastic bins as possible, to thwart the foxes, Iris suddenly heard someone cough behind her. Turning round, she could see no one there.

'Hello?' she called out. Then, more robustly, 'Billy, is that you? Because if it is, I want you to know I don't appreciate being followed.'

Nothing. Angry more than scared this time, Iris walked round the perimeter of the cottage garden. Beyond it lay open fields and the river on one side, and the slope up to Mill House on the other. There were no obvious hiding places, and the garden itself was clearly empty.

I must have imagined it. It could have been anything. An animal or a bird moving in the hedgerow. She was about to head back inside when she noticed that Dom and Marcus had stopped. Their two silhouetted figures against the skyline were clearly arguing, heatedly if the body language was anything to go by. Marcus was gesticulating wildly, sticking his head out and making jabbing motions at his father with his fingers. Dom started with his arms out wide, in a gesture of innocence, but as Marcus got closer, he, too, became aggressive. A few seconds later Iris was astonished to see Dom push his son, hard, in the chest. After staggering backwards, Marcus regained his footing and glowered at his father, before the two of them stormed off in opposite directions, out of Iris's view.

Bloody hell, she thought, hurrying back inside. *What was all that about?*

Oh well. The Wetherbys could sort out their own problems. Iris had enough of her own. Steeling herself for the high possibility of the phone being answered by a drunken Ian, she called home and was so relieved to get the answerphone that at first she couldn't think of what to say.

In the end she blurted, 'I got your message. I've been asleep most of the day. Sorry. Anyway, I wanted to at least say hello and merry Christmas. I'm not sure when I'll be back. The portrait's coming along . . .' She stalled, painfully aware that she was rambling. 'Look, Ian, I know we need to talk. I'll call you in the week, OK?'

She hung up, not satisfied exactly, but glad that an unpleasant task had been accomplished. Just a few minutes later she was rewarded by a new message on her mobile that *wasn't* a drunk, angry husband but a kind and thoughtful new friend.

'Hope your hangover wasn't too awful this morning,' the text read, followed by a sad face. 'Just wanted to wish you a happy Christmas from rainy London. Love, Graham. P.S. Can I see you again?'

A new friend? Iris laughed at herself. Who was she kidding? She was horrified by how happy she felt suddenly. It wasn't so much Graham himself, lovely as he was. It was more the realisation that life after her miserable marriage might actually be out there. Happiness. Romance. New experiences. Hope. These things didn't have to be fantasies, not if Iris didn't want them to be. Last night at the Wetherby party, and right now, reading Graham Feeney's message, they all felt not just real but tantalisingly close.

'I want to see him again,' Iris said aloud, trying the words out to see how they sounded.

'I will see him again.' The new, assertive Iris tried harder.

After all, as of today Graham Feeney *was* a friend, nothing more. After the year she'd just been through with Ian, Iris Grey needed all the friends she could get.

CHAPTER TEN

At first Iris thought the sound came from the television.

It was around six, and she should have been painting, working on the wood-panelled background in Dom's portrait that for some reason she couldn't seem to get quite right. Having slept through most of Christmas Day, she'd been determined to do something constructive (and also not to text Graham Feeney back until tomorrow morning at the earliest. Her life might *be* pathetic and lonely, but that didn't mean she had to act pathetic and lonely. Desperation was never a good look). But before she could reach for her brushes, she saw in the 'Culture' section that Alibi was showing back-to-back reruns of *Lewis* all evening, and the lure of the aptly named Laurence Fox proved too strong.

The episode had only just started, and Iris had nipped into the kitchen to grab a fortifying handful of Quality Streets when she heard it.

A scream, distant but utterly blood-curdling.

Hurrying back to the TV, she was annoyed to find the adverts were already on. Typical of her to miss the bloody murder! But then she heard it again, louder and longer and more distressed, and she realised with a lurching stomach that it was coming from outside. From the river. Someone must have fallen in!

It was pitch-dark outside and below freezing, but without thinking, Iris grabbed a torch and opened the door, racing towards the sound. She wasn't the only one. Tearing down the hill from Mill House came Marcus's wife, Jenna, followed by Marcus and a ghostly-white Ariadne, who appeared to be in some sort of nightgown.

'Lorcan!' Ariadne shrieked, her own voice raw with terror. 'Lorcan, what's happened? Where are you?'

The screams were louder now and more continuous, mingling with the constant rush of the river. Then suddenly their source became apparent – Lorcan, wild with panic, erupted over the top of the riverbank, sprinting for his life like a hunted animal. His head was thrown back, and his mouth was wide as the awful, anguished cries poured out of him. Iris reached him first and was almost mown over as he careened into her arms, still wailing.

'Lorcan! It's all right. It's all right.'

'*No!*' the boy bellowed. His eyes were white with terror, and his clothes were wet. Had he fallen in and panicked? It must be freezing in that water, and terrifying in the dark, all alone.

Before Iris could say or do anything else, Jenna, Marcus and Ariadne arrived. Bolting from Iris to his mother, Lorcan calmed slightly, but was still in a hysterical state.

'Thank God you're all right,' said Ariadne, hugging him tightly and rocking him back and forth in a soothing motion, as one might a baby. 'What happened, my darling?'

Suddenly, out of the blue, Lorcan screamed again, a deafening, keening, awful sound.

'Lorcan.' Marcus took charge. 'Calm down. Tell us what happened. Did you fall into the water?'

'He's *dead*!' Looking from Marcus to his mother, Lorcan burst into uncontrollable tears.

'Who's dead, Lorc?' Marcus asked calmly.

'Oh my God, it's Billy!' Ariadne gasped under her breath. 'He's found Billy!'

Her legs began to buckle underneath her. Instinctively, Iris and Jenna moved in, supporting her under each arm.

'We don't know that,' Jenna whispered.

'Who's dead, Lorcan?' Marcus asked again.

'He's in the river!' the terrified boy babbled. 'It's my fault!'

'*Who?*' Gripping his little brother's shoulders, Marcus tried to jolt him into coherence. 'Who's in the river, Lorcan?'

Iris would never forget the wide-eyed horror etched on poor Lorcan's face as he uttered the single, fateful word.

'Dad.'

PART TWO

CHAPTER ELEVEN

'So?'

Detective Inspector Roger Cant looked at the medical examiner impatiently. Dr Linda Drew was a decade his senior, a tall, angular woman with a razor-sharp intellect and elbows to match, who made no effort to hide her disdain for over-promoted, wet-behind-the-ears detectives like Cant. She resented answering his questions, but she had to.

'Suicide,' she said curtly.

'Are you sure?'

'Quite sure.' Dr Drew turned to go, but DI Cant stopped her.

'How?'

'*How?*' The older woman looked down her long nose at him like a racehorse spotting an unwelcome fly. 'He drowned, Detective Inspector. Tied a bloody great stone round his legs and jumped into the river.'

'I know that,' Cant shot back, irritated. 'I mean, how can you be sure it was suicide? There was no note. No obvious reason for him to top himself.'

The doctor winced at his crass turn of phrase, but DI Cant ignored her. He couldn't have given a frog's fart for her opinions, other than the medical ones.

'Couldn't somebody else have chucked him in?'

'No.' Linda Drew looked at him witheringly. 'They couldn't. I mean, theoretically it's possible. But there were no signs of struggle. No bruising anywhere, no ligature marks, no scratches, nothing under the nails. The physical evidence is clear. This was a calm and intentional act. I'd say Mr Wetherby had a peaceful death,' she added, unusually for a woman who rarely offered any sort of non-scientific opinion.

'Blood tests?' asked Cant.

'The lab's closed today,' said Dr Drew, looking at her watch impatiently. 'We'll have to wait for the more detailed stuff. But I did the basics here, drugs and alcohol.'

'And?'

'He'd had a few Christmas drinks. Not enough to incapacitate him. The coroner will make a final ruling, of course, but all signs point to suicide.'

'OK,' said Cant. 'Thanks.'

Dr Drew disappeared down the corridor, her shoes clack-clacking imperiously as she went. *Like Rosa Klebb*, thought the inspector. *Uptight bloody feminist.* Pressing his snub nose against the glass in front of him, Roger Cant looked again at Dominic Wetherby's uncovered face on the examination table. The ME was right. The famous author did look peaceful. Peaceful but white and waxen and very definitely dead.

Why would a guy like that, a rich, famous writer with a lovely house and family and life, want to kill himself? It seemed so wrong. Not morally wrong but incongruous. Jarring. It was simply hard to imagine that Dominic Wetherby's problems, whatever they were, could have been *that* bad.

But then Roger Cant thought about other suicides he'd worked on and realised what nonsense that was. What about Lisa Kenny, the pretty fifteen-year-old straight-A student who'd hung herself in Deerham Woods because her boyfriend dumped her? Or James McPhee, a thirty-year-old surgeon, popular and newly married with no history of depression, who'd walked into the sea one morning, leaving a note for his family that simply read, 'Life is not for me.'

Life is not for me? What did that even mean? Such terrible, senseless waste was hard to contemplate, but the awful truth was, it happened all the time.

Yes, Roger Cant was young to be in this job – not much older than poor James McPhee, in fact – but he was experienced enough to know that when it came to the human psyche, anything was possible. Dom Wetherby may have had the perfect life on paper, and his problems may have seemed inconsequential to others, but that told you precisely nothing about the man's inner life. Every suicide was a mystery. An unnatural act. It was supposed to feel jarring.

Outside the medical examiner's office, on the outskirts of Winchester, the car park was empty. It was two o'clock in the afternoon on Boxing Day, and the rest of Hampshire's finest were at home with their families, eating turkey curry and sleeping off their hangovers. *Lucky sods.* Only Roger and his well-meaning but useless sergeant, Pete Trotter, were working. (Roger Cant liked his sergeant, despite knowing exactly what Pete Trotter referred to him as, just like the others, whenever his back was turned. He didn't take it personally. You couldn't go through thirty-four years on earth with the surname Cant and have a thin skin about it. Not if you wanted a career in the police force, anyway.)

Retrieving his keys from his pocket, Cant climbed into his Range Rover and turned the heating on full blast. Short and pudgy, rather than flat-out fat, with a snub nose and freckles that lent him an unhelpfully boyish air, the detective inspector was neither ugly nor handsome. If he had to describe himself, physically, in one word, Roger would probably have gone for 'unobtrusive'. Which *could* be helpful, particularly if one's business was either committing crimes or solving them. *Don't remember me!* Roger's reflection seemed to demand. *I wasn't here.*

As a look, it was less of an advantage when it came to women, although happily Roger had lucked out and married Dolly, his girlfriend from school, ten years ago, punching (as his friends frequently reminded him) well above his weight. They'd never had kids – Dolly couldn't – but apart from that, their life together had been happy and solid and mercifully drama-free. DI Cant's job provided all the drama and conflict he needed.

The drive back to Hazelford would take about thirty minutes, maybe less on today's quiet roads. Thinking time.

It was only twenty hours since poor old Dom Wetherby had been hauled out of the water. The youngest son had found him. Some awful story about the child's boat getting caught in the corpse's hair, like something out of a horror film. But it was Marcus, the eldest, who'd managed to pull his father out, stone and all. His wife had helped, apparently, dragging the body up onto the banks of the Itchen. Both were wet and exhausted by the time Cant met them.

He himself hadn't arrived on the scene till eight fifteen, a full two hours later, having been rudely ripped away from a night on the sofa with Dolly by a call from the dispatch office at eight. But everybody had confirmed the sequence of events surrounding the finding of the body. The wife (widow now) and the lawyer son and the lodger, Iris Grey, who'd heard the youngest boy screaming at around six o'clock on Christmas night and rushed out to try and help.

Only now did Roger realise that he'd forgotten to ask Dr Drew to confirm a time of death. *Bugger.* He considered turning the car round, but then thought better of it. After all, it didn't really matter anymore. Dom Wetherby's death was suicide, not murder. Dr Drew had been quite sure about that. She might be lacking in charm, but Linda Drew was a damn good ME who never rushed to judgement. A couple more days of paperwork, a rubber stamp from the coroner and the case would be closed.

And yet Roger's mind still turned things over as he sped through the frosty Hampshire countryside. Dom Wetherby was a writer, a man of words, and yet he'd left no note. Was that odd? Perhaps not. But it felt odd.

With hindsight, the family's reactions felt odd, too. Of course, they'd all been in shock last night, when DI Cant had turned up at the Mill and his guys had cordoned off the scene and removed the body. And yet, apart from the lad with Down's, who'd actually found him, nobody had cried. Not the oldest son, or the wife. There'd been no hysterics, no obvious emotion of any kind, in fact. Just an eerie calm.

Cant found himself wondering how the Wetherbys would take today's news.

He'd know soon enough.

'It was you, wasn't it? It was bloody well you!'

Marcus grabbed Billy by the shoulders and shook him forcefully, his usually controlled expression contorted with anger and strain. As if the last twenty-four hours hadn't been terrible enough, now scores of news reporters had begun gathering outside the Mill, their vans and camera crews and microphones already clogging up Mill Lane and starting to draw a small crowd of curious onlookers.

'What was me?' Billy asked coolly. 'What are you accusing me of, big brother? Go on, spell it out. I dare you!'

'You called the press,' Marcus raged on, still clutching his younger brother's lapels. 'It had to be you. How could you?'

Billy had returned home early this morning, remorseless as ever and offering no explanation for his absence, to be greeted with the awful news about Dom. Ariadne had told him in the kitchen, still white and numb with shock herself. 'We're not sure exactly . . .' Her voice trailed off. 'The police are still down there. But poor Lorcan. I thought it was you in the river!' she blurted, when Billy turned to leave the room.

Billy had paused then, bitten his lip and said, 'OK.' That was it. *OK*. After that he'd gone upstairs to find Lorcan, who everyone was worried about because he hadn't said a word since he woke up this morning and was refusing to move from Dom's favourite armchair, where he'd spent the last four hours watching back-to-back *Scooby-Doo* cartoons.

'Get off me!' Stirring himself belatedly, Billy broke free of Marcus's grip. 'I didn't call anyone, you prat. Why would I?'

'W-well, who else?' Marcus stammered.

'How should I know?' snapped Billy. 'There's a dozen police techs down at the riverbank, not to mention half a mile of orange tape. Any passing dog walker could have rung the papers. Or had you forgotten Dad's the local celebrity?'

'Stop arguing! Both of you.' Ariadne's voice was high and tight with strain. The reality hadn't sunk in yet, not fully. Dom, her Dom. Dead. That last, ghastly image of his drowned face, eyes rolled back, lips slightly parted, his skin slick and cold and grey as ashes. That would stay with her for ever. And Marcus, frantically tugging, dragging his father up out of the reeds and silt only to find that stone tied fast round his legs. *Oh God, that stone!* The stone that meant Dom's death was no accident, a dead weight of guilt that must surely now drown Ariadne just as surely as it had drowned Dom.

She couldn't bear it. Or at least, she couldn't bear it without Marcus.

Ariadne needed Marcus now, more than ever. He couldn't fall apart, couldn't lose it, with Billy or with anyone else. He was the last solid, wholly good thing she had left.

He and Jenna had both been troupers this morning, getting the children up and making breakfast for Ariadne's father and trying to create some semblance of normality and routine in the surreal nightmare their lives had suddenly become.

'Sorry to disturb you all.'

It was the policeman, the detective inspector with a face like a naughty schoolboy, all freckles and chubby cheeks, and his gangly sergeant. *When did they arrive?* Ariadne thought. Jenna, who was hovering behind him in the doorway, must have let them in.

'We've had some preliminary results back from the medical examiner,' the detective inspector said.

Cant. That was his name.

'I thought you'd want to know right away.'

'Of course,' said Marcus, smoothing down his ruffled hair and taking charge once more, his loss of temper with Billy forgotten. 'Do sit down, Detective Inspector.'

'That's all right.' Cant waved away the offer politely. 'I won't intrude for long. But I thought you'd want to know we found no sign of foul play. No bruising, no struggle of any kind.'

For a moment no one said anything.

Billy was the first to break the silence. 'So it *was* suicide?' he asked bluntly.

'The coroner will have to make an official ruling,' said Cant, 'but we found nothing that suggests otherwise.'

Ariadne let out a stifled sob.

'Who'd have thought it?' said Billy archly, lighting the cigarette he'd been rolling. 'The first genuinely unselfish thing Dad ever did turns out to be the last thing he ever did.'

Marcus turned on him. 'What? What on earth do you mean?'

'Only that now we'll finally be able to take our inheritance and leave this hellhole,' Billy replied deadpan, blowing smoke out through his nose like a louche dragon. 'Thanks, Daddy dearest.'

Jenna gasped, glaring at her brother-in-law. 'Have you no shame?'

'Apparently not,' Billy grinned, winking at her. He was clearly trying to provoke Marcus into losing it again and hitting him, but it didn't work this time. Instead, turning away in disgust, Marcus thanked Detective Inspector Cant for his time and for letting them know and walked him to the door.

'Your brother didn't get along with your father, I take it?' Cant observed as he took his leave.

'My brother doesn't get along with anyone,' Marcus replied. 'Billy has a lot of problems, I'm afraid. He wasn't always like that.'

'He's probably still in shock,' DI Cant said kindly. 'People say all kinds of things they don't mean in these sorts of situations. I wonder if I might take a look around your father's study?'

'Of course,' said Marcus, calm again now. 'I'll show you where it is.'

A few minutes later Cant and his sergeant were alone in the cosy panelled room where Dom Wetherby had spent so much of his time.

'Is this where he wrote the books, then?' Sergeant Trotter asked, gazing at the shelves stuffed with Grimshaw titles as well as photos and memorabilia.

'I imagine so,' said Cant, running a gloved finger slowly along the edge of Dom's desk. The dead man's laptop was still open, but when Cant hit 'return', he found the battery was dead. Closing it carefully, he handed it to his sergeant. 'Put this in an evidence bag. And find the charger. When we get back to the station, have Sally open it up straight away.'

'Yes, sir.' Trotter took the MacBook Air without comment. Checking the deceased's computer was standard practice with any suspicious death. Dom Wetherby was no different. Meanwhile Trotter's boss began systematically opening and emptying drawers, looking for other devices.

'Phone.' Cant handed the iPhone to his sergeant. 'And here's his tablet.'

'At least he was organised,' Trotter observed, placing both items in sealed bags. 'I usually think of writers as being scatterbrained sorts of people, don't you, sir? Always spilling their tea down their fronts and tying their trousers up with string. But this place is neat as a pin.'

He's right, thought Cant. Wetherby's office was remarkably neat. Not that he'd ever been the tea-spilling type. But even so, it was uncanny how absolutely *everything* was *exactly* where it should be. Almost as if Dom's things were waiting for the police to find them.

You're making something out of nothing, Cant told himself, shaking his head to dislodge the suspicious thought, like a dog with water in its ear. So Dom Wetherby was organised. So what? The guy could be allowed one virtue at least, couldn't he, without having it picked apart?

'Keep a lookout for diaries, letters and any bills or credit-card statements,' Cant instructed his sergeant. 'The rest we can leave. We need to give the family some space.'

Sergeant Trotter nodded dutifully and the two men got to work.

Fifteen minutes later Marcus Wetherby smiled thinly and waved as the policemen got into their car. The detective inspector was empty-handed, but the junior man was carrying three large sealed evidence bags under his arm.

Did that mean anything? Was it normal to compile evidence after a suspected suicide? As a lawyer, he ought to know, but his mind had gone blank. Or rather it was overloaded with other, more pressing thoughts. Like had his father really been *that* unhappy? And what the hell was going on with Billy? Marcus couldn't stop thinking about the argument he and Billy had had on Christmas Eve. There was no way the police could know about that. Could they?

Despite the detective's comforting words earlier, Marcus knew that Billy had meant what he said today, just as he had meant it the night of the party. Every hateful, outrageous word had been loaded with intent.

It wasn't till later that night, in bed, that Jenna and Marcus had a chance to talk about it.

'Are you all right?' Reaching out, Jenna touched Marcus's cheek gently. The scratch on his face was still there, but it had lost its power to hurt her now, overshadowed by the terrible shock of Dom's drowning. 'I mean, I know you're not all right,' she corrected herself. 'But can I help?'

Pulling her to him, he hugged her tightly, closing his eyes and breathing in the familiar, comforting smell of her hair. 'You are helping. You've been amazing with the children today and with Clive and Lorcan. Do you think he'll be all right?'

'Lorcan? I don't know,' Jenna said truthfully. 'I think he needs to see someone.'

'A shrink, you mean?' Marcus's knee-jerk British disapproval of all psychotherapy usually irritated Jenna. As a trained psychologist herself, it was frustrating and demeaning to have one's experience dismissed. But under the present circumstances she could hardly expect him to be tactful.

'I mean someone who understands how kids his age with Down's get through this kind of stuff,' she explained. 'We're in uncharted territory here.'

Marcus sighed heavily. 'I know. I just . . . I can't believe it. I *don't* believe it.'

Jenna sat up in bed, suddenly animated. 'Oh my God, I am so glad you said that. Because I was starting to worry. After the inspector left, and your mom was all, like, "At least now we know," I kept waiting for someone to say something, but then I figured you probably just didn't want to upset her any more and—'

'What are you talking about?' Marcus frowned, cutting her off.

'The suicide thing,' said Jenna, surprised. 'I mean, we all know Dom wasn't suicidal, right? Not remotely! He wasn't even depressed.'

'Well, clearly he was,' Marcus replied, his voice suddenly brittle.

Jenna opened her mouth to say something, but then closed it again. Had she misunderstood? 'But I thought you just said you didn't believe it.'

'I don't,' said Marcus. 'But the fact is, Dad *is* dead.' He shuddered at the memory of his father's limp, frozen, waterlogged corpse in his arms, remembered the awful weight of it.

'I know, honey' Jenna tried to sound soothing. 'But suicide?'

'You heard the police,' Marcus said sullenly. 'No struggle, no bruising. No signs of foul play.'

'But, Marcus, you don't really think that Dom would—'

'What's the alternative?' Marcus shouted, cutting her off once more. His stress levels were clearly rising exponentially. 'You think somebody murdered him? Tied a rock round his legs and threw him in the Itchen while he just sat there and let them do it?'

'Don't get upset, darling,' said Jenna, wishing the conversation had not taken this turn. Besides which, Marcus did have a point. When you put it like that, it did sound nonsensical. 'I'm sorry.'

Sighing, relaxing a little, Marcus pulled her back into his embrace. 'No, I'm sorry. I shouldn't be shouting at you. I don't want to accept that Dad killed himself either. It's an awful thought and I can barely wrap my head around it. But sad as it is, that's what happened. It won't help Mum or Lorcan or anyone else for people to start second-guessing it.'

Jenna let it go, lying patiently in Marcus's arms until he finally fell asleep. Then she wriggled free and back to her own side of the bed, eyes wide open, thinking. About Dom. And about Billy, and his vile outburst today. A deep feeling of unease possessed her. Something was wrong, very wrong. Something that it was outside Jenna's power to control.

It took her a very long time to fall asleep.

Iris Grey blew on the top of her frothy hot chocolate and took a contemplative bite of her Chelsea bun as she leafed through the *Daily Mail*. The warm fug of Hambly's teashop enveloped her, the air smelling of a heady combination of yeast and sugar and freshly ground coffee and wood polish and the intermingled perfumes of the handful of customers who'd braved the cold on this dismal December morning.

Iris herself had walked into the village to escape the oppressive atmosphere at Mill Cottage since Dom Wetherby's death. Boxed in by reporters who, not content with blocking Mill Lane and the drive that led to both Mill House and Iris's cottage, thought nothing of knocking on Iris's door at all hours asking for interviews and then ringing her phone repeatedly when she said no, Iris had started climbing the walls. And if the press interest weren't oppressive enough, there was Mill House itself, looming over Iris's tiny cottage like some great sad, lost giant whose heart had just been ripped out. Before Dom's death, Iris had always thought of the big house as a benevolent, protective presence, but now its mellow stone walls seemed grey and bleak, a study in sadness, just like the faces Iris glimpsed in its windows. The bright light that had been Dom Wetherby had been extinguished, and overnight it was as if the house and everyone inside it had been unplugged. Plunged into darkness. Stopped dead. As if Dom's energy had been their energy and without it they were like dolls in Iris's doll's house or puppets in a play. Empty shells.

''Scuse me, love.' A heavyset man carrying a tray laden with tea and scones squeezed past the back of Iris's chair. Setting the tray down with a clatter on the next table, he nodded towards Iris's open newspaper. 'Awful business, isn't it? Like one of his books. *Grimshaw the Great*, wasn't it, where the fella drowned? The scientist? Or was it *Grimshaw's Gift*?'

Dom Wetherby's shock drowning was the tabloids' top story, a gift to editors wondering how on earth to fill their pages during the 'dead' week between Christmas and New Year, when all normal news ground to a halt. Naturally the interest levels in Hazelford were at fever pitch, with the village revelling in its fifteen minutes of notoriety. But the idea that the creator of the much-loved Grimshaw crime series should be found dead on Christmas Day in such grisly and mysterious circumstances seemed to have gripped the whole of Britain. So far, somewhat miraculously in Iris's view, no one in the media had got hold of the detail about the body being weighted down. As a result, most papers were still speculating about some sort of 'tragic accident', while being careful not to rule out the juicy possibility of something more sinister.

Iris found the whole thing salacious and distasteful. Or did she? She could practically hear Dom's voice in her head, laughing, *'You're still reading it, though, aren't you? It's no good playing the saint with me, Iris. We all love a bit of gossip.'* Which, of course, was true. It was also true that Dom himself would have delighted in the intrigue and attention surrounding his death. This sort of drama would have been right up his street.

'Wait a minute!' The man next to Iris pointed at her suddenly. 'You're that painter, aren't you? Don't you live down at the Mill?'

'I rent the cottage, yes,' said Iris wearily. 'I don't live there full-time.'

'Was you there when it happened?' the man asked eagerly, forgetting his cooling tea in his excitement at meeting someone with first-hand knowledge of the Wetherby tragedy.

'No,' Iris lied.

'You weren't staying there at Christmas?' The man sounded disappointed.

'Well, I . . . I was at the cottage,' Iris found herself explaining.

'So you *was* there! Is it true what they're saying in the papers? About the boy with Down's syndrome finding his dad's body?'

Iris looked at him witheringly. 'Excuse me.'

Leaving a twenty-pound note on the table, Iris grabbed her coat and handbag, and left, hurrying into one of the side lanes off the hill before anybody had a chance to come after her, then slumping back against a crumbling brick wall.

Ian was right. There'd be no escape from prying eyes and intrusive questions in Hazelford. Surely now was as good a time as ever for Iris to go back to London. Escape the media circus at the Mill. Start the difficult marital conversations that she'd been putting off for months. See friends like Annie and Joe, and her gallery, and her agent, Greta, whose calls Iris had been failing to return for weeks. Go to a hairdresser whose repertoire went beyond blue rinses and shampoo-and-sets. After all, she couldn't hide out here for ever. And with Dom Wetherby dead, she no longer had the excuse of her portrait commission to fall back on.

Ian had been surprisingly kind in the last few days, since it happened. He'd rung to ask Iris how she was and how he could help, sentiments she hadn't heard from him in a very long time. And while he'd suggested she come home, for once he hadn't pushed or insisted or threatened. It was a welcome change, but it had taken Iris by surprise, plunging her back into confusion about her marriage where only a few days earlier there had been resolve.

To add to the confusion, Graham Feeney had also called, twice.

'Such an awful thing. And you were there when they found him?'

'Yes.' Iris found herself confiding in Graham, pouring out emotions she never even knew she had about that terrible night. Her fascination with what had happened to Dom Wetherby had rather taken her by surprise, consuming her mental energy and feeding her natural curiosity to a degree she wouldn't have thought possible before. As if a long-dormant part of her had suddenly been awakened. In some ways, it was exhilarating. But beneath her intellectual curiosity lurked some real, painful feelings. 'Lorcan's screams. I'll never forget them. Just the most harrowing sound.'

Graham hadn't said much, but he'd understood, instinctively. How she was finding it hard to sleep, or focus. How even painting had become difficult. He had lost his own brother to suicide years before, so he was no stranger to family tragedy and its impact.

'Yes, but it's not my family, though,' Iris reminded him. 'Not my grief. I mean, I liked Dom, of course, but I barely knew him. It's not even as if we were close friends.'

'Doesn't matter,' said Graham, with a confidence that immediately made Iris feel better. 'It's the shock. You can't go through something like that and expect not to be affected.'

'I feel like an intruder,' said Iris. 'Like I shouldn't be here. The problem is, I don't know where else to be.'

'You could always come and stay with me,' Graham offered. 'Come to London. Get away.' It was said semi-playfully and Iris couldn't tell if he was serious.

'I'm not sure that would be the wisest idea right now,' she answered cautiously. She couldn't come to London and *not* stay at the flat with Ian. Or at least, if she did, she'd be making a statement about the marriage and her intentions that she wasn't yet ready to make. And if she was staying with Ian, she could hardly meet up with Graham. Even a friendly lunch would look wrong, for someone who was supposedly still trying to save their marriage.

But is that what I'm trying to do?

Somehow, Dom Wetherby's death had brought all the dilemmas of Iris's 'real' life back to the fore and into sharper focus. Painfully sharp, at times.

'Iris, isn't it?'

Iris looked up, startled. A car had pulled up beside her, slowing to a halt in the middle of the tiny lane where she was still standing, leaning against someone's garden wall.

'Sorry, did I spook you?' A blonde woman a few years younger than Iris stuck her head out of the driver's-side window. Iris recognised her, but she couldn't remember where from. 'It's Jenna Wetherby,' the blonde explained helpfully. 'Marcus's wife?'

'Of course it is. Sorry.' Iris shook her head, embarrassed. 'I'm afraid I was in a world of my own.'

Jenna hesitated for a moment. Then she asked tentatively, 'Are you busy? Like, right now?'

Iris shook her head. 'Not at all. I was trying to get away from the mayhem back at the Mill, but it's easier said than done. Why?'

'I just wondered . . . I'd like to talk to you,' Jenna said. 'I had to get out myself. I left the kids with Ariadne and made up an excuse about needing more logs!' She laughed nervously. 'Stupid, I know, but it was the first thing I could think of. I'm off to Betcheman's Farm to put in an order. D'you wanna ride with me?'

It was an odd invitation. Friendly but definitely odd. Iris barely knew Jenna. Didn't know her, in fact. Then again, it wasn't as if she had anything better to do.

'Sure.'

Five minutes later the two women were bumping slowly along the single-track potholed lane that wound through Betcheman's Woods. Hazelford was behind them, its rooftops out of sight, and rural Hampshire lay spread out in front of them, a green-and-brown patchwork of muddy fields after a wet autumn followed by a suddenly freezing winter.

Jenna and Marcus's Volvo was oven-warm and comfortable, despite being littered with the typical detritus of family life: packets of baby wipes and empty crisp wrappers were everywhere, and in the back, the car seats were strewn with half-built McDonald's Happy Meal toys and *Dora the Explorer* sticker books.

'You probably think this is weird, right? Me kidnapping you like this?' Jenna's American accent had been softened after so many years in London, but Iris noticed it came out more strongly when she asked questions. Her artist's eye took in both Jenna's beauty – natural, wholesome, radiant – and her exhaustion, as evidenced by the storm-cloud-grey shadows under her eyes and the deep, weary grooves running from her nose to the corners of her mouth.

'You said you wanted to talk.'

'Yeah. I just . . .' Jenna exhaled deeply, unsure where to begin. 'You knew my father-in-law.'

It was a statement, not a question, so Iris didn't respond.

'What I mean is, as a portrait artist, I assume you try to get to know your subjects? You talk to them; they talk to you?'

'Yes,' Iris agreed, cautiously. 'Some talk more than others, obviously.'

'I'm guessing Dom was a talker,' Jenna laughed.

'He was,' Iris smiled. 'But in all truth, I didn't know him well. We'd only had four sittings together before . . .'

'Before he died.'

'Yes. *Jesus Christ!*'

Jenna slammed on the brakes, sending the car into a noisy, terrifying skid. A stag had suddenly leaped out of the woods on Iris's side and landed in the middle of the road, right in front of them. It was a huge, magnificent monster of an animal, with antlers that must have stretched five feet across. Iris saw its eyes widen with shock, its powerful legs frozen in fear as the Volvo careered directly towards it. For a dreadful moment she felt certain they would hit it. That it would come flying through the windscreen, antlers first, and impale them like lambs on a spit. Jenna closed her eyes and winced. Leaning across, Iris grabbed the wheel on instinct and jerked it to the right, swerving so violently that they mounted the steep grass verge. In the same split second, the deer made his own move, scrambling up the opposite bank and disappearing into the thick of the trees as suddenly and silently as he had appeared.

The Volvo wobbled back down off the verge before finally coming to a stop. They had spun a hundred and eighty degrees and were now effectively parked lengthwise across the deserted lane, blocking it completely like a fallen tree. Both women sat silent for a moment, in shock.

Jenna spoke first. 'Are you OK?'

Iris nodded. 'Fine. Are you?'

'Yes, I think so' said Jenna, before promptly bursting into tears. 'Oh God, I'm sorry,' she sniffed, wiping her eyes on her sleeve. 'It's not the stupid deer. It's everything. What happened to Dom.'

'I'm sure it must be terribly stressful, staying in that house,' said Iris sympathetically.

Jenna shook her head, still crying. 'It's like living in a Dalí painting, I'm telling you. It's surreal. Marcus. His mom. The two of them exist in this sea of denial. They refuse to see what's staring them right in the face.'

'Which is?' Iris probed.

Jenna turned to face her head on. 'Let me ask you this, Iris. Did my father-in-law ever come across to you as suicidal? In those four sittings you guys had?'

Iris shook her head.

'Or ever?'

'No.'

'Did he seem depressed to you?'

'No,' Iris admitted. 'But like I said, I didn't know him well. And I'm not a psychologist.'

'Well, I am,' said Jenna. 'Not that you need a psychology degree to know that the idea of Dom Wetherby taking his own life is nuts. It's just *nuts.*'

'But that's what your husband thinks? That it was suicide?' asked Iris.

'It's what the police seem to think,' said Jenna. 'Which is shocking enough, if you ask me. But the way that Marcus and Ariadne have just accepted that idea. Like, "Oh, he killed himself, did he? Oh. OK." That's what really gets to me. They must know as well as I do it isn't true. They just can't face admitting the alternative.'

Iris frowned, trying to get to the heart of what Jenna was saying.

'So you're saying you believe Dom was killed?'

Jenna gave her a pleading look. 'Don't you?' Grabbing Iris's hand, she went on. 'That's why I needed to talk to you, Iris. To talk to someone outside of that asylum who actually knew Dom, who saw him in the weeks before he died, saw what was going on in that house.'

What was going on in that house . . .

Iris wondered if Jenna was thinking the same thing that she was.

'Do you believe Dom Wetherby killed himself?' Jenna asked bluntly.

Iris paused before answering. Not because she didn't know the answer, but because she was afraid of having Jenna Wetherby, or anyone, rely on her. Whatever battles Jenna was having with her husband's family, or the police, they were her battles, not Iris's.

'For Dom's sake,' said Jenna, sensing Iris's hesitation. 'Please just tell me truthfully. *Do* you believe it was suicide?'

'No,' said Iris. 'I don't.'

Jenna exhaled, visibly relieved to have found an ally, albeit an unwilling one.

'Which means he was killed.'

'I suppose so,' agreed Iris.

'But Marcus and Ariadne will never admit it. Not now the lazy-ass police have decided it was suicide before they've even started a freaking investigation!' Jenna seethed. 'Because admitting it would mean admitting that he's a monster.'

'Who's a monster?' asked Iris, although she already knew the answer.

'Who do you think?' said Jenna. 'Who was the one person who wanted Dom dead?'

Was there only one person? thought Iris.

'The one person evil enough and bold enough actually to do it? The one person that Marcus and Ariadne would risk everything to protect, even if it means poor Dom gets blamed for his own death, and his killer never gets justice?'

'You mean Billy?' Iris clarified.

'Of course Billy!' Jenna sounded increasingly agitated. 'Who else?'

She hadn't realised quite how much she'd feared and disliked her brother-in-law until now, when all the evidence pointed to this most heinous and unnatural of crimes. On some deep subconscious level, she also knew that her hatred of Billy was linked to her resentment of Marcus and his constant idealising of his family. Now, at last, Marcus would *have* to face the truth, to wake up to the reality of who his brother *and* his mother really were.

'Even if you're right,' Iris said after a long pause, while Jenna restarted the car and began a laborious seven-point turn to get them back on track, 'and even if I agree with you, I'm not sure what you want me to do.'

'I want you to help me,' Jenna said simply. 'Marcus may choose to live in a fantasy world, but I won't, not anymore. I can't just close my eyes to the truth. I'm hoping you can't either.'

Au contraire, thought Iris, ironically. Little did Jenna know that the last year of Iris's life had been almost exclusively devoted to closing her eyes to the truth. Although admittedly this was different.

This wasn't a slowly crumbling marriage.

This was murder.

'We owe it to Dom,' said Jenna, her eyes now back on the road. 'Not because he was a great guy. He wasn't. But he's dead, and he didn't deserve that, and everybody's lying about it, even his own family, and it's just . . . it's wrong.'

She was right. It *was* wrong.

'I can't do this alone,' Jenna went on. 'Marcus and I will have to go home eventually – soon. Lottie has school, and Marcus has work. He hates the thought of leaving his mom, but we both know it's coming. And when it does, there'll be no one left here, no one looking for the truth. Except you.'

Except me.

Iris's mind whirred.

She could stay on in Hazelford and help Jenna. That would be her reason. Because she owed it to Dom. Because it was 'right'.

She could stay.

'Help me, Iris,' Jenna drove the point home, not realising she'd already won. 'Help me prove Billy Wetherby murdered his father.'

CHAPTER TWELVE

Shivering on the porch outside Mill House, Iris screwed up her courage and pulled back the heavy brass knocker, rapping it three times loudly against the weathered oak front door.

It was the first week in January, a time for fresh starts, for leaving the past behind. Only this year, it seemed, the past was refusing to let go, clinging to the Mill and everyone in it like the cold tendrils of mist coiling themselves round Iris's legs. Iris had brought Dom's unfinished portrait over from the cottage, covered in an old canvas cloth to protect it from the elements. She'd been meaning for days to ask Ariadne what she wanted her to do with it, now that Dom was gone, but the time had never felt quite right. Now, though, with her promise to Jenna still fresh in her mind, it seemed as good a moment as any to step into the lion's den.

'Billy won't let anything slip to me,' Jenna had told Iris on their drive home from Betcheman's Farm. 'He's too smart for that. He knows I can't stand him.'

'We aren't exactly best friends either,' said Iris, filling Jenna in on her awkward encounter with Billy at the cottage at the beginning of Christmas week.

'Doesn't matter. He likes you. I can tell. Plus you're not a family member, which automatically puts you in a better position where Billy's concerned. Just see if you can get him to tell you where he went on Christmas Eve, after the row. If we knew that, we'd have a place to start.'

Iris wasn't sure she shared Jenna's confidence in her abilities to get Billy Wetherby to 'open up'. But she certainly wasn't going to get anywhere, with Billy or anyone else, unless she found an excuse to go back inside Mill House.

Still no answer.

Iris was about to knock again when the front door slowly opened, creaking like a haunted house in one of Lorcan's *Scooby-Doo* cartoons.

'Oh! Hello.' Ariadne gave Iris a weary smile. 'I wasn't expecting you.'

She looked tiny and positively frail, standing in the doorway in a black polo-neck sweater and wide-legged woollen trousers that swamped her petite frame, her wild grey-blonde hair swept up in a messy bun. Iris wondered whether the black was mourning dress or just a coincidence. Either way, it made her look ghostly and ill.

'Is this a bad time?' she asked hesitantly. 'Because I can come back if it is.'

'No, no, not at all,' Ariadne reassured her, swinging the door wider. 'And I see you've brought the painting with you. How lovely. Do come in.'

The house was quiet. Eerily so.

'Is everybody out?' Iris asked, following Ariadne down to the kitchen and propping the portrait against the larder wall while Ariadne put the kettle on.

'Almost everybody,' Ariadne sighed. 'Billy's around somewhere. Marcus took the children and Lorcan to some ghastly indoor-play place near Southampton, bless him. It's the first time Lorcan's been out of the house since . . . since it happened.'

'How is he?' asked Iris.

Ariadne shrugged sadly. 'Withdrawn. Jenna's the only one he talks to at all, as far as I can tell. I don't know what I'll do when she and Marcus go back to London.' Reaching up to a shelf above the Aga, she pulled down two teacups and a red-spotted pot.

'When will that be?' asked Iris.

'After the funeral. Although heaven knows when *that* will be, as the police still haven't released Dom's body.'

Iris frowned. 'Haven't they? Why not?'

She was no expert in these things, but ten days seemed an awfully long time to hold on to a body, especially when the autopsy had been performed within hours of death.

'Don't know.' Ariadne sounded unconcerned about this detail as she poured the tea. *Perhaps she's relieved*, thought Iris, *as it means Marcus will have to stay for a little longer*. Although surely she would want the closure of a funeral, for Lorcan if not for herself.

'Marcus said he'd ask what's going on tomorrow if we haven't heard,' said Ariadne, adding milk to Iris's cup. 'But anyway, enough about all of us – it's too depressing. How are *you*? Have you been painting again, now that those dreadful reporters have finally found something else to do?'

'A little,' Iris replied. 'Although not much outside. It's still too cold.' She nodded towards the covered portrait. 'I have added a few touches to Dom's portrait here and there. I wanted to ask you what your plans are with that. If it's not too painful.'

Ariadne looked perplexed. 'Plans?'

'Well, you can have it as it is, of course. Unfinished. *Or* I can try to finish it, using photographs and home video if you have any, as well as from memory.'

'Can you do that?'

'It's not ideal, obviously,' Iris said. 'But it is possible to work that way if there are no other options. Just like you might sculpt an animal from pictures.'

Ariadne shook her head. 'I couldn't do that. No, no. That wouldn't work at all. I need the living creature in front of me. I need to feel it under my hands.'

'Or I could just . . . get rid of it,' Iris offered. 'If it's too painful for you now. I'd pay you back your commission fee, obviously.'

'Heavens!' Ariadne held up a horrified hand. 'I wouldn't dream of it! And of *course* you mustn't destroy the picture. For one thing, it's a work of art in its own right. And for another, finished or not, it's the last record we have of Dom. May I see it?'

She stood up, animated now, and walked towards the draped canvas. Although framed as a question, it was clearly rhetorical. Whipping back the cover, she found herself staring straight into her dead husband's eyes.

'Dear God!' she gasped, stepping backwards and steadying herself on the kitchen table.

'You don't like it?' Iris asked, worried. 'Because really, Ariadne, you don't have to . . .'

'It's not that,' Ariadne whispered, her eyes still glued to the portrait. 'It's just that it's so *real.* I mean . . . it's him! It's him, looking right at me. Right *through* me. It's like he's alive. How do you do that?' She turned to Iris in genuine wonder.

'I don't know,' Iris said modestly, but also truthfully. 'It just sort of happens. Not every time, and not with every subject. But Dom *was* very alive. I saw him as this bright light.'

'He was,' Ariadne agreed, adding, almost to herself, 'He could be blinding sometimes. Blinding and blind.'

Iris watched and listened. Was this Ariadne the grieving wife talking or Ariadne the artist? Could the two even be separated? There was definitely a detachment about her, about the way she stood staring at the portrait, head cocked to one side, that seemed frighteningly cold to Iris for a woman who'd just lost her partner of thirty-five years. All dressed in black, for an instant Ariadne looked like Billy's description of her – *the wicked witch.*

But then, Iris thought, hadn't Dom been every bit as detached, in his own way? Every bit as selfish? Graham had described him jokingly as 'a thoroughbred narcissist', and he was right, at least in Iris's view. Perhaps that was part of what had attracted Dom and Ariadne Wetherby to each other: that uniquely artistic self-centredness that they both shared.

Like Ian.

Like me?

'Can I ask you something?' Ariadne turned back to Iris. 'Was he happy? During his sittings with you. Would you say he seemed . . . content?'

'He seemed to be. Yes.'

Iris waited for the obvious next question – didn't she think it strange that Dom would have killed himself? – but it never came. Instead, once again, Ariadne turned the conversation back to Iris, asking her about her own life, and Ian, and what her plans were for the next few months.

'I thought I might stay on here, just for a bit. I could try to finish the portrait, if you wanted that.'

'I do. Definitely,' Ariadne asserted. 'Once we've had this tea, I'll search for some photos and whatnot for you. Or you can come back and delve through Dom's things by yourself if you prefer. Either way, you'll have plenty of material. He was so vain, he adored having his picture taken.' She laughed, warmly, and for the first time Iris detected unmistakable affection in her voice. Then, catching Iris off guard, she added, 'Don't let things slip away with your husband, Iris. You're welcome to stay here as long as you like. But if you do still love him, you must go and see him. Life's so hideously short.'

'I will,' said Iris. 'I mean, I am. This weekend, in fact. I've said I'll come to London. We still have a lot of things to try to work out.'

'Good.' Ariadne took her hand and squeezed it, relieved. 'That's very good.'

Twenty minutes later, weighed down under three shoeboxes stuffed full of loose photographs, rolls of film and old VHS cartridges with labels like 'France' and no date, Iris set off back towards the cottage, not sure what, if anything, she'd learned from her encounter with Ariadne.

Like Jenna, Iris found it weird that Ariadne seemed so willing to accept the verdict of suicide. She'd said nothing about Dom being down or worried, and seemed devoid of curiosity about what his motives for such a terrible act might be.

Unless she already knows his motives? She knew him better than anyone, after all.

Perhaps the suicide wasn't a shock to her. But in that case, why ask Iris about Dom's mood during the sittings? That question definitely suggested Ariadne had her doubts.

And yet despite all these unexplained reactions, her detachment and her desire to let sleeping dogs lie, it seemed clear to Iris that Ariadne Wetherby had loved her husband. Deeply. If Jenna was right and Ariadne was sweeping the truth under the carpet to protect Billy, then she must love Billy very, very deeply, too.

'Need a hand?'

Iris jumped out of her skin so violently she might even have screamed. Billy, all in black like his mother, with a heavy duffel coat and scarf over drainpipe jeans, had sprung out from behind the kitchen garden wall as silently and suddenly as a panther.

'Did I scare you?' He smiled wolfishly. The idea seemed to delight him.

Fighting back her natural anger and dislike for him, Iris decided to seize the opportunity. She might never have a better time to strike up a conversation with Billy, and losing her temper with him now might ruin everything.

'Yes, you scared me!' she replied, but she did it with a smile. 'You almost gave me a heart attack. Where on earth did you come from?'

'The dark wilds of your imagination!' Billy responded in a flirty, mysterious voice, pleased and surprised by Iris's warm reception. 'Not really,' he chuckled. 'I actually just got back from London. Here, let me take those. What are they, anyway?'

'Photos,' said Iris, handing him two of the boxes and holding on to one herself as they fell into step together. 'Of your father. Your mum just gave them to me. She wants me to try to finish the portrait.'

Billy looked surprised, although, slightly to Iris's bemusement, not angry. Usually almost any allusion to his father or mother seemed to elicit an angry response. Today, however, Billy seemed in a mellower mood.

He's happier, thought Iris. *Relieved because the deed is done? And he thinks he got away with it?*

It didn't take long to reach Iris's cottage. Still carrying the boxes, Billy followed her inside.

'So what were you doing in London?' she asked, as casually as she could. Taking off her coat, she threw it over the back of the single kitchen armchair. Billy did the same. Iris noticed that both his coat and his sweater looked new and expensive. Cashmere.

'Visiting my lawyer,' Billy responded, equally casually. Pulling out a vintage silver cigarette case, he flicked it open and took out a smoke. It was the first time Iris had seen him smoke straights rather than rollies, never mind the affectation of the case. Who did he think he was, Jay Gatsby?

'Do you mind?' He reached for the matches next to Iris's scented candle.

'Be my guest.'

'Do you want one?'

'No, thanks.'

She passed him a ramekin dish as an ashtray.

'So, the lawyer meeting,' she began, probing gently, like a zoologist approaching a snake with a stick. 'Was that about your case? Your parole must be almost over now, isn't it?'

'Next month.' Billy blew smoke languidly through his pursed lips. He had his father's dark colouring and strong jaw, Iris observed, but that was where the physical similarities with Dom ended. They were both attractive men in their different ways, but if Dom Wetherby was light, then his second son was darkness. 'It wasn't about that, though. It was about Dad's will. I wanted to know how soon it will pay out.'

It was said so bluntly, so completely without apology, Iris wasn't sure how to react. In the end, she decided to echo Billy's own neutral tone.

'You're expecting a large bequest?'

Billy smiled smugly. 'That's for me to know.'

His confidence that Dom had left him money struck Iris as deeply odd, given how estranged they'd been before Dom's death. Not to mention the fact that, in normal circumstances, a living widow would be expected to be left pretty much everything. But she kept the thought to herself and tried to steer the conversation back to the million-dollar question: where had Billy been on Christmas Day?

'It must have been dreadful for you, coming back on Boxing Day to hear the news,' she began tentatively.

The smug smile faded. 'Yeah,' Billy mumbled, fiddling with a button on his cuff. 'It was.'

Iris hesitated, unsure how far she could safely push him. There remained a latent threat with Billy, a constant, lurking possibility that he could suddenly turn and pounce, as he had once before, either sexually or in some sort of violent rage.

Screwing up her courage, Iris opted for the direct approach.

'Do you regret not being there?' she asked bluntly. 'On Christmas Day?'

After what felt like an endless silence, at last he said, 'No. Not really. I don't think there's anything I could have done. When someone's determined to kill themselves, they do it.'

Was he acting? If so, he was damn good at it. Anyone listening would have believed that Billy thought his father's death was suicide. Iris knew she ought to ask him where he was that day, but instead she changed tack.

'Why do you think he did it?' she asked.

This time he looked up, completely animated. 'Because of *her*! Why else? Because he couldn't stand it anymore. I'm just amazed he cracked before I did.'

'Because of your mother?' Iris frowned. 'Had they been fighting?'

Billy's eyes widened and then he laughed, apparently genuinely, coughing on smoke and wiping his eyes. 'Sometimes I forget you don't really know our family very well,' he told Iris. 'It feels as if you've been here for ever. But of course you haven't. Anyway.' He stood up suddenly, stubbing out his cigarette. 'I'd better go.'

Damn it, thought Iris. She was close to something, something important, but whatever it was, she knew she'd barely scratched the surface. And now he was leaving.

'So where were you?' She threw out the question on the doorstep, hoping it didn't sound as desperate as it felt. 'On Christmas Day?'

Billy looked at her curiously. 'I can't remember. I'd gone over to a friend's house the night before and started drinking. I expect I was somewhere passed out cold for most of it.'

'But you must know *where*,' Iris pressed him. 'Where did you wake up?'

Billy's curious expression became irritated. 'Why the third degree?'

Iris shrugged and let it go. There wasn't much else she could do, not without further arousing his suspicions. 'Just curious, I suppose,' she told Billy.

He started to walk away, then at the last moment relented. 'If you must know, I woke up in Winchester A&E. Apparently, I was playing chicken with a moving car and got myself this.' Pushing back his mop of dark curls, he revealed a bruised gash to the head, interspersed with spiky white stitches. 'Maybe Dad wasn't the only one trying to end it all?' he added, laughing emptily.

Iris watched him go. Only once he was completely out of sight did she pick up the phone.

Jenna's mobile went straight to messages.

Iris kept it short and sweet. 'It's me. I spoke to Billy. Call me when you can.'

Exhausted suddenly, she picked up one of Ariadne's photo boxes and sank down on the couch, leafing through old pictures of Dom.

How sad that he's dead, she thought. *How wrong. He shouldn't be dead. I should be painting him, not reimagining him through a box of old photographs.*

Maybe she and Jenna would never know the real truth about what had happened to Dom Wetherby. But Jenna was right. They owed it to him to try.

Somebody had to try.

CHAPTER THIRTEEN

'What the hell? What the bloody buggering hell . . .?'

DI Roger Cant paced his cramped office, beads of sweat forming on his wide brow and trickling down his back and chest, leaving ugly patches on his blue Marks & Spencer shirt.

'What does she think she's playing at?'

Nobody else was in the office, but Cant was speaking aloud, like an actor rehearsing lines in his dressing room. He already had two murders on his desk, a stabbing outside a pub in Alton and a probable domestic in Beaulieu. Apparently, the New Year's resolutions of the good denizens of East Hampshire did not include peace and goodwill to all men. Or women, for that matter.

As if that weren't enough, his sergeant had informed him yesterday that the lab reports on Dominic Wetherby's suicide had somehow managed to 'go missing' from forensics, delaying the coroner's report, which meant it was only a matter of time before the press started sniffing around the case again, making trouble. And to top it off, DI Cant had just got off the phone with a deeply traumatised young woman named Susan Frey, the victim in the *Billy* Wetherby stalking case, claiming she was being harassed by

Jenna Wetherby, Dom's daughter-in-law, and demanding that DI Cant, as the officer in charge, 'call off that bloody American Rottweiler'.

As if he'd sent her! Or even knew the first thing about it! Apparently Dom Wetherby's daughter-in-law had got it into her head that Dom had been murdered and that his son Billy was the killer. Armed with this theory, she'd taken it upon herself to turn up on poor Susan Frey's doorstep and demand that Susan relive all the painful and traumatic details of Billy's harassment, which must have been a lot more than a bit of heavy breathing since the lad was given two years for it.

Cant sighed heavily. He didn't have time for this crap.

'Sir?' The useless Sergeant Trotter stuck his useless head round the door. 'There's a Marcus Wetherby here to see you. He says it's urgent.'

Marcus. That was Jenna's husband. *Perfect timing.*

'Show him in,' Cant said grimly, taking a seat behind his desk and doing his best to look authoritative, if not stern.

'Detective Inspector.' Dom Wetherby's son strode in in lawyer mode: tall, well dressed in an expensive suit and tie, and projecting an air of mildly irritated confidence. He got straight to the point.

'I'd like to know what's going on with my father's body.'

'What's going on with it?' Cant played for time. He did not want to have to get into the missing lab reports if he didn't have to.

'Yes. When is it going to be released?' Marcus clarified brusquely. 'Naturally my mother wants to arrange the funeral as soon as possible.'

'Naturally.'

'It's been a terrible time for her, as I'm sure you can imagine, and these unexplained delays only make things worse.'

'I understand, sir,' said DI Cant. 'I have chased the medical examiner and the coroner's office. I understand some of the post-mortem testing has taken longer than usual. But I do appreciate your frustration, and I'm trying to get an official verdict and release as soon as possible.'

It was a fudge and they both knew it. Marcus opened his mouth to press the DI further, but Cant cut him off.

'Mr Wetherby, may I ask, are you aware that your wife's been in contact with Susan Frey? That she's been to see her, in fact?'

Marcus blinked and did a visible double-take. 'My wife?'

Ha! Cant thought childishly. *Who's on the back foot now?*

'Jenna Wetherby. That is your wife?'

'Yes. But—'

'And you're aware who Miss Frey is?'

'Of course,' Marcus snapped. 'She's the poor girl that Billy . . .' He searched for the appropriate words. It was ridiculous how embarrassed he still felt by what Billy had done. As if his brother's actions reflected in some way on him. As the older brother, the truth was, Marcus had always felt responsible for Billy to some degree when they were growing up. Now things were different. But the shame still lingered. Marcus hated it. 'My brother was jailed for harassing her,' he said eventually.

'That's right,' said DI Cant. 'And I just had Susan Frey on the phone, not five minutes before you walked in here, complaining that your wife was now harassing her, and asking me to do something about it.'

'That's ridiculous,' said Marcus, irritated again. 'What possible reason would Jenna have to bother Susan Frey?'

'Apparently,' Cant replied, 'your wife believes that your father was murdered.'

Marcus stared at him blankly.

Cant gave this a few moments to sink in, before adding, 'She seems to think that your brother Billy may have killed him. My understanding is that she wanted Susan Frey to provide evidence to support this theory. And that when Miss Frey declined to get involved, your wife became . . . agitated.'

Cant watched the blood drain from Marcus's face. All the lawyerly confidence was gone now. His knuckles were white from gripping the arms of his chair so tightly. The poor guy looked as if he might be about to have a heart attack.

Cant took a more conciliatory tone. 'Look, Mr Wetherby, I really do understand what an awful time this must be for all of you. I don't want to make things worse by talking to your wife formally. But Susan Frey's been through a lot, too, and she does have a right to privacy.'

'Of course she does,' muttered Marcus, clearly still in shock. 'I'm sorry. I had no idea.'

'Perhaps if you have a quiet word with Jenna yourself?' Cant suggested.

Marcus nodded, standing up awkwardly. 'I will. Of course. Thank you, Detective Inspector.'

'Mr Wetherby?' DI Cant called after him. 'You should know, the ME had no doubts that your father committed suicide. No doubts at all. Your wife's barking up the wrong tree. Whatever your brother may have done in the past, he didn't do this.'

Marcus looked at Cant gratefully. 'I know he didn't. Thank you again. I'll deal with this.'

'Have you any idea, any idea at all, how foolish you made me look?'

Marcus and Jenna were in their Volvo, parked in a layby at the top of Hazelford Hill. With the last shred of his self-control,

Marcus had waited till his mother could watch the children and he and Jenna could be alone together before he erupted, anger and resentment spewing out of him.

'Going into the police station, guns blazing, demanding Dad's body back, only to learn that my own *wife* has been running around the county behind my back, spreading rumours about Dad being murdered and trying to dig up dirt on Billy! That poor woman could have pressed charges, you know, Jenna. What were you *thinking*?'

Despite her rapidly beating heart – she hated confrontation with Marcus – Jenna defended herself.

'I don't know, Marcus. Perhaps I was thinking that there are more important things in life than how you look! You or your supposedly perfect family! Perhaps I was thinking that *someone* ought to give a shit about getting justice for your father, seeing as the police have clearly given up and so have *you*. And your mother.'

'No one's "given up", for God's sake. Dad killed himself!'

'No, he *didn't*.'

'Yes, he *did*, Jenna! He did.'

Jenna shook her head vehemently. 'I'm sorry. I don't believe it. Why would he?'

Marcus turned and stared out of the window. He was shaking, actually physically shaking, although whether from anger or fear Jenna couldn't tell.

'You didn't even know him.'

He said it so quietly that at first Jenna wondered whether she'd misheard. But then he said it again, and she had the feeling that maybe finally, at long last, they were approaching a breakthrough. Approaching the truth.

'What don't I know, Marcus?' she asked, her tone softening to match his. 'What about Dom don't I know? Please. Tell me.'

Marcus's jaw stiffened. Still staring out of the window, unable to meet her eye, he shook his head.

'I can't.'

Jenna's eyes welled with tears. 'You mean you won't.' The bitterness slipped out. Marcus pounced on it like a cat on a mouse.

'You're right,' he shot back. 'I won't. Because he was *my* father, not yours. And because I loved him and I owe him . . . certain things. My God, Jenna, you didn't love him. You didn't even like him most of the time!'

Jenna winced. This was true. But why couldn't Marcus see that it wasn't the point?

'You claim to love me,' he went on, his voice trembling with emotion.

'I do love you!' insisted Jenna.

'Then I am asking you – begging you – let it go. Just let it go. For me. For our marriage. *And* for Dad, although I know you don't see it that way.'

How can I? Jenna wanted to scream. *How can I see it that way when you won't open up to me? When you won't tell me the truth? When my choices are a marriage based on secrets or no marriage at all?*

Yesterday had been frustrating enough, with Susan Frey clearly too terrified of Billy to say one word on the subject, and Iris Grey unable to get anything out of Billy directly other than some bullshit excuse about blacking out and waking up in hospital the afternoon Dom died.

'I'm tired, Marcus,' Jenna said quietly. 'I'm tired of all the Wetherby family secrets.'

Not as tired as I am, Marcus thought darkly.

*

Two days later, on Saturday night, Iris found herself sitting awkwardly at a beautifully laid table at Chez Bruce, Clapham South's only Michelin-starred restaurant.

'*A votre santé!*' Ian raised his champagne flute to Iris's. 'It's amazing to see you.'

Oh God, thought Iris. *Oh God, oh God, oh God.* She'd tried hard to get Ian to agree to meet somewhere more low-key. More casual. Less pressured. Less self-consciously romantic and date-y. Chez Bruce was where they'd celebrated Ian's fiftieth, and Iris's thirtieth, and countless anniversaries in between. It was where they came after Ian's last West End opening night, and on the first day of Iris's exhibition at the National Portrait Gallery.

Tonight it was all part of Ian's 'making an effort'. He was trying to remind her, remind both of them, of happier times. He was trying to do something special, to make amends. He'd met Iris earlier at the station, and they'd gone for a walk on the common together, Ian asking her kindly about her life and her work and all sorts of things, talking only a little about himself and touching as lightly as he could on his own recent professional disappointments. Iris noticed all of it. The clean-shaven face, the fact he hadn't had a drink, the expensive restaurant, the smiles, something she hadn't seen from him in months, if not years.

He's trying. He's trying really hard.

She wasn't sure why that made everything so much worse.

'So.' He took another sip of champagne. 'What's happening with the portrait?'

The portrait. It had become code for 'our marriage'. 'What's happening with the portrait?' really meant 'When are you coming home?' and they both knew it. Iris felt her heart rate quicken with anxiety.

'Ariadne wants me to finish it. She's given me boxes of photographs and home movies. I started sorting through them this week. It feels weird.'

'That's because it is weird,' said Ian, handing Iris a menu but then proceeding to order starters for both of them. 'From what you describe, it sounds like the whole family's a few sandwiches short of a picnic. Still, at least that means you can work on it wherever you like. You don't *have* to be there anymore.'

Iris swallowed hard. It wasn't a question, but it may as well have been.

When are you coming home?

Are you coming home?

She didn't have an answer for either except 'Not yet', which was exactly what Ian didn't want to hear.

'Tell me about your writing.' She changed the subject. 'What's the new play?'

Ian began talking as they ate their *moules marinières*, and continued as they switched from champagne to Château du Cléray Muscadet de Sèvre et Maine, the wine helping both of them slip back into their natural rhythm, and out of best-behaviour mode, a relief to Iris. By the time the main courses arrived, however, the Wetherby family dramas were back on the agenda.

'What are the kids like?' Ian asked, genuinely curious. 'Can't have been much fun being raised by a narcissist like Dom Wetherby.'

'Dom didn't raise them. Ariadne did,' said Iris, biting back comments about narcissism, pots and kettles. 'She *is* a bit weird, you're right, but she's a devoted mother. And the kids are all different. Marcus is quite serious and stiff, but I think he's a nice guy overall. Billy's very dark. And Lorcan has Down's, as you know, and he's such a sweetheart.'

Her eyes lit up when she spoke about Lorcan in a way that Ian found he didn't like. Or perhaps he just didn't like that Iris was still avoiding having a real conversation with him. He tried again. Reaching across the table, he took her hand.

'Why are you still there, Iris? Why won't you come home?'

Because I'm afraid to go back to the way things were.

Because I'm afraid of us.

Afraid of you.

Ian was being so sweet tonight, so kind. But how long would it be before the cruelty came back? The professional jealousy, the resentment of her career, her life, her friends? Iris knew she was using Dom Wetherby's death as an excuse. But it was a good excuse, and she wasn't ready to let it go. Not yet.

'I can't come home. Not till I know more. There are things going on in that house, Ian. In that family. Secrets. I'm not convinced Dom Wetherby killed himself.'

Ian pushed a piece of artichoke around his plate in a detached, angry way.

'Because?'

'Because he had no reason to.'

'I disagree.' Ian took a big slug of wine and grinned. 'He probably read one of his own novels.'

Despite herself, Iris laughed.

'I'm serious.'

'So am I. Why do you *care*, Iris?' Ian pushed her. 'If something sinister happened to Dom Wetherby, surely that's the police's job.'

'Well, yes, but that's the whole point. They're not doing it.'

The wine had loosened Iris's tongue as well, and she found herself telling Ian about her bizarre car ride with Jenna Wetherby, and their shared suspicions about Billy.

'I tried to talk to him, to get him to confide in me. Jenna thinks he fancies me and I think she's right. He is *so* creepy.' She prattled on, apparently unaware of Ian's darkening expression. 'Anyway, he gave me an alibi of sorts, although the friend he said he stayed with . . .'

'Iris.'

Ian's voice was so quiet she didn't hear, and continued explaining about Billy's drinking problem and his supposed Christmas Day visit to A&E.

'*Iris!*'

This time there was no mistaking it. Diners from around the room broke off their conversations to turn and stare. Lowering his voice, Ian said, 'Do you realise that all you've talked about for the last twenty minutes is Dom Wetherby and his damn family?'

'You asked,' Iris said defensively, sobering up at a rate of knots.

'I asked when you were coming home.'

Iris stared down at her empty plate. 'I don't know, Ian. I just don't know.'

'Have you met someone else?'

Iris looked up and met Ian's embittered gaze. She hadn't expected that question. The first question had been hanging over them like a raincloud from the moment they sat down, but this took the conversation to a whole other level.

She hesitated. *Had* she met someone else? Did Graham Feeney constitute 'someone else'? Surely not. Nothing had happened, after all. Well, almost nothing.

'You bitch!' Iris's pregnant pause was the last straw for Ian. 'Here you are spinning me all this Nancy Drew, "I must find the truth" rubbish and all the while you're having a bloody affair.'

'I am not!' protested Iris, her voice rising to match his.

'You let me book tonight. You let me hope!' he lashed out. 'Thank God we never had a child, that's all I can say.'

Iris flushed an ugly deep purple with an emotion she couldn't name.

Downing the last of the wine, Ian added spitefully, 'At your age, it would probably have come out duff, anyway, like Lorcan Wetherby. Nothing wrong with that boy that an abortion wouldn't have fixed.'

Iris didn't remember leaving the table. She didn't remember grabbing her coat and taking a cab straight back to Waterloo. The first thing she was fully aware of was sitting in an empty carriage as the last Winchester train hurtled through the darkness, the rhythmic rattle of the tracks echoing her own thoughts as she pressed her face to the cool, dark glass.

Over and done, over and done, over and done.

'I'm getting a divorce,' she whispered aloud to the empty carriage, trying the words on for size.

It was terrifying how comfortably they fitted.

CHAPTER FOURTEEN

Graham Feeney tossed his Italian leather overnight bag onto the four-poster bed and looked around the room admiringly. It struck him that the humble British pub had changed beyond recognition since his student days, when rooms over the bar would have been spartan, linoleum-floored affairs and the menu downstairs would have run to fish and chips and steak-and-kidney pudding if you were lucky.

On the other hand, the Black Swan at Hazelford, aka the Mucky Duck, had probably never been your run-of-the mill boozer. For as long as Graham could remember, Dom Wetherby's adopted home village had always suffered from delusions of grandeur. *Not unlike the man himself*, Graham thought wryly. His room at the Swan was lovely, beautifully appointed yet unassuming, like the best sort of boutique hotel. He was gladder than ever that he'd taken Marcus Wetherby's advice and decided not to stay at Mill House.

'Believe me, you'll need some space by the end of the day,' Marcus warned him. 'The emotional pitch in that house right now is at a level only bats can hear.'

It was only thanks to Marcus's phone call that Graham was in Hazelford in the first place. The police still hadn't released

Dom's body, 'Which worries me,' Marcus told Graham. As a fellow lawyer, it worried Graham, too. Something was up there. 'But Jenna and I need to get back to London. I have work, and Lottie's due back at school on Monday. We need to get back to some sort of normality. Try to, anyway.'

The strain in his voice was evident. Graham surmised that all was not well between Marcus and Jenna, and he felt bad if this were the case. The two were well suited, in Graham's opinion. Of all the Wetherby children, he'd always felt closest to Marcus, perhaps because he'd been named after Graham's beloved older brother.

'I'm desperately worried about Mum,' Marcus went on, 'alone there with Billy and Lorcan, dealing with it all.' He briefly described Lorcan's ongoing nightmares about finding Dom's body and his obsession with 'bad ghosts', whom he thought were responsible or had harmed Dom in some way. 'And Billy doesn't help, always banging on about money and the will, as if he doesn't care that Dad's dead, which of course he does. As usual he blames poor Mum for everything. But he still stays on at the Mill. By the way, did you know Dad left him half the royalty rights to Grimshaw?'

Graham hadn't known that. He'd just assumed that Dom's literary estate would pass to Ariadne. Those rights must be worth a not-so-small fortune.

'Who got the other half?' he asked.

'Me,' said Marcus, adding awkwardly, 'Mum hasn't said anything about it, but I don't think she knew.'

Graham had agreed that he would 'stop by' and stay for a few days on his way back up to Edinburgh. He would check in on everyone, report back to Marcus, and see if he could get any information whatsoever out of the stunningly useless Hampshire

Constabulary, and hopefully help Ariadne begin the work of planning Dom's funeral.

Truth be told, Graham Feeney also had another, less altruistic motive for returning to the Mill. According to Marcus, who'd heard it from Jenna, Iris Grey and her horrid-sounding husband, Ian McBride, were heading for divorce. Graham knew one shouldn't look on somebody else's marital misery as a good thing. He also knew that the early, painful stages of a divorce were generally not considered the most auspicious time to begin a new relationship. But he couldn't entirely extinguish the small flicker of hope that Iris's divorce had ignited within him.

As terrible as it was to say it, under the circumstances, this was already shaping up to be a happy New Year for Graham Feeney.

After a shower and a quick change of clothes, Graham headed downstairs to the Swan's cosy residents' lounge and ordered a fortifying pot of lapsang and a toasted teacake before plucking up the courage to call Iris and invite her to have dinner with him tonight.

'I expect things will be tricky up at the Mill this afternoon. According to Marcus, his mother is in pieces. I could use a glass of wine afterwards, and some non-Wetherby company. What do you say?'

To his surprise and delight, Iris had agreed without hesitation.

Graham had had a few 'serious' relationships over the years, but none that had ever felt right enough to propel him to marriage. He'd been accused of being a commitment-phobe, and perhaps he was. Although truthfully, he didn't feel afraid of marriage so much as uninspired by it. He'd never wanted children, and never felt that lightning bolt of lust and passion that seemed to bring such turmoil into the lives of other men.

And yet with Iris Grey there'd been something. Not full-on lightning perhaps, but definitely something. A real spark. Perhaps it was only now, in this moment, that Graham had become ready for true love. A bit late in the day, some might say. But better late than never.

He hung up the phone feeling profoundly happy.

Graham Feeney's luck was on the change.

Ariadne was in the kitchen, drying the same cup for at least the fifth time, when Graham walked in. In a wood-green polo neck and corduroy trousers, and with his newly washed hair smelling of old-fashioned Floris shampoo, he looked like a creature from another world. A world not haunted by death. A world where life continued.

'Graham!' Dropping the tea towel, she hugged him warmly. 'What are you doing here? And how did you get in?'

'The front door was open,' he said, hugging her back. 'You should be careful about that, you know.'

Ariadne gave him a look that implied Hazelford wasn't the sort of place where one needed to lock one's front door and offered him a seat. He explained that Marcus had been worried about her, about everyone, and that he'd offered to spend a few days in the village on his way back up north, 'Just to see if I can help.'

'How sweet of you.' Reaching across the table, Ariadne squeezed his hand. She looked thin and ill and old. No wonder Marcus was worried.

'I saw a woman driving off in a red Polo just as I arrived,' said Graham, unsure for a moment where to begin. 'I wondered if she was from the police, or the coroner's office. Has there been any news?'

'Eugh. No.' Ariadne sighed heavily. 'The woman you saw was Dana, Lorcan's therapist. They just finished another session together.'

'How was that?' asked Graham.

Ariadne's lower lip began to wobble. She bit down on it to stop herself from crying. 'I don't know, honestly. I feel like it's one step forwards, two steps back. He's still so anxious. And this obsession with ghosts . . . It started before Dom died, but since then it's got out of control. He used to open up to Jenna a bit about it, but he won't talk to me at all.'

'That must be hard,' Graham said soothingly.

'It is. It's awful. I mean, Billy never talks to me, and now Marcus has gone. To lose Lorcan, too. And Dom, of course . . .'

The tears came then, silent but unstoppable, a steady salt river of grief. Graham handed her a handkerchief, which she took gratefully.

'Since Jenna and Marcus left, Lorcan's taken to pestering poor Iris down at the cottage,' she sniffed, dabbing her eyes. 'He knocks on her door at all hours of the night. Sometimes he's screaming. I think he's still half asleep.'

'Night terrors,' said Graham. He'd suffered from them himself after his brother, Marcus, killed himself. But he'd been twenty years old and of sound mind. How much worse, how much harder to process must this be for Lorcan, a traumatised child. 'What does Iris do when he turns up?'

'Oh, she's been wonderful,' said Ariadne, sincerely. 'She calms him down and brings him back home. Sometimes she gives him a cup of warm milk and a ginger snap. She's a sweetheart.'

'And what does the therapist say? About Lorcan?' said Graham, who suddenly found he didn't want to talk about Iris, not in front of Ariadne.

'That he's feeling guilty.' Closing her eyes, Ariadne leaned back and pinched the top of her nose, clearly emotionally exhausted. 'That he blames himself for Dom's death in some way, probably because he found the body, and that these "ghosts" are a projection of that.'

'So creating these imaginary friends, so to speak, gives him someone to blame, you mean?' asked Graham.

'Exactly. Except in this case he's blaming them for something he *hasn't* done.'

'But he thinks he has?'

She nodded wearily. 'That's the theory.'

'You don't agree with it?'

'Oh God, Graham!' Ariadne exhaled loudly, frustration and anger pouring out of her now like pus from a lanced boil. 'I don't know. I don't know what to think anymore. All I want is to have the funeral and put this to bed and try to rebuild our lives. Meanwhile Billy's wandering around the house with a pen and paper like a bloody debt collector, itemising everything: Dom's watches, the Lowry he bought for his fiftieth. Anyone would think he wanted his father dead,' she blurted, the tears threatening to come again as soon as she realised what she'd said.

'*Did* he want Dom dead?' Graham asked. He had the barrister's ability to say the unsayable, but in such a softly spoken, matter-of-fact manner that it didn't seem shocking at all.

'No,' Ariadne responded in kind. 'Me, perhaps. But never Dom. He loved his father. No, he's just doing his level best to hurt me.'

'And succeeding, by the sounds of it,' said Graham. 'Look, I'm happy to talk to him if you think it would help. Or Lorcan. But I think in all honesty the most use I can be to you is in trying to get the police to pull their finger out and issue a death certificate, so you can have a funeral.'

'Oh, Graham!' Ariadne looked across at him gratefully. 'I can't tell you how much that would mean. I'm sure it would help Lorcan, too, to have some sort of closure. I know it's a terrible cliché to talk about "laying someone to rest", but that's what it feels like. Dom can't *rest* until there's a funeral. None of us can.'

Iris walked into the pub and scanned the room looking for Graham. She wondered whether it was scientifically possible for other people to actually *hear* your heart beating through a crowded bar, with Robbie Williams' 'Angels' playing loudly in the background. Hopefully not. On the other hand, Iris had failed GCSE biology twice, so what did she know?

She still remembered how disappointed her dad had been when she got those grades. 'I know you're clever, Iris. You're just not trying.'

Robbie Grey was right: Iris hadn't been trying. After a deeply chequered school career in her early teens, an unhappy period that had been heavily overshadowed by her older sister Thea's bipolar disorder, no one had been more surprised than Iris's teachers when she went on to achieve 'A's in A-level English, art and history of art and won a place to read English at St Hilda's College, Oxford. Her mother, Helen, had burst into tears of joy the day Iris got her acceptance letter, which Iris still kept in a drawer at Mill Cottage.

Dear Miss Grey, We are delighted to inform you . . .

Less than five years later, both Iris's parents were dead, her mother from heart complications and her dad from lung cancer. Iris knew it was irrational, but she couldn't help blaming her sister for the stress she'd put their mother under, and the misery she'd made of everybody's lives for so many years. There was something else Iris blamed Thea for, too – something that only the two of them knew about, or ever would know about. Something too painful for Iris to recount, even now.

The last time the sisters had seen each other in person was at their dad's funeral. Iris rarely thought about the estrangement these days. Thea lived in Holland with her doctor husband, apparently stable, and Iris had made a life with Ian. Only now that that life had unravelled had she begun to think about her sister again. Getting to know Billy Wetherby had also brought back memories of the painful depths of Thea's illness, although it all felt like lifetimes ago now.

The pub smelled of spilt beer and sawdust, and Iris felt her stomach start to churn in accompaniment to her thudding heart.

Get a grip, she told herself sternly.

Ever since Graham's call inviting her to dinner, Iris had been plunged into a flat-spin panic. Two solid hours spent rearranging her doll's-house furniture had failed miserably to produce its usual calming effect, as had the single shot of tequila she'd poured herself at six o'clock, which instead had left her feeling dizzy and sick and with an uncomfortable burning sensation in her windpipe that refused to go away. Throwing every item of clothing she possessed down onto the bed, she'd tried each one on in turn, every dress, every sexy skirt, every sparkly top, only to end up back in the jeans and Zara Breton sweater she'd been wearing all day and racing out of the cottage in a panic she'd be late.

And now here she was, *not* late – not very late – and no sign of Graham Feeney.

'Boo.'

Graham stole up behind her, his long arms snaking down around her tiny, doll-like waist. Iris let out a little yelp of shock.

'Oh my God, don't do that!'

Graham smiled, then laughed. 'Sorry. I didn't know you were so easily spooked. It's great to see you, Iris.'

The smile reached all the way to his eyes, just as it had on Christmas Eve, the night they met.

'You too.'

Stop it! the voice in Iris's head commanded. *Stop mooning at him like a lovesick adolescent.* Iris ignored the voice. After all, she'd listened to it diligently throughout her long and mostly miserable marriage to Ian, and where had it got her? Nowhere, that's where. Allowing Graham to take her hand and lead her into the dining room, then beaming up at him as he pulled out the chair for her to sit down, Iris decided to throw caution to the wind.

Unlike her gruesome meal with Ian at Chez Bruce – had that really only been a week ago? – with Graham the conversation flowed as easily and pleasurably as the wine. Of course, it helped that they had a ready-made topic to hand in poor Dom Wetherby's death and the family dramas that had followed, all of them more gripping than even the best Grimshaw mystery.

'Marcus tells me you and Jenna have become friends,' said Graham, flagging down the teenage waitress to ask for another carafe of house red to go with the plate of deep-fried whitebait they were sharing.

'I wouldn't say that, exactly.' Iris flicked a stray hair out of her eyes and swirled the wine round her glass contemplatively. 'I mean, she seems nice, but I don't really know her. It's more that we bonded over Dom and just how awful and lax the police are being.'

'Not releasing the body, you mean?' Graham casually scooped up the last forkful of whitebait from Iris's plate and ate it. 'I agree they have been a bit slow on that. Poor Ariadne was in a dreadful way about it this afternoon.'

'It's not that,' Iris corrected him. 'I mean, there is that, but that's the least of it. It's the way they jumped to the conclusion Dom drowned himself without any investigation, any interviews, any anything. And the family just accepted that without a whisper. Jenna thought there was more to it than that and so do I.'

Graham put down his fork carefully. *All his movements are careful*, Iris thought. *His words, too. Careful and thoughtful and measured*. It was hard not to contrast this to Ian's volatility and rage.

Looking at her curiously now, Graham asked, 'So you and Jenna think, what? That somebody killed Dom?'

'Yes.' Iris lowered her voice. 'At least, Jenna definitely does. She thinks Billy did it.'

'Billy!?' Graham spluttered, momentarily losing his cool. *Jesus. No wonder Jenna and Marcus were arguing, and Marcus had bundled his family back to London, sharpish.*

'Is that such a crazy idea?' Iris asked. The waitress brought their wine and refilled both their glasses.

'Frankly, yes,' said Graham robustly. 'Why on earth would Billy Wetherby kill his father?'

'For his inheritance?' Iris offered. 'Dom left him and Marcus the book rights, you know. That's millions.'

Graham shook his head. 'No way.'

'Why not?' Iris challenged him. 'Don't people kill for greed all the time?'

'Not often, actually. And not their own parents. Have you and Jenna got any other motives up your sleeve?' He was teasing her, playing the barrister, but Iris didn't mind. It was a relief to have someone to bounce ideas off for a change. Someone who wasn't two inches tall and made from a wooden clothes peg.

'Maybe they'd had an argument. Let's not forget, Billy's an angry, violent obsessive with a volatile, sadistic streak.'

Graham shook his head. 'No, he isn't. I've known the boy all his life, Iris. I grant you Billy's had his problems. Still has a lot of problems. But he's not a killer. I'm sorry but I just don't buy it.'

He seemed so very confident, Iris found her own doubts resurfacing.

'But you *do* buy the idea that Dom Wetherby was suicidal? Come on, Graham. We were both there on Christmas Eve.'

'I wasn't focusing on Dom's mood on Christmas Eve,' said Graham, leaning forward and, totally spontaneously, planting a kiss on Iris's lips. Sitting back in his chair afterwards, he smiled, his eyes twinkling, apparently delighting in her discomfiture.

'OK,' said Iris, collecting herself. 'So you tell me. Why would Dom have killed himself? At the top of his career, great friends, good health, happy family life, loads of money, beautiful house. What reason could he possibly have had to throw all that away?'

Graham considered the question.

'All right. Well, this is all speculation, obviously, but off the top of my head . . . One: affairs. Maybe one of his extra-curricular romances went spectacularly wrong.'

'Dom was having an affair?' Iris wasn't surprised by the idea. She could absolutely imagine Dom Wetherby to have been the cheating type. But surely when he was younger? Not *now*.

'I didn't say that,' said Graham. 'Dom did *have* affairs. But I'm just throwing out possibilities here. Two: depression.' He counted Dom's imagined problems off on his fingers one by one like a shopping list. 'Grimshaw was coming to an end. His life's work. Plus he was about to turn sixty. Maybe he felt the best was all behind him. Three: physical health. Maybe he was ill and none of us knew it.'

Iris frowned. Surely this was clutching at straws.

'All right, maybe not. But there was Billy,' Graham went on. 'The stress of his conviction, of dealing with him at home after his release. I know Dom came off as confident to outsiders—'

'Arrogant, more like,' Iris interjected. 'The man wasn't just confident. He was cocky.'

Graham didn't correct her.

'He could be at times,' he conceded. 'But underneath that façade, for all we know Dom may well have felt profoundly over-whelmed. You have to remember, Iris, suicide is an irrational act, by definition. That's the nature of the thing. We're all programmed to live, to survive, to save ourselves. To do the opposite suggests an unbalanced mind. Looking for "rational" answers might not be the way to go here.'

'Hmmm.' Iris clearly wasn't convinced. 'That's almost exactly what Marcus said to Jenna before he shut her down.'

Now it was Graham's turn to frown. 'What do you mean, "shut her down"?'

'He basically insisted she stop asking questions,' said Iris.

Graham took this in. 'Well, maybe Marcus was right.'

'Maybe. But maybe Marcus was wrong,' Iris retorted. 'And shouldn't Jenna be allowed to make her own decisions?'

She told him about Jenna's visit to Susan Frey and the row with Marcus that had followed. 'I think she felt she *had* to let things go for the sake of the marriage. That's not right.'

'I suppose not,' Graham observed mildly. 'You don't have that problem, though, do you?'

'No,' said Iris. 'I don't.'

'You're free to do as you please.'

'Yes.'

Their eyes met. It was a clear allusion to Ian, and Iris's own situation. *So he knows*, Iris thought. *Marcus must have told him. He knows I'm getting a divorce.*

Good.

I'm glad he knows.

'Let's say you're right and there was foul play in Dom's death.' Graham deftly changed the subject before the mood became too intense. 'Do *you* think Billy did it?'

It was a question that had been preoccupying Iris for the last week, distracting her from what she ought to be doing trying to move forward with her divorce and deal with her train wreck of a life. Instead, she'd contacted Winchester Hospital trying to find out if Billy Wetherby really had been treated there on Christmas Day.

'Are you a family member?'

'Er, n-no,' Iris had stammered. 'No, I'm not. I'm a friend.'

'I see. Well, I'm afraid we can't give out patient information.'

Less than an hour later, displaying a resourcefulness she never knew she had, Iris called back posing as Billy's parole officer.

'I'm following up on an offender we have reason to be concerned about. William Wetherby. He missed an important hearing two weeks ago and then failed to show up to mandated check-in with me on Christmas Day. He claims he was in A&E.'

'Let me have a look.' It was a different operator. Iris held her breath. Just making this phone call was almost certainly a crime, possibly a serious one. But she needn't have worried. When the woman came back on the line, she couldn't have been more helpful.

'William Wetherby. Yup, he was here, Christmas Day, checked in at one twelve p.m. Looks like the doctor saw him at three forty-five, but I couldn't tell you when he left. What time was his parole appointment?'

'It was at two,' Iris blurted. 'So it looks like he was telling the truth. Thank you.'

She'd hung up, her heart pounding from her lie. So there it was. Half an alibi. Presumably the hospital CCTV would reveal more detail on Billy's movements, but getting hold of that would have been a bridge too far for Iris.

Still, the fact that Billy had been drunk enough to wind up in hospital just a few hours before Dom drowned surely made it unlikely that he'd made his way back from Winchester to Hazelford, found his father, subdued him somehow and tied a sodding great stone to his legs.

'No,' Iris told Graham now, answering his question. 'I don't think he did it. Part of me wants to think it. I really don't like the guy at all. But no.'

'Well,' Graham said cheerfully, 'if you want a partner to help you solve the mystery, I'd be happy to offer my services. I do think it's important that Jenna stays out of it, though. Somebody's marriage needs to survive this mess.'

'Yes,' agreed Iris. 'It does.'

It was odd the way Graham talked sometimes. *Solve the mystery.* As if he hadn't known the man at all. On the other hand, he clearly did care, not just about Dom but about the whole Wetherby family. After all, he'd taken three days out of his life and work just to check on Ariadne and try to help out. Perhaps not having a family of his own made the bonds closer. That and losing his only brother.

'Not that I agree with either of you, just to be clear,' Graham continued, unaware of Iris's racing thoughts. 'I think it was suicide. But we lawyers know how to keep an open mind.'

'As do we artists,' countered Iris wryly. 'Open mind, open eyes. Those are essential in my line of work.'

Graham paid the bill. Iris let him. It was nice to be taken care of for a change, even if it was only dinner. He signed the credit-card receipt, sexual tension hanging over the table like a thick, heavy fog.

Ever the gentleman, Graham broke the silence first.

'I'd ask you up for a nightcap, but I'm afraid it would sound too cheesy.'

'It would,' Iris grinned. 'It's not that I don't want to,' she added hastily. 'It's just . . .'

'Too soon,' Graham finished for her, laying a warm, surprisingly rough hand over hers. 'I understand.'

Where did a rich barrister come by so many callouses? Iris wondered. *Rock climbing? Gardening?* She looked forward to finding out. There was so much Iris wanted to know about Graham Feeney. But he was right. It was too soon, and not just for sex. The end of her marriage had come on in awful, lurching stages, like a lift that falls a few floors, then stabilises, then falls again. You know you're going to hit the ground eventually. You just don't know when, or whether you'll survive the fall.

Iris had survived it, barely. But what came next she had no idea. *Baby steps.*

Focus on Dom Wetherby. One task. One distraction. Focus on finding the truth. 'Solving the mystery', as Graham put it.

Outside on Hazelford Hill, beneath the swinging Black Swan sign, Graham helped Iris on with her coat.

'Isn't that . . . what's-his-name? From the party?' he asked her suddenly. Iris followed his gaze across the road to where Harry Masters, the piano teacher, was standing next to his parked car, arguing with a woman. *No, not arguing. Pleading.* It was too dark to see Harry's face and too far across the road to make out what he was saying, but his tone of voice and body language were both submissive. Desperate. Distraught. He was holding the woman by the hand, but all at once she pulled away, releasing herself angrily from his grip and stalking off down the hill. As she turned, the street light lit up her features, just for a second.

There was no mistaking it.

'Ariadne!' Iris whispered to Graham. 'Did you see that?'

'Yup,' Graham whispered back. 'She didn't look too happy.'

'Neither of them did,' said Iris.

It was a short walk back to Mill Cottage. Ignoring her protests, Graham insisted on walking Iris home.

'It's dark, and according to you, there might be a killer on the loose.'

'It's not a game, you know!' she chided him, punching him jokingly on the arm.

'I know it's not,' he said seriously. They discussed Ariadne and Harry, and what on earth their heated meeting might mean. When they reached her front door, Graham pushed the hair back from Iris's eyes and stooped to kiss her forehead. It was such a tender gesture that for an awful moment she thought she might be going to cry. But then she pulled herself together.

'I'll see you in the morning?' he asked, a sweet note of vulnerability creeping into his voice. *He's anxious, too*, thought Iris. *He doesn't want to mess this up.*

'Of course.' She smiled reassuringly. 'I'll be here.'

Graham Feeney walked back to the pub alone.

Iris was right. He was anxious. But there was another feeling inside him, too, fighting to be heard. Was it hope? Was a dark, lonely chapter in his life coming to an end?

It would be up to him to write his own story.

The following evening at just gone six, Jenna was upstairs bathing Lottie and Oscar when the telephone rang.

'Will you get it, Marcus?' she yelled downstairs.

No answer.

'*Marcus!*'

She knew he was home from work because she'd heard the door open and close about ten minutes ago, just as she was squirting *Sofia the First* bubbles into Lottie's end of the bath and *Thomas the Tank Engine* bubbles at Oscar's end, near the taps. (Apparently it was the crappy plastic bottles they were poured out of that made all the difference.)

Wrapping a slippery Oscar up in a towel and cursing Marcus under her breath, Jenna dashed into the bedroom and picked up. 'Hello?'

'It's Ariadne.' Even in those two words Jenna could hear the tight, clipped strain in her mother-in-law's voice. 'Is Marcus—'

'I'm here.' Marcus had finally deigned to pick up the phone downstairs. Irritated more than she ought to be, Jenna hung up her end and returned to the children.

Five minutes later she was in Lottie's room, wrangling pyjamas, hairbrushes and detangling spray, when Marcus walked in. He looked ashen.

'What is it?' Jenna asked, her irritation forgotten. 'What's happened?'

'They didn't release Dad's body because some lab reports had gone missing.' His voice was the dead, flat monotone of somebody in clinical shock. 'Now they've been found.'

Jenna waited.

'There were high levels of chloroform in Dad's blood when he died.'

Jenna held her breath.

'He was unconscious when he went . . .' Marcus's voice broke. He looked down at his shoes, unable to meet his wife's eyes. 'When somebody put him into the river. You were right, Jen. Dad didn't kill himself. He was murdered.'

CHAPTER FIFTEEN

'For God's sake.'

DI Roger Cant rolled his eyes at the PC family liaison officer sitting beside him and exhaled deeply as he turned into Mill Lane. He'd hoped, naively, that they'd be able to arrive quietly for these initial family interviews. No such luck. The entire approach to Dom Wetherby's house was jammed solid with press vehicles, almost as badly as it had been after the body was found.

Bloody parasites.

After the coroner's report Cant had had no option but to release a statement to the media: that Dominic Wetherby's death was now being treated as murder, and that anybody with any relevant information should come forward immediately. Cant had taken a gamble and also asked that any locals who might have seen anything suspicious in the vicinity of the Mill or the river on the afternoon of Christmas Day contact the police on a special crime number. Nine times out of ten, all those sorts of 'tips' wound up being useless and a tremendous waste of time and resources. But the manner of Dom Wetherby's death – being drugged and dragged to the riverbank, painstakingly weighted down and then drowned, not in some remote, hidden location but practically in his own back garden – gave DI Cant hope that perhaps this time he might get lucky.

Slapping on the blue lights on the roof of his Range Rover, Cant steamrollered through the television crews like a bowling ball, sending news reporters and sound crews scrambling out of the narrow lane before they were hit like skittles. PC Sally Rogers silently gripped the handle on the passenger door.

'You all right?' Cant asked her, sounding more irritated than concerned.

'I'm fine, sir.'

'Good.' He skidded to a halt, putting the car in park. Behind them, a second squad car drew up, driven by his sergeant. 'You wait here till I need you,' Cant told Sally.

'But, sir,' Sally protested, 'I really ought to be present when you speak to the family, especially given the sensitivity of Lorcan's needs.'

'I'll call if I need you,' Cant insisted. 'Same goes for Sergeant Trotter.'

As soon as he stepped out of the car, crunching across the gravel alone towards Mill House, the questions flew at him like arrows.

'Detective Inspector! What can you tell us?'

'Do you have any suspects yet?'

'Why has it taken so long to launch a murder inquiry? What went wrong?'

'Inspector!'

Ignoring them all, Cant knocked on the front door and was instantly admitted by a tall, distinguished-looking man in his fifties whom he hadn't met before.

'Graham Feeney,' the man introduced himself. 'I'm a family friend. Ariadne's asked for my help organising the funeral and with . . . all this.' He gestured to the swarms of reporters gathered beyond the garden walls.

Cant shook his hand.

'Can I take your coat?' asked Feeney.

'Thank you.' Cant shrugged out of his ugly black waterproof jacket.

'Ariadne's in the drawing room,' said Feeney efficiently. He'd have made an excellent butler, Cant thought. 'I'll take you through.'

Ariadne Wetherby had looked unwell the first time DI Cant met her, but she looked immeasurably worse today. Her eyes were pink and puffy from crying, and her whole face seemed drooped and sunken with stress and lack of sleep. She was wearing a crumpled grey sweater and a pair of pink corduroy trousers that Cant suspected must have fitted her until recently, but now hung off her like a scarecrow's rags.

'Good morning, Mrs Wetherby.' Cant offered his hand, but she seemed to miss the gesture, continuing to stare at the press outside with a glazed expression. Cant turned to Graham Feeney. 'Perhaps you'd better draw the curtains. Just for now, while we have a chat.'

Graham nodded and did so, taking a seat on the sofa next to Ariadne. Resting a hand on her bony knee, he said, 'The detective inspector needs to talk to you, Ariadne. Ask you some questions. Is that all right?'

'Hmm?' Ariadne looked up as if seeing both men for the first time. 'Oh yes, of course. Did you talk to him about the funeral?' she asked Graham.

'We – the family – were hoping to hold the service next week,' Graham explained to DI Cant. 'Obviously it's been a long wait for the body to be released, and Ariadne would like some closure. For the children's sake, especially.'

'Of course,' Cant said kindly. 'That's no problem from our side. I'm sorry it's taken so long to reach this point, Mrs Wetherby. But I want to assure you we will do everything in our power, everything, to find out who did this to your husband.'

'Thank you.' She was looking him in the eye, but there were no tears. No visible emotion of any kind, in fact. Instead, the glazed look was back. She was there and not there.

'The first thing I'm going to need is everybody's movements on Christmas Day,' said Cant.

'*Our* movements?' Ariadne sounded surprised. 'You mean the family's?'

'Well, yes, as a starting point.'

'I don't see how that's going to help you find Dom's killer.' She was becoming agitated.

Graham Feeney placed a calming hand on her arm.

'It's just routine, Ariadne,' he assured her.

'You and your immediate family were the last people to see your husband alive, Mrs Wetherby,' Cant explained, 'and your son found the body. Piecing together a picture of that day, and perhaps the days prior, will provide crucial evidence.'

Ariadne stared at him in panicked silence.

Once again, Graham Feeney filled it. 'If it would be useful, Detective Inspector, I could help Mrs Wetherby put down a time-line of Christmas Day on paper, what everyone was doing when and so on?'

Cant's eyes narrowed. 'What did you say you do again, Mr Feeney?'

'I'm a barrister,' Graham replied politely. He watched the policeman's expression intensify, although whether Cant viewed this information as good or bad was hard to tell.

'A timeline would be helpful,' Cant said stiffly.

Ah, thought Graham. *It's bad.* In Graham's experience, a lot of police didn't like lawyers, which was odd given that, as long as they weren't corrupt, both professions were supposed to be on the same side, that of justice.

'When do *you* last remember seeing your husband, Mrs Wetherby?' Cant refocused his attention on Dom's widow.

'After the present-giving,' said Ariadne, answering quickly and with certainty. 'Dom put batteries into Lorcan's toy boat and made sure it was working. Then he went out for a walk. Marcus went with him.'

'What time was that?'

'I'm not sure. Around three o'clock or a bit later?'

'And did you see them leave the house?'

Ariadne frowned for a moment, trying to remember exactly. 'I don't think so. No. I went into the kitchen to start clearing up. Jenna was with the children and my dad, and Marcus and Dom went out for some air. But I didn't actually see them leave.'

'Your father was here that day?' DI Cant was taking notes.

'Yes. He always comes for Christmas,' said Ariadne. 'Is that important?'

Cant smiled, he hoped reassuringly. 'All we're trying to do is build a picture, Mrs Wetherby. Who was here, who wasn't. Now, your son Billy, he was *not* at home that day, correct?'

Ariadne visibly stiffened. 'Correct.'

'He'd had an argument with your husband?'

'No!' Ariadne sat forward, suddenly insistent. 'Who told you that? No. Billy had an argument with *me*, the day before, and he went to a friend's house to cool off. He never argued with Dom.'

'Never?' DI Cant raised an eyebrow. But Ariadne doubled down.

'Never. It was me Billy was angry with, not his father.'

'All right. Well, I'll need to speak to him, and your other sons.' Ariadne looked as if she were on the brink of saying something, but then thought better of it. 'I'll leave you in peace shortly,' DI Cant went on. 'I realise all this must still be a terrible shock and I don't want to overwhelm you. But I have to ask, Mrs Wetherby, did your husband have any enemies that you were aware of? Anyone who might hold a grudge against him, or want to do him harm?'

Ariadne shook her head vehemently. 'Everybody loved Dom. Everybody.'

'Perhaps in his business life?'

'No,' she insisted. 'Dom would walk into a room and light it up, Detective Inspector. Ask anybody.'

'There were tensions in the village, I understand? Some council members objected to your husband's chairmanship?'

'Well, yes.' Ariadne looked pained. 'Unfortunately, one can never completely escape envious people. The ones determined to dislike a man purely because he's successful. But Dom was well liked, DI Cant. He was a wonderful husband and a wonderful man.'

'I'm sure he was,' Cant said diplomatically, getting to his feet. 'Are any of your sons at home, Mrs Wetherby?'

Ariadne sighed. 'Billy's here somewhere.'

'And your oldest son?'

She shook her head. 'Marcus lives in London. I'm not expecting him now till the funeral.'

'What about your youngest boy?'

Ariadne looked away sadly, unable to meet the detective's eye. 'Lorcan's in his room,' she said quietly. 'He's always in his room these days. I'm afraid it's been a terrible shock for him.'

'I'll take you up there, Detective Inspector,' Graham Feeney offered, getting helpfully to his feet.

'That's all right, sir,' Cant said politely but firmly. 'You stay with Mrs Wetherby. I'll pop outside first and have my child liaison officer come and join me. I'm sure the two of us can find our own way.'

Cant couldn't say why exactly, but there was something about the lawyer's ever-helpful manner that he didn't trust. Or maybe he just didn't trust lawyers full stop. Either way, he wanted to interview each of Dom Wetherby's sons in private and without an audience.

Lorcan Wetherby's bedroom was a typical little boy's room, only with a big boy in it. He had a bunk bed with a *Scooby-Doo* duvet cover, a floor littered with Lego and other toys, and walls plastered with cheap Blu-tacked posters of puppies and spaceships and cartoon characters, as well as photographs of family members. DI Cant and his liaison officer, the kind but inexperienced Sally, found Lorcan sitting on a beanbag, plugged in to his iPod and staring out at the waterwheel and river below through the elegant floor-to-ceiling sash window.

'Hello.' Cant tried to sound cheerful and unthreatening, then realised that the boy couldn't hear him through the music. Tapping him on the shoulder, he tried again.

Lorcan turned round and took off his earphones.

'Hello.' He smiled briefly, before turning back to the window.

'I'm a policeman,' said Cant, sitting down next to him and wishing he had more experience – any experience – of people with Lorcan's condition. 'And Sally here's a policewoman.'

'OK,' Lorcan said blankly.

'Do you know what that means?'

Lorcan looked from Sally to Cant and nodded. 'Catch baddies,' he said, seriously.

'That's right,' Sally jumped in. 'DI Cant and I catch baddies. Would it be all right if we asked you some questions, Lorcan?'

Lorcan shrugged. He didn't look happy, but Cant pressed on. 'Do you know why I'm here?' he asked.

The boy shifted uncomfortably on the bag. 'Dad?'

'That's right. I'm here about your dad.'

'Hair,' Lorcan mumbled. He was starting to sound increasingly distressed. 'The boat got stuck!'

'Take your time. We know it's hard to talk about,' Sally said kindly, earning herself a 'back off' look from her boss.

'You were the one who found the body,' Cant resumed bluntly. He felt as sorry for Lorcan Wetherby as the next person, but they had a murder to solve.

'It wasn't me!' Lorcan's voice was rising. He stood up, panicked.

'No one's accusing you of anything.' Cant tried to sound reassuring.

'It was the ghost! I saw the ghost!'

The boy was rambling wildly now, but Cant jotted the word down anyway: 'Ghost.'

'What ghost was this, Lorcan?'

'White ghost. By the water!'

Billy Wetherby suddenly appeared in the bedroom doorway in tracksuit bottoms and an Eton College hoodie. Elbowing past Sally, he squared up to Cant with a belligerent glare. 'What's going on in here?'

Cant took in Billy's appearance. He had the same hollow-eyed, brooding good looks that the detective remembered from their first meeting, two weeks earlier, although something seemed to have changed about Billy since that encounter. His cheeks looked fuller, his clothes cleaner and his general demeanour healthier and more confident, despite his obvious anger.

'What do you think you're doing, upsetting my brother?' he demanded, putting a protective hand on Lorcan's shoulder.

'We need to ask Lorcan a couple of questions, sir,' Cant replied calmly.

'Why?' Billy retorted, eyeing first Sally and then Cant disdainfully. 'Nothing my brother tells you will stand up in court. He's non compos mentis, Detective Inspector. Or hadn't you noticed?'

Sally blushed, but Cant looked at Billy poker-faced. He was thinking how odd it was to be considering what would or wouldn't 'stand up in court', versus what might help catch their father's killer.

'Lorcan's a key witness,' Cant replied patiently. 'And this is a murder inquiry. He might have seen something.'

Turning away from them both, Billy ruffled Lorcan's hair affectionately, as one might pet a dog. The boy seemed comforted by the gesture, smiling up at his brother with relief before putting his headphones back on.

Cant contemplated arguing the point and insisting on resuming his interview with Lorcan, but instead decided this was as good an opportunity as any to ask Billy some questions. Jump in and catch him unawares, before he had time to rehearse his responses.

After sending Sally back to the car, he asked Billy what he knew about Dom's movements on Christmas Day, or the days leading up to it. 'Is there anything you can think of that might be relevant?'

'Such as what?' Billy leaned one shoulder against the wall, affecting a look of profound boredom and looking every inch the spoilt public schoolboy, especially in that hoodie. 'As you know, I wasn't here when it happened. Drunk and disorderly in a hospital waiting room, I'm afraid.' He leered, looking anything but afraid.

'Did your father have any enemies?' Cant asked, trying not to let it show on his face how much he disliked this sulky, poisonous young man.

Billy laughed loudly. 'You'd better sharpen your pencil, old boy. How long have you got? Dad's enemies . . . let me see. There were the villagers he belittled. That's a long list in itself. Then there were the writers and producers he stiffed on Grimshaw over the years. You'll want to talk to them. The spurned mistresses. Are you getting all this?'

He thinks this is a game, Cant thought, disgusted. But he was professional enough not to rise to Billy's taunting, or to interrupt his flow.

'The most recent was that dumb bint Rachel Truebridge. She turned up at the Christmas Eve party off her tits apparently, embarrassing herself and poor old Dad. And he clearly had his eye on his portrait painter, Iris Grey. No doubt you've met Iris. She's renting the cottage. I can't say if she'd reached the point of wanting to drown him yet, but I'm sure she would have eventually.' Noticing the detective's obvious distaste, Billy's smile broadened. 'You don't appreciate my sense of humour, Detective Inspector? That's all right. Not many people do. Now, where was I? Oh yes, Dad's enemies. Well, there's my mother, of course. I'm sure I don't need to tell a man of your intellectual insight not to be fooled by Ariadne's sweet, saintly, artistic exterior. She hated my father. Hated his lies, his affairs, his success, hated that everybody loved him. I don't suppose she thought to mention that she has a shed full of chloroform out in our woods?'

'What are you talking about?' Cant was beginning to lose his temper.

Billy explained about Ariadne's sculpting shed and how she used drugs to gas and subdue animals she wanted to sculpt. 'Other sculptors use carcasses, but not Mum. She likes the control of having the animal alive but powerless. Totally at her mercy. Creepy, isn't it?'

Cant said nothing. It *was* a bit creepy, but nothing compared to Billy.

'Is the shed locked?' he asked.

'No idea.' Billy yawned. 'I doubt it, but Mum would know. In any case, if Dad had chloroform in his system, you can bet that was where it came from. See how helpful I'm being, Detective Inspector? I believe that's what you call a "lead".'

'And you, Mr Wetherby. How did you feel about your father?'

Billy cracked his knuckles, a look of wry amusement creeping back over his face. Glancing to make sure that Lorcan was completely tuned out, he leaned forward and stage-whispered, 'Oh, I hated him, Detective Inspector. It could have been me! Could have been any of us. Did you know, as children, he used to play "no escaping" games with Marcus and me, where we'd tie weights to our feet in our swimming pool in France and then have to try and swim up to the surface? Dad called it "Houdini". We used to beg him to play it with us. We loved the adrenaline, you see. That and knowing we were pleasing him. Everyone always wanted to please my father, Detective Inspector.'

Not everyone, thought Cant. *Not in the end.*

'Of course, Mother hated the game. She banned it. Used to scream at Dad for being "wildly irresponsible". But Dad just ignored her. He did stop in the end, but that was because of Lorcan.'

Billy looked down at his brother with affection. 'He freaked out one time. Panicked. He almost drowned. That was the end of the Houdini game. Well' – Billy raised an eyebrow ironically – 'almost the end. So you see, Detective Inspector, it could have been any one of us who finally did for Dad. Or any one of a hundred other people burned by the great Dominic Wetherby. I wish you all the best in unravelling the mystery and bringing his killer to justice, but I'm afraid you'll be spending a good deal of time chasing your tail. And I do so *hate* to see police time being wasted.'

Cant gave him a look that would have turned a lesser man to stone.

'Don't leave Hazelford without letting us know, Mr Wetherby. We'll need to talk to you again.'

'Leave Hazelford?' Billy mocked. 'Heaven forbid. Why would anybody want to do that?'

Outside, Cant collared his sergeant.

'Call forensics. There's a shed in the woods over there.' He pointed down towards the river. 'Mrs Wetherby uses it for sculpting. Apparently she has a supply of chloroform in there.'

Sergeant Trotter looked puzzled.

'Don't ask,' said Cant. 'And don't go in or touch anything till forensics have checked it out.'

'Sir.'

'I'm nipping over to the cottage.' Cant nodded towards Mill Cottage, where a thin stream of grey smoke was winding its way up from the chimney into the chill winter sky. 'Ms Grey's our last witness for today.'

*

Iris saw DI Cant making his way towards her cottage from the kitchen window. Like the rest of the world, she'd heard the news this morning, about Dom Wetherby's death being reclassified as murder. *Not before time*, had been her first thought. Her second thought was not so much who, or why, but *how* had a killer managed to subdue a big man like Dom, weight him down and dump him in the Itchen on Christmas Day and within yards of scores of possible witnesses? There were still far too many unanswered questions, and Iris couldn't help but wonder whether the baby-faced DI Cant was really the right man to answer them. She'd only met him once, but Cant had seemed both young and plodding, quite lacking in the insights and instincts that helped one look deeper into human nature, and the dark heart within us all.

Five minutes later, sitting opposite Cant at her kitchen table to give an impromptu witness statement, Iris saw nothing about the detective inspector to change her mind. His questions were routine – how long had she known Dom? When had she last seen him? What had her own movements been on Christmas Day, and had she noticed anything unusual in the days prior? That much was understandable. But the utter lack of curiosity, the apparent boredom with which Cant noted down her answers, never pressing or challenging or once asking her to elaborate, left Iris with the strong impression that he was merely going through the motions. Poor Dom deserved better.

After providing DI Cant with a detailed description of the Wetherbys' Christmas Eve party, including her own perceptions of the Rachel Truebridge 'incident', Iris had some questions of her own.

'I understand he was drugged, that you found high levels of chloroform in his blood?'

'I'm afraid I can't comment on that.' Cant blew out his cheeks pompously.

'You don't have to,' said Iris, feeling herself getting cross. 'It's all over the papers. Ever since you invited that lot to set up camp here, putting us all under siege.' She gestured in the vague direction of Mill Lane and the assembled media.

'"That lot" don't need an invitation, Ms Grey,' Cant responded, matching Iris's tetchy tone. 'As for releasing a statement to the press, it gives us a chance to manage the flow of information. If we're lucky, we may get some helpful leads.'

Iris raised a sceptical eyebrow. 'You know about the chloroform in Ariadne's sculpting shed, I assume?'

'Of course,' said Cant, somewhat defensively, as his forensics team had not even had time to arrive yet. 'Is that common knowledge?'

Iris took a sip of tea. 'Well, it's not a secret. Everybody at the Mill knows about it, and I daresay a number of Ariadne's friends and clients. I suppose Billy told you, did he?'

Cant's eyes narrowed. How on earth would Iris Grey know that?

'As a matter of fact, he did, yes. Not that we take that young man's evidence at face value, mind you.' He made no attempt to hide his dislike of Billy, which struck Iris as odd. Weren't policemen supposed to be impartial?

Leaning back in her chair, she asked boldly, 'Is Billy a suspect?'

'I can't answer that,' mumbled Cant.

'I think you just did!' Iris laughed. Because the laziness *was* laughable. Day one and already the police were zeroing in on Billy, just because he had a record and wasn't likable. Of course, Jenna had done the same. But then it wasn't Jenna's job to look at all the evidence in a balanced and thoughtful manner, or to see past Billy's vicious, prickly exterior to the wounded and much more complicated boy within. It wasn't Iris's job either, for that matter. But somebody had to do it.

'I can save you some time there, Detective Inspector,' she announced, admittedly a little smugly, refilling Cant's mug of tea. 'Billy couldn't have done it.'

She told him about Billy's story of being picked up drunk and taken to A&E on Christmas Day and how she'd verified it by calling the hospital pretending to be his parole officer. 'There's no realistic way a profoundly drunk, disoriented man could have got back to Hazelford from Winchester in an hour, and then pulled off the sort of elaborate murder you're talking about. Even if you were starting from the premise that Billy wanted to murder Dom. And truthfully, there's scant evidence for that.'

Cant sat and listened to this monologue in stunned silence. He was so angry it took him a moment to regain his composure. When he finally spoke, his voice positively quivered with indignation.

'Let me get this straight, Ms Grey. You took it upon yourself to *pose* as a parole officer illegally in order to obtain a set of medical records?'

Iris flushed. When he put it like that, it did sound bad. Less resourceful, more . . . fraudulent.

'Not his records,' she countered defensively. 'Just his admission times.'

'Why?' Cant demanded furiously.

'Why?' Iris echoed, deciding that in this instance the best form of defence was probably attack. 'To check out his alibi, obviously. Because the police weren't doing anything. You hadn't even worked out it wasn't suicide, for God's sake. No one had even bothered to investigate.'

Cant felt a small muscle in his jaw begin to twitch. The *arrogance* of the woman!

'Let me make myself very clear, Ms Grey.' His voice was ominously quiet. 'If I hear so much of a whisper about you playing Miss Marple again, if you do *anything* to compromise or jeopardise *my* murder inquiry, whether that meddling is downright illegal or not, I will have you charged with perverting the course of justice, wasting police time, interfering with a witness, unlawfully obtaining personal data and anything else I can think of. This isn't a game of bloody Cluedo!' he added, losing his cool. 'Professor Plum didn't do it in the library with a sodding candlestick.'

'I'm surprised you're old enough to have heard of Cluedo, Detective Inspector,' Iris retorted cheekily. In fairness, he had a point, but she wasn't about to be talked down to by a man she suspected was younger than some of the unidentifiable lumps of cheese in the back of her fridge.

'I'm serious, Ms Grey. Next time there'll be consequences. Do you understand?'

'Perfectly,' said Iris.

Cant stood up and walked to the door.

'But it *is* a free country, Detective Inspector,' Iris called after him, her chin jutting forward defiantly, despite her shaking hands. 'Last time I checked. I'm entitled to ask questions. To approach people. Especially if I believe the police are doing a sloppy, half-hearted job.'

No one was more surprised than Iris by this sudden burst of feistiness on her part. As a general rule, Iris hated confrontation, loathed it, and had spent most of her adult life trying to avoid it. And yet here she was, picking a fight with a man who could no doubt quite easily have her thrown in jail. She wondered where on earth this newfound confidence was coming from.

'If you really want to help find Dom Wetherby's killer, Ms Grey, and to have that person brought to justice, back off,' Cant responded sharply. 'Go back to your paintings. You're out of your depth.'

He was right. Iris was out of her depth.

But surely the only thing to do when out of one's depth was to keep swimming?

She couldn't turn back now.

'He actually called you "Miss Marple"?'

Graham Feeney had 'dropped in' at Mill Cottage for a cup of tea, which turned into drinks, which turned into supper. Now he and Iris were on the sofa, replete with a Tesco Finest mushroom risotto and a slightly ropey bottle of Argentine red, eating Lindt chocolate and dissecting the day's events.

'He did,' Iris confirmed. 'Which I thought was a bit rich coming from a James Corden lookalike with all the razor-sharp investigative acumen of a mollusc.'

Graham laughed loudly. Not many people became more articulate the drunker they got, but Iris Grey seemed to be one of them. She was a riot of contradictions: quiet but pushy, reserved but passionate, observant yet refreshingly slow to judge. (Except perhaps in DI Cant's case.) It frightened Graham how much he enjoyed being around her.

'Anyway, I'm not that old.' Iris frowned at her distorted reflection in the empty wine bottle.

'You're not old at all,' said Graham. 'More importantly, Miss Marple never had a sidekick, did she? I prefer to think of you as Holmes. Then I can be Watson.'

'I'm not sure that's much more of a compliment,' said Iris, snapping off a third piece of chocolate and dispatching it with relish. She, too, was having far more fun than she ought to be, given that poor Dom Wetherby was dead, murdered, and her own divorce proceedings were continuing apace. If ever there were a time to be at home, sobbing into her soup, this was surely it. But instead she seemed to be spending her time pissing off senior police officers, coming within a whisker of being arrested and now happily flirting with a rich, handsome, single man. Dom Wetherby would definitely have approved.

'So Cant thinks it was Billy too?' Graham clarified, relieving Iris of the chocolate.

'Yup. He's everybody's favourite suspect,' said Iris. 'Cant's clearly going to waste weeks trying to pin it on Billy.'

'But we're ruling him out?'

Iris nodded. 'I think so, yes. It's just too unlikely.'

'Good,' said Graham. 'Agreed. So what's our next line of inquiry?'

'I'm not sure.' Iris sipped her wine contemplatively. 'I'd like to know more about Rachel Truebridge. She was here the night before and might have stayed in the area. It was clear at the drinks party that she and Dom weren't the best of friends.'

'Yes, I'd like to know more about her, too. Although she wouldn't be number one on my hit list.'

'Oh?' Iris cocked her head curiously. It was so adorable it took all of Graham's willpower not to lean in and kiss her then and there.

'What about our friend from the other night?' he said. 'Harry Masters.'

'The piano teacher?' Iris looked sceptical. 'Really?'

'Why not? We know he had a long-standing grudge against Dom. Something to do with village politics.'

'The chairmanship of the parish council, yes,' said Iris. 'Dom stole it from him, apparently. But that's hardly a motive for murder.'

'I disagree,' said Graham. 'Small resentments, carefully nursed and cherished, can grow into obsessional loathing. I've seen it in court, more times than you can imagine. One minute you're bickering over a hedge and the next somebody's·plunged a pair of clippers into your sternum.'

Iris frowned again. It was hard to see sweet old Harry as the type.

'What if he's having an affair with Ariadne?' Graham went on. 'That's motive.'

Again Iris's instinct was to reject the idea. Harry was too old, too sexless. On the other hand, even before the party she'd heard the bitterness and resentment with which Harry spoke about Dom and the admiration, bordering on adoration, he seemed to feel for his enemy's wife. And Harry and Ariadne *had* looked close the other night. Yes, they'd been arguing, but from a distance at least their encounter had looked a lot more like a lovers' tiff than a dispute between two acquaintances.

'As a local with intimate knowledge of Mill House and its grounds, Harry would have had ample opportunity, both to plan and to execute.' Graham looked at Iris and, without thinking, placed a hand on her knee. 'He'd make my suspect list.'

Mine too, thought Iris. Although shamefully her mind had already begun to wander away from Harry Masters and into an intense consideration of how good (and how terrible) it would be for Graham's hand to start moving upwards.

She swallowed, and found her throat was horribly dry all of a sudden.

'OK,' she croaked. 'I'll talk to Harry tomorrow.'

There was a moment – or perhaps she'd imagined it? – when the closeness between her and Graham felt so intense it was almost palpable. When he took back his hand, Iris half expected to see its imprint permanently branded on her skin. *I've grown unused to intimacy*, she thought sadly. *I can't read the signs anymore.*

'I'd better go.' Graham stood up and Iris felt a wave of loss and regret wash over her. 'I'm leaving for Edinburgh in the morning.'

'In the morning? I thought you were staying longer?' Iris hated the disappointment in her voice.

'I was, but my trial date got moved up,' said Graham. 'Don't worry. I'll be back down here soon to check in with the family. And to hear how your sleuthing's getting on.' He smiled, and kissed her on the cheek.

'The police might have solved it by then,' said Iris, forcing herself to sound cheerful.

'Somehow I doubt it,' said Graham. 'Stay in touch, Iris.'

She closed the door behind him, leaning back on it heavily as soon as he'd gone.

'I will,' she murmured to herself. *I shouldn't. But I will.*

CHAPTER SIXTEEN

Harry Masters closed his eyes and pulled the pillow over his head to block out the noise of the church bells.

Five peals. Five o'clock in the morning.

Harry had lived at Church Cottage for more than twenty years now and had long since learned to tune out the bells during the night. But recently his sleep had been so fitful and fractured, he'd begun waking on the hour and then struggled to fall back off again. Perhaps, unconsciously, he was resisting sleep, afraid of returning to the nightmares that had haunted him ever since Christmas Day. The ghoulish image of Dom Wetherby's drowned face, his cruel, taunting eyes rolled up to just the whites. Harry himself, trapped in a glass box in which the water was rising, unable to escape, scrabbling frantically at the smooth closed lid. Ariadne beyond the glass, coolly passive, watching him drown. When he awoke from these dreams, Harry wasn't sweating, like people did in films. Instead, it was as if every ounce of moisture had been sucked out of him. His mouth and throat felt painfully dry, his skin burned, and his eyes stung, devoid of tears, yet still full of the horrors of the night.

He rolled over, daring sleep to reclaim him, but as the first thin rays of dawn started streaking the sky, he realised the attempt was futile. Night was over. He may as well get up.

After his usual breakfast of two crumpets with marmalade and a large mug of very sweet tea, followed by a couple of peaceful hours pottering about in the garden – in Harry's youth, the Hampshire soil had been frozen solid in January, but these days the winters were so mild there was no excuse not to get out and dig – he felt revived enough to wander up the hill and buy a paper. He saw at once that the *Mail* was back on the Wetherby murder story in its usual tasteless way and was running an interview with some raddled old slapper claiming to be a former mistress of Dom's. Curious, but too angry to buy it (Harry Masters wasn't about to put another penny in the pocket of these greedy, shameless journalists, trying to make entertainment out of tragedy), he opted for the *Guardian* instead, hurrying back home before the heavens opened.

Iris Grey, Ariadne's artist tenant, was coming to see him this morning at nine, to talk about starting piano lessons. Harry had explained over the phone that he was retired now and rarely, if ever, took new pupils. But she'd offered to do a free sketch for him in return – a portrait, if he wanted it, or a picture of his beloved garden – and Jim Agnew, Harry's friend from the bowling club, had convinced him to accept.

'She's had exhibitions in famous London galleries, you know, Harry. And this portrait she's doing of Dom is bound to be big news, especially since the murder. She's up and coming, Iris Grey. This sketch might be worth a fortune in five years' time.'

Harry Masters wasn't really interested in fortunes. But he had other reasons for making an exception in Iris's case. Living at Mill

Cottage, she must see Ariadne every day. He could resist indulging in the latest gossip from the *Daily Mail*, but Harry needed to know what was really going on up at Mill House.

Luckily, almost as soon as she arrived, Iris seemed happy to talk about it. In fact, she barely mentioned the piano at all.

'It's nice to get out of the house for a bit,' she told Harry, removing a thick, fluffy duffel-coat-cum-cardigan that swamped her tiny figure and hanging it on the back of Harry's front door. Underneath it, she wore black trousers tucked into boots and a black sweater that made her look like a diminutive cat burglar. 'The telly crews all left yesterday morning and we thought – hoped – they'd gone for good. But they're all back today, worse luck. Like some awful rash you can never quite get rid of.'

Harry shook his head angrily. 'It's because of the *Daily Mail* interview.' He told Iris about this morning's piece by 'one of Dom Wetherby's tarts. This one was from decades ago.' He made it sound as if there were hundreds of other women rattling around in Dom's past. Perhaps there were, but Iris found it odd that someone like Harry Masters would be privy to that sort of information.

'As if her opinion's remotely relevant to the case, or to anything,' Harry added bitterly. 'I think it's shameful the way these people harass poor Ariadne in her own home. The police should do something about it. They should move them on.'

'I agree,' said Iris, who'd been wondering how, exactly, she was going to steer the conversation with Harry around to the Wetherbys when he helpfully did it for her. 'Although I'm afraid I've rather lost my faith in the police since all this happened. They've been useless.'

'Really?' Harry threw another log into the woodburner, which was already crackling away merrily. His cottage struck Iris as cosy and charming up to a point, although it could have used a woman's touch. Weeks' worth of newspapers remained in piles on the table and windowsills, still not jettisoned, and the fake plastic flowers gathering dust in a vase on the bookcase spoke of a life with more than its fair share of loneliness. Church Cottage was also very much a modest home, containing nothing of any real value as far as Iris could see. Being here, in Harry Masters' private space, she could imagine how profoundly his feelings must have been hurt when a rich, famous, glamorous man like Dom Wetherby swept into town and 'robbed' him of his parish council position. Dom, who had everything, had casually stolen something precious from Harry, who had nothing. *I'd hate him too*, Iris thought.

'In what way?' Harry asked, still talking about the Hampshire Constabulary and its failings.

'Well, apart from the press siege at the Mill, which is miserable to live with, as far as I can tell they're not doing much actually to solve Dom's murder,' said Iris.

'I'm surprised,' said Harry cynically. 'It seems to me people are as obsessed with Dominic Wetherby in death as they were in life. Haven't the police devoted many resources to the investigation?'

'Oh, there are tech teams there and forensics and God knows what.' Iris told Harry briefly about the focus on Ariadne's sculpting shed as the likely source of the chloroform used to drug Dom. She scanned his face for a reaction, but there was none. 'They put on a good show for the media,' Iris went on. 'But Cant, the fellow in charge, seems convinced that Billy Wetherby did it. He's determined to cobble together enough evidence to charge him.'

This time, the change in Masters was clear. His face went from ruddy to ashen, and Iris was fairly sure that she saw his hands start to shake, although it became harder to tell once he started wringing them together.

'Poor Ariadne! Poor, poor Ariadne,' he muttered, pacing the room and shaking his head with evident distress. 'She lives for those boys. Loves them unconditionally. Even Billy, who treats her terribly badly. If any of her sons were to be charged with Dom's murder, I don't think she'd survive it. Truly I don't.'

'Do you think one of the boys might have done it, though?' Iris asked, casting a line out across the water.

'No idea,' Harry said brusquely. 'I know I wouldn't blame them if they had. But I'm surprised they'd be considered prime suspects. Dom Wetherby had more enemies than you and me and the rest of Hazelford put together. For all I know, it was the developers whose plans for the meadows he thwarted who finally did for him. Nasty bunch they were.'

'Did you know them?'

'Only by name,' said Harry. 'Gardievski, the fella's name was. Igor Gardievski. He was far too grand to hobnob with the likes of me, but I think Dom Wetherby knew him socially. They used to play poker together, apparently. Gardievski blew a gasket when Wetherby stopped him building his housing estate across the river from the Mill. He thought he was owed a favour and Dom stabbed him in the back. But frankly, Miss Grey, I don't care who killed him. I just hate to see dear Ariadne going through it.'

'Are the two of you very close?' Iris asked as casually as she could, happy for the subject to be looping back to Ariadne.

To her surprise, Harry looked her in the eye and said with blunt honesty, 'I love her. I've always loved her, Miss Grey. Just as I've always loathed her bullying bastard of a husband. Sadly for me, the feeling isn't mutual.'

Iris was silent, leaning forwards and adopting what she hoped was her best sympathetic-listener pose while she waited for him to go on. It wasn't a long wait. Clearly Harry Masters lived to talk about Ariadne Wetherby. The woman had him wrapped round her little finger.

'I would say we've become close friends,' Harry continued. 'Even before all this mess. Ariadne leans on me, Miss Grey. Perhaps she's mentioned me to you?'

The hope in his voice was pathetic.

'I've never really had an intimate conversation with Ariadne.' Iris chose her words carefully, hoping to draw Harry out. 'I would say we're friendly, rather than friends. I spent more time with Dom. Because of the portrait,' she clarified.

It was almost comical how quickly Harry's face clouded over when Dom Wetherby's name was mentioned. As if he retained the power to wound him, even in death.

'Well.' Collecting himself, Harry forced a smile. 'Perhaps now you and Ariadne will have more of a chance to get to know one another. You're both artists, after all.'

'That's true,' said Iris.

'And I think she could use a friend,' Harry added. 'Especially a female friend. Not many people know this, Miss Grey, but Ariadne Wetherby's had a terribly difficult life. As a child, or a teenager, her father—' Harry stopped and looked away, realising he'd gone too far. 'Well. We won't go into all that.'

'I met her father. Clive,' said Iris, willing him not to stop at such a crucial moment. 'He stayed with them for Christmas. He seemed rather a sweet and harmless old boy to me.'

'Hmm. Appearances can be deceptive,' Harry muttered gruffly.

'Do you know Clive?' Iris asked, intrigued.

'Not really. Look, I've said too much already,' Harry murmured, somewhat anxiously. 'It's not my place. Ariadne told me certain things in confidence. But if the two of you were to become friends, perhaps . . . I don't know. It might help her to have a woman to talk to. That's all.'

'I'd be happy to try,' said Iris.

They agreed a date for Iris to return for a first piano lesson, and Harry led her out into the garden. He'd decided he preferred a picture of Church Cottage from the rear over a sketched portrait, rather to Iris's relief, as she still felt she hadn't got a clear read on Harry Masters' character. She realised, belatedly, that she hadn't managed to worm an alibi out of him either for Christmas Day afternoon, but there was no way to wrench the conversation back to Dom's murder now without it looking awkward and crass.

Next time.

For now, Harry's insinuations about Ariadne's childhood and past were more than enough food for thought. *'As a child, or a teenager, her father—'* How had Harry planned to finish that sentence? What, exactly, was he accusing Ariadne's father of having done? Was it really possible that frail, doddery old Clive had abused her in some way? Sexually, or physically? Or what else might Harry have meant? He'd also implied that Dom Wetherby might have hurt his wife, but Iris thought that sounded very much like wishful thinking on the piano teacher's part. He was angry with Dom for other reasons, and besotted with his wife, so he was hardly an impartial observer.

Even so, you never know, thought Iris. It was astonishing the things that went on behind the closed doors of other people's marriages. Her own marriage to Ian was a case in point.

She took her leave, shaking Harry's limp, smooth hand, and headed straight to Hazelford Stores for her own copy of the *Daily Fail*, as Ian always used to call it. With a jolt Iris realised that it no longer automatically caused her pain to think about Ian. Was that progress? Or denial? In either case, the interview with Dom's former mistress would be a welcome distraction. Yes, it was prurient. But Iris was barely painting these days. Solving the mystery of Dom Wetherby's murder had become the focus of her life during this turbulent time, her reason to get up in the morning. And she wasn't likely to earn her Miss Marple stripes by taking Harry Masters' high road and refusing to read the *Mail* piece. Whoever killed Dom Wetherby must have either hated him or had something to gain by his death, or both. Hatred that deep didn't pop up overnight. Whatever the truth turned out to be, it had its roots somewhere in the Grimshaw author's past. Iris must wade through the lies and the dross until she uncovered it

'You'll be wanting the *Mail*, then?' Jean Chivers asked Iris, retrieving a copy from the giant pile stacked beside the stockroom and handing it over before Iris had a chance to answer. 'Terrible, isn't it?' Jean leaned forward conspiratorially, revealing a light bristle of chin hairs poking out from beneath her heavy make-up. 'Poor Mrs Wetherby, still grieving, and all his fancy pieces crawling out of the woodwork. Of course, I don't think anyone's that surprised. He was a charmer, wasn't he, always with a twinkle in his eye? And you know they're saying it's the son as did it? Billy. The stalker. Drugged and drowned his own father – can you imagine?'

Iris replied firmly that she couldn't. She wouldn't have thought it possible a few weeks ago, but she was starting to feel genuinely sorry for Billy.

Alan Chivers emerged from the stockroom, eager as ever to join in the gossip.

'They've got police techs crawling all over the property now, looking for fingerprints and whatnot, something to link Billy with what happened,' he announced confidently. 'Apparently Ariadne Wetherby keeps chloroform up at the house. I mean, that's a bit weird, isn't it?' Alan looked at Iris, whom he now considered a friend of sorts. 'Who has chloroform in their house?'

Iris could have answered this, but instead mumbled something noncommittal and left. She liked Alan and Jean, and didn't want to get into an argument with either of them. Besides, she'd been in Hazelford long enough to know that the rumour mill would keep on turning whether she corrected the shopkeeper's facts or not. She wanted to get home to read the article by Dom's former flame in peace.

Back at the cottage, she read the *Mail*'s two-page spread quickly at first, then again in more detail. The woman being interviewed, Caroline Clarkson, was in her late forties now and looked nothing like your typical kiss-and-tell bimbo. With her sleek blonde bob, understated make-up and professional skirt suit, Ms Clarkson actually looked a lot like a corporate, uptight version of Ariadne. Dom clearly had a type.

She was also articulate and thoughtful in the answers she gave the reporter, stressing Dom's charisma but how he also had a dark, depressive side. How, despite their affair, he remained devoted to his family and could never break free from the guilt he felt towards his wife. Ms Clarkson also expressed guilt and regret over their affair – although Iris couldn't help but feel that a paid interview in a tabloid newspaper might not be the most obvious way for a mistress to make amends to a wife.

'I wasn't shocked when I read that Dom had taken his own life,' she said. 'Saddened, obviously, but not shocked. But the idea that someone could have murdered him, and in what seems to have been such a terrible, calculating way? That, I can't imagine. Dom had many faults, but he was a hugely likable man, with a big talent and a big heart. I will miss him for ever.'

Iris closed the paper and closed her eyes, letting the events of the morning wash over her, like waves lapping her consciousness, until the sediment settled and the water became clear.

What had she learned from Harry Masters today?

That Dom had made an enemy of a powerful property developer. That could be important. Ought to be important. And yet somehow it didn't feel as if it were, not really.

So what was important?

As she sat and contemplated, one word floated to the surface. *Ariadne.*

There was more, much more, to Mrs Dom Wetherby than met the eye. If Harry Masters was right and her father had abused her, then she'd spent a lifetime concealing dark secrets. Her father's. Her husband's. Her son's. And perhaps her own? She had such a gentle way about her, such a kind, soft, feminine, artistic manner. But was there someone else underneath? Another, very different Ariadne – the one that Billy was constantly alluding to, the dark side, *the witch*, that no one, including Iris, had been willing to believe in?

What if Billy had been right all along?

Dom Wetherby had had a dark side, after all, beneath the warmth and light and bonhomie. Iris had seen it when she painted him, and his mistress had seen it when they made love. Was it that much of a stretch to imagine that Dom's wife might be the same? What if all Ariadne's softness and forgiveness and calm were a mask, hiding a very different side to her nature? A side formed, perhaps, by childhood abuse?

Or was the abuse story a red herring, a tall tale Ariadne had spun to Harry Masters to justify . . . what? Her anger towards her husband? Towards men in general? Iris believed Harry Masters when he claimed the two of them were just friends, that there was never any attraction on Ariadne's side. But she also believed him when he said he loved her. The thought crystallised shockingly then in Iris's mind: *Harry Masters would kill for Ariadne Wetherby. He'd do anything she asked of him.*

Iris opened her eyes and checked herself. She had no evidence – none – to think that Ariadne Wetherby was involved in Dom's death. And yet the very fact that Ariadne cultivated friends like Harry – loyal, devoted, fanatical and not remotely her equal – implied that there was, at a minimum, a missing piece in her marriage.

That missing piece was the next piece in the puzzle.

The next clue for Iris to follow.

I need to get close to Ariadne.

Graham Feeney was in his favourite greasy-spoon café in an alley behind the Edinburgh High Court when he got the call.

'Can you talk?' Marcus's voice was brittle with tension, so much so that Graham felt his own stomach lurching.

'Of course. What's wrong?'

'I need your help. I think Billy needs a lawyer and I . . . It can't be me.'

'OK. Calm down,' said Graham. 'Take a breath and tell me what's happened.'

For the next eight minutes straight Marcus kept talking, the words tumbling out one after another as he unleashed his list of grievances against both the press and the police.

'They sent a bloody inept female liaison officer to the house to interview Lorcan. *Lorcan!* No one cleared it with Mum first or even asked her; they just showed up this morning and started grilling him about the stupid Houdini game we used to play with Dad.'

'Houdini game?'

Marcus explained. Graham frowned. What a breathtakingly irresponsible game to play with young children, and how typical of Dom to come up with something like that. For all his many strengths, there had always been an element of the overgrown child about Dom, an impish, Peter Pan side to him that Graham had never liked. He kept his thoughts to himself this morning, however, and let Marcus go on.

'Billy told the police about the game last week and how Lorcan and the rest of us used to play it. I mean, can you credit it? As if our stupid childhood pranks had anything to do with Dad's death.'

Graham noticed that Marcus still couldn't bring himself to use the word 'murder'.

'Why did Billy mention it?' asked Graham.

'Good question,' Marcus said bitterly. 'I think it was his idea of a joke – let's throw the moronic police an obviously false lead – but it's not bloody funny. Poor Lorc was already cut up enough about Dad and finding the body. Now he's going to worry that it might have been his fault. Lorcan can't separate the past from the present the way the rest of us can. He remembers playing that game with Dad and he remembers Dad being dead. Once he hears adults connecting those dots, he does the same. He's so traumatised, Graham.'

'I'm sorry to hear that,' Graham said seriously. Billy clearly had a lot to answer for.

'Luckily, a local couple were out flying their model aeroplane on Christmas afternoon and saw Lorc playing with his torch and his boat, for almost two hours, so he has an "alibi".' He injected the word with as much disdain as possible. 'As if Lorcan would hurt a fly. Meanwhile Mum's in pieces, Lorc's still a wreck from the whole interview thing, and the cretin in charge, Cant, is leaking stuff to the press like a sodding sieve. Not to mention the fact that he's clearly after Billy. They brought him in under caution the other day because his prints and Dad's were all over Mum's sculpting shed. I mean, all our prints must be in there, for God's sake. And in the meantime, the bastard who actually did this to Dad is still out there, probably laughing his head off.' His voice broke. Graham could hear that he was fighting back tears.

'Anyway, the long and the short of it is, we need you. Is there any way you can come back down?'

Graham took a moment to process everything Marcus had just told him. Eventually he said, 'All right. Look, I can't come down before the funeral. I have a trial finishing up here and I can't just cut and run.'

'No.' Marcus sounded deflated. 'Of course not.'

'But that's only a week away,' Graham reminded him. 'It's really not long. And after that I'd be happy to represent Billy, if that's what he wants. Although bear in mind he hasn't been charged yet, Marcus. Things may not be as dire as you think. Having said that, it would be helpful if someone could get him to stop playing silly buggers with the police between now and your father's funeral. From what you describe, he's not helping himself.'

'Since when does my brother ever help himself?' Marcus sighed heavily. 'Mum's absolutely panicked that he's going to do something stupid at the wake in front of all the press. Our family does seem to have an uncanny knack for turning a tragedy into a farce.'

'It'll be all right,' said Graham. 'Once the funeral's over, things will calm down. The police will realise soon enough that Billy's innocent and with a bit of luck they'll find whoever did it. Have faith.'

Marcus gave an empty laugh.

'Thanks, Graham. I'm sorry to dump on you. It's just Jenna and I are . . . Well, things are not great. I feel as if it's all on me to sort everything out, but I have to work and—'

'It's OK,' Graham interrupted. 'I'm happy to help. In fact, I'm looking forward to it.'

He hung up and an image of Iris Grey's delicate, doll-like face floated into his mind

Iris had been in touch twice in the last couple of days, filling him in on her meeting with Harry Masters and what the piano teacher had told her about Ariadne, all very interesting developments. Graham found he loved to listen to her voice, to hear her quick mind working and her artist's eye seeing beneath people's façades.

Has she seen through mine? Graham wondered nervously. At some point, she was bound to realise that he was nowhere close to good enough for her. *Not yet, though. Not yet. There's still time.*

In one week he would see her again.

Was it wrong to be looking forward to Dom's funeral?

Probably. Gulping down the last of his tea, Graham left the café, happier than he had any right to be.

CHAPTER SEVENTEEN

St Anne's Church in Hazelford was one of the most exquisite baroque churches in the whole of the south of England. Although not a grand edifice like Winchester Cathedral, St Anne's nevertheless boasted some of the most intricately carved stonework and elaborate tombs and side chapels of any village church in the country. Built on the banks of the Itchen, surrounded by model-village-perfect almshouse cottages and set against a backdrop of idyllic rolling Hampshire countryside, even in the depths of winter Hazelford's church rose up from the frozen earth like a beacon of beauty and peace.

It's a nice place to be buried, thought Jenna, following a stony-faced Marcus through the enormous throng of media lining Mill Lane as they made their way inside. Her father-in-law's funeral was always going to be a big event. The Grimshaw books and TV adaptations had made Dom a household name and something akin to a national treasure. But the fact that Dom had been murdered, and that the case remained unsolved, had turned today's service from a sideshow into a full-blown circus. Someone had drugged Dom Wetherby and drowned him in the grounds of his idyllic estate. It was a case worthy of the great detective Gerry Grimshaw, whose final television outing – *Grimshaw's Goodbye* – had been postponed from New Year's Day following Dom's death, and was now being shown this Sunday night. Naturally, it was predicted to pull in record audiences, with Carl Rendcombe, the actor who played the great detective, being hounded day and night by the media to spill the beans about the plot.

Inside, the church was packed like a rush-hour Tube train. Mourners from all the different pieces of Dom's life – family friends, school friends, university friends, literary friends, TV friends, local friends – jostled for space among the polished elm pews. Jenna recognised many of them from the Christmas Eve drinks party, including Rendcombe. Next to him stood Dom's agent, the portly Chris Wheeler, looking sombre in his heavy three-piece suit. John Pilcher, the TV producer who'd taken over the Grimshaw franchise from Rachel Truebridge, had opted for a considerably more casual ensemble of drainpipe jeans and a thick black sweater. Rachel was there too, somewhat to Jenna's surprise given how little love had been lost between them on Christmas Eve. In a dull sludge-coloured dress and wearing next to no make-up, she looked far from her usual glamorous best. Unlike Iris Grey, who somehow seemed to be glowing in a burgundy skirt and jacket teamed with flat riding boots, squeezed into the third row next to a dapper Graham Feeney. *I must catch up with her properly later*, thought Jenna, as the organist struck up a lugubrious rendition of 'Jerusalem', Dom's favourite hymn. She and Iris had spoken briefly outside, before the service, but Jenna was too scared of Marcus overhearing them to ask anything meaningful about Dom's murder, such as how the useless police were getting on or what, if anything, Iris had discovered since they last spoke.

It was awful, the distance that had grown between Jenna and Marcus since they left the Mill. Not that things had been peachy before. But it was ironic how Jenna's instincts being proved right, and Dom's death now being treated as murder, had made everything a thousand times worse. Ever since then Marcus had been behaving in an inexplicably childish and hurtful way, ignoring poor Jenna completely, shrugging off her every attempt to talk or bridge the gulf between them, almost as if he blamed her for Dom's murder. As if Jenna *suspecting* his father had been killed had somehow magically made that happen. As if she'd betrayed him.

Looking up at him now, his back ramrod straight, staring straight ahead as he belted out 'Jerusalem', Jenna thought bitterly that it was he, Marcus, who was the betrayer. Even now, after everything that had happened, he couldn't stop himself putting on an act. *The Wetherby family is fine. United. There's nothing to see here, folks. The show must go on.* He'd shown an astonishing, and to Jenna's mind borderline psychotic, lack of interest in who may have killed his father or why, instead focusing wholly on 'protecting' the family and 'moving on'. Whatever that meant.

Across the aisle, Jenna noticed, Ariadne was doing the exact same thing, singing, rigid and dry-eyed, immaculately turned out in a black Dior wool dress and lace mantilla veil. Image, apparently, was everything. Only Billy spoiled the illusion, off message as usual in a crumpled shirt and jeans, resolutely closed-lipped, his expression making it plain that he would rather have been anywhere than here.

Because you killed him, Jenna thought, furiously. *You killed him and you got away with it, and now all you want to do is run off and spend his money.*

As the hymn finished and the congregation took their seats, Jenna witnessed a flash of what could only be described as white-hot rage pass across Marcus's features. For once, however, it wasn't directed at her. Leaning forwards, Jenna's stomach lurched when she saw who the recipient was: Rachel Truebridge, who met Marcus's death stare with a defiant scowl of her own.

What the hell's going on between those two? They barely know each other.

Jenna gripped the pew for support as it all came flooding back to her. The unexplained scratch on Marcus's face before Christmas, conveniently 'dropped' as a subject in the wake of Dom's murder. His horrified reaction when Rachel turned up drunk at the Christmas Eve drinks, and again today.

Were they having an affair? Was that the real reason for Marcus's distance, for this sudden, terrible change in him? Suddenly Jenna found it hard to breathe.

'Jenna doesn't look well,' Graham Feeney leaned over and whispered in Iris's ear.

Iris glanced across the aisle. 'God, no. She doesn't,' she whispered back. Catching Jenna's eye, she smiled encouragingly, receiving a weak nod in return. She'd promised to chat to Jenna later, privately, about the latest developments, but perhaps their first conversation should be about the obviously dire state of affairs between her and Marcus.

No one understood better than Iris the strain that a disintegrating marriage could put on the body, not to mention the soul. She had received a bitter letter from Ian in the post this morning, ironically enough, in response to receiving the divorce papers from her. Only a few short weeks ago that would have been enough to plunge Iris into a barely functioning state of despair. Yet now, thanks in part to the distraction provided by trying to solve Dom's murder – and perhaps thanks also to Graham Feeney – she felt bizarrely yet blissfully isolated from the pain. Almost as if Ian, her husband and partner for so many years, had become a fictional character, a figment of Iris's imagination. Whereas Graham, with whom she had still not slept or even kissed properly again since that first time, had become hyper-real, a constant, vivid, worryingly important presence in this new life Iris seemed to be embarking on.

A few days ago, when Graham was still up in Scotland, Iris had once again had the strong sensation that she was being followed. Twice it had happened in the village, when she was out shopping or running errands. Nothing tangible, just shadows and noises. And once at home, when Iris could have sworn she heard a door open and close downstairs while she was in the shower. She had no hard evidence for any of these incidents, other than a disturbing and increasingly pronounced sixth sense. Not like December, when someone had broken into Mill Cottage and left her that creepy 'gift', but still, it had bothered her enough to call Graham.

'You think I'm being silly, don't you?' said Iris, embarrassed by the silence on the other end of the line.

But Graham had insisted otherwise. 'You should be careful. If you're going to go out hunting a killer, then you're putting yourself at risk. Even innocent people don't appreciate having their skeletons rattled.'

Thinking of secrets, Iris had spent the last ten minutes watching Ariadne's elderly father, Clive, at the end of the family pew. If anything, he looked even frailer than Iris remembered him, a tiny, stooped, shrunken person whose every breath seemed to shake him from within like a mini earthquake. Was there any truth to what Harry Masters had implied about Clive mistreating Ariadne as a child? Again it was hard to picture, although Iris could think of no reason for Harry to lie. Watching Clive throw occasional sidelong glances at Ariadne, and Ariadne do the same to Billy, who looked skittish and possibly even high beside the rigid-backed Marcus, it struck Iris what a strange triangle they made. The perfect mother, the age-ravaged father and the fallen son. *Something's binding them*, she thought. *Some tie, some current flows through the three of them that the rest of the family can't see.*

The vicar had started his eulogy. Iris was too busy people-watching to listen properly, but the regular ripples of laughter suggested the speech must be good. About six rows behind her, Iris saw Harry Masters, also watching, his eyes mostly glued to Ariadne but occasionally turning round to check out DI Cant, who stood at the back looking awkward and vaguely sinister, despite his chubby cheeks and freckles.

A few rows in front of Cant, sitting next to the London lawyer who was handling Dom's will, a slim, bald man in a cheap-looking suit suddenly began waving at Iris, discreetly at first, but becoming more and more animated as she failed to respond in kind. 'Do you know who that is?' She nudged Graham, who turned to look. 'I think he must have mistaken me for someone else. I've never seen him before in my life.'

'Good God.' The colour drained from Graham's face.

'You know him?' said Iris.

'Yes, I . . . yes,' Graham stammered, waving back briefly before turning to face the front. His throat felt tight and constricted all of a sudden, as if he'd swallowed a bee. He was having a tough time focusing and stared at the embroidered cross draped over Dom's coffin in a conscious attempt to steady himself.

'He . . . His name's Jago. He was . . . He knew my brother,' he explained disjointedly to Iris.

Calm down, Graham told himself. *Get a grip.* He didn't want Iris to see him upset like this. Didn't want anyone to see how much seeing Jago Dalziel had affected him, but especially not Iris.

He should have thought of this. Realised that some of Dom's old Oxford friends were bound to attend the funeral. But stupidly, it had never occurred to him. He'd been too excited about seeing Iris, and being back at the Mill, and too consumed with the prospect of representing Billy against the Hampshire Police.

But now here they were, here Jago was anyway, no doubt wanting to reminisce about Marcus and Dom, and what terrific friends they'd been, and how devastating to think that they were both now gone.

Graham felt panic rise up within him like a storm surge. He could not have that conversation. He physically *could not* have it.

'Are you OK?' Iris touched his hand lightly and he jumped as if he'd been stung.

'I'm fine.' He smiled, convincingly he hoped. 'Surprised to see him, that's all. It's been a very long time.'

Iris squeezed his hand. Graham returned the pressure gratefully. She really was the most wonderful woman. *Just don't mess it up.*

DI Roger Cant stood on the edge of the crowd gathered round the graveside for Dom's internment. There were enough people present for the vicar's voice to be a distant hum, the familiar words merging one into another like a windswept mantra: 'Let us commend Dominic's body to the mercy of God . . .'

Whoever had 'commended' Dom Wetherby's body to the Itchen had done so without mercy and while Dom was still alive. The water flooding his lungs left no doubt that the cause of death was drowning. Unfortunately, seven weeks after Wetherby's murder, this one bald fact was just about the only certainty DI Cant had. The loathsome Dr Drew was 'quite sure' the victim had been heavily drugged, based on the toxicology report, and 'ninety-nine per cent sure' that the toxin of choice was chloroform. Apparently the body broke chloroform down so quickly into its component chemicals that there could never be an absolute guarantee. Worse, fatal or near-fatal doses of chloroform could be administered in a variety of ways, including ingestion via food or drink, injection into the bloodstream, inhalation through a mask such as the one Ariadne Wetherby used on her animal subjects or even in some cases through the skin. Cant had had high hopes that a thorough examination of Ariadne's sculpting shed would turn up a wealth of evidence. His working theory was that Billy had lured his dad there, somehow managed to drug him with his mother's supply of chloroform and then carried him, unconscious, to the riverbank under cover of darkness.

As it turned out, however, there was no sign of any struggle having taken place in the shed, nor was there any compelling evidence that large amounts of chloroform had in fact been taken from Mrs Wetherby's supply. All Cant had to show for his efforts was a bunch of family fingerprints, but as all the Wetherbys had been in and out of the shed multiple times over the years, that was hardly remarkable.

Cant's attempts to 'squeeze' Billy into a confession based on such flimsy evidence had ended predictably in failure, and he still had no witnesses placing Billy in or near Hazelford for those crucial hours, never mind in the shed or along the riverbank. Yet Cant remained stubbornly sure that Billy Wetherby was the killer. Just watching him twitch and smirk through the service, at one point actually winking at the detective on his way out, strengthened his conviction still further. Someone here today must have seen something, or heard something, or must know something that could firmly tie Billy to the murder. Out of all these hundreds of mourners, surely someone had cared enough about Dom Wetherby to want to tell the truth? So Cant had come to the funeral and watched and waited.

The service seemed to go on for ever, and by the end St Anne's had felt like a furnace, a combination of a slightly dodgy old heating system and hundreds of human bodies pressed together in a confined space. It had been a relief to step outside into the cool, crisp air of the churchyard, and enlightening to watch people's reactions as Dom's coffin was lowered into the ground. Most people stood and watched silently, even the flashy TV types who'd turned up in jeans and been so chatty during the funeral service, as if this were a wedding or a cocktail party. Iris Grey was there, the meddlesome portrait painter from Mill Cottage who'd taken it upon herself to ride roughshod over Cant's case, impersonating parole officers and God knows what else. She too looked sombre, although Cant was more interested by the fact that she'd clearly become very buddy-buddy with Graham Feeney, the Wetherbys' ubiquitous lawyer friend. That, in Cant's view, was a dangerous combination. Barristers always thought themselves above the police. The last thing Ms Grey needed was any more encouragement in that department.

Most interesting to Cant, however, was the family itself. Billy stood aside from his mother and brothers, having attached himself like a louche limpet to the lawyer in charge of Dom's estate. Meanwhile Marcus Wetherby looked grim and frozen beside his mother, as stiff and rigid in his formal suit as any corpse. Ariadne let out a single, stifled sob as the coffin sank from view, her only display of emotion so far. But standing on her other side, it was poor Lorcan Wetherby who lost it completely.

'No!' he screamed, as handfuls of earth were thrown and the vicar started reciting the 'ashes to ashes, dust to dust' part. 'Daddy! No!' He lunged forwards, and it was only thanks to lightning-quick reactions on Marcus's part that he didn't fall head first on top of the coffin. Grabbing him by the shirt, Marcus pulled his brother back and tried to restrain him, but Lorcan struggled frantically. 'Ghost!' he screamed hysterically, his voice becoming louder and louder. 'White ghost did it! I saw him. I *saw*! No one believes me.'

It was awful to watch, tragic and embarrassing at the same time. Nobody knew where to look. In the end, Cant noticed, it was Jenna Wetherby who succeeded in calming Lorcan down, eventually managing to prise him away from Marcus and lead him gently back to the house, still crying and shaking and rambling about ghosts.

Iris felt as dismayed as everyone else – poor, poor Lorcan – although clearly Graham felt worse, squeezing her hand so tightly during the whole episode Iris worried her fingers might crack. He'd obviously been shaken by his brother's old friend from Oxford showing up today. Perhaps Dom's funeral was stirring painful memories from that time. Or perhaps he'd been closer to Dom than Iris realised.

Iris squeezed back, trying not to think about how fond she was becoming of this sweet but complicated man.

*

Iris was one of the last to arrive at Mill House for the wake, having nipped home first to change into more comfortable shoes and to pick up the videos and photographs of Dom that Ariadne had lent her. Dom's portrait was almost finished now, and Iris wanted to return the prints before she accidentally spilled coffee on them, or singed them with a candle, or otherwise lost or ruined such precious mementos. Perhaps today wasn't the right time to bother Ariadne, but she could always nip into Dom's study and leave them on the desk.

An added advantage of the trip home was that it allowed her to retouch her make-up, spray on some scent and generally freshen up – not that she was trying to impress anyone in particular. Not at all.

Definitely not.

As usual, Ariadne had laid on an impressive spread. The house looked as immaculate as ever, albeit quieter and less dazzling without Dom's presence. Fresh vases of white lilies graced every table and mantelpiece, fires crackled away invitingly in all the downstairs rooms, and a simple but delicious feast of poached salmon, wild rice, salad and some sort of Moroccan chicken stew awaited the cold and hungry mourners on three vast trestle tables arranged along the hallway. A fourth table provided a full bar, already swamped by the time Iris arrived. The whole thing had been professionally staffed by a team of local caterers. *I suppose this is how the rich do funerals*, thought Iris. *Effortlessly*. Money might not be the answer to everything, but it was the answer to a lot.

Glancing around in vain for Graham, Iris helped herself to a small plate of salmon and a glass of red, and headed towards Dom's study. Pushing open the door, she set the padded envelope of photographs and home movies down on the desk and took a moment to look around her at the familiar oak-panelled walls. It was odd to think that only three months ago, she'd entered this room for the first time for her initial sitting with Dom. How utterly and profoundly everything had changed since then! Iris had always loved the room, loved its warmth and richness and history, all of which on some level reflected the nature of its occupant. *Former occupant.* Dom's presence was still heavy here, tangible in the soft indent his body had made in the desk chair, and the lingering smell of cigar smoke and cologne that clung to the heavy velvet curtains. The shelves were full of his books, including *Grimshaw's Discovery*, *Grimshaw Moves On*, *Grimshaw's Nemesis* and his last novel, *Grimshaw's Goodbye*. Pulling one of the books out – it turned out to be Dom's debut, *Inspector Grimshaw* – Iris flipped open the cover curiously. The dedication read: 'For Marcus, who's always been behind me. With thanks.'

He must have been referring to Graham's brother, Marcus. Iris was deeply curious about the legendary Marcus Feeney, adored brother, loyal friend, Oxford superstar by all accounts. And yet this beloved, blessed individual had taken his own life, and at such a hideously young age. All of that potential wasted. Lost for ever.

Iris was still pondering this when something outside the window caught her eye. Two figures, both in black, stood very close together beneath the yew tree at the bottom of the kitchen garden. Iris recognised Ariadne at once, but it took her a moment to ascertain that the second figure, once again, was Harry Masters. *That's the second time in two weeks I've seen the two of them together.* This time, however, they weren't arguing. Instead, Ariadne was leaning into Harry, pressed against his shoulder. And he was bending down, apparently stooping to hear something she was saying. From this distance, it was hard to see accurately, but it looked very much to Iris as if Ariadne were whispering in Harry's ear.

And then his arm shot around her, and he was comforting her, holding her, saying something back.

'There you are! I've been hunting for you everywhere.'

Jenna, looking less deathly pale than she had in the church, suddenly burst in. Perhaps she'd been fortified by the large glass of white wine she was holding.

'If you're searching for clues in here, I'd be careful if I were you,' she told Iris, lowering herself into Dom's favourite armchair, and apparently not registering Iris's shock. 'That knob-end Cant's only a few feet down the hall. He's already complained to Marcus about "busybodies" hampering his investigation. I assume that means you, as I've been well and truly put back in my box.'

She said it with a smile, but Iris could tell that Jenna's jokiness hid a real pain.

'I'm not searching for anything,' said Iris, perching on the desk opposite her. 'I was just returning some mementos Ariadne gave me. I didn't want to bother her.'

'Oh no,' Jenna said bitterly. 'Heaven forbid my mother-in-law should be bothered. By anything. Ever.'

And with this caustic remark, the dam burst. It all came out then: how dreadful the last couple of weeks had been with Marcus. How Jenna knew he was lying to her, knew he was keeping secrets, yet he persisted in treating *her* like the enemy. Finally she told Iris about her suspicions regarding Rachel Truebridge – their furtive, hostile glances in church earlier, Marcus's overblown reaction when Rachel turned up drunk to the Christmas Eve party, his late-night disappearance before Christmas and the still-unexplained scratch on his face.

'I think he's having an affair. On Christmas Eve I assumed he was worried about Rachel upsetting his mother. I just assumed it was Dom having the affair, and Marcus didn't want Ariadne to find out or be embarrassed or whatever. I mean, Rachel was Dom's producer, and Dom's type, and that was the sort of thing Dom *did*. And Marcus barely knew her, right?'

'Right,' said Iris.

'No! Wrong!' Jenna was getting agitated again. 'He knew her. He *knows* her. I don't know how, but I am telling you, what I saw in that church – my husband knows that woman, intimately. He's having an affair, Iris. I know it!'

'You don't know it,' said Iris. 'You suspect it. And maybe you're right, I don't know, but there's a big difference. You suspected Billy, remember? We both did. But we were wrong.'

Jenna frowned. This was news to her. 'Were we? Why? What's happened since I left?'

Iris gave her a potted history of the last two weeks, culminating in the fact that, unlike Billy, Harry Masters had no alibi for the afternoon in question and more than enough motive.

'Harry wouldn't have been strong enough to overpower Dom alone,' Iris admitted. 'But if Dom were drugged, and if he had help?'

Jenna looked sceptical.

'I'm not saying it's likely. Just possible,' said Iris. 'Harry's also very close to Ariadne, closer than people think.' She told Jenna about seeing the two of them together, and about Harry's insinuations that Ariadne might have experienced some childhood abuse at the hands of her father.

Jenna's eyes widened. 'From Clive?! Are you sure? That sounds highly unlikely to me.'

'I'm not saying it's true,' said Iris. 'Only that Harry Masters thinks it is. And only one person could have put that idea into his head.'

Jenna digested this.

'I think Ariadne has Harry wrapped round her little finger,' Iris went on. 'In Harry's mind, she's a damsel in distress and he's her knight in shining armour. Her hero. Her saviour.'

'Yes, but . . . even if that's true . . . Ariadne didn't want Dom dead,' said Jenna. 'She and I have our differences, heaven knows, but I'm certain she loved Dom. More than he deserved, actually.'

A commotion outside the study door stopped both women in their tracks.

'What on earth . . .?' said Iris.

Jenna opened the door just in time to see a man in a suit roll past her, flying down the corridor like a bowling ball. Next came Billy like a fury, his shirtsleeves rolled up ready for the next punch, shouting loudly.

'You shit! You bastard! You won't get away with this.'

The man in the suit scrambled to his feet, revealing himself to be James Smythe, Dom's executor. A thin trickle of blood ran down to his chin from his swollen lower lip, where a purple bruise was already forming.

'You're a bloody madman,' Smythe swore at Billy, wiping the blood on his sleeve. 'Touch me again and I'll call the police.'

'No need for that.' DI Cant stepped forward from the huddle of spectators who'd gathered to watch the drama. 'Step back, please, sir.' He glared at Billy. 'And put your hands where I can see them.'

Billy complied, still yelling at the lawyer. 'I swear to God you won't get away with it! How much is my brother paying you?'

'What on earth's going on?' Ariadne arrived on the scene, followed swiftly by Marcus and Graham.

Billy turned on her furiously. 'As if you don't know! Marcus has only gone behind my back and challenged the will. He's trying to cut me out of the Grimshaw rights. He's claiming I'm "mentally unfit", and you're helping him!'

'That's not true,' said Ariadne, distressed. 'I *am* worried about your mental state. Managing Dad's literary estate is a huge pressure, Billy. But no one's trying to "cut you out" of anything. You'd still maintain a life interest in the money. Marcus would simply be managing your share.'

'*Liar!*' snarled Billy.

Cant rounded on him. 'One more word out of you and I'm taking you down the station. Do you understand? Zip it.' Turning to James Smythe, he asked, 'Would you like to press charges, sir?'

The lawyer looked from the still-glaring Billy to Ariadne, who appeared close to tears, to a shell-shocked Marcus. 'No,' he said quietly. 'That won't be necessary. But someone needs to get him under control.'

Graham Feeney stepped forward and took Billy by the arm, catching Iris's eye briefly as he led him away. 'Come on,' Graham said kindly. 'Let's get some air.'

'I don't want some fucking air,' Billy muttered, although he allowed himself to be guided by Graham. 'My so-called brother just robbed me of two million pounds!'

The drama over, people began to drift away. Jenna put an arm around Ariadne as they returned to the drawing room, and Marcus was about to follow them when Cant laid a restraining hand on his shoulder.

'Could I have a quick word, sir?'

'Of course.' Marcus smiled tightly, clearly wanting to get back to the guests, but not wishing to antagonise the policeman any further. 'How can I help?'

'Is it true your brother's being cut out of your father's will?'

'No.' Marcus frowned. 'Of course not.'

'But the two of you were left the rights to his literary estate? In equal shares?'

'Yes.'

'And that must be worth, what? Four million? Five?'

'Something like that,' Marcus snapped, wondering how the detective knew so much detail about Dom's estate. 'But everything's been left in trust, and it's part of the trustees' job to ensure that all beneficiaries are in a fit mental state to be able to manage money. I appealed to the trustees to have Billy assessed by a psychiatrist. That's all. He's perfectly at liberty to make the same request about me.'

'I see.' Cant's expression darkened. 'And you didn't think that the family questioning Billy's sanity might be something of interest to the police? Given that your father has just been murdered, your brother has a criminal record, and we know the two of them were at odds in the days before your father died?'

'No,' Marcus replied bluntly. 'I didn't. Because I know for a fact that Billy had nothing whatsoever to do with Dad's death.'

'Oh really? How do you know that?'

'For one thing, he wasn't even here on Christmas Day,' said Marcus.

'But you were,' said Cant. 'Run me through your movements that afternoon again, Mr Wetherby.'

Marcus sighed impatiently. 'You already know this, Detective Inspector. We finished giving out the presents. Dad and I went for a walk. I came home first to see if Mum needed any help. Dad went on by himself and that was the last time I saw him.'

'At four o'clock?'

'Around then. I can't remember exactly, but I'm sure it's all in my statement. Listen, Detective Inspector, it's my father's funeral. People have come a long way to be here and I'd really like to get back to our guests.'

'Of course,' said Cant. 'One last thing. How did your father seem on that walk? Was he happy? Troubled? How were things between the two of you?'

'They were good,' said Marcus. 'Dad was happy. Looking forward to the last Grimshaw coming out. A bit nervous about retirement, maybe. But he was fine. It was a nice walk. Now, if you'll excuse me.'

Iris, who'd stayed behind in Dom's study, watched from the shadows as first Marcus and then DI Cant walked away.

Marcus had just lied. And he'd done it so well, so smoothly, it was chilling.

It wasn't a 'nice walk'. Dom hadn't been happy, and things between the two of them weren't 'good'. Iris remembered vividly seeing the two of them arguing from Mill Cottage. And then how she'd seen them both at the top of the rise, Dom gesticulating wildly, before Marcus turned and stalked back to the house.

She thought back to her conversation with Jenna earlier. If Marcus *was* having an affair with Rachel Truebridge, could that be what the two of them were arguing about? Was it possible that both men, father and son, were involved with Rachel? And if they were, would that constitute a motive for murder?

Marcus Wetherby's own wife was convinced he was hiding something. And now he was making moves to cut Billy out of the will, presumably for his own financial benefit.

Perhaps it's time to look more closely into Mr Perfect, thought Iris.

Graham was very close to Marcus, so she would have to tread carefully there. But with Jenna's help, Iris was sure they could uncover the truth.

Marcus. Ariadne. Harry Masters.

All three of them were pieces of the puzzle.

All three were hiding something.

Iris closed the study door and slipped unnoticed back into the crowd.

CHAPTER EIGHTEEN

Ian McBride sat in the waiting room of his lawyer's offices on Cheapside, flipping through the 'Review' section of the *Guardian*.

Grimshaw's Goodbye, the final instalment in Dom Wetherby's crappy, banal, derivative 'opus', had aired last Sunday and been watched by a record eleven million viewers. *Eleven million!* That was more than the *Downton* finale, the highest live ratings figures for any drama in modern TV history. Ian felt a fresh rush of loathing course through his veins, and tried to take comfort from the fact that the bastard Wetherby was dead and had not lived to witness this latest undeserved success.

Much good your ratings will do you now that you're a rotted corpse.

Dom Wetherby had destroyed Ian McBride's life. That was how Ian saw things now. True, he and Iris had been struggling before she took the cottage at the Mill. But show Ian a couple who weren't struggling after ten years of failed fertility treatments. They had problems, but it was only since Iris started hanging out with Wetherby, sucked into his web by the charade of the portrait commission, that everything had unravelled. After that, nothing Ian did was good enough. Not his writing. Not *him*. Iris had become a different person, and Dom Wetherby was to blame. But Dom was dead and buried now, beyond Ian's reach. Which left only Iris to be punished.

Ian's divorce lawyer, Lisa Schaech, opened her office door and smiled. 'Sorry to keep you, Mr McBride. Do come in.'

Lisa's office was warm and welcoming, full of floral prints and comfy armchairs and objets d'art. *No family photographs, though. She's too smart for that.* Ian had consciously chosen a female divorce lawyer because he believed in fighting fire with fire. Women were more Machiavellian than men, more crafty, more spiteful. Who better to help him defeat Iris at her own game?

'I've read all the papers you sent me, and been through the accounts,' Lisa began, all business. 'Before we go any further, I have to ask you: are you sure you want to do this?'

Ian frowned. 'Do what? Divorce?'

'No,' said Lisa. 'That part I understand. And besides, it was your wife who filed, so to a large extent that ship has sailed.'

'Fine by me.' Ian leaned back and cracked his knuckles.

'I mean your financial strategy: trying to cut her out of the flat and your savings; this whole argument about her plundering your joint accounts for IVF treatments without your consent or knowledge; requesting spousal support. That's a very aggressive line to take, and once we go down that route, it might not be easy to turn back.'

'I've no intention of turning back,' snapped Ian. 'Are you saying you don't think you can succeed?'

'No. I'm not saying that.'

Lisa Schaech slid her glasses down her nose and looked thoughtfully at the bitter, broken, dangerously angry man sitting opposite her, wondering where it had all gone wrong.

'We may succeed. We may not. What I'm asking you is if you're sure you *want* to succeed in that way. You're effectively trying to leave your wife penniless, Mr McBride, after an almost twenty-year marriage. Not all judges will like that. And you may also come to regret it, once the dust settles.'

'The only thing I regret is wasting twenty years on that disloyal, ungrateful cow in the first place,' muttered Ian. 'She started this war, but I'm going to finish it.'

Lisa frowned. 'Mr McBride, as your lawyer, I can't advise you strongly enough to try and lose the toxic rhetoric and be—'

'She's already with someone else, you know,' Ian interrupted furiously. 'She's having an affair. Some rich barrister from Scotland, a friend of Dom Wetherby's. Can we use that against her?'

'How do you know Iris is having an affair?' Lisa asked calmly.

'I just do,' snapped Ian. He was getting tired of being second-guessed by a woman he was paying hundreds of pounds an hour to be on his side. 'People tell me things.'

'So it's rumour?'

'Oh, don't worry. I can get proof if you need it when the time comes,' Ian asserted confidently. 'She isn't even trying to hide it. What you don't seem to grasp, Ms Schaech, is that my wife does not give a shit. She's laughing at me. Laughing at us. I want you to wipe the smug smile off her face.'

They finished the meeting and Lisa watched her client go, apparently relieved that his instructions had been received and understood. She wondered briefly about Ian McBride's estranged wife, the much younger celebrated portrait artist Iris Grey. Was she really the heartless monster Ian made her out to be? Lisa highly doubted it. In her experience, all divorces distorted reality to some degree. But the really bitter ones, like this, blew all objective reasoning clean out of the water.

It was perfectly obvious to Lisa that Ian McBride still loved his wife.

What fools love makes of us all.

'I'm up here! In the bedroom.'

Iris hovered awkwardly in the flagstoned hallway at Mill House with the finished portrait of Dom in her arms, while Ariadne called down the stairs.

'Do you want to come up? I'm sorting through some of Dom's things.'

Hesitantly, Iris mounted the stairs. She'd visited Mill House countless times, but had never seen the upper floors, which seemed to represent the family's private space. It felt odd and like an intrusion somehow to be walking into Dom and Ariadne's bedroom, although at the same time Iris was deeply curious. Today would be her first chance to probe deeper into Ariadne's *real* relationship with her husband, not to mention the other men in her life: her father, her sons, Harry Masters.

Ariadne looked up from the mountainous pile of clothes on the bed and smiled warmly as Iris walked in, leaning the painting gently against the wall.

'There you are! And there it is. How exciting. May I?' She walked over to the painting.

'Of course,' said Iris. 'It's yours. I'm sorry it's taken so long.'

Holding the portrait at arm's length, Ariadne stared directly into Dom's eyes, not moving for a full twenty seconds. Then she took it back over to the bed, propping it up on the pillows and stepping back, to get a more removed perspective. Another twenty seconds passed, maybe more, and she still hadn't uttered a word.

For God's sake, say something, thought Iris, her stomach churning with nerves like the water beneath the Mill's waterwheel.

'Well. That's quite an achievement, my dear,' Ariadne said eventually, still gazing at the portrait. 'I think you got him. You pinned him down. And that, as we both know, was *very* hard to do.'

'Thank you,' said Iris, relieved. 'I'm so glad you like it.'

'I do,' said Ariadne, smiling again and turning back to Dom's clothes, which she was folding and sorting cheerfully into piles. Something about her had changed profoundly since Iris had last seen her, at Dom's funeral. The sadness, the heaviness, the anxiety that had gripped her since Dom's death all seemed miraculously to have lifted, blown away like mist rolling off the ocean. It was uncanny.

'You look well,' Iris observed.

'Thank you.' Ariadne kept folding. 'I'm feeling better, I must say. I was awfully worried when Billy moved out.' Picking up a pile of Dom's sweaters, she placed them neatly on the floor to her right. 'But ever since Graham called and said he's been in touch, I've been able to relax a little. Exhale. To be perfectly honest, it's been a relief *not* to have him in the house for a while. I love him, but he's so . . . well, you know.'

Iris did know, although it was a surprise to hear Ariadne, the saintly, perfect mother, express such an honest opinion about her difficult second son. Especially as, according to Graham, Billy had not so much 'moved out' as had a complete breakdown, storming out of the house and going AWOL over the family's challenge to the will. 'He was a no-show at the psych eval,' Graham told Iris, over the phone from London, where he was working this week. 'I suspect because he's using drugs again. He was definitely on something when I spoke to him. He feels Marcus in particular has stabbed him in the back and he's just shattered by it.'

Evidently Graham must have painted a more tactful, positive picture to Ariadne for her to be able to 'exhale' about Billy.

'I think having the funeral over and done with has helped as well,' Ariadne went on. 'It does offer some sort of closure.'

'Yes,' said Iris. 'Although I imagine it must be hard to move on with the murder still unsolved . . .'

Ariadne stopped folding for a moment – just a beat – then resumed her work in silence, without looking up.

'It was lovely to see so many people at the service,' said Iris, changing tack in response to the unspoken but distinct shift in mood.

'It was,' Ariadne agreed. 'Dom was very much loved.'

'Graham said there were lots of old Oxford friends there.'

'Yes.' Ariadne kept folding.

'And your father made it, which must have been nice for you. It can't be easy travelling long distances at his age.'

At last Ariadne looked up. 'Do you know my father?'

It was almost an accusation. Having hit a nerve, Iris tried to make light of it, while at the same time hoping to trigger some sort of revelation from Ariadne, some chink in the armour or crack in the façade.

'Oh no, not really,' she said. 'We said hello, that's all. Your friend Harry Masters pointed him out to me.'

'I see.'

Ariadne turned back to the clothes pile. If she felt any emotion at all, she took pains not to show it. After another awkward silence, she suddenly turned to Iris and asked casually, 'How long do you think you'll want to stay on at the cottage?'

The question was a surprise. Ariadne's voice was its usual soft, gentle, sing-song self, yet Iris couldn't help but detect a veiled threat in her inquiry, a menacing edge that hadn't been there before.

'I hadn't really thought about it,' she replied. 'Did you want the cottage back?'

Ariadne shrugged. 'At some point, I suppose. It's more that now that the portrait's finished, I imagine you'll want to return to your own life.'

And stop asking awkward questions, thought Iris.

'Actually, I'm perfectly happy here for the time being. I'm still painting. I've just done a sketch for Harry Masters, as it happens, in return for some piano lessons.'

'Yes. He mentioned it,' said Ariadne casually.

'Perhaps I could paint you one day, Ariadne?' said Iris.

'Me?' Her eyes widened. 'Oh, I don't think so. You did a wonderful job with Dom's portrait, but that was for a reason. Dom was a well-known writer. Why would anyone want to do a portrait of me?'

'Well, it's like you said,' said Iris. 'A good portrait should capture someone's essence. How did you put it? "Pin them down." It's about finding a truth and recording it. Preserving it. From my perspective, you're every bit as fascinating as Dom was.'

Ariadne smiled stiffly. 'You're very kind, Iris. But I wouldn't want to be painted. Dom was always the extrovert, happy to be on show. I'm not like that. Not at all.'

Ain't that the truth, thought Iris.

'Thank you for bringing the painting.'

It was a dismissal. Not rude, but equally not open to interpretation.

'Of course. I'll let you get on.'

Iris smiled and walked towards the door.

Ariadne called after her, 'And I'll let you know on the cottage. Once I decide what I want to do with it, going forward.'

So it wasn't an empty threat, thought Iris. Ariadne Wetherby genuinely wanted her out.

She must be closer to the truth than she'd realised.

'Are you writing this down, young man? 'Cause if you ain't writing it down, I'd like to speak to whoever's in charge. This is evidence, this is. It might be important.'

The rude, overweight woman leaned forwards across DI Cant's desk, her pasty arms quivering grotesquely like the thick, fatty layers on a pork chop. Her whole face seemed to wobble when she spoke, as if made of some ghastly, partially set milk jelly. As if, warmed only slightly, she might melt into a rotten, sickly puddle of self-righteousness, right there on Cant's office floor. Beside her sat a silent stick-insect husband, whose facial expression seemed to have been permanently set to defeat. *Poor bastard*, thought Cant. *Imagine being married to that blob.*

'*I'm* in charge of the investigation into Mr Wetherby's murder, Mrs Jones,' Cant responded curtly. 'I'm not taking notes because in a moment I'm going to ask my sergeant to take down a full statement from you and your husband.'

The woman harrumphed in a vaguely mollified manner.

'In the meantime I want to make sure I've understood you correctly,' said Cant. 'Are you certain that the car you saw belonged to the man you saw arguing with Dominic Wetherby?'

'That's what I said, isn't it?'

'You actually saw the man driving?'

'Not driving. He was parked up on the lane, but we saw him get out, didn't we, Bob?'

The stick insect nodded obediently.

'He hops over the gate and sets out across the field. Marches right up to Mr Wetherby and starts having a go at him.'

'Verbally?' Cant raised an eyebrow. 'Or physically?'

'You what?' Mrs Jones looked confused.

'Was the man shouting at Mr Wetherby or hitting him?' Cant asked patiently.

'He was pushing him. Waving 'is arms about. I daresay he was shouting, but we couldn't hear much, could we, Bob, on account of the wind?'

'And you've described the man as tall and thin, wearing a black Barbour jacket and boots?'

'And a hat. One of them trendy woolly hats without a bobble.'

'A beanie?'

Mrs Jones shrugged, an unspoken 'If you say so.'

'He was having a go at Wetherby, and Wetherby was having a go back, and they sort of scuffled a bit, and then Wetherby walked away.'

'So this man let him go?'

She nodded. 'He was shaking his fists and that. He wasn't happy. But yeah.'

'And there's nothing else you remember about him?' asked Cant. 'Nothing you can tell us about his face, his age?'

'Don't you think I'd have told you if there was?' Mrs Jones said rudely. 'What I'm telling you is, this bloke looked like he wanted to kill Dom Wetherby. Isn't that enough?'

Cant sighed. 'Unfortunately, there are a lot of tall men wandering around Hampshire wearing jackets and hats.'

'I remember the car,' the downtrodden Bob piped up for the first time, earning himself an astonished look from his wife. 'It was a Volvo XC90.'

Cant visibly brightened. That, at least, was information they could use.

'Are you sure, sir?'

The little man nodded. 'Silver. L-reg.'

'Thank you, Mr Jones. That's very helpful.' Cant smiled. 'I'll have my sergeant look into it.'

'Is that it?' The gelatinous Mrs Jones sounded as if she'd been cheated. 'You'll "look into it"?'

'Yes.' Cant stood up, signalling the interview was over. 'The more detail you can give to my sergeant in your statements, the higher our chances of finding this man. If only to rule him out of our inquiries.'

'Rule him *out*?' Mrs Jones looked as if she might be about to explode. 'Why would you want to rule him out? We reckon he did it, don't we, Bob?'

Cant opened his office door and forcibly ushered her through. 'Thank you again for coming in. Goodbye, now.'

After the Joneses had gone, Cant sat back down at his desk. It was a lead. A genuine lead, and a new one. He'd have been happier if it had pointed directly to Billy Wetherby, whom he still felt was their most likely suspect. But beggars couldn't be choosers, and at this point in the investigation, DI Cant needed all the help he could get. There was, after all, a theoretical chance that someone other than Billy Wetherby had killed Dom. But with no arrests, no charges brought and no physical evidence to go on other than the chloroform in the body itself, the case was growing colder by the hour. And Roger Cant's career was cooling with it.

Meanwhile he still had the media second-guessing him at every turn, not to mention the meddlesome Iris Grey, who only yesterday had called his office to complain that she thought she was being followed and that she was afraid her mysterious 'stalker' might be connected in some way to Dom's murder.

'Perhaps it's a ghost, Ms Grey,' Cant had replied scathingly. 'The same one that Lorcan Wetherby's been telling us about, the white ghost of Mill House.'

'I'm serious, Detective Inspector,' said Iris.

'So am I,' said Cant. 'I don't suppose it's occurred to you that if you'd mind your own business and go back to painting or whatever it is you do, no one would have any reason to follow you?'

'So you're not going to do anything?'

'About what, Ms Grey? You haven't given me any evidence of any crime having been committed. I can't send my men down to police your woman's intuition.'

Cant knew that making an enemy of Iris yesterday probably hadn't been smart. She and that slick lawyer friend of hers, Graham Feeney, were just the type of posh know-it-alls who would like nothing more than to make him look foolish and incompetent.

He needed a break.

Could the dreadful Mrs Jones's mysterious man-in-the-field be it?

Iris stepped out of the shower and dried herself off. Fastening the towel turban-style over her newly washed hair, she rubbed moisturiser all over her body before stopping to take a critical look in the mirror.

She'd never loved her body. It was too boyish, too straight up and down to be considered beautiful, at least in Iris's opinion.

On the other hand, having never had children, she still had the smooth, flat stomach of a woman in her twenties, and her boobs, by virtue of their smallness, were still round and relatively sag-free. *Could be worse*, she thought. *Like the rest of my life.*

Everything was pluses and minuses. No baby: minus. Blossoming career: plus. Collapsed marriage: minus. Meeting Graham: plus. Moving to Mill Cottage: that was a tough one. Lots of things about Hazelford and getting to know the Wetherbys had been a plus, and yet clearly Dom's murder was a terrible thing, a destabilising thing. In an awful, ironic way, though, Dom's death had helped to bring Iris back to life. It had awakened something in her – a curiosity, an intelligence, a courage – that had been asleep for so long, she'd forgotten she ever had it.

Brushing her teeth, her thoughts returned again to her encounter with Ariadne this morning. When was Iris going to give up the cottage? When was Iris going to go away, to move on? To 'mind her own business', as DI Cant had so crassly put it when Iris made the mistake of ringing him yesterday. Why on earth she'd imagined for a second that Cant would help her, or take her seriously about being followed and spied on, she couldn't imagine now. The man was a sexist idiot, with all the imaginative breadth of an amoeba. But the truth was, Iris was frightened. Living here alone, in this isolated spot, far from help should she need it and with, one had to assume, Dom's killer still out there somewhere on the loose.

Unwrapping her hair, she ran a comb through it, then padded naked into her bedroom to grab the nightdress she'd laid out earlier on her bed. Slipping it over her head, she suddenly froze.

A noise, coming from behind her. A low, keening moan.

Very quiet. Very quick.

Very human.

Oh my God. Someone's in here!

Iris spun round. She felt her stomach liquefy with fear and adrenaline course through her veins so powerfully she could almost hear it, a great rushing river of panic, of fight or flight. Where could she run? If she made a dash for the bedroom door, whoever was in the closet could jump out and grab her. Strangle her. Rape her. Drown her. Whatever they'd come here to do.

The moan came again, louder this time, and before Iris had a chance to do anything, the wardrobe door swung slowly open. Inside, curled up at the bottom in the foetal position and rocking gently to and fro, was Billy. As soon as Iris saw him, the dynamic changed and her fear turned to pity. In dirty clothes and with his dark curls heavily matted, he looked as if he'd spent the last several days at least on the streets. His grimy face was streaked with tears, and when he turned to look at Iris, there was such utter desperation and desolation in his eyes that she couldn't help but feel sorry for him.

'Billy. What are you doing in there?' She approached him slowly, extending a hand, as one might move towards an injured animal that needed help but that still might bite you.

'I wanted to see you,' Billy whimpered. 'I didn't know where else to go. But I thought you might . . . you might . . .' He started moaning and rocking again, screwing up his eyes tight and shaking his head, as if willing the tears away.

'It's OK,' said Iris, crouching down and patting his head gently as one would a frightened dog. 'It's fine for you to be here. Come on out. Let's get you cleaned up.'

Clearly he needed psychiatric help. But in the first instance he needed reassurance, a hot shower and something to eat. Iris helped him into the bathroom, handed him a clean towel and some soap, and went down to the kitchen, still shaken, to warm up some soup. Ten minutes later Billy shuffled downstairs, back in his dirty clothes but looking cleaner and calmer and marginally less deranged.

'Thank you.'

'Of course,' said Iris.

She put a bowl of Heinz tomato soup and two thick slices of toast in front of him, and watched in silence while he ate. It felt so strange to see him reduced to this weak, helpless creature. Ever since her first encounter with Billy, Iris had felt there was something dangerous about him, something predatory. The same thing, presumably, that made the police so convinced he must have had a hand in Dom's death. But looking at him now, she saw a different Billy. Tonight he was not predator but prey. Hunted. Haunted. Afraid.

When he started to talk, the words came out in snatches, a disjointed torrent of emotion. 'I needed to see you,' he blurted, in between slurps of soup. 'No one believes me. No one's ever believed me. But *you*. You see things. You *notice* things.'

'What does no one believe, Billy?' Iris asked.

'That she hurt me. Bullied me. Told me I was weak, I was stupid, I would never be anything, not like Marcus. I suppose she was right about that.' He laughed, then grimaced, pushing away his empty plate. 'She used to hit me when she got angry.'

'Ariadne hit you?' said Iris.

'And worse. Look at this.'

Rolling up his sleeves and twisting his left arm, he showed Iris what looked like a row of cigarette-burn scars between his armpit and elbow.

'I was nine. I made a sculpture of a horse for Dad and she hated it. Hated me. She said no one would believe me. She was right about that too.' He rolled his sleeve back down, calmer now. Perhaps it was a relief to talk.

Iris winced. Because she could see it, absolutely. She could see Ariadne doing it, lashing out in a fit of jealousy.

'Did you tell your father?' Iris asked gently.

Billy shook his head. 'No point. You couldn't get a cigarette paper between my parents. Ever. Dad was unfaithful; he needed the ego massage. But he loved her. He'd never have believed me.'

'So who . . .?'

'I told the teacher at school. Miss Kenny. She said I was attention-seeking. That was my first psych referral.' A small, ironic smile passed his lips, then died, withered into bitterness. 'And I told my brother.'

Iris took this in. 'You told Marcus that Ariadne abused you. And he didn't believe you?'

'He still doesn't.' Billy started shaking. 'That's why he got the will changed. He wants to make it my fault, to "prove" I'm crazy all over again. Because what's the alternative? Admit Mum's a monster? He'll never do it, Iris. And why should he? She was always the perfect mother to him. She loved Marcus, just as much as she hated me.'

Iris sat back, thinking. There was no proof of any of this, no evidence even. And Billy did have a history of mental illness. He could be making the whole thing up. And yet, in her bones, Iris knew he wasn't. She just knew it.

'Why do you think she hated you?'

Billy shrugged. 'Because I wasn't Marcus, I suppose.'

Iris frowned. Not much of a reason. But then abuse often stemmed from irrational emotions. Particularly if the abuser had themselves been a victim. Harry Masters' heavy hints about Ariadne's father, Clive, came rushing back to her.

'Do you think your father ever suspected?' she asked Billy. 'You never said anything, but did he never see any of this behaviour?'

'Never,' Billy said bitterly. 'My mother may be a witch, but she's not stupid. She was always patient with Dad. The loving, forgiving wife.' After a pause he added, 'When Dad was alive, I was convinced he had no idea of the truth. But after he died, I started to wonder. I mean, he included me in the will. He didn't have to do that, right?'

'No,' Iris agreed. 'He didn't.'

'And not just included me. He put me *above* her. She got the house, but he left me and Marcus the Grimshaw rights, equally. That's a hell of a lot of money.' Billy was becoming agitated again now, Iris noticed, pulling at the threads on his cuff in a distinctly manic manner. Looking up at Iris, he blurted, 'So maybe he *did* know? Maybe the will was his way of saying sorry? Of making things right?'

It was a question. He was willing Iris to confirm this, begging her to offer him that small comfort at least. That Dom knew. That Dom had believed him. That Dom was sorry. But Iris couldn't do that. The truth was, she had no idea what had been in Dom Wetherby's mind when he made his will. The last thing Billy needed now was for someone else to lie to him, so she said nothing.

'Do you believe me?' Billy asked, once the silence became unbearable. 'About Mum.'

'Yes,' Iris said, without hesitation. 'I do.'

It was as if the floodgates had suddenly been opened. Billy let out a terrible moan and crumpled forwards over the kitchen table, his whole upper body racked with sobs. Not sure what to do, Iris acted on instinct and walked over to him, pulling up a chair and wrapping her arms around his thin, convulsing torso. For a few seconds Billy did nothing, passively accepting her embrace as his own emotions reached a peak. Then suddenly he sat up, wrapped his arms tightly around Iris and kissed her passionately on the mouth. Horrified, Iris tried to pull back, but Billy's grip tightened. His hands were everywhere now, down her back, in her hair, grabbing and clawing at her, mistaking her pity for attraction.

'Iris,' he murmured. 'Oh, Iris.'

'*No!*' she shouted, elbowing him as hard as she could in the ribs and literally wrenching her face away from his. 'Billy, stop! I don't want this. *Stop.*'

He stopped, instantly, like a robot whose power supply has just been switched off. Iris jumped up and scrambled back away from him, to the other side of the table.

'But you . . . you came to me.' Billy looked at her, confused.

'I felt sorry for you,' said Iris, perhaps more truthfully than was wise under the circumstances. 'I still feel sorry for you.'

Now it was Billy who got up and backed away. 'You encouraged me! You led me on.'

'No,' Iris said firmly. 'You misread the signs, that's all. You made a mistake.'

'I trusted you,' Billy hissed, turning and bolting for the door as if the house were on fire.

'You *can* trust me,' Iris called after him. 'I'm your friend, Billy. Where are you going?'

But it was too late. He'd already taken off into the night, swallowed by the shadows that were waiting for him.

Iris closed the door behind him and leaned back against it. Only then did she realise that she, too, was shaking. *Did that just happen?* This entire evening had been surreal. Terrifying and enlightening and sad and—

'Aaaaagh!' Iris screamed. The door at her back had been swung open forcefully from the outside, sending her flying across the room. Landing with a thud on the stone tiles, next to the Aga, she banged her head on the bottom oven door. Pulling herself up to her hands and knees, the first thing she saw was her own blood dripping onto the floor. Then she turned and saw a man's figure looming in the doorway. Then everything went black.

'Iris? Iris! Thank God.'

Graham Feeney's face hovered above hers, a picture of concern. It took Iris a moment to piece things together and get her bearings. She was lying on the sofa at Mill Cottage, with a pillow under her head, a blanket over her and a packet of frozen peas resting semi-precariously on her forehead.

'Are you all right? You've been out cold for more than a minute. I'm so sorry, Iris. Do you think I should call an ambulance? I'm sorry. I . . . I didn't know what to do.'

'Stop saying sorry for a start.' Iris smiled weakly. 'I don't need an ambulance. Ow,' she winced, gingerly moving the peas aside and touching the gash on her head. 'So it was you who broke the door down?'

'I didn't break it down,' Graham gabbled wretchedly. 'At least, I didn't mean to. I opened it suddenly because I was worried. I'd just pulled up when I saw someone running hell for leather away from the cottage. I know you're being followed, or you think you are, and I thought . . . I was afraid that maybe this person had tried to hurt you. I didn't know you were leaning on the door. Are you sure you don't need a doctor?'

'Quite sure,' Iris sighed. Perhaps she was still feeling dizzy from the blow. Or perhaps the difficult, painful encounter with Billy had messed with her head. Whatever the reason, she found herself reaching up and stroking Graham's face.

He hesitated for a moment, smiled, then took her hand and kissed it.

'I think I might love you,' Iris said softly.

Graham's smile broadened. 'You think you might?'

Iris tried to nod, but it hurt her head. 'Yes,' she said quietly instead, closing her eyes.

'I think I might love you too,' said Graham.

Iris felt his lips on hers, and felt happy and safe and other things that she hadn't felt in a long, long time. She waited for the guilt to hit her and spoil everything, but it didn't.

'Will you stay?' she whispered between kisses.

'Try and stop me,' Graham whispered back. 'I think we've waited long enough, Iris. Don't you?'

Later, Iris would look back and remember the date: 12 February.

The beginning of the beginning.

The night Graham Feeney brought her back to life.

CHAPTER NINETEEN

Jenna Wetherby pulled her orange Zara wrap more tightly around her shoulders and tried to tell herself that she was shivering with cold rather than abject terror. It was certainly a possibility. The mercury in London this Valentine's Day morning had dropped to below zero for the first time in several years. Walking down the narrow lanes towards the Thames, past newsagents' windows full of cheesy Valentine's cards and naff teddies clutching sateen hearts, Jenna could see her own breath form into little clouds before her. It was the perfect weather for lovers to cling to one another, curled up indoors with a glass of champagne in front of a roaring fire.

For Jenna and Marcus, however, there would be no champagne, and no roaring fire. Because today was the day when Jenna could take it no longer. Today was the day she needed to know. The day she *would* know, she told herself firmly, stifling the frightened voice inside telling her to stop this nonsense now, immediately, before it was too late, to go back home and pretend everything was all right and 'drop it', as she'd promised Marcus she would.

Another promise broken.

But then Marcus knew all about broken promises, didn't he?

If Marcus had kept his promises, none of this would be happening.

Weaving through the Embankment traffic, Jenna crossed Waterloo Bridge, forcing her mind to go blank until she reached her destination, the nondescript grey-white tower block of Television Centre. Standing outside the traffic barrier, hopping from foot to foot against the cold, Jenna checked her watch: 11.50 a.m. It wasn't long before the first trickle of staff came out for their lunch breaks: gaggles of giggling interns in their cheap H&M boots and coats; older, seasoned technical workers, cameramen and sound guys and computer technicians, for whom the 'glamour' of a job in television had long since worn off; the occasional well-dressed presenter or producer, darting off for meetings at the Oxo Tower or one of the overpriced foodie restaurants along the South Bank.

It was twelve thirty on the dot when Rachel Truebridge emerged. Elegantly dressed in a long black wool skirt and matching polo-neck sweater, she was chatting to a female colleague as she passed the barrier, oblivious to Jenna's presence.

'Rachel!' Jenna called out. Her nerves were at fever pitch, but she'd come this far.

'Yes?' Rachel turned round and looked at her blankly. 'Can I help you?'

'I'm Jenna Wetherby. Marcus Wetherby's wife.'

Rachel's face darkened. 'I'm afraid I've nothing to say to you.' She started to walk away.

Jenna chased after her, grabbing her by the shoulder. 'Well, I have something to say to *you*,' she blurted angrily. 'I want to know how long you've been having an affair with my husband.'

Rachel's friend looked from Rachel to Jenna open-mouthed.

'It's all right, Angela. You go on,' Rachel said calmly. 'I'll see you back at the studio.'

She waited for her colleague to leave before turning back to Jenna.

'Let's walk and talk,' she said, her apparent confidence rather throwing Jenna off her stride. 'There's a park a few streets down. Come on.'

Not sure what else to do, Jenna followed in silence as Rachel headed towards the wrought-iron park gates. The small strip of green was almost deserted, and surprisingly quiet, given that it was wedged between busy roads and office blocks.

'I'm not having an affair with Marcus,' Rachel opened robustly. 'That's the first thing you need to know.'

Jenna eyed her suspiciously. 'Have you ever had an affair with him? A fling?'

'No!' Rachel laughed.

'I don't see what's so funny about it,' Jenna said, stung. 'It was obvious at Dom's funeral that the two of you know each other, and not just casually. And at the Christmas Eve party, the night before Dom died, when you showed up at the Mill, Marcus looked like he'd seen a ghost. Why?'

Rachel looked at Jenna's angry, anxious face and felt a wave of pity. She was an attractive girl, but the deep shadows under her eyes and worry lines on her gaunt face bore testament to how much she'd been torturing herself. It was time to put her out of her misery.

'I'll tell you why,' she said, earnestly. 'But only on the under-standing that this stays between us. I don't want the media sniffing around my door, or the police. This is my private life. OK?'

Jenna nodded curtly. She hadn't been prepared for liking Rachel, but there was an honesty about her, a directness that was hard to resist.

'I had an affair with Dom,' said Rachel, her boots crunching on the gravel path as she walked. 'I'm not proud of it, but it happened. We'd been working on Grimshaw together for a number of years. At the time, I was in love with him.'

Jenna listened in silence. If she found it strange that this poised, beautiful, articulate young woman should fall in love with Jenna's charismatic but much, much older father-in-law, she didn't say so. Dom's effect on the opposite sex was well documented, whether Jenna understood it or not.

'In any event, I had no expectations, as they say. I knew he wasn't about to leave his wife or anything like that. But I *was* shocked when it ended and Dom had me fired from the show. Shocked and, well, furious. I wasn't going to have that.'

'So how does Marcus come into it?' asked Jenna, who sympathised, if what Rachel was saying was the truth. And she could imagine it might be. Dom certainly had a ruthless streak when it came to work, or to protecting his own interests generally.

'I told Dom I would go to the press about our affair if he didn't reinstate me as producer on *Grimshaw's Goodbye*,' said Rachel.

'But he didn't,' said Jenna.

'No.' There was no hiding the bitterness in Rachel's voice. 'He didn't. The bastard called my bluff in the end. But he must have been worried enough to confide in his son about it, because one night in early December, Marcus came to see me. He just showed up at my flat unannounced and started shouting. Calling me a whore and a gold-digger and a blackmailer and God only knows what. He was vile, actually,' she told Jenna defiantly. 'I told him to leave and he refused. He became very angry and violent, pushing me, accusing me of trying to destroy his mother's life. This is in my own flat, mind you. We ended up fighting, physically. I scratched him on the face and a neighbour threatened to call the police and he left. I don't know to this day if Dom sent him, if he even knew about it. At the party on Christmas Eve, he claimed he didn't, but then Dom claimed a lot of things that weren't true.'

Jenna took all this in. It made sense. The timing, the scratch to Marcus's face, his lies about that. Jenna knew better than anyone how hard it would have been for Marcus to admit to her what she already knew: that his parents' marriage was far from perfect, that the blissful Wetherby family idyll at the Mill might be about to collapse around their ears like a house of cards in a breeze.

'Why was he so upset at the funeral?' asked Jenna.

'He thought I shouldn't be there,' said Rachel. 'I suppose he was right, in a way. But the thing is, despite everything, a part of me still loved Dom. We'd shared a lot together and I . . . I wanted to say goodbye.'

To Jenna's surprise, she saw that Rachel's eyes were welling with tears.

'I understand Marcus wanting to protect his mother, I do, but threatening me? The way he sees his mother . . .' she went on. 'I never wanted to hurt Ariadne, only to protect myself, my life, my career. The only real villain in all this was Dom. But your husband enabled him. I'm afraid I'm not a fan of your husband.'

The two women completed their circuit of the park, mostly in silence, and walked back towards Rachel's office. At a café on the corner, Rachel stopped. 'This is me,' she told Jenna. 'I still haven't eaten.'

'Of course,' said Jenna. 'Thank you for talking to me.'

They shook hands and Rachel went inside while Jenna walked back towards the river, oddly deflated. The interview had not gone at all as she'd expected. She felt a mix of emotions, chief among them relief. She believed Rachel when she said that she and Marcus had never had an affair. And that, surely, was the main thing. And yet much of the behaviour Rachel described still troubled Jenna deeply. Dom had always been a bully. Charming, but a bully nonetheless. But Jenna had always thought of Marcus as better than that. Kinder. More decent. And yet whenever his mother was concerned, all bets were off.

What had Rachel said? *'The way he sees his mother . . .'*

It's not normal, thought Jenna. *It's not.*

It was time to talk to Marcus. Whether he liked it or not.

As soon as the double doors closed behind her, Rachel tapped the familiar number into her phone.

'I can't talk now.'

His voice was the same as it had been the first time. Businesslike. Clipped. Dismissive. Yet for all his brusqueness, he was as deep in all this as she was. Deeper, in fact. And he knew it.

He'd started it.

'Call me back when you can,' Rachel snapped, her irritation mirroring his. 'And don't wait too long. It's important.'

She hung up.

To Jenna's surprise, Marcus took the news about her visit to Rachel Truebridge quite well.

'I knew something was up when you booked this place,' he said, glancing around the expensive Italian eatery Jenna had brought them to for a 'Valentine's Day dinner'. 'You hate Hallmark holidays.'

'I do,' she admitted, relieved for the second time that day that her marriage was apparently not about to unravel after all. 'But I thought we should talk out of the house. In case things got heated.'

'Heaven forbid,' said Marcus, smiling back and taking her hand. 'So what did she say?'

Jenna recounted their conversation close to verbatim, only slightly toning down the part where Rachel cast aspersions on Marcus's relationship with Ariadne, mostly because it sounded so much like Jenna's own point of view she worried he wouldn't believe the words came from an outsider.

Marcus listened patiently, frowning occasionally but not interrupting. Like Jenna, he felt battered and exhausted by their estrangement in recent weeks, especially with the added pressure of the murder investigation still hanging over everything. It was imperative he tread carefully tonight. That he pull his wife closer, not push her away.

'OK,' he said, once Jenna had finished. 'So a lot of what she told you was true. I'll admit that.'

'I liked her,' said Jenna. 'I didn't expect to, but I thought she was honest. Brave, even.'

'Well, hold on,' said Marcus, raising a finger in caution. 'Before you go awarding her the Nobel Peace Prize, there was stuff she left out, Jen. Important stuff.'

Jenna raised an eyebrow. She was prepared to believe this new, calmer, kinder Marcus, or at least to hear him out. 'Such as?'

'Such as the small matter of her blackmailing Dad.'

'You mean threatening to go to the press about the affair if Dom sacked her?' said Jenna. 'She told me about that. Although I'm not sure I'd call it blackmail. More self-defence. What your father was doing was outrageous, Marcus. And anyway, she never went through with it.'

'Not that,' said Marcus, taking a fortifying sip of wine. 'Months before the sacking thing, before the affair was even over, she was threatening him. Touting around some cock-and-bull story about Grimshaw not being Dad's original work. About him stealing the idea from another writer.'

Jenna frowned. 'Come on. Really? What evidence did she have?'

'None!' said Marcus. 'How could she have any evidence? It's bollocks. Dad was writing notes for the first Grimshaw book in his teens, for God's sake. Mum still has those notebooks at the Mill.'

'Then why threaten him?' asked Jenna. 'It doesn't make any sense.'

'Sure it does. This is the British media we're talking about,' said Marcus. 'The tabloids. You don't need evidence. You need rumour. Insinuation. Let's face it, *ideas* are ten a penny. And it's not as if Grimshaw is an original *idea*. He's a detective, solving murders. Any Tom, Dick or Harry could say, "I thought of that plot", or, "I thought of that character. You stole it from me." A couple of sob stories in the *Daily Mail* is all it would have taken to destroy Dad's reputation. He knew it and so did she. I'm telling you, Jenna, that woman was extorting him. The only thing Rachel Truebridge ever wanted out of Dad was money. He didn't fire her because their affair ended. He fired her because she was a lying, scheming, manipulative bitch. He stood up to her. And I supported that, but at the same time I was worried about Mum. So yes, I probably handled it badly. But I'm not the bad guy here, and Rachel Truebridge sure as hell isn't the feminist heroine.'

Jenna sat back, thinking. Marcus seemed so plausible. But then so had Rachel, when they met today. They couldn't both be telling the truth.

'Why did you lie to me about the scratch on your face?' Jenna asked him directly.

'I don't know.' For the first time all evening he sounded unsure of himself. 'I shouldn't have. I panicked.'

'Why didn't you or Dom go to the police, if Rachel really was blackmailing him?'

'Dad wanted to,' said Marcus. 'I wouldn't let him. We fought about it all the time. We had the same argument the day he died.' He welled up then, swallowing hard to try and choke back the tears. It was the first vulnerability he'd shown Jenna since the whole nightmare started and she responded instantly, reaching across the table and taking both his hands in hers.

'I love you,' she told him. 'It will be all right, Marcus.'

He looked back at her gratefully. 'I just knew it would kill Mum to find out Dad had been having an affair. Whatever else was going on, I felt he owed it to her to protect her.'

'And if Dom wouldn't, you would?' Jenna prompted.

'Something like that. Yes.'

Later that night, in bed, they made love for the first time in months. It was emotional for both of them, not so much an erotic experience as a healing one, Afterwards, when Marcus was deeply asleep, Jenna snuck down to the kitchen and emailed Iris.

I have to step away from this now.

I'm not saying Marcus has told me the whole truth. I know there are still pieces missing. There were rumours about plagiarism, hidden things in his father's past that he's chosen to ignore, or at least not to tell me. But I think he's trying, and I know he didn't have an affair. For now, that has to be enough. I don't want to lose my marriage, Iris. I hope you understand.

Good luck,

J.

*

'Iris? Did you hear what I said?' Greta Brun, Iris's agent, waved exaggeratedly at her client, like someone trying to bring an errant plane in to land. 'The National Portrait Gallery have been calling me. Now, I know you've been shown there once before, but let's not get cocky. This is still a very big deal. Huge. Iris?'

'Oh, I know, I know. Sorry.' Iris turned away from the window, where she'd been watching an arthritic duck hold up traffic as it tried to waddle slowly across the road. Greta had a stunning Victorian villa overlooking Clapham Common, and she and Iris were meeting over tea and ginger biscuits in the house's grand drawing room. Snuggled into one of her agent's upholstered Edwardian armchairs, gazing out through the original sash windows, Iris felt as she always did at Greta's, like a character from *Downton Abbey*, some minor player in a rarefied, perfect, long-lost life.

Today her feelings of other-worldliness were intensified by the way her mind kept wandering back to Graham. Kissing Graham. Talking to Graham. Holding Graham. Lying in bed with Graham. Surely any moment now someone would pinch her and she would wake up to a world of nothing but doll's houses and divorce papers, debt and doom.

'Ordinarily I'd assume that all the ghoulish tabloid salivating over Dom Wetherby's murder was behind a request like this,' Greta went on, determined to hold on to Iris's attention for a full minute at least. 'But David Bone, the new curator there, is far too much of a purist for that. He must simply love your portrait.'

'But he can't have seen it,' Iris protested. 'It's still propped up against the wall in Ariadne Wetherby's bedroom.'

'Someone sent him a photograph.' Greta smiled conspiratorially. 'A fellow named Feeney. He's a family friend of the Wetherbys, apparently, and a donor to the NPG. Do you know him?'

Iris blushed like a schoolgirl.

'Yes. He's a friend. I'm meeting him for lunch today, funnily enough.'

Greta Brun's eyebrow shot up. She had good antennae for this sort of thing.

'Hmmm. What a small world,' she teased. 'Well, he must be quite a friend, to get you a gig like that.'

'He's lovely,' Iris admitted. 'But this isn't a done deal, Greta. The painting belongs to Ariadne. It will be entirely up to her whether to show it or not. And to be honest, I'm not sure I'm top of her Christmas-card list at the moment.'

'Why ever not?' asked Greta.

Iris looked out of the window again. 'It's complicated. I liked Dom, and I'm not convinced . . . I don't think his wife is quite what she seems.'

Greta looked puzzled. 'In what way?'

Iris shrugged. 'Maybe she was involved.'

Greta's eyes widened. 'In what? You don't mean in Dom's murder, surely?'

Iris stared down at the road, to the spot where the duck had been a few moments earlier, almost in a trance.

'Maybe,' she said eventually. 'I don't know.'

'But weren't they madly in love?'

'Maybe,' said Iris again, adding thoughtfully, 'The problem with being madly in love is that you're mad. And mad people do all sorts of terrible things.'

'Well,' Greta said robustly. 'See if you can get her to agree to exhibit the portrait *before* you accuse her of bumping off her husband. A show like this now, with all the Grimshaw publicity . . . It could make your career, Iris. Really take you to the next level.'

Iris smiled. Greta Brun was a lovely woman, but she was also an agent to the very marrow of her bones. What was a small matter of murder compared to a really splashy exhibition?

Not that Iris was complaining. She was grateful to have Greta in her corner, and even more grateful to have Graham.

Two hours later, at lunch off Piccadilly, she told him as much.

'One night of passion and you're already pimping me out,' Iris teased him, over a delicious plate of chilled oysters at Hartley's on Swallow Street.

'I wouldn't say that,' Graham purred, unable to tear his eyes away from Iris's.

'I would,' laughed Iris. 'I've got David Bone calling *me. He's* asking *me* about showing my work. That's not normal. And it's all thanks to you.'

Graham flashed her a smile of deep, profound contentment, mixed with more than a little wonder. How on earth had he managed to get a woman this beautiful, not to mention this talented, to fall for him, a plodding, awkward, ageing barrister? He was well aware that he didn't have a fraction of Dom Wetherby's charisma. Whatever modest good looks Graham may once have possessed had long since faded. True, he was well off. But Iris wasn't the sort of woman who gave a fig about money. And yet she was here, with him. Somehow, out of the tragedy and anxiety and stress surrounding Dom's murder, Iris had materialised in Graham's life, a shining, perfect pearl glinting through the shit, calling to him, *'Take me. Have me. I'm for you.'* And he had. For once in his life, Graham had been bold and impulsive and he'd reached out and grabbed her. And now here they were. Together. Happy. Eating oysters.

Magic.

They chatted for a while about the possibility of exhibiting Dom's portrait, then moved on to Ian, and his latest salvo in what was already becoming an increasingly bitter divorce.

'You realise he won't succeed?' Graham tried to reassure Iris. 'No family court judge on earth is going to give him the entire flat and your joint savings. It's a nonsense. The worst that can happen is that he'll waste a lot of both your resources trying.'

'I don't care.' Iris waved a hand breezily. 'He can have the flat. And the savings. I can always earn more. At this point all I want is my life back.'

'A noble sentiment, but a foolish one,' Graham upbraided her. 'And if I may say so, something only a woman would say. Of course you care about the flat! It's valuable and it's half yours.'

It was nice to be able to talk to Graham about this stuff, Iris thought. About Ian, and the divorce. She hadn't realised until now quite how lonely and isolated her life had become. She couldn't remember the last time she'd seen a friend socially, or even called someone for a long chat. When she lived in London, she used to drop in on Annie regularly, for coffee or just to talk. But ever since she took the lease at Mill Cottage, and started spending so much time in the country, the sad fact was that Iris had become a virtual recluse, letting all those old friendships drift. Graham was the first person she'd felt close to in a very long time. It felt good to have another human being around who was truly and wholeheartedly in her corner.

'I got an email from Jenna yesterday,' she told him, changing the subject as the second round of cocktails arrived.

'Oh?' Graham slurped down another sweet Kumamoto oyster. 'Things seem better between her and Marcus.'

'I'm glad,' said Graham.

'She said she met up with Rachel Truebridge. Asked her flat out if she and Marcus had had an affair.'

'Goodness! That was brave of her,' spluttered Graham. 'I'm assuming the answer was no?'

Iris nodded, taking a sip from her cocktail. 'She told me some very interesting things, though. Rachel and Dom were having an affair.'

'No big surprise there.'

'No,' agreed Iris. 'But Rachel and Marcus each told Jenna a different version of events. According to Rachel, Dom fired her from Grimshaw out of spite once he'd ended their affair. He tried to erase her completely from his life, which made her angry.'

'I can see how it would,' Graham observed mildly. 'Dom could be a shit when he wanted to be.'

'Absolutely' said Iris. 'But according to Marcus, Rachel getting booted off *Grimshaw's Goodbye* was nothing to do with the affair. *He* says she was blackmailing Dom.'

Graham raised a curious eyebrow. 'Threatening to tell Ariadne, you mean? About the affair?'

'Worse.' Iris shook her head. 'Apparently Rachel claimed to have evidence that Dom had plagiarised the very first Grimshaw book.'

'What evidence?'

'I don't know,' admitted Iris. 'But Marcus told Jenna that Rachel had asked Dom for money, a lot of money, to keep quiet about it. And when he wouldn't pay up, she threatened to ruin his reputation. I mean, can you imagine? If Dom really *had* stolen another writer's work and made all that money from it? He'd stand to lose everything, wouldn't he? His fortune, his royalties, not to mention his good name. Anyway, I suppose one must conclude that there was no smoking gun in the end, otherwise all this stuff would have come out before Christmas when . . . Graham? Are you all right?'

For the first time Iris noticed Graham's colour. His skin had gone from normal to white to a ghastly, almost translucent blue. His eyes were wide, and he had a hand on his neck, his throat, as if he were struggling to breathe.

'Graham?' Iris stood up, panicked. 'He needs help!' she shouted to the nearest waiter. 'Something's wrong!'

A nearby diner rushed over. 'I'm a doctor,' he announced, bending over Graham and immediately loosening his collar and tie. 'Can you breathe?'

Graham nodded, clearing his throat, then coughing profusely. 'I'm OK,' he said, looking anything but. Sweat poured from his forehead and had begun to soak through his shirt. 'I just feel . . . I think I'm going to be sick.'

Staggering up from the table, he ran into the gents', followed by the doctor and two restaurant staff. Iris sat at her place in shock. A few moments later the doctor emerged looking reassuring.

'He's all right. He's thrown up, but he already looks a lot better. I suspect it was food poisoning. Shellfish can get you like that.'

The manager ran over to Iris's table, his arms flapping, like a bird trying to escape a forest fire. 'I can assure you it was not food poisoning, madam. With respect to your medical training' – he nodded angrily at the doctor – 'our oysters are a hundred per cent fresh and we have never, *never* had a single case of poisoning.'

'It's all right,' said Iris, who really couldn't care less what it was as long as Graham was OK.

'Take him home and give him lots of fluids,' the doctor told her, ignoring the manager, who was now literally hopping from foot to foot, offering to waive Iris's bill while stressing 'very clearly' that he did *not* admit liability, in any way. 'He'll probably throw up on and off for a few hours,' said the doctor. 'If it's more than that, you might want to swing by A&E. But I don't think it will be.'

In the bathroom, Graham waited for the waiters to leave. When he was finally alone, and sure there was nothing left in his stomach to expel, he made his way to the washbasins and splashed ice-cold water on his face. Looking up into the mirror, he saw a ghost staring back at him. His complexion was white and deathly. He looked a hundred years old. Like a man in shock.

Iris is out there. Waiting at the table.

The best thing that ever happened to you is out there, waiting.

Pull it together, Graham.

Get a grip.

He waited until his breathing had calmed and the last wave of nausea had subsided. Then he rehearsed the conversation he and Iris would have back at the table in his mind as he dried his hands.

'I feel mortified. It all happened so suddenly.'

Then Iris would say something reassuring about food poisoning and how it could happen to anyone. And Graham would change the subject back to Marcus and Rachel, and Iris would let him, and he'd be as calmly dismissive as he should have been the first time around.

'Of course Rachel Truebridge must have been making it up. Sounds like classic woman-scorned stuff to me. If there were a smoking gun about Dom's authorship of Grimshaw, the press would have found it by now. They've dredged up everything else, after all.'

By the time he walked back into the restaurant, Graham looked and felt like himself again. But as soon as he sat down at the table, he saw that it was Iris who'd now become the ghost and knew that his rehearsed spiel would have to wait.

'What is it?' he asked, concerned.

Iris took a deep, steadying breath.

'Has something happened?'

'You're not going to believe this,' said Iris.

'What?' asked Graham, really worried now.

'I just received a phone call from Hampshire Police.'

Graham waited.

'Ian . . . my Ian's been arrested.'

Graham stared at her. He didn't like her use of the expression 'my Ian', but this didn't seem the time to say so. 'What? Why? What for?'

'They've arrested him on suspicion of Dom Wetherby's murder.'

CHAPTER TWENTY

'Interview resumed ten fifteen a.m. Present are the suspect, Mr Ian McBride, Mr McBride's solicitor, Mr Thomas James, DI Cant and Sergeant Trotter of Hampshire Police.'

Cant eased his ample backside into the hard plastic chair and leaned back confidently. He'd had a fractured night's sleep – the arrest of McBride was the biggest break in the case so far and his mind was racing – but he was prepared to bet he'd had more rest than the suspect. Ian looked terrible. His hair was dishevelled, his eyes bloodshot and hung with enormous bags that made him look every day of his fifty-seven years. It was hard to imagine this wreck of a man as Iris Grey's husband.

'Let's talk about the emails,' Cant began.

'What emails?' Ian shot back nervously.

'The threatening emails you wrote to Mr Wetherby, after your wife accepted the commission to paint his portrait.'

Ian glanced shiftily towards his lawyer. 'I don't know what you're talking about.'

Sighing deeply and dramatically, Cant reached into his briefcase and pulled out a small sheaf of printed pages, passing them across the table towards McBride and the solicitor.

'For the tape, I am showing Mr McBride and Mr James hard copies of emails retrieved from Dominic Wetherby's computer, sent anonymously from the same Internet café on Wandsworth Bridge Road in November and December of last year. You know, it would speed things up a lot, Mr McBride, if you would stop lying. We have both credit-card records and CCTV footage from the café consistent with the times these emails were sent, as well as logged server information proving that you wrote them. Quite apart from the multiple references made to your wife.'

Ian leaned over and whispered something to his lawyer, who frowned, then nodded.

'Mr McBride, do you admit that you sent these emails?' Cant pressed, irritated.

'Yes,' said Ian morosely. 'I didn't like him, OK? I didn't like the way he was sniffing around Iris.'

'I'd say that was obvious,' said Cant.

'But I didn't kill him,' Ian blurted. 'I swear! I never touched the guy.'

'On the first of December you wrote, and I quote, "Leave her alone or suffer the consequences. You can consider this a final warning. The time for words is past." What did you mean by that?'

'Nothing!' Ian sounded desperate, close to tears. 'I wanted him to leave her alone. That's it. That's all!'

'Except it wasn't all, was it, Mr McBride? You continued sending threatening notes for a further twelve days. But when those, too, failed to have the desired effect, you carried out your threat to take action. You hired a car, a silver Volvo XC90, from Cathedral Cars in Winchester on the thirteenth of December, a car you did not return until almost midnight on the twenty-fifth of December, the day of Dom Wetherby's murder. Is that true?'

Ian put his head in his hands. 'Yes, but—'

'Unfortunately for you, witnesses saw you park that car on a remote stretch of Rowan's Lane in Hazelford on the afternoon of Christmas Day, just hours before Mr Wetherby was drugged and dumped in the river to drown. You had followed Mr Wetherby and were seen approaching him in a field. You became violent—'

'No!' Ian interrupted. 'I was angry. I thought he was sleeping with my wife. But I never hurt him.'

'We have witnesses who say otherwise,' said Cant. 'Somehow I find their version of events easier to believe than yours, Mr McBride. Perhaps it's because only yesterday, you sat in this very room and swore blind you spent Christmas Day in London. That you were nowhere near Hazelford.'

'I panicked, for God's sake!' Ian snapped. 'You'd just arrested me for murder. I was frightened.'

'You should be frightened,' Cant growled ominously. 'Shall I tell you what I think happened, Mr McBride? I think you'd convinced yourself that Dom Wetherby was to blame for the breakdown of your marriage. I think you threatened him, and when that didn't work, you stalked him, just like you stalked your wife . . .'

'I wasn't stalking Iris. I was watching her.'

'In secret, without her knowledge or consent, following her around in the dark? Breaking into her house? That's stalking, Mr McBride.'

'She's my wife!'

'So what? So you own her? She belongs to you?'

'Mr McBride never said that,' the solicitor jumped in, placing a restraining hand on Ian's shoulder, apparently aware that his client was close to breaking point.

'It doesn't matter.' Cant waved a hand dismissively. 'This isn't about what he did to his wife. It's about him threatening Dom Wetherby, following Dom Wetherby, becoming violent with Dom Wetherby. Do you realise that the next time anybody saw Mr Wetherby after your encounter in the field, he was floating in the river, dead?'

'There's no way my client could possibly know that,' said the solicitor, but not even Ian was listening to him.

'I think you drugged him during that encounter, Mr McBride. Either you injected him or you gave him the chloroform dissolved in a drink. I think you came prepared.'

'That's not true.'

'You went back to your car to let the chloroform take its effect. You knew he'd be unconscious in seconds, a minute at most. You checked the coast was clear and you went back up to that field.'

'I didn't.'

'You carried him back to your car. Then you drove to the Mill, parked near the woods and waited for darkness to fall. Maybe you gave him a second dose, to keep him out, I don't know.'

'This never happened!' protested Ian.

'Is there a question here?' asked James, the solicitor.

Cant steamrollered over both of them. 'You dragged Dom Wetherby to the river, weighted him down and dropped him in there to drown. Then you waited a bit longer, to make sure he was dead, that he wasn't coming back up.'

Ian shook his head vehemently.

'You covered your tracks and you drove off. Got the car cleaned. Dropped it back. Hightailed it to London so you could establish an alibi. You planned every inch of it, didn't you, Mr McBride?'

'No.'

'No?' Cant scoffed. 'You even hired the exact make and model of car that Marcus Wetherby drives! So if anybody saw that Volvo, they wouldn't think twice. You blamed Dominic Wetherby for your wife leaving you and you killed him!' He jabbed an accusatory finger in Ian's direction.

A knock broke the almost unbearable tension. A young WPC put her head round the door.

'What?' Cant yelled at her furiously.

'S-someone's here for you, sir,' the girl stammered. 'It's important.'

'Who?' roared Cant.

The PC shook her head helplessly. Evidently she couldn't say the name in front of McBride and his lawyer.

'Fine. Interview suspended.' Cant flipped off the tape and beckoned to his mute sergeant to follow him. The solicitor heard him mutter, 'This had better be good,' to the PC as the three officers left the room.

As soon as they'd gone, he turned to Ian.

'We may not have much time.'

Ian was rocking from side to side, his head in his hands. 'This is awful. This is a nightmare. How did they know about the emails? The emails make me look so bad.'

'Forget the emails. What about the car?' Thomas James dragged him back to their biggest problem. 'Is there any possibility that they will find DNA evidence linking you to Dom Wetherby in that car? Think carefully before you answer.'

Ian's eyes widened with fear. 'No. Of course there isn't.'

'You're sure?'

'Yes, I'm sure. Don't you believe me?'

'I'm asking if you're sure,' James answered, in an impressive display of lawyerly obtuseness. 'That's my job. What about drugs?'

'Drugs?' Ian looked confused. The stress and exhaustion were clearly getting to him.

'Will they find any drugs in that car?' James spelled it out.

'No. At least, not from me,' said Ian. 'I mean, it's a rental car. People have used it since I did. And before I did. Oh God!'

'Don't panic.' The solicitor patted his hand 'And don't say anything else for the time being. They can only hold you for three more hours without charging you. Unless they've applied for an extension, but we should have been notified if they've done that.'

'What sort of extension?' Ian gnawed at his nails.

'They could ask for thirty-six hours instead of twenty-four, and they usually get that,' said James. 'Technically, they *can* ask for up to ninety-six hours.'

'Four days? They can keep me here for four days?'

The solicitor shook his head. 'It won't come to that. I think you'll be out by tonight, but do *not* rise to the DI's bait, and do not offer up any more information.'

'OK,' Ian nodded.

'And don't lie,' James added. 'If you feel the need to lie, say nothing. Just look over at me and I'll handle it.'

Ian nodded again, terrified and clinging on to his solicitor's words for dear life.

'*You'll be out by tonight.*'

Please, God, let that be true. Whether he deserved his freedom or not, he hadn't realised till now quite how deeply he cherished it.

How had everything unravelled so fast?

Iris had already been ushered into Cant's office and offered a cup of tea by the time the DI himself burst in, radiating a combination of self-importance and irritation.

'What can I do for you, Ms Grey?' He took a seat on his own side of the desk and stretched out his legs in front of him, a picture of confidence.

'What do you mean, what can you do for me?' Iris's own irritated tone punctured his ego bubble. 'Your sergeant called me to tell me Ian was in custody. I was asked to get here as soon as I could.'

'Hmmm.' Cant frowned dismissively, as if Iris having been summoned was by the by. In fact, he'd forgotten that he'd asked Trotter to bring her in. In all the excitement yesterday after his team found the rental car, it had seemed important to talk to Iris. To let her know that, far from being the lazy, stupid policeman of her imagination, Roger Cant had in fact been following new leads and was on the brink of cracking open the Wetherby murder case like a soft-boiled egg. The fact that it now looked like Iris's own husband had killed Dom – that for all her artist's intuition, or whatever the hell she considered to be her crime-solving 'gifts', she'd somehow managed to miss a murderer in her own family – only made Cant's triumph all the sweeter.

Today, though, Iris's presence was a distraction. He'd been close to breaking McBride earlier, and he highly doubted that Iris was going to be able to add much to his efforts to secure a conviction.

'I don't know where all this came from, or what evidence you have against him,' Iris began, filling the rather hostile silence between them, 'but you're making a mistake. Ian didn't kill Dom. My husband may be many things, but he isn't a murderer.'

'That's what your intuition tells you, is it?' Cant sneered.

'It's what twenty years with the man tells me,' said Iris hotly.

Cant rolled his eyes. 'You and the wives of just about every convicted killer since Jack the Ripper,' he said. 'Were you aware your husband was threatening Dom Wetherby? That he bombarded him with aggressive emails for weeks before his death?'

Iris did a double-take. 'No, I wasn't. Why would Ian do that?'

'Evidently he suspected some sort of romantic relationship between you and Wetherby.'

'Between *me* and Dom?' Iris's eyes widened.

Cant nodded smugly. He appeared to be enjoying himself. 'Did your husband have any grounds for those suspicions, Ms Grey?'

'No!' said Iris. 'None whatsoever.'

'I'm assuming you also weren't aware that Mr McBride was staying in Hazelford over Christmas? He's been staying here regularly, in fact, both before and after Mr Wetherby was murdered. Over at Whitman's Farm. Turns out the mysterious "stalker" you've been complaining about was your own husband.'

He said this triumphantly, as if it vindicated his dismissiveness of Iris's complaints and his own inaction.

'Funny, you not picking up on that. What with your sixth sense and everything.'

'I've never claimed to have a sixth sense, DI Cant,' Iris snapped, losing her temper. 'Only to make good use of the five God gave me. If you'd done the same, you might have learned weeks ago that I was indeed being followed, as I told you. I also told you that you were mistaken in focusing your inquiry on Billy Wetherby, something else you now seem to have accepted. Of course, you persist in barking up the wrong tree with Ian. But who knows, maybe you'll figure that out more quickly this time. I suppose we can only live in hope.'

Cant's eyes narrowed and his jaw clenched. He looked at Iris with something closely approaching hatred.

'Was your husband ever violent towards you, Ms Grey?' With a superhuman effort, he managed to keep his tone professional.

Iris was about to say no, then hesitated. Ian had never hit her, but he'd certainly behaved in a threatening manner, especially when he was drunk. More than once he'd broken her things, lashing out in rage, or intimidated her to the degree where she felt she needed to leave the flat.

'He lost his temper at times,' she answered cautiously. 'But he never physically injured me, if that's what you're asking.'

Despite his dislike of her, Cant read between the lines.

'Were you afraid of him?' he asked, less aggressively.

'Sometimes,' Iris admitted.

Then, to Cant's surprise, she asked, 'Can I see him?'

'No,' he answered on autopilot. 'He's still being interviewed.'

'On suspicion of Dom's murder?' Iris asked.

Cant nodded, and she shook her head vehemently. Clearly, Iris Grey was convinced her husband hadn't done it. Even though she'd left him, and he'd intimidated her and stalked her and God knows what else, McBride's wife still didn't see him as a killer. Despite himself, Cant felt the first seeds of doubt starting to stir. He didn't want Iris to be right about McBride. He didn't want her to be right about anything, at this point.

'Let me talk to him,' she pleaded. 'You never know, he might open up to me more than he would to you. It can't hurt, Detective Inspector.'

Could it hurt? Cant wasn't sure. McBride was already in a highly emotional state. Seeing his wife might push him over the edge. But in this case, that could be a good thing. It was just possible he would blurt out the truth to Iris. Without the tape and the lawyer . . .

'All right,' he said eventually, to Iris's frank amazement. 'I'll give you ten minutes.'

'Really?'

He nodded gracelessly. 'Just get on with it, Ms Grey. Before I change my mind.'

Thomas James left the interview room looking deeply unhappy.

'I'd rather stay with my client,' he told DI Cant.

'And I'd rather be married to Margot Robbie,' Cant quipped, 'but that's life, Mr James. Your client would like some time alone with his wife.'

The solicitor looked pleadingly at Ian, but it was no use. He'd clearly already made up his mind.

A few minutes later the door to the interview room opened and Iris walked in. Ian looked up and their eyes met. For a moment they both fought back tears.

'Hello,' Ian said gruffly.

'Hi,' said Iris, sitting down. 'They only gave me ten minutes.'

Ian nodded but remained silent, waiting for her to start. When she didn't, he cleared his throat and said awkwardly, 'I didn't do it.'

'I know that,' said Iris.

Ian's shoulders slumped visibly with relief. Simply to be believed was something.

'You look beautiful.' His voice started to falter.

Iris stopped him. 'Don't.' It was impossible not to pity him, seeing him sitting there looking so small and defeated and frightened. But pity only went so far. She was angry too. 'For one thing, we both know I look awful. I barely slept last night after I heard you'd been arrested. What the hell happened, Ian? You sent Dom threatening emails?'

Ian groaned.

'You followed him? You followed *me*? Have you any idea how terrified I was? I spoke to the police about it. I thought someone was trying to kill me!'

'I'm sorry,' Ian muttered. 'I thought you were having an affair. I would have hired a private detective, but I couldn't afford one, not with the divorce looming and my play cancelled. And I wanted to see for myself.'

'See what?' Iris sounded exasperated. 'There was nothing to see!'

'Not with you and Dom, as it turned out,' Ian admitted, adding bitterly, 'Although I'm not sure you get to play the innocent, Iris, seeing as you *are* having an affair.'

'You mean Graham?' Iris stiffened.

'Why? Are there others?' Ian shot back, instantly regretting it. 'Look, I'm sorry, OK? It just . . . it hurts. You moving on so quickly.'

This was the first honest, vulnerable thing he'd said to her in months. Iris found her anger evaporating. For a rare moment the two of them were still, floating on calm water.

'Are they going to charge you?' Iris asked. 'What evidence do they have, other than those emails?'

Ian told her the circumstantial case against him. The secret trips to Hazelford, renting the car and returning it in the dead of night, lying about his whereabouts, the witnesses to his Christmas Day argument with Dom. 'My solicitor thinks they won't have a case without some sort of forensic link. They're going over the car now, but there's nothing to find, obviously.'

It's obvious to us, thought Iris. But she wouldn't put it past Cant and his men to plant evidence, if they were truly convinced Ian did it. What he really needed, what they all needed, was some link to the real killer.

'Did you find anything out about Dom?' she asked. 'When you thought we might be sleeping together, all that snooping around you did. Did anything else come up that might be relevant?'

Ian smiled thinly. 'Well, he was an interesting guy. There were a string of mistresses, going way back, but that was an open secret. He had a lot of friends, but he had plenty of enemies too. Wronged husbands, disgruntled employees at the publisher and at ITV. And then there were his creditors. He was a gambler, your friend Dom Wetherby, in more ways than one. He owed a lot of money to a lot of people, some of them pretty unpleasant.'

'He had unpaid gambling debts?' Iris sounded sceptical. 'That doesn't make sense. According to his will, he was flush with savings. If he owed money, he could have paid it.'

'I'm not saying he couldn't,' said Ian. 'Only that he didn't. There were plenty of disgruntled poker players out there, fed up with Wetherby's welching. Apparently his nickname on the poker circuit was "Crime".'

Iris looked puzzled.

'As in "crime doesn't pay"?' Ian clarified.

Iris winced at the dreadful pun. 'That's awful!'

'I know,' Ian chuckled. 'And look, I'm not saying his creditors killed him, but some of those guys are serious players. They don't mess around.'

Iris suddenly thought back to her meeting with Harry Masters at the piano teacher's house. What had Harry said about the Russian property developer who hated Dom? And come to think of it, hadn't Dom himself said something to her once about Russians? Not trusting them, or words to that effect. None of it had seemed important at the time, perhaps because the manner of Dom's death – how and when and where it was done – seemed more intimate than anything related to a business dispute. Dom was drugged and drowned in the grounds of his own beloved home, a place he felt safe, the weight round his legs an echo of a game he once played with his children. On Christmas Day, a time of joy and peace, a time for family.

Family.

But perhaps there was more to it than that. Perhaps Dom's death had had nothing to do with family and everything to do with money, betrayal and revenge. Had Iris been guilty of the very thing of which she'd accused DI Cant? Lazy narrow-mindedness? Refusing to look at evidence that didn't fit her preconceived notions of what might have happened to Dom on that fateful Christmas afternoon?

'Have you told the police about this?' she asked Ian.

He shook his head. 'They haven't asked. My lawyer reckons I should stop talking to them altogether for the moment. What do you think?'

Iris hesitated. 'I think if they ask you a question, you should answer it,' she said eventually. 'Cant will dig his heels in even harder if he feels he's being stonewalled. But I wouldn't offer anything up that you don't have to. Is your lawyer good?'

Ian smiled. 'I hope so.'

'Because, if you needed it, I know Graham would—'

'No, thanks,' he cut her off, his smile evaporating. 'I'd rather be done for murder, if it's all the same to you.'

Iris looked him in the eye. 'He's a good man, you know. He's kind to me.'

'I'm happy to hear it,' said Ian. 'Truly. But I can't forgive him, Iris. In my heart, you'll always be my wife.'

He means it, thought Iris. For the second time, she felt herself tearing up.

'I did love you,' she blurted.

'I know you did.'

'I did try.'

'So did I.' Ian looked away. Her face, twisted in misery, was too painful to look at. 'Thanks for coming to see me.'

'Of course.'

Iris stood up, pushing out her chair with a clatter.

'Good luck at your portrait unveiling on Thursday,' Ian said graciously as she turned to leave. 'That's quite an achievement.'

'Thank you,' said Iris. She could barely remember the last time Ian had paid her a sincere compliment about her work. 'I'm excited, actually. Nervous and excited.'

'Are you happy with the painting?'

Now it was Iris's turn to smile. 'Of course not. When am I ever happy with a portrait? Everything can always be better.'

Everything could certainly be better now, thought Ian. He felt profoundly sad, suddenly. In this moment, so much of his life felt like a terrible, awful waste.

Iris felt something similar as she headed for the door. The anger she'd brought into the room with her was completely gone now. Something had been healed by this brief encounter with Ian. There was a new mood in the air, a new calm. Not forgiveness, exactly. But perhaps acceptance.

Cant knocked once on the door, a brisk, perfunctory rap, and walked in, swaggering like a silver-backed gorilla preparing to reclaim his territory. Behind him scuttled his sergeant, and an antsy Thomas James.

'My sergeant will show you out, Ms Grey,' Cant informed Iris imperiously.

'No need for that,' replied Iris, already halfway out the door. 'I know where I'm going. You have my mobile, if you need me.'

Cant opened his mouth to insist that he wouldn't 'need' her, but Iris was already gone.

The fact was that *she* needed this now, whatever the police or anyone else might think. She needed to know the truth, not just for Dom's sake or even for Ian's, but for her own. Unravelling the mystery of Dom Wetherby's murder, and the web of secrets and lies at the Mill, had transformed Iris into a new person. A person with a purpose, and perhaps even a gift. It was the same gift that made her a great portrait painter, only now she was using it not just to create beautiful paintings but to reveal the truth, to make the truth matter, make it count for something. She would demand justice for Dom Wetherby. And this time, she would get it.

It had taken an agonising divorce, not to mention a murder, for Iris to reach this point. But she was here now. She finally knew who she was.

It felt good.

Graham Feeney lay back in Iris's bed with his arm around her, staring up at the ceiling. It was bumpy and uneven, a symptom of Mill Cottage's great age, the white plaster rolling in undulating waves above him. There were cobwebs in the corners, and tiny hairline cracks in the paintwork and beams. Graham found himself noticing everything suddenly, each tiny shadow or stain, his senses heightened to a quiveringly high pitch. He couldn't easily place the emotions raging inside him. At times he felt something akin to panic, at other times elation. All he knew for sure was that being with Iris – talking to her, holding her, making love to her as he just had – had intensified everything, made him more alive and awake and present than he had been for many years. Not since before his brother's death.

'I'm so looking forward to Thursday night,' he said, stroking Iris's hair. 'I can't wait to be there at the portrait unveiling, by your side. Are you nervous?'

'A bit,' Iris admitted. 'I told Ian yesterday I'm nervous *and* excited.'

Rolling over, Graham shot her a wounded look. 'You and Ian sound awfully cosy all of a sudden.'

It was so petulant Iris stifled the urge to laugh. 'Hardly. I went to visit him at the police station. It wasn't a date.'

'I don't see why you had to go and see him,' Graham grumbled.

'Yes, you do,' Iris said gently. 'No matter what's happened between us, I can't stand by and do nothing while the police fit him up for murder.'

In fact, Ian had been released a few hours after Iris left the station yesterday. Evidently Cant didn't have enough to charge him . . . yet. But Iris knew from experience that when the detective inspector had a suspect in his sights, he became like a pre-programmed drone. Totally focused on the target. First it had been Billy. Now it was Ian. Iris might not love Ian anymore, but she couldn't allow the police to cobble together some cock-and-bull case against him.

'DI Cant's probably out there right now trying to find enough evidence to pin Dom's killing on the wrong man,' she told Graham. 'You don't want that to happen any more than I do.'

'Are you sure about that?' asked Graham.

'Sure about what?' said Iris. 'You not supporting a miscarriage of justice? Or Cant's total disregard for the truth when it doesn't fit his prejudices? I'm pretty sure about both, to be honest.'

'I meant, are you sure Ian's the wrong man?' said Graham.

Iris propped herself up on one elbow and looked at him with astonishment.

'Are you serious?'

'I am, actually. I don't see why it shouldn't be him,' Graham replied calmly. 'Look, I was with you on Billy – you know I was. I never believed he was capable of killing anyone, let alone his father. But your husband's different.'

'How?' said Iris.

'Because he's shown himself to be violent and vengeful,' Graham replied. 'He's also highly intelligent and an accomplished liar. He terrorised you and threatened Dom, physically as well as verbally, if Cant's witnesses are to be believed. And let's face it, they've no obvious reason to lie.'

Iris shook her head. 'You're wrong. I know Ian. He wouldn't. He couldn't. Not murder. You don't know him like I do.'

'Well, that's true,' admitted Graham, kissing her tenderly on the forehead. 'I don't. But perhaps that makes me more objective. Me and the police. You have to give Cant credit where it's due, Iris.'

'Give *Cant* credit? For what?'

'He got hold of those emails to Dom,' said Graham, counting off the detective's achievements on his fingers one by one and sounding more like a lawyer than ever. 'He tracked down Ian's rental car and his B&B, blowing apart his alibi, and he found those witnesses to the fight with Dom, all while we assumed he was sitting on his arse waiting for Billy to crack and confess.'

Iris's frown deepened. This was all true. And yet she didn't want to credit Cant, or to suspect Ian. She just didn't.

'Perhaps we've misjudged the detective inspector,' suggested Graham.

'Yes, and perhaps we haven't,' Iris snapped. 'Those emails must have been on Dom's computer for months, so he should have found them ages ago. The fact it took him this long is sloppy detective work, if you ask me.'

Graham smiled wryly. 'You're even more lovely when you're angry. Has anyone ever told you that?'

Iris blushed and swatted him away.

'By the way, did I mention Ariadne's decided to attend on Thursday night?' Graham threw in casually.

Iris's face fell. Ariadne had been giving her distinctly mixed messages recently, continuing to strongly hint that Iris's time at Mill Cottage might be up.

'What's the matter?' asked Graham.

'Oh, nothing.' Iris rolled over. 'I don't entirely trust her, that's all. I don't think she likes me.'

Graham looked surprised. 'Well, she sent me a very kind note about you yesterday, saying what a great job you'd done on the painting and how happy she is that you and I found each other.'

'Really?' Iris found this hard to believe. How odd of Ariadne to be so kind and complimentary to Graham and simultaneously so cold to her. The woman's moods were more changeable than the eddying waters of the Itchen.

'Really,' said Graham, kissing her.

After lying in companionable silence for a few minutes, Iris suddenly turned to him and asked, 'You remember when your brother and Dom were up at Oxford together?'

'Yes.' Graham frowned, disconcerted by the non sequitur.

'Did you ever go and visit him?'

'Once or twice, I think,' said Graham. 'It was a long time ago. Why do you ask?'

'No reason,' said Iris. 'I was just wondering what Dom was like in those days. I can't really imagine him as a young man. I mean, it must have been a hugely creative period, being around so much talent and inspiration. I know it was for me, in my own small way. But for Dom, writing the first Grimshaw book, conceiving the character that was going to change his entire life—'

'I barely remember him,' Graham said curtly, cutting her off, and wondering why, exactly, the conversation had gone off on this tangent. 'When I think of those days, all I remember is Marcus. *His* youth. *His* promise. *His* creativity.'

Realising she'd hit a nerve, Iris reached up and touched Graham's cheek.

'That was insensitive of me. Sorry. I wasn't trying to bring up painful memories.'

Graham covered her hand with his and consciously took two deep breaths.

'You didn't,' he assured her. 'And I'm the one who should be sorry. The memories – *those* memories, anyway – are mostly good ones. Marcus loved Oxford. He used to tell me hilarious stories about Professor Nevers turning up drunk for tutorials, and him and Dom trying to convince the old boy that he'd lost their essays, when in fact they hadn't bothered to write one.'

Iris laughed.

'That reminds me of my own Oxford days. Except for the fact that I was sleeping with my tutor and ended up marrying him!'

Graham forced himself to smile at this latest allusion to Ian. He mustn't come across as jealous. Women didn't like that. But deep down he felt aggrieved by how many of his and Iris's recent conversations seem to circle back to her poisonous, abusive ex. Almost ex.

Perhaps sensing his discomfort, Iris snuggled in closer.

'I'm looking forward to Thursday too,' she told him. 'It means so much to me, you being there.'

'I'm glad,' said Graham, exhaling. Turning off the bedside light, he held her until she fell asleep.

Then, in the darkness, he watched.

Iris Grey, he thought, gazing at her sleeping form in wonder. Even her name felt special, melodic and lovely, like a poem.

How lovely you are, my Iris. How beautiful and smart and perceptive.

Too perceptive.

Marcus would have loved Iris.

Marcus would have loved a lot of things, had he lived.

At last Graham fell into a fractured and shallow sleep.

CHAPTER TWENTY-ONE

Tucked away on St Martin's Place behind Trafalgar Square, hiding in the petticoats of the larger and grander National Gallery, the National Portrait Gallery was easily the most prestigious venue in Europe for portrait artists. Behind its grey, classical façade, dominated by the busts of its three founders, Stanhope, Macaulay and Carlyle, the NPG housed collections incorporating everything from Tudor oil paintings to modern digital photographs. There were portraits of monarchs and generals and movie stars, alongside many depicting ordinary people, their essence captured in one moment, one expression that the artist had somehow distilled and preserved, in that alchemy that was portraiture. The NPG was a celebration of fine art, but it was also, uniquely, a celebration of humanity. Of the human spirit, revealed through faces and bodies and reimagined through the brush or the lens.

For Iris, it had always been a Mecca, ever since her first visit as an A-level art student all those years ago. Tonight, though, it was not at its best. Renovations to the pillared portico had left the front of the building covered in ugly scaffolding, like a teenager's braces, and a relentless grey drizzle added to the depressing first impression.

Worse than the weather were the scrum of reporters huddled along the railings like wet rats, drawn to Iris's big night not for any love of art but because they smelled the rotten flesh of scandal. As if Dom Wetherby's gruesome death weren't salacious enough already, his portrait painter's *husband* had just been arrested on suspicion of his murder! True, Ian McBride had since been released without charge. But the story was still a tabloid editor's wet dream, especially as the portrait artist in question turned out to be properly attractive: another of Wetherby's conquests, perhaps? His last?

The jostling and shouted questions began the moment Iris arrived, bundled up in a trench coat and clutching Graham Feeney's arm for dear life.

'Have you seen your husband, Iris, since his arrest?'

'Why was Ian arrested? Do you think he might have done it?'

'Is Dom Wetherby the reason the two of you got divorced?'

'Is this your new boyfriend, Iris? What's his name?'

By the time they finally got inside and handed their coats in at the cloakroom, Iris felt close to a total panic attack.

'I can't do it!' she panted at Graham, doubled over in an attempt to calm her raging pulse and erratic breathing. 'I can't go in there and stand up in front of all those people with everyone thinking about Ian and Dom and what might have happened. I wanted tonight to be about the portrait.'

'It is about the portrait,' said Graham, rubbing a soothing hand in circular motions over Iris's back, the way one might calm a colicky baby. She'd reverted to her instinctively quirky look tonight, in a scarlet ankle-length dress with geometric cut-outs in the back teamed with a pair of 1970s platform boots in clashing burnt orange. It looked a bit bizarre, from Graham's conservative perspective, but at the same time it suited her. When he picked her up earlier, Graham had interpreted Iris's vibrant outfit choice as a sign of confidence. Perhaps it had been. But whatever positivity she'd been feeling back at Graham's London house had evaporated the moment the paparazzi descended.

'Those morons outside might be here for the soap opera, but everyone in that room is here for your art. People are excited: the critics, the family, everybody. Including me, I might add. I can't believe I still haven't seen the finished article yet.'

'I know,' Iris said weakly, straightening up and attempting to breathe more normally. 'I really hope you like it. Thank you so much for setting this up, Graham. I hope you don't think I'm ungrateful. I'm just nervous.'

'Of course you are, my darling.' Stooping down, he kissed her tenderly on the collarbone, an unexpectedly intimate gesture in such a public place. 'Having one's work shown here is a big deal, a huge honour. You'd have been nervous anyway. And it has been quite a week.'

'Iris! There you are. The woman of the hour. Do come through.'

Lena Carrington, this year's president of the Royal Society of Portrait Painters, was a warm, encouraging, generously curvaceous woman from Newcastle, with the sort of broad Geordie accent that had Americans reaching for the subtitle button on their televisions. Lena's own portraits, though technically brilliant, had never been to Iris's taste. All her subjects looked angular and reduced, somehow, as if in art Lena felt compelled to strip away the fleshy, human softness she struggled to control in life. But like everybody else, Iris adored Lena as a person, and was in awe of her immense energy and passion, as well as her generosity towards other artists.

'And you must be Graham?' Lena said, enveloping both of them in a waft of gardenia scent from beneath her soft cashmere poncho. '"Here's our Graham with a quick reminder." Always makes me think of Cilla Black, that name.'

Graham looked blank, but Iris got the *Blind Date* reference and smiled as she allowed Lena to sweep them through the double doors into the Wolfson Gallery.

'David Bone tells me we have you to thank for showcasing the Wetherby portrait here?' Lena turned to Graham. 'Not that he needed much convincing. David loves Iris. We all do.'

'And why wouldn't he?' said Graham, taking Iris's hand in his and feeling a warm glow run through him as they walked into a room already packed to the rafters with buyers, critics and fellow artists, as well as Wetherby family friends and supporters. Tonight marked the 'coming out' of Iris and Graham as a couple. But it was also a professional triumph for Iris, and one he felt delighted in which to have played a small part.

'I'm going to "ding, ding, ding" and give my little speech in a minute,' Lena informed Iris. 'Then I'll unveil the picture. And you can either do an official Q&A if you want to or just get pissed and mill about a bit, basking in the glow.' She chuckled. 'Cheer up, pet! You've done well. Have a drink and enjoy yourself.'

Taking Lena's advice, Iris swiped two flutes of champagne from the first passing tray and, handing one to Graham, downed hers almost at once. Feeling better, despite the stream of bubbles threatening to pour out of her nose, she helped herself to a sausage roll and a second drink, and had just started to scan the room for familiar faces when Lena took up her position next to the covered portrait and cleared her throat.

'Ladies and gentlemen, boys and girls,' she began, to a wave of drunkenly enthusiastic applause. 'I won't take up too much of your time. I know none of you came here to listen to me rambling on.

You're here to see a tremendous, important piece of work by one of our very best British portrait painters, the lovely Ms Iris Grey.'

Another ripple of applause as various eyes turned to seek out Iris, who wasn't difficult to find in her red cut-out dress and boots.

Graham stepped back slightly, to allow Iris her moment in the spotlight alone as the RSPP president continued extolling her virtues.

Glancing around the room, he honed in on a handful of familiar faces, observing their reactions to both the speech and one another. Some he'd expected to be here. Marcus and Jenna Wetherby seemed happier in each other's company. He looked like he'd come straight from work – crumpled suit, loosened tie – but Jenna had clearly made an effort in a bottle-green cocktail dress and heels, and was leaning back against him in a way that suggested intimacy or at least calm. *They've called a truce*, thought Graham. *That's good.*

On the other side of the room, just a few feet to the left of Lena and the portrait, Ariadne stood with Lorcan, holding hands. That was a more jarring pairing: Ariadne, in a pale pink kaftan and strings of beads, looking positively yogi-like and radiating peace, beside Lorcan, stiff and awkward in his sports jacket and chinos, and visibly distressed to be there.

Why did she bring him? Graham found himself thinking, almost angrily. *Why put him through this, poor kid?* But then it occurred to him that perhaps there was no one with whom Lorcan could be safely left. Ever since Dom's death, the boy's separation anxiety had become acute, and focused relentlessly on his mother.

Billy was a no-show. No surprise there, although Graham imagined that his mother and brothers must have wondered whether the public unveiling of Dom's portrait would be enough of a pull to wrest the family's black sheep out of the shadows.

Other faces, though familiar, were a shock to Graham. At the back of the room, hovering beside the door, presumably in case she should need to make a swift escape, stood Rachel Truebridge, the very last person Graham would have expected to show her face. In black cigarette pants and a dark grey sweater, she looked wan and much too thin and as if she'd aged a hundred years since Christmas Eve.

Turning back to Iris, he discovered that she'd wandered off, no doubt kidnapped by one of her many admirers. In her place, two women in cheap Next party dresses were huddled together, gossiping. Clearly neither of them knew that Graham was Iris's plus-one.

'I don't know how she's got the nerve to show herself,' the first woman observed in a stage whisper. 'With the family here and everything. As if poor Mrs Wetherby didn't have enough to deal with already, now she's supposed to make small talk with the killer's *wife*?'

'They released him, you know. McBride,' her friend observed, dousing the flames of the first woman's excitement with an unwelcome bucket of fact.

'Under caution,' woman one shot back. 'That means they still think he did it – they just can't prove it yet.'

The barrister in Graham had to smile at that. The great British public's lack of understanding of their own laws never ceased to astonish him. Not that he felt remotely inclined to leap to Ian McBride's defence. Whatever he may or may not have done to Dom Wetherby, he'd been vile to Iris, and that was crime enough in Graham Feeney's book.

Iris, meanwhile, had slipped towards the back of the room, where to her great delight she'd spotted her old friends Annie and Joe waving at her manically.

'I can't believe it!' Annie enveloped Iris in a hug, the fabric of her natural bamboo-fibre dress as soft against Iris's skin as a baby's blanket. 'It's been so *long*.'

'I know,' said Iris, inhaling the clove and cinnamon scent of Annie's hair. Somehow she always managed to smell like baked goods, perhaps the result of living above the shop at Joe's café. 'I'm sorry I've been so distant. I've been away a lot.'

'We know.' Annie's boyfriend, Joe, winked at her. 'We read the papers. And occasionally run into your miserable sod of a husband. I gather they released him?'

'Yes.' Iris rolled her eyes. 'The whole thing was ridiculous. Ian didn't kill Dom Wetherby.'

'Who do you think did?' Annie asked, as eagerly curious as a schoolgirl. 'All those intimate portrait sittings . . .' She nudged Iris knowingly. 'He must have given you *some* clues.'

If it were anyone else, Iris would probably have been irritated by this jokey tone, but she was so pleased to see Annie, she couldn't be angry and found herself responding in kind.

'The trouble is, he didn't know he was going to end up at the bottom of the river. If he had, I'm sure he'd have been a *lot* more forthcoming.'

Just as she made the joke, Iris noticed Lorcan Wetherby waving at her and trying to catch her eye. Feeling horribly guilty, Iris waved back. She was pleased that Lorcan seemed to want to communicate again, for the two of them to return to being friends. Not that they'd fallen out, but lately the poor boy had become borderline reclusive, rarely leaving his mother's side. At some point Iris needed to talk to him about the night Dom died. Finding an opportunity to speak to Lorcan alone was going to be the hardest part, and tonight clearly was not the right time. But there were things Iris needed to ask him, for Ian's sake, whether the police ultimately believed them or not.

Lorcan Wetherby's mind might be wired differently to everyone else's, but he was not stupid, especially when it came to the language of emotion. He knew more than he was telling, Iris was sure of that.

Up at the front of the room, Lena was wrapping things up, thanking Ariadne for loaning the painting and talking about the importance of truth in art, especially portraiture, and how none of us must allow the press's baser instincts and grubby interest in Dom Wetherby's death to detract from the value of his life or to sully our memories of who he 'truly' was.

'I never knew Dom myself, although I know many of you did, but I do know Iris Grey. And I know that you won't find a more truthful, more courageous artist than Iris anywhere. And so it is my honour and my great pleasure to reveal to you all tonight, for the very first time in public viewing, Iris Grey's portrait of Mr Dominic Wetherby.'

With one pull on a rather cheesy gold-tasselled rope, the red velvet drapery covering the painting fell away and there it was – there *he* was, Dom, his eyes as bright and searching as they had been in life, eagerly scanning his latest crowd of admirers.

It's actually not bad, thought Iris, as applause and murmured admiration rippled audibly around the room. The warm patina of the wood in Dom's study came over beautifully from this distance. The knickknacks behind him, the rich softness of his cashmere sweater, the deep fan of lines around his eyes, all came across better on canvas than Iris remembered. As for Dom, he looked like himself. Relaxed, and yet conscious of the impression he made, how he was sitting, the direction of his gaze, even the way his hands trailed along the back of the sofa.

Moving through the crowd, she tried to make her way back to the spot where she'd left Graham. Annie and Joe were lovely, but Iris realised with a sudden jolt that Graham Feeney was the one person with whom she wanted to share this moment. But when she reached the place where they'd been standing, he'd gone. Before Iris could track him down, a gaggle of private collectors swooped in to congratulate her on her latest 'masterpiece' and she found herself plunged deep into work mode, or what her agent, Greta, liked to refer to as 'the hustle zone'.

Oh well. I'll catch up with Graham later.

Outside in the lobby, Rachel Truebridge twisted her wrist, painfully trying to free herself from Graham Feeney's grip.

'Why did you come here?' Graham whispered furiously. 'What on earth did you hope to gain?'

'Nothing!' Rachel insisted. 'It's not about *gain*. I wanted to see it. I wanted to see the painting.'

'Well, now you have. So go.'

'Did you know?' Rachel challenged him. 'Did you know where she painted him? That room! The background!'

'Calm down.'

'You're sleeping with her, for God's sake. Iris must have shown you . . .'

'She didn't,' Graham insisted.

'I don't believe you.'

'Do you think I give a damn what you believe?' Graham snapped, his voice louder than he'd intended it to be. 'I am telling you, the first time I ever laid eyes on that portrait was two minutes ago. Just like you. Now, for God's sake, leave, before you draw any more attention to yourself. Or me.'

He let go of her wrist and she slunk away, grabbing her coat before disappearing into the night.

Graham took a moment to collect his thoughts. Then, straightening his tie, he walked back towards the bar. As he moved, he could feel Dom Wetherby's haunting eyes following him from Iris's canvas up on the dais, boring into him like twin lasers.

Don't you judge me, you old bastard, he chuckled to himself.

Iris's portrait was truly incredible. She'd captured Dom in all his complexity, like a soul-catcher imprisoning a spirit in a jar and hanging it up for all to see. Right there, in oil paint, was Dom's charm. His vanity. His warmth. His spite. There was his *life*.

It's as if he's still alive, thought Graham, suddenly realising what it was that was making the hairs on the back of his neck stand on end.

But Dom Wetherby wasn't alive. He was dead and buried, and his secrets would be buried with him. As long as Rachel Truebridge kept her mouth shut.

Extricating herself at last from her gaggle of admirers, Iris escaped to the ladies'. The loos in this part of the gallery were the posh kind, with white marble countertops and a woman whose job it was to hand people individual towels for drying their hands. This woman had a little bowl beside her into which people were dropping tips, usually a pound. Washing her hands, Iris found herself idly wondering how much you could make in an hour, handing out towels, and whether the loo lady made more or less than most of the wannabe artists and writers at an event like tonight's, when Ariadne suddenly appeared at the basin next to her, in unusually talkative mood.

'Iris, my dear.' She smiled the saintly smile. 'I've been meaning to talk to you all evening, but my lovely Lorcan won't let me out of his sight. I noticed you and Graham arrived together?'

'Yes.' Iris returned the smile. As usual she was never quite sure what to make of Ariadne. 'He was instrumental in setting this up, as you know. Thank you again for agreeing to loan the painting.'

'Oh!' Ariadne waved a hand dismissively, as if to say it was nothing. 'I'm just thrilled to see the two of you together. Dom and I both felt you'd make a wonderful couple, but it's rare that these things work out so perfectly, isn't it?'

Iris nodded awkwardly and threw her towel in the 'used' basket, reaching into her evening bag for some change. Had Dom really thought that she and Graham should get together? Had he put the idea into Graham's head before he came down to Hazelford for the Christmas Eve party, the same way that Ariadne had 'casually' mentioned Graham to Iris when she dropped by Mill Cottage that day? And if so, why did that idea trouble Iris so much? Matchmaking one's friends and acquaintances wasn't a crime, after all. So why did Iris feel so manipulated, like a puppet on a string?

'I noticed Rachel Truebridge was here earlier,' Ariadne observed casually. 'Did you invite her?'

'No!' Iris said vehemently. 'Why would I invite her? I don't know her.'

'Hmm.' Ariadne nodded, apparently satisfied with Iris's answer. But the whole exchange was very odd. 'Well, she's gone now, anyway. I saw her talking to Graham and then she just left. Here, let me.'

Ariadne dropped two pound coins into the attendant's bowl with a satisfying *clink, clink* and hugging Iris as if the odd, accusing Rachel conversation had never happened, headed back into the party.

Iris hung back. Looking up at her reflection in the mirror, she was surprised to see two frightened eyes gazing back at her. Each 'clink' had sounded ominous, somehow, like a key turning in a lock. A cage door closing.

Something bad is happening. Something's wrong.

Stepping back into the gallery, she was immediately accosted by a man she didn't know.

'Iris?'

'Yes?'

The man looked distinguished and was softly spoken, with a faint European accent of some sort. He had grey, slightly unkempt hair, and wore tortoiseshell glasses, a combination that gave him the look of a professor. Iris didn't recognise him, but assumed he must be either a critic or a collector.

'We haven't met.' He extended a hand politely. 'I'm Lars. Lars Berens.'

Iris looked at him blankly. Was the name supposed to mean something? Greta was always telling her she needed to remember people's names and try harder at networking, but Iris's brain was like a sieve for that sort of thing.

'Thea's husband,' he clarified.

Thea!

Iris's stomach lurched. She felt the room begin to spin and instinctively leaned against the wall for support. She hadn't seen or heard from her sister in decades, although she had started thinking about Thea again recently, ever since she began investigating Dom's death. It was astonishing how quickly the painful emotions came flooding back, opening a door to the past that Iris had hoped was shut for ever.

But this was worse than dredging up old memories. This was tangible. This was Thea's husband, standing right here in the flesh, touching Iris, talking to her. Worse, he seemed like a nice, decent sort of man.

'I hope you don't mind my coming tonight,' Lars went on, oblivious of Iris's inner turmoil. 'I happened to be in London for a seminar and I read about your exhibition in the paper. I have a good friend on the board at the National who was kind enough to arrange an invitation. Your work is—'

'What do you want, Mr Berens?' Iris interrupted coldly. She knew she was being rude, but she couldn't help it. She was angry. How dare her sister impinge on her special night like this? Iris didn't want to think about Thea, tonight or any night. She wanted to be happy. She deserved this moment, and now Thea and her softly spoken husband had ruined it! 'Why are you here?'

If Lars was affronted, he tried not to show it.

'I wanted to meet you,' he said, reasonably. 'Thea doesn't know I'm here.'

Iris snorted. 'I find that hard to believe.'

'She doesn't,' Lars insisted. 'But I know she wants to end the estrangement between you, Iris. It's been so many years.'

'No!' Iris could hear the fear in her own voice. She barked the word out in staccato, like a gunshot. 'I'm not interested in that.'

'Your sister has changed,' Lars continued patiently. 'She was very ill when she was younger, but that's all behind her now. With the right drug combination and therapy, she came back to life, Iris. She's a good person.'

No, she isn't. She isn't!

Please go away!

Iris closed her eyes, willing this well-meaning man to be gone.

'She's a good wife.'

No.

'A good mother.'

Each word was like a punch in Iris's stomach.

She opened her eyes and stared at her sister's husband. Everything stopped dead: the spinning room, the hubbub of the party. It was as if time itself had frozen to let Lars's last words hang in the air.

'Thea has children?' Iris croaked out the words in disbelief.

'Yes!' Lars smiled, mistaking Iris's horror for surprise. 'We have three, actually. Henrietta, Michael and Anton.' He pulled a laminated picture out of his wallet and handed it to Iris, who took it dumbly. She found herself looking into the faces of three blond, smiling children. The oldest, the girl, looked like a gap-toothed version of Thea. For an awful moment Iris thought she was going to be physically sick.

'I'm in the UK for a couple more days,' Lars continued blithely, retrieving the photograph from a dumbstruck Iris and replacing it with a business card. 'These are my numbers. I'm staying at the Dorchester. I know you're probably very busy, but if you had time for a coffee, I'd love to meet up. Fill you in on our lives, on the years you've missed.'

Iris opened her mouth to respond, but no words came out. She felt paralysed with rage. *The years I've missed? I haven't 'missed' anything! I've been living my life, away from that bitch, that liar.* How dare this man walk into *her* life, *her* exhibition, and have the audacity to tell *her*, *Iris*, that her sister was a 'good person'? She was nothing of the sort. No drug, no therapy in the world could take a black, spiteful heart and make it white. Nothing could erase what Thea had done. Not now, not ever.

Just then Greta Brun, Iris's agent, wafted over in a cloud of Chanel Cristalle and confidence. Iris couldn't remember the last time she'd been so pleased to see someone.

'Can I steal her for a moment?' she asked Lars, adding to Iris, 'There's an important Russian collector here I need to introduce you to.'

'Of course,' Lars smiled. 'I was just leaving. Take care, Iris.' And with that, mercifully, he was gone.

'He's attractive,' said Greta, guiding Iris back into the reception and through the crowds towards her Russian. 'Not cheating on the lovely Graham already, are you?'

Still in shock, Iris was only half listening. 'What? No!'

'I was joking,' said Greta. 'Are you all right, Iris?'

'She's back.' Iris had stopped suddenly. 'Ariadne said she left, but she's back.'

'Who's back?' Greta followed Iris's gaze to the double doors. Rachel Truebridge was standing just inside, talking animatedly with Chris Wheeler, Dom Wetherby's agent. Iris remembered that the two of them had clashed at the Christmas Eve party, the night before Dom's death, when Rachel had shown up drunk and made a scene. She'd been angry then and on the offensive. Tonight, clearly, the tables had turned. Wheeler was leaning over her, his finger wagging chastisingly, dominating and aggressive, while Rachel literally shrank back, cowering like a frightened dog.

'Really, my love,' said Greta, struggling to hide her impatience with Iris's random asides, 'I need you to meet Vasile Gretski. He spent over twenty million sterling on his collection last year alone and . . . Ah, speak of the devil! Vasile, you must meet Iris Grey.'

The man leaning down to kiss Iris on both cheeks looked more like a professional wrestler than an art collector. Tall, bald and built like a Sherman tank, Vasile Gretski radiated an unsettling combination of power and menace. Despite this, he was flanked by two goons in dark suits, both wearing earpieces, who were clearly some sort of security detail. *He must have some serious enemies. Or major paranoia*, Iris thought. A fistful of gold rings sparkled on his hands, adding to his overall 'gangsta' image, and he wore an expensive couture suit that looked ridiculous on his massive muscle-bound frame.

'It's a good portrait,' Vasile told Iris, nodding at his bodyguards to step back. 'You have captured him very well.'

He spoke slowly, which was just as well, as his Russian accent was so thick it was an effort to understand him.

'You knew Dom?' Iris asked, disconcerted to see that Greta had already scuttled away and abandoned her to her fate.

'Unfortunately, yes,' the big man growled.

'Unfortunately?' Iris looked at the Russian with renewed curiosity.

'He was a liar. Deceitful,' Vasile intoned, nodding towards Iris's portrait. 'He cheated many people out of money.'

'Is that so?'

'Of course. On the card tables and elsewhere. But I think you knew that, no? You show it in his eyes.'

'Do I?' Iris played for time. Her mind was replaying her discussion with Ian at the police station, about Dom's outstanding gambling debts to some angry and potentially violent people. 'Are you a poker player yourself, Mr Gretski?'

The big man grinned, revealing a set of surprisingly ugly crooked teeth. Vasile Gretski might have many vices, but clearly vanity was not among them.

'Sometimes. I play many games, Ms Grey.'

I bet you do, thought Iris.

'Did Dom owe you money?'

'Me?' Gretski let out a deep, booming laugh that made his broad chest shake. 'No! He wouldn't dare. But friends of mine, certainly.'

'You played him, though?'

The Russian nodded. 'Twice. In Oxford. We had some mutual acquaintances there.'

Oxford. Russians. Gambling debts.

Iris's mind raced. Half-remembered pieces of conversations – with the piano teacher, Harry Masters, and with Dom himself – drifted back to her, like parts of a puzzle.

'Wetherby was a wanted man in Oxford. At least for a while,' Vasile Gretski added. 'What was he like to paint?'

Iris didn't answer immediately. She was still trying to think about the Oxford connection. Hadn't there been a developer there, a Russian who wanted to build houses on Hazelford Meadows?

'Did he enjoy sitting for you? He was a very vain man, I believe. *Samovlyublennyy chelovek*, we say in Russian. "Narcissist."'

'He could be vain . . .' Iris replied, still dredging the recesses of her mind for the developer's name. Something beginning with 'G'. But not Gretski. She was just on the point of remembering when something in her peripheral vision distracted her.

Right next to the double doors leading out to the main lobby, Chris Wheeler had leaned forward and was whispering something in Rachel Truebridge's ear. Iris watched as Rachel recoiled, stung, burst into tears and then ran out of the room.

'Excuse me.' Iris disengaged from the Russian collector. She knew bullying when she saw it, and she wasn't going to stand for it, not at *her* unveiling night. 'It was lovely to meet you, but I must go and talk to someone.'

Making a beeline for Dom's rotund agent, she challenged him angrily. 'What did you just say to Rachel?'

Chris Wheeler smiled broadly, as if all were right with the world. 'Hello, Iris.'

'Don't "Hello, Iris" me!' Iris shot back. 'Answer me. What did you just say to upset her like that? I was watching you.'

'Nothing she didn't already know,' Chris said smoothly. 'Poor Dom couldn't shake the woman when he was alive,' he added, taking a cigarillo out of his inside jacket pocket and lighting it in defiance of the no-smoking signs. 'It seems a bit rich to keep stalking the bastard once he's dead. Don't you think?'

There was real cruelty in Wheeler's eyes. An expression of pure spite, like a cat toying with a mouse before the kill. Iris wondered how she'd failed to see it before, when she met the agent at the Mill. Had Dom known this side to him? Presumably he must have.

With a look of disgust, Iris left him and went outside in search of Rachel Truebridge.

There was no one at the coat check, and the lobby was deserted. Bracing herself against the cold, Iris pulled open the heavy front door of the gallery and stepped outside. The photographers and reporters had all gone home now, but Trafalgar Square was still busy with tourists and evening revellers, and it was difficult to make out anyone distinctly on the dark, crowded streets. Iris certainly couldn't see Rachel.

After a few more looks to left and right, she was just about to give up and go back inside when suddenly she spotted her, coatless and visibly distressed, on the opposite side of St Martin's Place. Her arm was raised, trying to hail a cab, but there were no orange 'for hire' lights to be seen.

'Rachel!' Iris shouted, but the din of the traffic drowned her out. She fought her way across the road, almost getting knocked flat by a bus. Infuriatingly, just as Iris made it to within shouting distance, a black cab pulled up and Rachel disappeared inside it, slipping off into the night.

Damn it!

Cold and frustrated, Iris stood on the kerbside as Rachel's taxi pulled away. Seconds later she saw two men in dark suits jump into an illegally parked Mercedes and speed after it. The same two men who'd been hovering protectively around Vasile Gretski just a few minutes ago.

They're following her! Iris felt deeply uneasy. Why would the Russian billionaire's goons be following Rachel Truebridge? What did she know that was making so many people so afraid?

It wasn't till she was back inside the warm fug of the gallery that it came back to her. Mill House. The Christmas Eve party. She didn't remember Vasile Gretski being there, but the two suited men definitely were! She only remembered because Graham told her he'd overheard them gossiping about Dom's unpaid debts or something like that, and she'd been amazed and impressed that Graham spoke Russian.

'There you are!' Graham wrapped his arm around her as soon as she walked back into the room. 'I've been hunting for you everywhere. I thought you'd left without me.'

'Sorry,' said Iris. She explained about Rachel, and the bullying she'd witnessed from Chris Wheeler. Then she told Dom about Vasile Gretski's two Russian goons tailing her in their car. 'They're the same two men from the Christmas Eve party at the Mill. The ones you overheard bitching in Russian about Dom buying that expensive car. Do you remember?'

'Vaguely,' Graham frowned. 'Are you sure it's the same guys?'

'Positive,' said Iris. 'I'm worried,' she added, leaning into him more closely. 'I actually think Rachel might be in some sort of danger. I'm certain they were following her, and they looked like thugs. Ariadne mentioned you were talking to Rachel earlier. Did she say anything to you? About being threatened or intimidated?'

Graham shook his head. 'No. Nothing like that. We talked about Dom. She was a bit upset and she left.'

'She came back, though,' said Iris. 'Why would she leave the party and then come back?'

Graham cupped Iris's face in his hands. 'I don't know, my love. But I do know Rachel Truebridge will be fine. She's a tough cookie. I also highly doubt the men you saw were following her.'

'They were! I saw them with my own eyes,' Iris insisted.

'You saw them get into a car and drive away,' Graham corrected her. 'That's all. You don't know where they were going. For what it's worth, I overheard Gretski talking earlier about going on to a private strip club in Mayfair after this. My guess is that he sent his guys ahead to check out the venue and make sure he'll be safe there.'

'Why wouldn't he be safe?' asked Iris.

Graham shrugged. 'He's an oligarch. When you're that rich, there are always people waiting in the shadows ready to slip polonium-210 into your green tea. Who were you talking to earlier, by the way? That grey-haired chap?'

It took Iris a moment to realise he was talking about Lars Berens, her sister's husband. For some reason, that bizarre encounter already felt as if it had happened ages ago, in the distant past. Too much had happened tonight. Too many connections were forming, or trying to form, in Iris's brain.

'Oh, he was just a journalist,' she lied. She was too emotionally exhausted to explain to Graham about Thea tonight, or about being randomly ambushed by her husband. Oddly, the one person she did want to tell was Ian. Especially the part about Thea having children. The unfairness of that, the hideous, ironic, unbearable *wrongness* of Thea getting to become a mother when Iris could not was a pain that only Ian would fully understand.

A wave of sadness overcame her suddenly.

'Are you all right, Iris?' Graham's kind eyes looked deeply into hers. 'You don't seem yourself, my darling.'

'I'm fine,' said Iris, pulling herself together. 'I need to go to Oxford.'

'Oxford?' Graham's frowned deepened. 'Why?'

'Because there's something going on with these Russians,' said Iris. 'And it's something to do with Dom's gambling debts, and the housing development he blocked in Hazelford, and Rachel Truebridge is connected somehow, and the whole thing started in Oxford.'

Graham kissed her softly on the forehead. 'You're not making much sense – you do know that?'

'It might be why Dom died,' Iris said simply. 'It might be the key to proving Ian's innocence.'

Graham stiffened.

'I know you don't like Ian,' said Iris, 'but this isn't about likes or dislikes. It's so much bigger than that, Graham. And I'll admit I don't see how any of the pieces fit together. Not yet. But if I'm going to stand a chance of working it out, I need to go to Oxford. I need to.'

Not for the first time Graham wondered what on earth went on in Iris Grey's chaotic but brilliant mind. He didn't want her to go to Oxford on some wild goose chase for her undeserving ex. He wanted her to stay here, in London, where the New Faces exhibition was about to start, with Iris's portrait as its centrepiece. He wanted her to stay with him. Always with him. But he knew that trying to stop her would be a mistake, not to mention futile.

Let her go. Let her reach a dead end on her own and come back to you.

'All right, my love,' he said resignedly. 'Whatever you need.

*

Ariadne Wetherby watched from an upstairs window as Graham Feeney put his arm around Iris's shoulders and walked her across the road to the taxi rank. Beside her, on a wide leather bench, Lorcan slept, using his mother's rolled-up scarf as a pillow. His breathing, deep and rhythmic, helped regulate Ariadne's own.

Tonight had been a risk. Calculated, but none the less terrifying for that.

Now, thank God, it was over.

It was over and everything was all right.

Rachel Truebridge had been frightened off. *Good riddance.*

Iris and Graham would walk off into the sunset together. They would fall in love and leave the Mill and never come back.

Never.

Turning away from the window, Ariadne placed a hand on Lorcan's chest, feeling it softly rise and fall. Dom had always said that a wise man should keep his friends close and his enemies closer. Well, tonight Ariadne had done just that.

'Are you proud of me, my darling?' she whispered aloud. 'I do hope so. I miss you, Dom.'

As she said the words, she realised they were true.

Covering Lorcan gently with her coat, she crept back down to the party.

CHAPTER TWENTY-TWO

Built on the banks of the Cherwell at the eastern end of the High Street, just over Magdalen Bridge, St Hilda's was certainly not the most beautiful of Oxford's colleges.

'Sturdy' and, at a pinch, 'handsome' were the kindest adjectives the various city guidebooks used to describe the solid late-Victorian brick buildings of the famous women's college, named after the patron saint of learning and culture.

Only of course it wasn't a women's college anymore, Iris remembered, doing a double-take at all the young men darting in and out of the porter's lodge to collect their college post, while she picked up her room keys. As a member of the college, she was entitled to stay in one of the 'guest rooms' for a nominal rent if she chose to. St Hilda's accommodation was far from luxurious, but Iris preferred the nostalgia of being back in her old stomping ground to the comfort of a hotel suite. She rarely came to Oxford, and she wanted to make the most of it, even if she was here under strange and difficult circumstances.

It all felt so different, though! According to the latest shiny St Hilda's prospectus, which Iris had been sent in the post, almost half the undergraduates matriculating last year had been boys.

In Iris's day, it had still been all girls, although even then the prospect of allowing men to apply had been a hotly debated topic. Iris herself had been passionately opposed at the time, although she couldn't totally remember why now. Possibly to impress Ian McBride with her left-wing feminist credentials.

Almost everything Iris did in those days came back to Ian, one way or another.

A cheerful elderly porter handed Iris her keys. 'Welcome back, madam,' he said. 'You'll be staying in the Wolfson Building. Two nights, is it?'

'Probably,' said Iris. 'I might need three.'

'Whatever you need, madam. We're delighted to have you.' The old man was so sincere Iris could have hugged him. 'Do you remember where you're going, or would you like a map?'

Iris said she remembered. Taking her keys and a sheaf of papers, most of them thinly veiled requests for money disguised as 'news-letters', she made her way across the quad towards her staircase.

A light snow had been falling for the past few hours, dusting the city in a bright white coating of icing sugar. It was three o'clock now and still light, with a pale sun hanging in a brilliant crisp-blue sky. It was the sort of day that demanded hope and optimism. Iris felt both, although they were mingled with other, more complex feel-ings of nostalgia and loss. Every doorway, every tree, every distantly pealing church bell reminded her of her youth, her student self. And that, in turn, brought back memories of her and Ian. Of how happy they'd been, how besotted, how utterly, helplessly, gloriously in love.

What had happened to those two people? Ian had changed beyond all recognition. But then, if Iris were honest, so had she.

God, it was cold! Having finally reached the Wolfson Building, she trudged up C staircase and blew on her fingers until they were warm enough to enable her to retrieve the key from her pocket and open the door to her room. Inside, a huge ancient radiator blasted out heat, transforming the spartan space into a mini furnace. Turning it down, Iris surveyed the room. There was a single bed, a battered chest of drawers and a desk with a bunch of plastic flowers on it. On the far wall, one door opened onto a minuscule bathroom consisting of a loo, a handbasin and a shower so cramped it was hard to imagine how a grown man could have used it. A second door led into a 'kitchenette', which was basically a countertop and a small sink. Iris saw a kettle and a toaster, as well as a microwave that looked dangerously old and decrepit, and would probably irradiate anyone foolish enough to try to use it.

It was all exactly what she'd expected. What she'd wanted. But now that she was actually here, she felt inexplicably depressed. Claustrophobic, and trapped, and just . . . sad.

She'd remembered the name of the Russian developer Harry Masters had mentioned to her, all those weeks ago. *Gardievski. Igor Gardievski.*

Tomorrow she would track him down. She would find out all she could about the aborted housing development, and about Dom's unpaid poker debts. She would ask about Vasíle Gretski, and the two men she'd first seen at Dom Wetherby's party who'd turned up to her portrait unveiling and taken off after Rachel Truebridge. She would make the puzzle pieces fit, somehow.

But not tonight.

Tonight she would go out and grab some takeaway, and eat it in this little room, and think about her life, and Ian, and what had gone wrong. She wanted things to work out with Graham Feeney. She really did. But for that to happen, she had to lay the ghost of her marriage to rest for good.

Was that part of why you needed to come to Oxford? Iris asked herself. *Part of what was pulling you back here? Was that the part you couldn't tell Graham?*

With a sinking heart, she realised that it was.

Iris had come to Oxford for closure, not just for Dom Wetherby but for herself.

Would she find it?

Lying back onto the single bed, she closed her eyes.

One step at a time, Iris. One step at a time.

Iris woke at five, feeling tired and hung-over. The bottle of Rioja had seemed like a great idea last night, especially after two chicken kebabs from the van on Iffley Road, but with hindsight it probably hadn't been her smartest move of all time.

After taking an Alka-Seltzer and going back to bed, she woke again at seven feeling slightly better. A shower, two strong coffees and a fried breakfast later, Iris felt strong enough to put on her coat, scarf and bobble hat, and walk to the Bodleian Library. The walk took longer than usual. Snow had continued falling through the night and yesterday's light dusting was now a thick, soft, clogging blanket of white that had slowed the entire city, blocking roads and making even cycling impossible in many places. Making her way past giggling, snowball-throwing undergraduates, Iris snagged herself a space at one of the Bodleian computers and got to work.

Finding Igor Gardievski's company address and phone number online took a matter of minutes. Spire Properties International were based on one of the large industrial estates on the Oxford ring road, although they also had premises in London, Moscow and Hong Kong. If Gardievski really was the kind of man who had people murdered over unpaid gambling debts or cancelled development contracts, then he'd done a good job of masking it beneath a legitimate, professional façade. Iris spent another hour and a half at the library, searching for articles, tweets, anything that might link Gardievski or his company to illegal activity: gambling, coercion, blackmail, violence. But there was nothing to find. Vasile Gretski had enough rumours flying around about him to launch a slew of libel actions, if he wanted to. But according to the Internet, his friend Igor Gardievski was clean as a whistle.

A small local article did mention the denial of Spire's planning application to develop at Hazelford last year. Gardievski was quoted as being 'disappointed', but that was it. Dom was quoted in the same piece, rambling on about the importance of 'grassroots activism' in preserving the nation's 'glorious green spaces'. There was a picture of him with Ariadne, arm in arm before the church, with a crowd of villagers apparently cheering in the background. Lorcan was standing in front of his parents, smiling at the camera as he always did. Iris looked at the picture for a long time, struck by something about it that she couldn't quite name. In the end she gave up. Whatever it was would probably come to her later, when she was less hung-over.

Packing up her things, she logged out, grabbed her coat and headed for the nearest taxi rank.

Igor Gardievski had just hung up on a difficult call to one of his investors in Moscow when his secretary bustled in.

'I'm sorry, Mr G,' the girl whined, in the nasal Birmingham accent that Igor somehow hadn't noticed when he interviewed her but that now grated on him daily, like a squirt of lemon juice in the eyes, 'but there's a lady outside who's refusing to leave the premises until she talks to you. I've told her your agenda's full and she needs to make an appointment, but she's not budging. Should I ask security to get rid of her?'

'Is she a reporter?' Igor scowled.

'I don't think so. She didn't say so.'

'Well, who is she?'

'Her name's Iris Grey. Says she's an artist.'

'An artist?' Igor's scowl deepened. 'What business can an artist have with me?'

'I asked her what she wants to see you about, but all she said was it's a "private matter".'

Igor gave an irritated grunt. In Russia, you could eject anyone you wanted from your own offices with no questions asked: artists, beggars, disgruntled investors, ex-lovers. Here, you could hire security, but if any of them actually laid a finger on someone, especially a woman, you risked lawsuits at dawn.

'Show her in,' he growled.

'Are you sure?' the secretary asked. 'Because I could—'

'I just said so, didn't I?' snapped Igor. 'Tell her she's got five minutes. And warn her in advance I'm not buying any damn art.'

As soon as Iris walked in, however, Igor's entire manner changed. This particular 'artist' was a strikingly good-looking woman, and very much his type. Igor liked his women tiny and breakable. His wife, Irina, had been that way once, before the children and middle age had thickened her waist into that of a babushka doll.

'Ms Grey.' He gave Iris his most ingratiating smile. 'I don't believe we've met. To what do I owe the pleasure?'

His English is a lot better than Vasile Gretski's, thought Iris. She'd pictured him as a Muscovite thug in the Gretski mould, when in fact he was anything but.

'I'm a friend of Dom Wetherby's.' Iris waited for him to flinch, but there was no discernible reaction. Even when she dived directly into questions about his relationship with Dom and the soured Hazelford housing deal, he betrayed not the slightest emotion. Instead, he waited patiently for her to finish and then said simply, 'I was shocked when I heard about Dom. Very shocked.'

Stretching out his long legs in front of him on the expensive leather sofa where both he and Iris were sitting, he seemed utterly at ease.

He's an attractive man, Iris thought, more handsome in person than in the pictures she'd seen online. There was a certain languid grace about him, a confidence of manner that oddly reminded her of Dom.

'Murder is a shocking thing, after all,' he went on, as unperturbed as if they were talking about the weather. 'And yet on the other hand I was not entirely surprised. It's no secret that Dom Wetherby and I were not friends. But many, many people had an issue with him.'

Iris's eyes narrowed. This comment echoed what Vasile Gretski and others had told her. It was uncanny how often, when she asked somebody about their own enmity with Dom, they would rush to draw attention to everybody else's.

'What was your issue, Mr Gardievski?'

'Igor, please. He owed me money,' he answered, matter-of-factly. 'And I found him to be dishonest in our business dealings.'

'Dishonest enough for you to want him dead?'

Igor's smile didn't waver. 'For me personally? No. But others may have wished that. Certainly. The man was dishonest in business and he was dishonest at the card table, which many consider to be worse. When I heard he was dead, I supposed that somebody, one of the many people he cheated, must have had enough and snapped.'

'Dom's murder was carefully orchestrated,' said Iris. 'Both in its execution and afterwards. The killer left almost no physical evidence. This wasn't a case of somebody "snapping", Mr Gardievski.'

Igor held out his arms in an innocent, 'if you say so' gesture.

'I imagine this must be painful for you, Ms Grey,' he said. 'You mentioned earlier that the two of you were friends. But I fear that perhaps you and I saw different sides of Dom Wetherby.'

'We weren't close,' Iris clarified. 'His wife had commissioned me to paint his portrait. We were halfway through when he died.'

Igor leaned forward, looking at Iris more closely. 'Wait a minute,' he said, belatedly putting the pieces together. 'Didn't I read about you in the newspaper? Aren't you the one whose husband was arrested? For Dom's murder?'

'Yes,' Iris admitted grudgingly. 'Except that he's my estranged husband, and he didn't do it. He's been released.'

'But you're still trying to help him?' Gardievski observed. 'How noble of you.'

Iris couldn't tell if he was angry or amused. Or perhaps he was just pleased to have manoeuvred her onto the back foot.

She was finding it altogether harder than she'd thought to get a handle on the Russian. He was certainly slick, and she imagined him to be not entirely trustworthy, but at the same time he appeared a long way removed from the brutal enforcer she'd expected, or perhaps hoped for.

'You mentioned Ariadne commissioned you,' he said. 'How is she doing? I always thought she was a good woman, a good wife to Dom. Better than he deserved, that's for sure.'

'She's doing well,' said Iris, cautiously. 'As far as I can tell.'

'And the boy, Lorcan. I imagine his father's death must have been especially hard for him.'

'Yes,' Iris agreed. 'It's hard to explain something like that to a child, particularly one with Lorcan's problems.'

The two of them sat in silence for a moment, mentally sizing one another up. *It's like playing a game of chess*, thought Iris. It occurred to her that Russians were supposed to be awfully good at chess.

'So you and Dom were social friends,' she said eventually. 'It wasn't only a business relationship. You knew his family.'

'We played poker together,' Igor confirmed. 'Mostly we played here, in Oxford. But I also visited Dom's house once or twice, around the time we were pitching the Hazelford development.'

'What happened with that?' asked Iris, pleased to have moved the subject on from Ian. 'I mean, I know Dom opposed it. The new houses would have spoiled his view from the Mill.'

Igor laughed loudly. 'Spoiled his view? I can assure you, Ms Grey, Dom Wetherby couldn't have cared less about his "view", or protecting the environment, or any of that crap he spouted to the parish council. The whole thing was about money.'

'In what way?'

'Wetherby was a greedy bastard,' Igor said simply. 'That's the bottom line. We'd agreed to cut him in from the beginning – ten per cent of the profits from the Hazelford Meadows development, if he helped us get it through planning. But at the eleventh hour he decided he wanted more. Twenty per cent, which is a preposterous figure, well outside industry norms.'

'You're saying you offered him a bribe?' asked Iris.

'Yes. And he took it, with both hands! Don't look so shocked, Ms Grey,' Igor smiled. 'This is the way the real-estate business functions. Although we prefer the word "incentive" here at Spire.

But in any event, in the end there *was* no incentive payment made to Wetherby, because I told him in no uncertain terms that twenty per cent was a non-starter. He was furious. I think he needed to raise money very badly at that time.'

'Why?' Iris asked.

Igor shrugged. 'I don't know. There were various rumours swirling around. Some mistress he had to pay off.'

Iris's mind immediately flew to Rachel Truebridge. Would she really have asked Dom for money?

'Personally, I think it's more likely his poker debts had got out of hand,' said Igor. 'He owed me six figures, and I know for a fact I wasn't the only one. In any case, he asked for more on the Hazelford deal, I told him no, and he voted down the development. That was it.'

'You must have lost a lot of money,' Iris observed.

'Yes,' Igor admitted.

Was it Iris's imagination or was his smile starting to look just a little more forced?

'That can't have made you happy.'

'No. It didn't,' he said. 'I set my lawyers on Wetherby for the unpaid poker debts. They sent him a bunch of letters, none of which he responded to. After that we tried to get a lien on his house.'

'Did you succeed?' Iris was curious. This was the first she'd heard that Mill House itself might have been under threat. She wondered whether Ariadne had known, or whether Dom had kept his legal troubles a secret, like so much else.

'Not so far. We're still trying,' said Igor. 'I'm pursuing Dom's estate at the moment, via a Mr James Smythe. Do you know him?'

Smythe. Iris remembered him vaguely. He was the lawyer Billy had assaulted at Dom's wake. The one who was helping Marcus and Ariadne challenge Billy's entitlements under his father's will. Cant had wanted Smythe to press charges, but the lawyer had refused, no doubt wanting to protect his lucrative relationship with Billy's mother.

'Look, Ms Grey,' Igor concluded, 'I think it's a noble thing you're doing, trying to clear your husband's name.'

'I'm trying to find out what happened to Dom,' Iris clarified. 'That's all.'

'You understand that there are some, myself included, who might argue Dom Wetherby deserved his fate?'

'No one should get away with murder, Mr Gardievski,' Iris said seriously.

'I agree,' said Igor. 'But I would caution you to beware of lazy stereotypes. Not all of us Russians are Putin's thugs,' he added, his tone warmer than his words suggested. 'Yes, I had a grievance against Dom, and yes, I disliked him. Not at first. But I came to dislike him, as I suspect you would have, had he lived. I didn't kill him, though, or pay anyone else to do so. I have nothing to hide.'

Iris left Spire Properties' offices thinking about Igor Gardievski's parting words. She strongly suspected that the smooth-talking Russian, with his perfect English and easy smiles, had plenty to hide. But at the same time, she had no reason to believe he was behind Dom's murder. Other than her deep need to believe that Ian didn't do it, she had not a shred of evidence.

There *was* something else, though, something swirling in her subconscious, trying to float its way up to the surface but not quite making it.

The picture she'd looked at earlier in the Bodleian.

Lorcan. Ariadne. Dom. All in front of the church, with the crowd of villagers.

Iris thought about Lorcan and his terror of ghosts. His insistence that it was a 'ghost' that killed his daddy. But the ghost of what?

Of Christmases past?

Of Dom's past?

Something that had returned to haunt him? Something he'd thought was dead and buried?

What had Igor said just now?

'*There were various rumours swirling around. Some mistress he had to pay off.*'

All at once Jenna Wetherby's words came back to Iris. '*There were rumours about plagiarism, hidden things in his father's past.*'

If that were true, it would be a scandal, a secret Dom would want to keep hidden at all costs. But *was* it true? And where would Rachel have heard about it? Surely it would have to have been here, in Oxford. Where Dom wrote the first Grimshaw book. Where everything started.

Her trip to Gardievski may have been a dead end, but Oxford itself had set Iris's mind racing. Where better than here to hunt for Dom Wetherby's ghosts?

Iris hailed a cab.

'Christ Church College, please. Main gate.'

As a university member, Iris was free to wander around any Oxford college, including the parts that were closed to tourists or off limits to the general public. Christ Church was Oxford's largest, and some felt grandest, college, famous for Great Tom, the bell in Tom Tower on St Aldate's, as iconic an image of the university as any and a backdrop for countless movies from *Brideshead Revisited* to *Harry Potter*.

Iris didn't know it well, however. Ian had been at Balliol, and her own undergraduate life had revolved exclusively around St Hilda's, Balliol, the union and the library. Graham once told her that Dom and Marcus used to share rooms in Peck, and Iris was about to head there just to walk through the quad and get a feel for it when a name on the porter's lodge board caught her eye.

'Professor Nevers.' She cornered one of the undergrads milling around. 'That isn't William Nevers, is it? The English don?'

The girl nodded. 'Prof. Nevers is a legend. He's been here longer than the gargoyles.'

'Is he still teaching?' Iris asked, trying to fathom how old this man must be, if he'd taught Dom and Graham's brother.

'He's ninety-eight.' The girl grinned. 'There's an active book running on whether he'll make his century. But yes, he still takes tutorials, and he's sharp as a tack apparently.'

Excited, Iris hurried to the staircase leading to the professor's rooms, a large suite overlooking Christ Church Meadows and the river. To be able to talk to Dom's old professor, the man who knew him back when he wrote the very first Grimshaw book! It was more than Iris had hoped for. When she got to Professor Nevers's rooms, however, the heavy wooden outer door was locked, and the old-fashioned sign outside it, next to the professor's name, had been switched to 'Out'.

'If you're looking for Prof. Nevers, 'e's gone to his daughter's in Burford for the weekend,' an apple-cheeked scout, or college cleaner, informed Iris helpfully in a broad Oxfordshire accent. 'Won't be back till Monday now, my lovely.'

Iris bit back her disappointment.

Oh well. It wouldn't kill her to stay in town for the weekend. There was no way she was going to miss out on the chance to talk with Dom's old professor. While she was waiting, she could visit her favourite art supply store in Summertown and go to the Identities exhibition at the Sarah Wiseman Gallery. She might even manage to unearth some other leads relating to Dom's Oxford days, although for the moment she couldn't think where to start.

Later, back at St Hilda's, Iris checked her messages. There were two from Ian, 'just checking in'. Iris tried not to be irritated. Was he checking in on *her* or on whether she'd made any progress identifying Dom Wetherby's real killer? She told herself it was normal for Ian to be anxious, with the cloud of public suspicion still hanging over him, and DI Cant doing everything he could to try to connect him to the murder. Of course clearing his name would be his priority. Even so, it felt strange and irksome to be being hounded for progress reports by the man whose divorce lawyer was still trying to rob her blind.

After Ian's messages there was a long voicemail from Graham, telling her how much he missed her and how cold and lonely London was without her.

'I hope you're being careful, Iris,' he ended. 'I know you don't want to believe your ex is involved in any of this, but Ian's out of custody now, and I know I'm not the only one who's worried about what he might do. Call if you need me, night or day. And for God's sake, lock your doors.'

Part of Iris wanted to laugh. *Lock your doors? Against Ian?*

But another part of her felt disconcerted. She knew Ian was innocent. But somebody had killed Dom. If she was getting closer to finding that somebody, or to unearthing secrets that they or other, powerful people wanted to stay buried . . . perhaps she *was* in danger.

Standing alone in her tiny college room, Iris felt the hairs on her forearms stand on end. As if Lorcan Wetherby's murderous ghost was passing over her grave.

CHAPTER TWENTY-THREE

Professor Nevers' rooms reminded Iris strongly of Dumbledore's study. There was an age-worn high wooden schoolmaster's desk complete with a working inkwell and fountain pen, a long refectory table sporting an antique Victorian globe, various stuffed animals in glass cases and endless piles of books and papers, all in various stages of disarray to the naked eye but no doubt organised according to some precise and peculiar pattern known only to the professor himself. In the corner, a day-bed strewn with dusty kilim cushions and animal hides looked suspiciously as if the professor might have spent the night on it.

The old man assured her that this wasn't the case, however. 'June drove me in from Burford this morning,' William Nevers informed Iris in the wheezy, high-pitched whisper that passed for a voice in his tenth decade. 'She's a good girl, June. Well, I shouldn't say "girl", I suppose. She's seventy-three now, if you can believe it.' He smiled, a broad, gummy affair that lit up his whole face and made Iris want to paint him immediately. 'Funny to think of one's children being that sort of age. Do you have children, Miss Grey?'

'Er, no,' said Iris, feeling stupidly flustered. 'No, I don't.'

For years she'd dreaded that question. Or rather, she'd dreaded her answer, dreaded the doom-laden sound of the word 'no' on her own lips. But recently she found she'd begun not to care, or at least not to care as much. Leaving Ian, and perhaps finding Graham, had given her a new sense of purpose and possibility, outside of the concept of motherhood.

'Never wanted them, or couldn't have them?' the professor asked in his clipped upper-class voice, pushing the nail deeper into Iris's side with the refreshing bluntness that was the prerogative of the very old and very young.

'Couldn't have them,' Iris answered, managing a smile.

'Pity,' said the professor.

'Yes,' agreed Iris, thinking how much he reminded her of a 1950s television announcer.

Changing the subject, she asked, 'Professor Nevers, would it be all right if I asked you a couple of questions about a former pupil of yours? Dominic Wetherby?'

'Of course, my dear, of course!' Rising up out of his chair slowly, his knee joints creaking audibly as he moved, the old man shuffled over to the kettle. 'May I offer you a cup of tea?'

Iris nodded.

'Builder's all right?'

'Fine, thank you,' said Iris. 'You remember him, then?'

'Wetherby? Hard to forget him, I'd say.' Professor Nevers gave a dry, deep-throated cackle. 'Even if you wanted to, if you know what I mean. I remember all my students, Miss Grey. But Wetherby never tired of telling people how brilliant he was and how he was going to change the world. I suppose, in his own small way, he did.'

Shuffling back across the room with two mugs of tea, he handed one to Iris and creaked down into his chair, like a leaky galleon easing itself unsteadily into the water. 'He was never the star of that tutorial group, though. I think perhaps the hubris was a bit of an act. Overcompensating, you know.'

Iris wasn't sure she did. 'Dom didn't stand out among his peers?'

'Not as a writer, no.' The professor sipped his tea contemplatively. 'No, it was his friend who was the bright light. Marcus Feeney. Quite brilliant, that chap was. Meeker than Dominic, but by God, he had talent. As a poet, an essayist. He was a remarkable young man. So very sad what happened to him. It was here, you know, in Oxford, that he died.'

Iris looked perplexed. The old boy must have got his dates wrong.

'Actually, I think Marcus committed suicide the year after he and Dom went down. Or possibly even two years after. Marcus's younger brother, Graham, is a close friend of mine, so I know some of the story.'

'Some but not all, it would appear.' The professor raised an eyebrow knowingly. 'It was two years after *Wetherby* went down. The same year that that dreadful potboiler of his came out and caused such a sensation, if memory serves. But Feeney stayed on to do his PhD. He jumped from a seventh-floor flat in one of those horrible blocks on Cowley Road. Leaped off his balcony. No warning. No signs of depression. No *reason*. I'll never forget it.'

It would be easy enough to check the details, but Iris had no reason to believe Professor Nevers wasn't correct. As the undergraduate had told her, the old man was still sharp as a tack. What troubled her was why Graham *hadn't* told her that his brother had died in Oxford. No wonder he had bad memories of the place and hadn't wanted her to come. But why wouldn't he just say so?

'Did Dom ever come back here?' Iris asked. 'For gaudies or to give talks or whatever?'

'No.' Professor Nevers rubbed his rheumy eyes with gnarled fingers. 'I daresay the place held bad memories for him after that awful business with Feeney. They were very close as young men.'

Iris nodded, thinking.

'His wife, I believe, has visited. I introduced the two of them, you know. Ariadne Hinchley, as she was then. I knew her father, Clive. Nasty piece of work, in my opinion, but the daughter always seemed charming.'

He was rambling, but Iris let him go on. She was curious to hear that Professor Nevers had disliked Ariadne's father, given the dark past that Harry Masters had hinted at. Perhaps old Harry had been on to something after all?

'In any case, Ariadne Wetherby has visited and she's also donated money to the college on at least two occasions. Once shortly after Feeney died and again just recently.'

'Really?' Iris was surprised. She'd have imagined Ariadne's causes of choice to be something to do with animals or the arts, and she knew the family donated to Down's syndrome charities. But Dom's old college must have one of the biggest endowments of any educational establishment in the world. Why Christ Church? And if she was going to donate to Oxford at all, why not her own college, St Anne's?

'The papers say that Wetherby was murdered.' Professor Nevers looked questioningly at Iris.

'He was,' she said. 'Somebody drugged him unconscious, then tied a weight round his feet and drowned him in the river, just yards from his house.'

'I see.' The old man seemed unfazed by these details, no doubt having read them before. 'And how did you know him?'

Iris recounted the details. Her work as a portrait artist seemed to fascinate Professor Nevers considerably more than Dom Wetherby's murder.

'I've always considered there was an alchemy to good portraiture. Don't you agree? There's a certain magic to it, because of the *layers*.'

'The layers?'

'Yes. The picture you paint on the surface – the recording of the subject's features and expression and whatnot – and then the picture that emerges underneath.'

'You mean the sides of people's character that they don't want you to see?' asked Iris, curious.

'Partly that,' said the professor, 'but also the background. The little details. *Where* a person chooses to be painted, for example. What room they're in, what chair, what position. What are the objects behind them? The shadows? The clues? I always feel that the best portraits are the ones in which every brush stroke has meaning. Yes, you're trying to capture a person, but none of us exists in a vacuum, do we?'

Iris cocked her head to one side and looked at him differently. This was an incredibly perceptive comment, and a true one. Dom hadn't existed in a vacuum. He'd chosen to be painted in his study, at home at the Mill. That place, that background, had meant something to him.

And what about Iris? What had *she* chosen to pick up on in that room? What elements of Dom's background had spoken to her strongly enough to warrant a brush stroke, to be committed for ever to canvas and posterity, to be preserved as 'shadows' or 'clues'?

And that was when she remembered.

She closed her eyes. In her mind, the dominoes fell, one by one.

The portrait.

The study.
The background.
Her stomach lurched.

'Are you all right, my dear?' The old man leaned forward, concerned. 'Can I get you something? A glass of water?'

'No. Thank you.' Iris stood up, dazed. She wanted to be wrong. *Please, please let me be wrong.* 'I have to go. I've an exhibition just starting in London and I . . . I need to speak to my agent. Thank you for talking to me, Professor. Goodbye.'

She shook his hand and hurried out of the room, out into the cold, misty air of Christ Church Meadows. Her fingers shook as she dialled Greta's number.

'Do you have a photograph of Dom's portrait on your computer? A high-res one?'

'Hello, Iris!' her agent answered happily. 'Funnily enough, I just got off the line with David Bone. They've had record attendance for the New Faces exhibition, all thanks to you, Iris. He even asked me whether—'

'Greta, I'm sorry, but this is urgent. I need a photo of the painting.'

'But surely you have one? On your phone or somewhere? You must do.' Iris's agent sounded baffled.

'I don't. I'm sorry. Do you?'

Greta gave the sigh of a woman used to dealing with artists and their panic attacks but still irritated by them. 'Of course. I'll send it to you in a mnute. But, Iris, you do realise it's too late to make changes now? The painting doesn't even belong to us.'

'I know that,' Iris snapped. 'I don't want to change it, Greta. I just need to see it again. As soon as possible.'

Sixty seconds later a 'ding' on her phone indicated the image had arrived. Iris opened it, her heart in her mouth. She thought she remembered, was pretty certain, in fact, but she needed to see it to be sure.

There it was.

A tiny, insignificant detail. Just a few brush strokes. But it was enough.

It was everything.

CHAPTER TWENTY-FOUR

Lorcan Wetherby held his mother's hand as they walked up the kitchen stairs together, along the flagstoned hallway to the front door. Lorcan had learned to fear the ring of the doorbell. It meant that the Mill, his home and long his sanctuary, was under threat. It meant that outside things wanted to come in. Outside things should not come in. Outside things, Lorcan had learned, could hurt you. But as long as his mother was with him, he could manage his fears. Her hand was a talisman. Her long, cool fingers entwined in his were like a force field of love and safety.

His mother would save him.

Ariadne opened the door, smiling serenely. 'Oh! It's you. I thought you were away.'

Iris stood against a backdrop of a bright blue March sky, the first properly sunny day of the spring. In the front garden at the Mill, a few brave crocuses were beginning to poke their heads above ground, while the snowdrops hung theirs, acknowledging the end of a long winter. Iris herself still looked wintery in black corduroy skinnies and a deep maroon sweater, teamed with a thick, puffy black coat. A geometric-print pink-and-green scarf was the only pop of real colour, but it wasn't enough to lift her pale, make-up-free complexion or to distract from her tired, swollen eyes.

'I was,' she said. 'In Oxford. Is it all right if I come in?'

'Of course.' Ariadne threw her arms wide and stepped back in a gesture of welcome. Lorcan, who'd always liked Iris, smiled shyly from his position of safety, pressed against his mother's side. Unthinking, Ariadne kissed the top of his head as she closed the door behind them.

Whatever happened between her and Billy, whatever her failings as a mother, she adores that kid, thought Iris. *And he her.*

As so often with Ariadne, Iris felt her emotions swing from distrust back to warmth, and from admiration to condemnation, like a pendulum. She believed what Billy had told her that night in her cottage. That sort of misery and desperation couldn't be faked. And yet Billy's version of his mother wasn't any more true than the love Iris saw in Lorcan's eyes right now, or the overprotective adoration Marcus constantly displayed towards his mother. Was it possible for someone to be both a really good mother and a really bad one at the same time?

Perhaps it was. And really, who was Iris to say otherwise? She would never be a mother.

'Would you like a cup of tea?' Ariadne asked, holding out a hand for Iris's coat.

'Biscuit!' Lorcan shouted excitedly, relieved that today's 'outside person' had turned out only to be Iris.

'Lorcan and I just made a batch of shortbread,' Ariadne explained, adding, sotto voce, 'He's doing *sooo* much better.'

'I'd love one,' said Iris, returning Lorcan's smile. 'But I actually came by . . .' She swallowed nervously, suddenly not sure how to bring it up. In the end, she opted for the direct approach, not because she felt confident in it but because she couldn't think of anything cleverer to say. 'I wondered if I could see Dom's study again. The sofa where he sat for our portrait sittings.'

'Certainly.' Ariadne turned left and led the way. If she considered Iris's request a strange one, she didn't show it. Iris followed, with Lorcan trotting along at Ariadne's side like a sweetly affectionate puppy. 'Here we are.'

Iris took a moment to reconnect to the room. The smell, Dom's smell, was still there, but it had grown fainter. Someone had dusted, and opened the windows. The desk had been lightly tidied, but otherwise everything was the same.

Almost everything.

Iris looked again at the shelves behind Dom's Chesterfield, which had formed the backdrop to his portrait. And then she looked again, up and down, left to right, as if looking might make the missing object reappear.

'Is something troubling you, Iris?' Ariadne asked.

'No,' Iris lied, hoping her smile didn't look as fake as it felt. 'I was just trying to visualise something, about the portrait. Do you know, has anything been moved in here since D—' Clocking Lorcan's curious face, she checked herself. 'Since Christmas?'

'I don't think so,' Ariadne said breezily. 'I mean, there were unopened bills and things that Marcus dealt with. He went through Dom's post that first week, before he went back to London.'

'Other than that,' said Iris. 'Has anyone else used the room?'

'Well, after the coroner's report, the police were in here,' said Ariadne. 'But I must say they were very respectful and put everything back where they found it. Is it something specific you're looking for, my dear?'

Ariadne seemed unruffled, but Lorcan was looking up at Iris with big, worried eyes.

'Oh no. Nothing specific.' She smiled at him reassuringly, adding with a wink, 'Does the offer of a biscuit still stand?'

As soon as they left the study, Lorcan seemed happier, and was positively delighted in the kitchen, laying the shortbread out on his favourite *Scooby-Doo* plate.

'So how are things with you and Graham?' Ariadne asked, delicately pouring milk into her cup of Earl Grey.

'Fine.' Iris smiled noncommittally. 'We haven't seen each other for a few days. I've been away, and he's working.'

'I know,' said Ariadne. 'He called me yesterday, bless his heart, to tell me he'd heard from Billy. He's in London, apparently, at some sort of rehab, halfway-house place. Graham said he sounded better. I must say it was a huge relief.'

'I can imagine,' said Iris. An image of Billy, shaking and rocking in her bedroom closet, leaped unbidden into her mind. Then another, of him rolling back his sleeve to reveal the row of cigarette burns. *No one's ever believed me . . . She hurt me. Bullied me.*

'Having a child like that, who self-harms . . . there's never an end to it,' said Ariadne. 'The worry, I mean.'

She sounds so believable, thought Iris. But then so did Billy. Talking to the Wetherby family was like trying to find one's way through a hall of mirrors. Everything was distorted somehow. Nothing was certain.

'He won't let me see him.' Ariadne stared down into the tea leaves at the bottom of her cup. 'But Graham said he'd pop in and visit at the end of the week. He really has been a saint through all this. I'm so glad the two of you have found one another.'

'Well, it's early days,' Iris said awkwardly. She finished her tea and took her leave, promising to come back and play Jenga with Lorcan soon.

Ariadne walked her to the door. As they passed the study, she casually observed, 'Of course, there is one person who's used Dom's room regularly.'

Iris stopped and turned to face her. 'Oh?'

'Graham.' Ariadne smiled, pleased to have remembered.

'Graham?' Iris's brow furrowed.

'Yes. After Marcus and Jenna went back to London. You remember when he came and stayed in the village and helped me organise everything with the police and the funeral and Dom's will?'

Iris remembered. Graham had taken a room at the pub in Hazelford. But he had spent huge amounts of time at Mill House.

'Dom's study was his little command centre,' Ariadne continued. 'Or perhaps it was his escape from all of us – I'm not sure which.' She laughed softly. 'But you should ask Graham if he can help you. He'd know if anything had been moved around since you painted in there.'

'Thank you,' Iris said stiffly, feeling the knot in her stomach tighten. 'I will.'

Outside, she took three deep, calming breaths and checked her watch: 1.15 p.m.

If she hurried, she could still catch the two o'clock train to Paddington.

Ian met Iris at a swanky bar on Piccadilly. Despite the jacket and tie – he'd attempted to make an effort – he looked drawn and haggard. Clearly he hadn't slept properly in days.

'You don't look well,' Iris said, ordering a much-needed double gin and tonic for herself and a Virgin Mary for Ian, who wanted her to know he was still on the wagon.

'I've been better.' He tapped his fingers nervously on the bar. 'Yesterday I had a bunch of deranged Grimshaw fans hanging around outside the flat yelling, "Murderer!" up at the bedroom windows.'

'That's harassment,' said Iris angrily. 'Did you call the police?'

'The police?' Ian scoffed. 'Who do you think leaked my address on the bloody Internet? That bastard Cant's determined to ruin me, by hook or by crook, and the truth be damned.'

Iris put a comforting hand on his shoulder, then withdrew it quickly. After the whole debacle with Billy, she didn't want to be accused of giving out any more 'mixed messages'.

'How was Oxford?' Ian asked gloomily. 'Did you meet with the Russian developer?'

'Gardievski. I did,' said Iris. 'Dom wasn't top of his Christmas-card list, that's for sure. From what he said, Dom royally screwed him over the Hazelford development project. But I don't think he had anything to do with Dom's murder.'

'Why not?' Ian sounded almost petulant. 'He's a nasty guy, you know. I looked into his last two businesses before Spire and he's been accused of all sorts: intimidation, threats. Back in Moscow, he allegedly sent his goons to rough up a supplier who owed him money. The guy was beaten so badly he lost the sight in one eye.'

'I'm not saying he's Mother Teresa.' Iris sipped her drink. 'Just that there's no evidence tying him to Dom's drowning.'

'I'm not saying he drove down to Hampshire and did it himself.' Ian was becoming exasperated. 'He'll have had people, paid hitmen . . .'

Iris shook her head. It wasn't beyond the imagination that Igor Gardievski might do such a thing. But the plain truth was, he hadn't done it, much as both Ian and Iris might wish he had.

'I need to talk to you about Rachel Truebridge.' Iris cut to the chase.

'Rachel?' Ian was not yet ready to drop the Russian thread. 'I don't think Rachel's the one we need to focus on. The police have already eliminated her from their inquiries. Unlike me.'

'Did the two of you ever meet?' asked Iris, beginning to tire of his self-pity. 'Back when you were sneaking around Hampshire, following me and trying to make trouble for Dom?'

'And what about the trouble the bastard made for me?' Ian whined. 'And Rachel! Dear God, Iris, the way he treated that poor woman. I don't know why you insist on defending him.'

'I'm not defending him,' said Iris. 'Did the two of you meet?'

'Not in person. No.' Draining his deeply unsatisfying mocktail, Ian signalled to the barmaid for another. 'We emailed and spoke on the phone. Both of us were trying to be discreet. She had her own axe to grind against Wetherby, as you know.'

'Where did she first hear the plagiarism rumours about Dom and Grimshaw? Did she ever tell you the story on that?'

'Not really,' said Ian, picking desultorily from a small bowl of peanuts. 'I believe she said she'd heard it from a lawyer. Someone "very close" to Dom. She'd seen papers or something, letters that proved it.' He put down the nuts suddenly. 'Oh my God. You don't think it could be the son, do you? Marcus? He's a lawyer. And he knew Rachel. He'd been to her place!'

Iris could practically hear Ian's mind working.

'Isn't he, like, the sole largest beneficiary from Dom's estate? Oh my *God*! Maybe the son teamed up with the mistress. They try to blackmail the dad; Dad won't pay, so the son bumps him off. He was there, opening presents, nice as pie. And the two of them go off for a walk and—'

'And then *you* come along,' Iris reminded him, '*after* Marcus has left Dom and walked back to the house alone.'

'So he says,' said Ian.

'I saw him with my own eyes,' said Iris. 'I was in the cottage, remember? I saw them rowing. Marcus went home. The next person to see Dom was you. And the next person was poor Lorcan, God help him, fishing his father's corpse out of the river.'

'No,' Ian said firmly. 'Someone else saw him, after me and before Lorcan. His killer saw him, Iris. Because it *wasn't me*! I didn't kill Dom Wetherby, for *Christ's sake*!' His shouts drew hostile stares from around the bar. Iris sat reactionless. Putting his head in his hands, Ian forced himself to calm down.

'Marcus went home,' he said eventually, in the face of Iris's silence. 'But for how long? He could have gone out again. Picked up the argument where he left off, but then finished it this time. It's possible, Iris. Admit it. It *is* possible!'

Reaching into her purse, Iris left a twenty-pound note on the bar. Grabbing her coat off the back of the chair, she kissed Ian perfunctorily on the cheek.

'Where are you going?' he asked.

'I'll call you later,' said Iris, slipping on her coat and scarf. 'Try not to worry. I know you didn't do it, OK?'

'Wait! I should come with you,' said Ian, belatedly showing some concern for her safety. 'Wait, Iris! Where are you *going*? For pity's sake.'

But by the time he weaved his way through to the exit and out onto the street, Iris had already gone.

*

Jenna Wetherby pulled Iris into a bear hug, genuinely delighted to see her.

'Oh my goodness, why didn't you call?' she berated her, dragging Iris into the kitchen and depositing her coat and scarf on an already overloaded Heal's sofa. 'I didn't know you were in London. What's going on? I barely saw you at the unveiling party. I wanted to but you were being mobbed. How's the exhibition going?'

It took well over five minutes for Jenna to draw breath at all. Not that Iris minded. It was wonderful to see her looking so much happier. Clearly her marriage problems with Marcus had been straightened out. Or perhaps just being away from the Mill and Ariadne and all the drama had revived her. Either way, Iris hoped she wasn't about to undo all the good work and plunge Jenna back into the deep, dark pit of a few weeks ago. It was ironic to think that it was Jenna who had got Iris involved in the first place. Jenna who'd insisted Dom's death must have been murder and that it was their moral responsibility to discover who did it.

Amazing how moral responsibility fades when one's life and marriage are at stake, thought Iris. Not that she felt bitter. Jenna still had a chance at happiness and she'd chosen to grab it. Why not? She couldn't bring Dom back from the dead, after all. Iris had only continued trying to solve the riddle because she needed a distraction. And because she'd had nothing left to lose.

Until Graham.

'Marcus is still at the office,' said Jenna, plonking both her children in front of a cartoon in the living room and cutting herself and Iris a large slice of Tesco's Smarties caterpillar cake each. 'Was it him you were after or me? What brings you here, in fact, if not your exhibition?' She narrowed her eyes, then asked playfully, 'Is it Graham? Have you come to town for a night of hot sex with everybody's favourite lawyer? Second favourite lawyer in my case,' she corrected herself.

It was, finally, Iris's cue to speak. But she found herself tongue-tied. A few weeks ago she would have come clean with Jenna, told her what she was looking for and why. And Jenna would have helped her. But now it was harder.

'What are you doing here?' Marcus, bursting in and taken off guard, sounded considerably less thrilled to see Iris than his wife.

'Don't be so rude!' Jenna chided cheerfully. 'Anyway, what are *you* doing here? It's only just gone five.'

'Case meeting finished early,' muttered Marcus.

'Well, Iris just popped in to say hello en route to a night of un-bridled passion with your godfather,' teased Jenna. 'Isn't that right?'

'That'll be hard,' said Marcus dryly, before Iris could respond. 'I spoke to him earlier and he's still up in Edinburgh. I'd have thought Iris would have known that.'

'I did,' said Iris, equally dryly. 'I believe Jenna was joking. I fear she imagines my life to be considerably more exciting than it actually is. The boring truth is that I'm in town on business.'

'Mm-hmm,' said Marcus, turning his back to both women as he took off his coat and suit jacket and opened a bottle of wine on the counter. Iris could have sworn she saw a tiny muscle twitching at the top of his jaw, just below his left ear.

He's nervous.

Pointedly getting two glasses down from the cupboard, not three, Marcus composed himself before turning to face Iris.

'Well, it was nice of you to stop by, but I daresay you'll want to be getting on. Jenna and I have a dinner tonight, you see, so I'm afraid it's not a terrific time.'

'Marcus!' A mortified Jenna glared at her husband. 'What on earth's got into you? Our dinner's not till eight thirty, for heaven's sake. We've plenty of time. I'm so sorry, Iris.'

Just then Lottie ran in wailing, conveniently breaking the tension. 'Oscar's been sick. It's all on the sofa, and the iPad. It's disgusting!'

'Oh God, not again.' Jenna raced into the living room, grabbing a J-cloth from the sink on the way.

Alone with Marcus, Iris seized the moment.

'I need to talk to you.' She kept her voice low.

'You don't give up, do you?' Marcus bristled with hostility. 'Why can't you just go back to your own life and leave us all alone?'

'Did you remove something from your father's study?' Iris asked, ignoring him. 'A photograph?'

'It's none of your damn business whether I did or didn't!' Marcus snapped.

'Did you?' Iris pressed him.

'No.' Marcus glared at her. 'As it just so happens, I didn't. Now please leave.'

'I don't believe you,' said Iris, her heart pounding.

'Frankly I don't give a toss what you believe,' said Marcus.

'I think you took it, and I think you know exactly what picture I mean,' Iris continued. 'I'd be happy to ask you about it again in a minute, in front of Jenna. She'll be back in here any second.'

Iris watched the colour drain from Marcus's face. He hated her in that moment, and Iris saw hatred and fear fight a brief but intense battle within him.

Fear won.

'Come into my study,' he hissed, putting his wine glass down on the counter and leading the way up the narrow stairs. Iris followed him into a tiny room, little more than a cupboard, into which was crammed a desk, a bookshelf and an old-fashioned filing cabinet.

'Close the door,' Marcus instructed.

Iris did. He pulled open the desk drawer and took out a photograph in a heavy gilt frame. It was the frame, the iridescent glint of gold, that Iris had captured in her portrait of Dom, an unexpected flash of light in the background. But it was the photograph inside it that interested her now. It showed Rachel Truebridge, her head thrown back, laughing. The picture had been taken at some sort of event, perhaps a TV wrap party, and was officially a group shot, although clearly the photographer's main focus had been Rachel. There were various revellers behind her, most holding champagne flutes, the men in formal jackets and the women in cocktail dresses. Rachel herself looked radiant in a short red off-the-shoulder number, not looking at the camera directly, yet clearly aware of it, aware of the effect she was having on whoever was behind the lens.

'Why did you take this?' Iris asked Marcus.

'To protect Mum,' he replied bluntly.

'From what?'

Marcus's eyes narrowed. 'Oh, come on. I'd say that was pretty clear, wouldn't you? Dad had it up on the bookshelf in that study, in pride of place. He said it was just a shot of the Grimshaw production team at last year's wrap party. But I mean, look at it.' The anger in his voice was unmistakable. 'It's obvious why he kept it. Mum never gave it a second glance while he was alive, but after he died, with all the rumours swirling around and that bitch of a woman, his old mistress, going to the papers . . . I was worried she'd see it in a different light.'

'So you took it?' said Iris.

'Yes. I don't think Mum noticed. Although apparently you did.'

'I need to borrow it,' said Iris, holding out a hand. 'Just for a day or so.'

'Why?' Marcus frowned.

Downstairs, Jenna's voice floated up to them. 'Marcus? Iris?'

'I'll bring it back, I promise,' said Iris, without answering his question.

Marcus hesitated for a moment, then handed her the picture, watching nervously as Iris slipped it into her handbag.

'Look, I have no idea why this is important, or why you think it is,' he whispered, conscious of Jenna's footfall coming up the stairs. 'But Jenna already suspects me of having an affair with Rachel. If she knew I'd taken the picture – this picture, especially – she might get the wrong idea. I'd appreciate it if this stayed between us.'

'Of course,' said Iris.

The door opened.

'There you are!' Jenna stood there smiling. 'I wondered where you'd both got to. I hope Marcus has apologised for being such a Grinch before.'

'Yes, sorry about that,' Marcus said to Iris. 'I'm afraid I had a bad day at work. It wasn't you.'

'Oh, no need to apologise,' said Iris breezily. 'To be honest, I'm not big on being dropped in on either.'

'Well, sick-gate's over, for now,' said Jenna cheerfully. 'Would you like to come down and have a drink?'

'I actually can't,' said Iris, making a show of looking at her watch. 'I have a dinner myself. It's a work thing. Potential commission. I just wanted to say hello, as I was nearby.'

A few minutes later Marcus stood with his arm around Jenna, watching Iris walk down the road and jump into a cab.

'That was sweet of her,' said Jenna, leaning into him. 'To stop in like that. She's a nice woman.'

'Yes,' said Marcus. 'Very nice.'

'You shouldn't have been so rude to her,' said Jenna.

'I know,' said Marcus. 'I'm sorry. But I think she's all right. I don't think she took it to heart.'

He hoped he was right about that. He wasn't sure exactly what he felt about Iris Grey. But he knew she was not a woman he wanted to make an enemy of.

What the hell does she want with that picture?

Iris arrived at Bell & Mason's offices just as they were closing. Dom's publishers were based in a charming converted Victorian mansion, tucked away behind St Martin's Lane, a few doors down from the Ivy. It was a part of London better known for its nightlife than for the daily grind of office work, and the bars and restaurants around Bell & Mason were already starting to fill up with early revellers by the time Iris hopped out of her cab.

'Is Raymond Beatty still here?' she asked the receptionist, briefly stating her business. Beatty was the senior publisher, and had been with Dom from the beginning, signing Grimshaw to Bell & Mason when both men had been in their twenties. 'It's about Dom Wetherby. I'm a family friend.'

'He *is* here,' the girl admitted hesitantly, 'but I believe he's about to head home. If you don't have an appointment, perhaps—'

'Iris?'

Iris turned to see Raymond Beatty smiling at her broadly. A contemporary of Dom's, it was astonishing how much older Raymond looked, with his stooped shoulders and face so blighted with liver spots he looked like a speckled Cotswold egg. Even more astonishing was that he recognised Iris and remembered her name. As far as she knew, the only time he'd ever seen her before was at the Wetherbys' Christmas Eve party, and then they'd had the briefest of introductions.

'Raymond.' She smiled back. 'I'm sorry to ambush you at work. I wondered if you had a second?'

'Of course, of course.' He turned back towards the lifts, gesturing for Iris to follow. 'Katie, send up some tea, would you? Or would you prefer a drink?' he asked Iris. 'As it's after six?'

'Tea's fine,' said Iris. The buzz from her afternoon gin and tonic had worn off, thank God. She needed to keep her wits about her.

The receptionist watched her boss and his guest return to his office with a sinking heart. Now she'd have to stay too, probably till seven. She called catering and ordered the tray of tea, then sat down sullenly to wait.

Forty minutes later Iris emerged, followed by a still-smiling Raymond.

'I'm sorry I couldn't be of more help,' he told Iris, helping her on with her coat. 'It was all such a long time ago.'

'That's all right,' said Iris. 'And you did help. Thank you for seeing me.'

'Of course, of course,' the old man beamed. 'Anytime. You know, I'd like to know what happened to Dom, too,' he added, almost as an afterthought. 'He had his faults, but he was a good friend. Stay in touch, would you? Let me know if you find anything?'

'I will,' promised Iris.

Outside, the streets were packed with people, but Iris felt nothing but dark and cold. She'd been planning to stay in London tonight and had booked a room at Soho House in Chiswick, but suddenly she felt an overwhelming urge to get home to Mill Cottage and go to sleep in her own bed. *Home.* The cottage had become home, she realised. But the thought made her sad, because she knew she couldn't stay there for long. Especially not now.

For the first time in weeks she thought about her doll's house, and how calming it would be to take out all the tiny, perfect furniture and rearrange it. To create order and beauty, in this world of chaos and sadness. Such incredible sadness, for Dom and for herself.

She'd wanted to be wrong so very badly.

But she wasn't wrong. She knew. The picture burning a hole in her handbag might not prove it, exactly, but it was the biggest missing piece in the puzzle. And so *obvious* now! Now that she knew.

Her mobile rang, number unknown, and she answered it.

'Hello, gorgeous.' Graham's voice was soft, soothing, full of love. 'I'm done with my case up here. When can I see you? Are you still in London? I could come down first thing tomorrow.'

Iris told him she was heading back to Hampshire and he agreed to meet her there.

'Are you all right, my love? You sound terribly tired.'

'I am tired,' Iris admitted. 'Is it all right if we talk tomorrow? I'm just rushing for my train.'

'Of course,' said Graham. 'You go. I'll see you then.'

He hung up and for a moment Iris stood rooted to the spot by the entrance to the Tube, oblivious to the passengers jostling her as they swarmed in and out. Then she dialled the one number she really, really didn't want to.

'Hello? . . . Yes. I'd like to speak to Detective Inspector Cant, please. Tell him it's Iris Grey.'

CHAPTER TWENTY-FIVE

Bizarrely, Iris slept deeply and well that night, not waking up until mid-morning to a bedroom flooded with spring sunlight. Her exhausted body had demanded rest and had taken it, almost as if it were drugged. Long after her morning coffee, her arms and legs still felt heavy and limp with sleep, but in a good way, a way that filled her with warmth and a slowly stirring energy for the day ahead. Unfortunately, her mind was a different story. Every time she thought about what she was doing – what she was about to do, what she had to do – she could practically hear her brain buzzing, her emotions stretched and taut with tension like a live electrical wire about to snap. Too anxious to eat breakfast, she forced herself to swallow a piece of dry toast at lunch, washed down with a mug of sweet tea. She went for a walk, which helped, until she saw Lorcan waving at her from an upper window at the Mill and felt choked with tears and regret for everything that poor child had been through. Everything he still had to go through.

Oh God, oh God, oh God. I can't do it. I can't!

Graham's train got in at three fifteen and he would be at Mill Cottage by four. Iris had to get a grip by then. After more mind-less pacing, at two she started cleaning the larder cupboard out, desperate for any sort of task to distract her. By three she was attempting to bake cookies, searching for recipes on the Internet. The first batch were burned by three thirty, filling the kitchen with acrid and bitter black smoke. By the time Graham arrived, ecstatic to see her and bearing a stunning bouquet of spring flowers, Iris had got rid of most of the smell and was elbow-deep in flour, having started on a second round, probably unwisely.

'I don't think I've ever seen you cook.' Walking up behind her, Graham kissed the back of her neck. Iris closed her eyes, feeling goose pimples break out all over her body.

'I'm not very good at it,' she said, pushing the mixing bowl aside and turning on the kettle.

'Well, you look delectable in an apron,' Graham assured her adoringly. 'That's the main thing, I always think. I'll be down in a sec.'

He dragged his suitcase upstairs while Iris made the tea. Forgetting the cookie dough, she shoved two crumpets in the toaster on autopilot and laid the table with spotty Cath Kidston mugs and a flower milk jug she'd bought at Hazelford Stores, going through the motions of domesticity like some deranged Stepford wife.

She'd just put the butter dish and Marmite on the table when a cough from behind made her turn round.

'Oh my goodness!' Iris gasped.

Graham was at the foot of the stairs, on one knee. In his left hand, he held open a ring box, lined with plush black velvet. A diamond-and-ruby engagement ring, as elegant and simple as Iris could have dreamed of, sparkled inside like a talisman.

Only a week ago she would have been so happy at this moment. Now it took all her strength to exhale a single word: 'No.'

Graham's face fell. 'I know it's a shock. And I know it's too soon, and you're not even divorced yet. But don't say no, Iris. I've waited my whole life . . . too long. But I've never felt like this. Never met anyone—'

She held up her hand. 'Stop,' she said gently. 'Please stop. I know, Graham.'

He turned his head to one side curiously, like a dog hearing a strange sound.

'You know?' He smiled at her fondly. 'What do you know, my darling?'

Iris opened the drawer of the kitchen dresser and pulled out the photograph of Rachel Truebridge she'd taken from Marcus yesterday. Removing the picture from its frame, she handed it to Graham.

Still on one knee, he looked at it, then at Iris. With a sigh, he closed the ring box. Then, after what felt like hours, he slowly got to his feet.

'Where was it?' he asked quietly. 'Where did you find it?'

'Marcus had it,' said Iris. 'He took it out of Dom's study to try to protect his mother. He didn't understand its significance.'

'But you did.' Graham looked at her then, his expression a mixture of affection, admiration and sadness.

'Yes,' said Iris.

They sat down at the tea table, as if this were any other afternoon and they were about to discuss art or politics or the weather, not a brutal murder. The calm atmosphere was surreal, yet at the same time quite normal. Graham was always calm. It was one of the things Iris had been drawn to about him. So different from Ian, whose hot temper had burned her many a time. But cooler tempers could also be more calculated, she reflected now.

'I looked everywhere for this, you know.' Graham ran a finger round the edge of the photograph. 'I turned Dom's study upside down. I looked in his bedroom, his briefcase, his dressing room. Ariadne thought I was searching for legal papers. She even thanked me for tidying up afterwards. Dom would never have done that.' He smiled ruefully.

Iris poured the tea, letting him go on. She wanted him to tell her. She wanted him to tell her without being asked.

'She sent him the picture herself, you know. Rachel. Stupid girl.' He shook his head, more in sadness than in anger. 'It was over between them, but she was still obsessed with Dom. She thought she looked good, sexy. She wanted him to see her like that. I don't think she even noticed I was in the shot, standing right behind her.'

'But Dom noticed,' said Iris.

Graham gave a wry smile. 'Oh yes. Dom noticed. And that was the beginning of the end.' He sipped his tea contemplatively. 'I might not have had the balls to go through with it if Dom hadn't challenged me directly. He pulled me aside on Christmas Eve, after the party, drunk and angry, demanding to know how I knew Rachel, accusing me of sleeping with her, threatening this, that and the other. Bullying, basically, as only he could. I agreed to meet him on Christmas Day to "explain".'

A dark shadow fell across Graham's face then, and his features tightened and contracted as the anger and hatred came flooding back.

'He wanted *me* to explain.' He shot Iris a 'can you believe it?' look. 'He *knew* what he'd done. *Knew* who he was: a liar and a thief. Everything he was, everything he had: his fame, his wealth, his family, his friends, this beautiful house. All of it was stolen from my brother. And yet the bastard had the gall to summon *me* to explain my actions, my imagined affair with his mistress – his discarded mistress at that! He truly was the most revolting man.' Graham looked deep into Iris's eyes. 'He deserved to die.'

With an effort, Iris reserved comment. She wanted Graham to go on, needed him to go on, however painful each word might be.

'When did you first learn about the plagiarism accusations?' she asked calmly.

'Late. Very late. About two years ago,' he replied bitterly. 'Marcus never told me. He never told anyone. I can only imagine he was too hurt by what Dom did, too shocked and ashamed to confide in us.' He shook his head angrily. 'But a couple of years ago I began hearing rumours, from Marcus's Oxford contemporaries. It started as the odd comment on Marcus's in memoriam Facebook page. Snide little snippets about Dom, and how much he "owed" to my brother. Nothing was spelled out. At first I dismissed the posts out of hand as straightforward envy. Don't forget the Wetherbys had always been good to me and my family. We were close friends, and my mother adored Dom till the day she died. But when I mentioned these comments in passing to Dom at dinner one night in London, his reaction was visceral. He was furious, not just with the person who wrote them but with me. I should be "grateful" to him. How "dare" I repeat these comments? Who did I think I was? That sort of thing. We fell out, and that was when I dug deeper.'

'You went to see Raymond Beatty,' Iris prompted.

Graham looked at her admiringly. She was as clever as she was beautiful. Was he really going to lose her now, after all this?

'Yes,' he said aloud. 'I always liked Raymond. He was one of the good guys. Of course, he gave me Dom's version of events, but he gave it in good faith. That was all he knew, after all. He said that when Dom first came to him with a Grimshaw manuscript, he admitted he'd conceived the original idea with a friend. Raymond asked at the time whether the friend might have any claim to the work, but Dom was adamant he'd written the novel alone. Raymond took him at his word. No friend ever came forward claiming co-authorship, so he had no reason not to.

'But by now I was suspicious. My brother had no history of depression, Iris. No reason to kill himself that any of us knew about. It was true he was unhappy in his first job out of university, but he quickly jacked that in and returned to Oxford for his PhD, and as far as we knew, he was fine. But of course he wasn't fine.' Graham's frown deepened. 'After I met with Beatty, I went back to Oxford myself and spent almost a month tracking down anyone and everyone who knew and remembered my brother. It was a terrible time.'

His eyes welled with tears. Instinctively, without thinking, Iris placed her hand over his.

'Marcus was crushed by Dom's betrayal. They came up with that book together. They wrote the synopsis together, co-wrote the early chapters. They spent weeks and weeks developing the Grimshaw project. But then summer vac came around and Marcus landed a top internship at one of the big consultancy firms. They agreed he would take it and Dom would go travelling and they'd resume the book in the autumn. But instead Dom dashed off a manuscript in secret, shopped it around to publishers and got a deal behind Marcus's back.

'They fell out about it of course at the time. But they were lifelong friends and Dom apologised and, I don't know, they worked it out, I suppose. Marcus was a deeply forgiving person,' he mumbled bitterly. 'But of course we weren't talking big money then. Neither of them imagined for a moment that the book was going to sell the way that it did. When Dom began to make millions and was feted all over the literary world, Marcus asked to be credited. He wasn't even asking for money, just a thanks in the book, a dedication or whatever. Something that would tell the world that he, too, had conceived this character, that he had been a part of it.'

'But Dom said no.'

'Worse than that,' Graham seethed. 'He started acting as if their collaboration had never happened. He made my brother out to be delusional, told him he needed to see a shrink, that he had never been an integral part of the book. That was what pushed Marcus over the edge. Literally. I mean, Dom came to his funeral, Iris! He stood there, next to my parents, and sobbed. He put his arm around me and promised to act like a "big brother". And he did! And I let him! Because I didn't know. But *he* did, the bastard. He knew all along.'

'That must have been a terrible shock for you. Finding out,' Iris said understandingly.

Graham laughed, and took another long gulp of tea.

'You could say that. Yeah. The problem was, I didn't have any proof. This was long before computers or emails, remember, and whatever paper records my brother might have left were long gone, scattered on the wind. I had no chapters I could show, no synopsis with his name on it, no letters between him and Dom, nothing. I knew I needed to punish Dom, to get justice for Marcus. But I couldn't see how. So I started digging around for allies, people whom Dom had made an enemy of, who might be able to help me bring him down.'

'And you found Rachel Truebridge.'

'And I found Rachel Truebridge.' Graham smiled again, the storm of his immediate anger passed, for now. 'Poor Rachel. She was out of her depth from the beginning. Any fool could see that Dom was going to screw her over. But she loved him, and he cared enough for her to confide in her. I don't know whether it was looming retirement, or the prospect of turning sixty, or all the pain they'd been through with Billy and Lorcan. But he was tormented with nightmares during their time together, and sometimes he would yell out in his sleep. Evidently the bastard was doing some soul-searching, or whatever it is you call it when someone doesn't have a soul. Introspection, I suppose. Anyway, I suppose he felt guilty, but he told Rachel he'd done something terrible as a young man, something he would always regret. And he hinted there were letters, documents, some sort of tangible proof that he had, something that he'd stolen and hidden, that could expose him as a fraud if anyone were to find them. He was deeply fearful.

'But he was also deeply spiteful, and as soon as their romance was over, he wasted no time firing Rachel from her job, ruining her life and career just as nonchalantly as he had discarded my poor brother.'

'So the two of you teamed up?' asked Iris.

Graham nodded. 'I suggested she go to the papers. The police would have needed more evidence than we had, but a life can be destroyed by innuendo and scandal. And perhaps, in time, I'd have enough to file a civil suit against Dom at least. Take his house. His savings. Crush him, the way he crushed poor Marcus.'

Iris sat back and exhaled slowly, running a hand through her hair. For the first time since Graham had walked through the door, she allowed her emotions to get the better of her. Looking from him to the ring box that was still sitting forlornly on the table, her eyes welled with tears. For Dom, but also for Marcus Feeney, broken by betrayal. And for Graham, the brother who'd wanted to avenge him. And finally for herself. Because for a moment, a brief, shining, lovely moment, Iris had glimpsed a happy future. No Ian, wounding and belittling her with his rage. No ties. Just her and Graham, together. Married perhaps, although that wasn't a necessary part of the fantasy. Iris no longer cared much for white dresses and rings. But companionship, friendship, humour, sex. Those things still mattered. Those things she still wanted, passionately. They wouldn't have children, Iris and Graham, but they'd have each other and their work and Iris's art and their love, and it would be enough.

It could have been enough.

'So why didn't you?' Iris threw out the question in anger. 'Why didn't you sue him or go to the press or . . . anything? Why did you have to kill him, Graham?'

'Oh, my Iris.' Graham looked at her with eyes filled with compassion. 'It was this, my darling.' He held up the photograph again. 'This picture! You were the one who saw it, Iris, who recognised it as the missing piece, and you were right. Rachel and I were working together. She'd already tried to blackmail Dom about the plagiarism, hinting she knew more than he'd told her, but he had no idea I was involved. I'd recently been brought back into the Wetherby fold, you see. Invited to the Christmas Eve party no less. So I was still an insider, with access. Rachel was an outsider, banished for ever. She was never supposed to be at that party, still less to be sending Dom sexy photographs of herself. But she was coming unglued.'

Iris shook her head. She didn't want to hear about Rachel.

'I came down to the Mill for that party full of hope and excitement,' said Graham, correctly sensing Iris's impatience. 'I was hoping to find proof of what Dom did to Marcus. I planned to search the house while the party was going on downstairs. If I didn't find anything, I thought maybe Billy could be persuaded to spill some secrets. Clearly things between him and his parents were very strained. Or perhaps dear, sweet Lorcan might unwittingly help me and give something away. Daddy or Mummy's "secret places"? Because make no mistake, Ariadne was up to her neck in this too. She was there at Oxford, stood by Dom through it all.

'Anyway, the point is, Dom eventually spotted me in that damn photograph of Rachel's and demanded an explanation, and so on Christmas Day we met. He'd already had a set-to with Marcus, about his affair with Rachel, followed by another argument with your horrible husband. I assume about you.'

Iris shrank in her seat. 'Yes.'

'So by the time I met him down in the woods, he was in a foul mood, punchy and obnoxious. He got into my car and asked me flat out if I was sleeping with Rachel. Despite the way he'd treated her, he still seemed to view her as his property in some repellent, sexist way. I shut him down, obviously. I confronted him with the truth about what he'd done to my brother. Everything I knew, and Rachel knew, everything I'd learned in Oxford and from his own publisher. I asked him how he'd lived with the guilt for all these years, of knowing he caused Marcus's suicide. I asked how he could have befriended me, and our parents.'

'And how did he respond?'

Graham's expression darkened again. 'He was all over the place. First, he denied it, if you can believe that. He actually defended himself to me. It was the same self-justifying crap he'd fed to

Beatty: yes, he and Marcus had come up with the idea together, but that was all. And ideas were ten a penny in publishing. According to Dom, he'd done all the writing, every word. I can hear his voice now.'

Graham screwed up his eyes against the memory, rubbing balled fists over his ears as if he could somehow eradicate the sound.

'"Marcus didn't *want* to be a writer, Graham. He took a safe consultancy job because he didn't want to take the risk."' Graham did an eerily accurate impression of Dom, right down to the outstretched, innocent arms and 'what could I do?' hand gestures. '"*I* took the risk, Graham. *I* did the work. And then when Grimshaw took off and I began to reap the rewards, Marcus regretted his decision and tried to blame me for it. It was his own regret that pushed him into depression, Graham, not me. You must believe me."'

'I knew then that I could do it.' Unballing his fists, Graham laid his palms on the table, looking at Iris with restored calm. 'And not just could. I wanted to. I mean, I'd prepared, of course. I always prepare, as you know. As soon as I received my invitation to the Christmas Eve party, I knew that that was my chance. But planning something and dreaming about it is not the same as actually screwing your courage to the sticking point and *acting*. It was Dom's own words that night that pushed me over that edge.'

So he was responsible for his own death? Is that your twisted logic? It wasn't really you? Iris thought. But she remained silent, waiting for him to go on.

'I had a hip flask of single malt with me, heavily diluted with liquid chloroform,' Graham continued. 'And yes, I did pinch it from Ariadne's creepy sculpting studio. I knew that would implicate her with the police, should Dom's body ever be found, and should anyone suspect it wasn't suicide. Although of course I did my best to make it look like it was. But if Ariadne had ended up in prison, I wouldn't have been sorry. Don't forget that bitch did everything she could to protect Dom and hide the truth about my brother. She deserved punishment, too.

'We were still in the car and I told Dom that I knew he felt partly responsible for Marcus's suicide, whatever he said. Rachel had told me about his nightmares, his regrets. And then, of course, he started snivelling, embarrassing crocodile tears about how Marcus had always been his dearest friend and how he'd never really been able to enjoy the Grimshaw money, knowing Marcus's pain. How he wished he'd credited him, as he should have, but he was young and ambitious and blah, blah, blah.'

There was a coldness to Graham's voice now, a thin, ruthless edge that Iris had never heard before.

'I let him go on. I told him I forgave him. I passed him the hip flask and let him drink. He was so over the top by then that he downed the lot, stupid, maudlin bastard. He was out cold in less than thirty seconds.'

Iris listened, transfixed. Graham, too, seemed to be almost in some kind of trance, reliving the moment, but not for Iris. Not for anybody. The words just continued to flow, like somebody reading a story into a tape recorder.

'After that I got my kit out of the boot. I'd bought plastic contamination overalls from a company that supplies hospitals up in Edinburgh – bodysuit, gloves and a sort of bath-cap job for your head. They made all the suits for the Ebola crisis, if you remember that? And I had a length of rope and a suitable stone. I took those to the riverbank first. Found a spot that was quiet and hidden by trees but where you could still see the house and dumped them there. The house was important, you see.' Graham looked at Iris, willing her to understand. 'The Mill, Dom's dream, bought at the bargain cost of my brother's life. I wanted him to die there. And that's what happened.' He leaned back and exhaled, smiling. The story had come to an end. A happy end, or at least a neat one. He could switch off the tape and turn back to Iris.

'It was so simple in the end,' he said. 'He was heavy, but I didn't have far to carry him. Tying the stone on was easy. So was sliding him into the water. He never stirred, not once. It was over in moments. I'd studied the currents and the weight and all of that beforehand. I had no reason to believe he'd pop back up again the way he did, like a bad penny. Or an unflushable turd,' he added wryly. 'The suit meant I left no fibres, no hair, no footprints. The whole thing was . . .' he searched for the right word, 'satisfying.'

Iris looked at him aghast. 'Satisfying?'

He wasn't even boasting. In his mind, he was simply stating a truth, to someone he trusted. Someone he seemed to believe would understand. As if what Graham had done could ever be understood. As if it could ever, ever be excused.

'It was a shame, what happened afterwards,' Graham went on, apparently oblivious to Iris's reaction. 'Poor Lorcan. Such a darling, innocent child. I feel terrible that he was the one to find Dom. I can only imagine how terrified he must have been.'

'He'll never get over it,' Iris said with quiet anger.

'No,' Graham admitted. 'I don't expect he will. Then again, who knows what really goes on in Lorcan's mind? I panicked a little bit when he started talking about seeing a "white ghost" in the woods on Christmas afternoon. Clearly that must have been me in my overalls. I bought a set for me and a set for Ariadne to sculpt in. That was a nice touch, I thought: the gift.' He smiled. Iris felt her blood run cold. 'But of course the moronic police never picked up on it. Who's going to trust the word of a traumatised boy when they have a murder to solve? Not to mention so many easy, lazy suspects to choose from.'

Iris stood up and walked to the window. It was dark outside now, and she had to press her face right up against the glass to see anything beyond her own reflection.

To her surprise and dismay, Graham walked up behind her, pressing himself against her and dropping a tender kiss on the back of her neck.

'I'm not sorry I killed him, Iris. I'm sorry I had to lie to *you* about it. But Dom Wetherby deserved to die.'

Iris spun round, her face a picture of anguish.

'You don't get to decide that, Graham! Who deserves to die and who deserves to live? That wasn't your choice to make. And even forgetting about Dom for a minute, you were prepared to implicate Ariadne . . .'

'I told you. I had good reason for that.'

'And Ian! What about Ian? My husband, whom you barely know.'

'I know enough.'

'No, you *don't*!' Sobbing, Iris pounded a fist against Graham's chest. 'You would have let Ian go to prison, for life, for a murder he didn't commit. A murder *you* committed! And then what? Marry me? Live happily ever after? What the hell is wrong with you?'

'Iris, listen to me.' Graham put both hands on her shoulders, not threateningly but firmly, willing her to look at him. 'Ian was a bully and a drunk. He treated you appallingly for years, then tried to rip you off financially in the divorce *he* caused. Why shouldn't he be in prison, hmm? Why shouldn't he be punished? He's a bad man.

'Dom Wetherby was a bad man, too. The worst. He drove my brother to suicide, stole his work and lived off the profits like a king for the rest of his miserable, lying, cheating, rotten life. I'm not like Dom, Iris. And I'm not like Ian either. I'm not a bad man. I'm not a bully or a liar or a cheat.'

'You're a murderer!' Iris reminded him, tears streaming down her cheeks.

'No,' said Graham. 'I avenged my brother's death. It's different. Iris, please. I love you. I love you so much.'

'I thought we had a future together,' Iris whispered, her voice hoarse from crying. 'I really did.'

'So did I,' Graham said eagerly. 'And we still do. We still *can*.'

Her eyes widened. 'What do you mean?'

'Think about it,' said Graham. 'You're the only one who knows. The only one who figured out the truth. If you didn't go to the police . . . we could destroy that photograph.'

'No.' Iris mumbled, shaking her head.

'Or give it back to Marcus, or to Rachel. Cant would never put the pieces together, never in a million years. We could carry on with our lives, just as we were.'

'And what? Let the police pin it on Ian?'

'That won't happen.' Releasing her, Graham waved a hand dismissively. 'They need proof, something substantial or physical to make it stick. Trust me, Iris, the case will be closed unsolved. No one needs to go to jail here. You did what you set out to do. You solved the riddle. Even with me beside you, doing my best to misdirect you. You did it, Iris. But do you really want to throw away our future together? Everything we've hoped for?'

Taking her silence for acquiescence, or at least possible wavering, he walked back to the table and picked up the ring.

'We could still be married, Iris. We could still be happy.'

Behind Iris, the door opened. DI Cant, flanked by three armed constables, walked slowly in. 'I don't think so, sir,' Cant said quietly to Graham.

There was no scene. No shouting, no struggle. Instead, Graham gave a last, long look to Iris that was at once sorrowful, defeated and forgiving. 'You already called them.'

'I had to,' said Iris, her throat dry as dust. Part of her wanted to add, 'I'm sorry,' but when the time came, she couldn't do it.

Graham nodded. He made no move to run or resist when Cant's men handcuffed him.

'Graham Feeney.' The words rolled off Cant's tongue. 'I'm arresting you for the murder of Dominic Wetherby. You do not have to say anything, but it may harm your defence if you omit to mention something you later rely on in court.'

Iris turned her head as Graham was led away, out to the waiting police car.

DI Cant lingered for a moment. 'Thank you, Ms Grey.'

Iris stared at the flagstoned floor. 'You got it, then?'

'Oh yes. Every word. Although something tells me he'll be happy to give us the same statement himself. He's a cool customer that one, isn't he?'

Iris sank down onto a kitchen chair. All of a sudden her knees felt weak.

'Will you be all right?' Cant asked. 'I can get a PC to come and sit with you if you like?'

'No, thank you,' Iris said firmly. 'I'll be fine.'

Cant left and the kitchen and the cottage returned to an almost deafening silence.

Iris sat for a long time in the dark.

I'll be fine.

Only of course she wouldn't.

At that moment she knew with complete certainty.

She would never be fine again.

PART THREE

CHAPTER TWENTY-SIX

Iris sat behind her easel at the top of the rise, looking down at the bucolic scene below. Mill House glowed golden and warm in the late May sunshine, shimmering slightly through a haze of early summer heat. Beside it, the River Itchen flowed lazy and sluggish, turning the wooden waterwheel at a slow, steady pace. From where she sat, Iris could just make out the roof of her cottage on the far side of the river. Much clearer and more detailed was her view of Mill House's walled kitchen garden, and the big lawn that lay between the front door and the gate out to the lane.

Lottie, Marcus and Jenna's daughter, was playing some form of tag on the grass, her shrieks of laughter carried on the breeze as her blonde plait flew behind her like the tail of a kite. She and Lorcan, also giggling, were running away from Billy, who was almost unrecognisable in preppy knee-length shorts and a Hackett T-shirt, and with his hair cut short. He'd returned home to the Mill almost three weeks ago now, after a long spell in a London rehab, and seemed far happier and calmer, albeit in a numb, medicated sort of way.

Not that Iris had had much to do with Billy since he came back. She'd been too busy packing up to leave for Scotland, where her next job – a commission to paint a rich laird's young socialite wife – awaited her. But on the few occasions their paths had crossed, Billy had made no further mention of the things he'd told Iris back in February, about Ariadne's abuse of him as a child and the anguish of not being believed.

Perhaps he made them up after all, Iris wondered now, dabbing flecks of deep purple onto her canvas in an effort to capture the riotously flowering buddleia, smothered with butterflies, beside Mill House's front door. He had been very confused back then, his mind addled from a mixture of anger, grief and, it now emerged, a chronic addiction to pain pills. Whatever the truth, there could be no denying he seemed markedly happier now than he had before he left the Mill, calmly accepting his mother and brother as trustees of his interest in Dom's will and submitting meekly to their decisions.

Iris continued to paint and watch as various Wetherby family and friends drifted in and out between the house and the garden. Schools around the country were off for half-term, which explained Marcus and Jenna's presence in Hazelford. Less clear was why Ariadne's father, Clive, should suddenly have turned up. Perhaps he wanted to see his great-grandchildren. Or perhaps not, as he was certainly doing an excellent job of ignoring Lottie, settling down into an old wicker bath chair under the shade of the big sycamore, while she tore past him, with a large glass of Pimm's in his hand and his nose firmly jammed into an old copy of *Horse & Hound*.

Iris couldn't help but think back to what Harry Masters had told her about Clive – well, not told her exactly but hinted – about Ariadne's father abusing *her*, perhaps beginning a terrible cycle. Had that all been fantasy as well? Certainly from up here, at a distance, the Wetherbys were putting on a convincing performance of being a happy family. Albeit one still recovering from a hideous trauma.

Ariadne wandered out with a tray of drinks for the children, helped by Marcus. *He's aged*, thought Iris, watching Dom's eldest son hover attentively at his mother's side. While Ariadne looked far better than she had a few weeks ago, plumper and softer and visibly more relaxed, Marcus seemed to have suffered the opposite effect. Even so, he, too, was back in the fold, stepping forward to hand out refreshments to his brothers and daughter, an integral player in the new-look 'Team Wetherby'. Only Jenna struck a jarring note, hanging back under the shadow of the portico, removed from the rest of the happy group.

Looking up, she caught Iris watching her and waved, beckoning Iris down.

Leaving her paints, canvas and easel where they were – it was too glorious a day not to keep painting – Iris wiped her hands on her apron and walked down the steep slope leading to the garden.

'I thought it was you.' Jenna kissed her on both cheeks. 'I didn't know if we'd see you. Ariadne said you were giving up your lease on the cottage?'

'Yes,' said Iris. 'I have a new job coming up, quite a big commission in Scotland. After the exhibition at the National Portrait Gallery, I got a number of offers. And, you know, it was time for a change.'

She cringed at the forced heartiness in her own voice. As if a bright smile and a pull-your-socks-up attitude could heal the deep wounds of the last few months. And before that, the last God knew how many years.

'Can I come and see you? Privately?' Jenna whispered. 'I could get over to the cottage after lunch if you're free.'

For the first time Iris noticed Jenna's nervousness. Even as she spoke, she maintained a fixed smile, directed in the general direction of Marcus and Ariadne. She was behaving like a spy at a dead drop, passing secrets to the enemy.

Except that they were supposed to be past secrets now. Graham had confessed and pleaded guilty to Dom's drowning, allowing for a swift sentencing and closure. For the briefest of moments, scandal had whirled around the possibility that Dom Wetherby might have 'stolen' the idea of Grimshaw, or part of it, from his killer's brother. But when the judge dismissed this idea and no evidence was ever put forward to support it, the spark of interest soon fizzled and died. The news cycle moved on and the press dropped the Dom Wetherby murder story. It was over.

'Of course,' Iris told Jenna. 'Not a problem. Around two o'clock?'

Jenna nodded, scurrying away to join Marcus and Ariadne, who turned and waved to Iris.

'Would you like a drink?' Billy called out to her. 'This is elderflower, but there's Pimm's inside.'

'No, thank you,' said Iris, who was beginning to feel more and more fake, as if she'd wandered onto a film set, possibly *The Stepford Wives*. 'I'd better get back to work.'

She turned and hurried back up the hill, hot and bothered and impatient now to talk to Jenna alone. Something was obviously eating at her, something that she couldn't – or wouldn't – tell Marcus.

'Wow. So you're really going, then?' Jenna cast an eye over the crates and packing cases lined up against the wall in Iris's tiny sitting room. In the largest one, marked 'Fragile', she could see Iris's treasured doll's house, with scores of tiny bubble-wrapped figurines and pieces of miniature furniture stacked in neat rows along the top. 'When does this new commission start?'

'Not till July,' said Iris, removing a folded pile of laundry from the sofa so that Jenna could sit down and opening the windows to let whatever breeze there was outside into the stiflingly hot cottage. 'But I want to get settled up there. Find a place to live, explore the area a bit.'

'So I see,' said Jenna, holding up a copy of *The Rough Guide to the Scottish Highlands* from the coffee table. 'Are you excited?'

Iris poured them both a glass of iced lemon squash and considered this. 'I suppose I am, in a way.' She sat down next to Jenna. 'I need a new professional challenge. And the last year's been so intense.'

'Has your divorce been finalised?' Jenna asked tentatively.

'Yes, thank God.' Iris leaned back into the soft sofa pillows. After Graham's arrest, Ian had been so relieved and grateful to Iris that he'd dropped all of his punitive financial demands and allowed the divorce to go through uncontested and lawyer-free. As a result, Iris was now sitting on a small nest egg of savings. Their Clapham flat had sold almost instantly and for above asking price, a welcome bonus in what had been a very hard year for both of them. Ian and Iris had gone out for a drink to celebrate, a small moment of shared happiness that had offered a glimpse of what might be possible between them in the future. Civility, at a minimum. And perhaps, one day, even friendship.

'And what about Graham?' Jenna asked.

Iris's face fell.

'Have you heard from him since the sentencing?'

'Yes. Two letters.' Iris grimaced. 'That's been hard. He asked me to come and visit him.'

'And you don't want to?'

'Eeeeugh.' Iris put her head in her hands. 'I do and I don't. I mean, I still care for him. You can't just switch all those feelings off, can you? But I can't forgive what he did either. I mean, poor Dom.'

'Yes.' Jenna looked away, out of the open window. 'Poor Dom.'

Sensing the change in mood, Iris seized the moment. 'So what is it, Jenna? What did you need to talk to me about?'

'Oh God.' Jenna put down her glass and reached for her handbag. Iris noticed that her hands were shaking. 'I didn't know if I should say anything. I mean, I did know. But things have just started to get better between Marcus and me, just started to heal, and I couldn't bear . . .' Her words trailed off. Pulling out some neatly folded papers, she handed them to Iris. 'You can read for yourself. These are photocopies. I found the originals quite by accident when I was cleaning up in the spare bedroom. Lottie spilled some juice on the carpet, and when I lifted it to clean it, a loose piece of floorboard came up. I found an old diary of Dom's and a stash of letters inside.'

'Where are the originals now?' Iris asked, still reading the papers in her hand.

'Still there,' said Jenna. 'After I copied them, I put them back.'

She waited anxiously for Iris to finish reading. When at last Iris looked up, aghast, Jenna asked, 'What should we do?'

We? thought Iris. *You found them!*

'I could give them to the police, I suppose,' Jenna said miserably. 'I could ask them not to tell Marcus. But would they do anything?'

'I highly doubt it,' said Iris. 'The case is closed. Cant isn't going to open up a fresh can of worms based on this.' She waved the papers. 'Nobody is.'

'So what, then?' Jenna looked at Iris pleadingly.

Iris sighed.

She could walk away if she wanted to. Make this Jenna's problem, or the police's, or somebody else's. Anybody but hers.

She could go to Scotland and pretend she'd never seen what Jenna had just shown her. She could leave Dom's secrets where they'd been all these years: buried, along with the dead.

It's not my responsibility.

None of this is my responsibility.

But she already knew it was hopeless, just as Jenna had known when she came over here.

'All right,' Iris said at last.

'You'll look into it?' Jenna's relief was palpable.

'I don't know if I'll find anything,' said Iris, checking her enthusiasm. 'I probably won't. It was so long ago, Jenna. But I'll look. I'll go back to Oxford.'

CHAPTER TWENTY-SEVEN

Iris reread the letter for the hundredth time as her train rattled through the Oxfordshire countryside. It was another unseasonably hot day and all the carriage windows were jammed open, so that the papers fluttered and danced on the table in front of her, the corners curling up and struggling for escape beneath Iris's pressing hands.

Marcus Feeney's handwriting was bold and forceful, his distinctive loops and flourishes echoing both the confidence and anger of his tone.

15 March 1980

Dear Dom,

I received your reply to my letter of 1 March. To be clear: I also have no desire to end up in court. We've been friends for a long time. As long as you agree to make me whole, and to pay me my equal share in the monies you have received for our book, I have no wish to shame you, or expose your deceitful behaviour towards both me and your publisher to the wider world. Unlike you, I've never been interested in fame. I am perfectly content to live a quiet life. What I am

*not prepared to do is to sit here and do nothing while you
and Ariadne blatantly rip me off.*

*What I said in my letter was that I have more than
enough material to take this to court, should you fail to meet
your obligations. This is the simple truth, and indeed I have
provided you with copies of much of this material to prove it,
although by no means all. I have chapter plans, notes, whole
sections of the book, very clearly in my hand. I also have six
letters from you, in two of which you promise explicitly not to
move forward with the novel – our novel – during the
summer of '78 when I took my internship.*

*Dom, I feel I have been both forgiving and patient, in a
situation where you have readily admitted to me in private
that you were in the wrong. But enough is enough. This will
be the last letter I write to you before instructing my
lawyers. I will give you two weeks to reply, and to send me
a cheque for fifty per cent of your combined advance and
royalties.*

Yours,

Marcus

*P.S. The fact that you and A decided to buy a bloody great
Hampshire pile using money that you knew was half mine is,
I'm afraid, your problem. Please, Dom, no more excuses.*

At this point Iris already knew every word by heart. Every
phrase, every nuance. The letter had been written only a week
before Marcus Feeney's death, yet there was nothing remotely
suicidal about his tone. Quite the opposite, in fact. And Dom
clearly knew it, judging by his diary entry of a few days later,
also photocopied by Jenna.

The Mill, Tuesday, 6 p.m.

Terrible day, sick with worry. M clearly serious about a lawsuit and determined to ruin me. Nothing I say gets through. Ariadne's agreed to go up to Oxford tomorrow and try to talk some sense into him. Praying she succeeds, as every time I open my mouth, the red mist descends and M explodes on me.

He claims to have enough material to make a case, and perhaps he does, legally. I don't know. All I do know is that I wrote the damn book, while he thought about writing it, and some grasping lawyer somewhere seems to have convinced him that makes us co-authors! Christ, it's sad. Years of friendship down the drain. I'd pay him off if I could, rotten and unfair as it is, but the money's gone. Between this house and the poker, I'm tapped out.

Must give up the cards. Promised A. She's forgiven me a lot this year, but I need her now more than ever.

And a day later, 21 March, the day of Marcus Feeney's suicide:

3 p.m.

Call from A. Saw M for lunch and he listened, apparently. She's going over to his rooms for drinks later. Hopeful.

The last entry Jenna had copied was for two days later, 23 March. Dom hadn't written anything on the 22nd, the day he would have learned of Marcus's death. No doubt he was too upset.

M has killed himself, jumped from the window of his flat. Two days ago.

No words. Want to feel more, but I can't seem to. Just . . .
numb. A saw him about an hour before it happened. She said
he seemed fine. Happy, even. He was still angry with me, but
she'd convinced him to drop the lawsuit. That it was better to
talk calmly as old friends and come to some sort of arrange-
ment in private. She said he seemed relieved.

And then this!

Terrible day. Poor A can't stop crying. I think she blames
herself.

Everyone's in shock.

Dom's horror and bafflement rang true to Iris. She could hear
his voice echoing off the page, authentic and tortured. And yet
something was wrong with the picture of Marcus Feeney's suicide.
A number of things were wrong, in fact, going by these letters
and diary entries.

Firstly, and most obviously, there was the disconnect between
Marcus's apparently confident mood and his decision to take his
own life. But that wasn't the only jarring note.

If Marcus really had had chapters, written proof of some kind
that gave him a claim to the Grimshaw series, and if he'd already
spoken to a lawyer about that, as he claimed, surely he would have
filed those documents away with a lawyer. And surely the beneficiaries of his estate – specifically Graham – would have known about
them and filed a claim against Dom Wetherby and the publishers.
Graham had mentioned 'rumours' to Iris. Dom's mistress, Rachel,
had said the same. But if Marcus Feeney had been on the brink of
going to court, there should have been a lot more than rumours.

Who was Marcus Feeney's lawyer? And where did those 'chapters' go?

Of course, it's possible that there was no proof, Iris thought, as the train rattled on its way. *No lawyer, no chapters. If Marcus Feeney was bluffing, and Ariadne called his bluff, could that have pushed him to suicide? In the frustration and heartbreak of the moment?*

Maybe.

Tucking the letters into her handbag, Iris leaned back against the headrest and closed her eyes. Her last trip to Oxford had helped her to solve the mystery of Dom's murder. It was Professor Nevers, talking about the art of portraiture and the importance of the background, that had helped Iris see what had been right in front of her all along.

The professor's voice drifted back to her: '*What are the objects behind them? The shadows? The clues?*'

What was the background to Marcus Feeney's death? What details, what shadows had Iris missed? Had everybody missed?

The train arrived in the city at just after three, and by four Iris had checked into the Randolph. Her room was overpriced for what it was – Oxford's most famous hotel had become a study in faded grandeur, with a heavy emphasis on the faded – but it was at least clean and bright, with a comfortable bed and a mercifully powerful shower. After washing and changing into a light cotton sundress and espadrilles, Iris headed straight to the coroner's office on Tidmarsh Lane.

A low grey concrete building with all the warmth and charm of a nuclear winter, the Oxford Coroner's Office was a fitting structure in which to house the business of death. By contrast, the sixty-something woman at the front desk was as bubbly and bright as her surroundings were dour, defiantly injecting a much-needed note of colour in her yellow flowery dress and rainbow-hued bangles as she beamed helpfully up at Iris.

'Our records are open to the public, of course, and we're organised chronologically. Computers are free, but you need the Wi-Fi password.' She handed Iris a printed sheet of paper, with this and other details on it, including a detailed map of the building. 'Your case was in the 1980s, you say?'

'Yes,' said Iris.

'So that'll be housed here – we go back to 1960 in this building – and we should have a corresponding paper file. Just type the deceased's name and the date into the search engine and you should be directed. You can't make copies here, although we can order one for you, if you need it. There's a charge for that, I'm afraid. Anyway, do come back and see me if you have any problems, my love.'

Iris didn't. 'Marcus Feeney, March 1980' swiftly produced a six-digit code, corresponding to a room, aisle and shelf number. Five minutes later Iris was sitting at a desk, carefully reading every word of the coroner's report into Marcus's death, and how the verdict of suicide was reached.

'Rolf Carnaby.' Iris returned to the desk on her way out. 'He was the coroner at the time of the case I'm interested in. I don't suppose you've any idea where I could find him?'

'Sorry.' The receptionist gave an apologetic shrug. 'Mr Carnaby was well thought of here, I know that, but he was before my time. You could try the public records office. If he's still in Oxford and a registered voter, he'll be in there. Or if he's died. They close at six, and they'll be open again at ten tomorrow morning,' she added helpfully.

Iris arrived at five thirty and, after a little negotiation, persuaded the clerk to let her in. Again, the office was almost empty and its computer systems, though archaic, were surprisingly efficient.

Within twenty minutes Iris had discovered that Rolf Carnaby was indeed still alive, still registered to vote and still living in Oxford, at an old people's home off the Witney Road.

Ironically, the home was called 'Mill House'.

Tomorrow, thought Iris. Tomorrow morning she would pay the old man a visit, see if he remembered Marcus Feeney's case. At almost ninety, there was of course a chance that he didn't remember anything at all. But a first-hand account was worth more than a thousand pieces of paper.

On her way back to the Randolph, Iris took a cab to Marcus's old block of flats on Cowley Road. It was starting to get dark now, although the warmth of the day persisted as she stood on the pavement and stared up at the seventh-floor windows. All the flats were the same, with full-length windows opening out onto tiny balconies, which were really little more than ledges, big enough for a small planter or windowbox and perhaps a single chair. Tenants, most of them students, streamed in and out of the building as Iris watched, some talking on mobiles, others laughing or calling out to friends, all of them caught up in the hubbub of daily life. The same noisy, youthful life that had ended for Marcus Feeney here, violently and, for his family at least, quite unexpectedly.

She wasn't sure what she was looking for exactly.

Background. Shadows. Clues.

Nothing came to her.

She returned to her hotel, ate a light supper of soup and salad, and fell into an overheated and fitful sleep.

From the outside, 'Mill House' was an ugly 1980s brick building, a vast sprawling bungalow that spread out in long tentacles from a central hub, like a rather rigid octopus. Once inside, however, visitors were immediately struck by the bright and cheerful atmosphere. For one thing, the whole place was flooded with light. Each 'tentacle' contained ten rooms or suites, all of which opened out directly onto the gardens. In the central hub, the body of the octopus, was a foyer complete with flowers, gaudy artwork, comfortable armchairs and a rocking horse, toy corner and (perhaps unwisely) upright piano, for the entertainment of visiting grandchildren. Also there was a large refectory-style dining room, with tables draped in red-and-blue gingham cloths, a residents' lounge, containing a large television, a games area and a help-yourself snack bar, and a small whitewashed non-denominational chapel, like the ones you get in airports only more welcoming.

If I ever wind up in an old people's home, I hope it's like this one, thought Iris, remembering the soul-crushing home her grandmother had been dispatched to in east London, with its grey walls, miserable staff and hallways smelling of cabbage and disinfectant. Clearly Rolf Carnaby was one of the lucky ones.

As it turned out, his luck extended beyond his family's choice of care home. The smiling nurse who showed Iris into Mr Carnaby's room introduced her to a man who, though physically frail, was clearly in full possession of his mental faculties, and seemed delighted by this unexpected chance to reminisce about his old professional life with an attractive young visitor.

'I'd like to tell you I remember all my cases, Miss Grey,' the old man said, offering Iris a Bourbon biscuit from the plate by his chair. 'But I was a coroner for twenty-two years. Eight in Harrogate and fourteen here in Oxford. That's rather a lot of corpses, I'm afraid.'

'This was a suicide,' said Iris, declining the biscuit but taking a sip from the cup of tea the nurse had poured for her. 'It was

1980. A young man named Marcus Feeney fell from the balcony of his flat.'

'Oh God.' Carnaby frowned. 'Terrible case that. Of course I remember it. He jumped at about nine at night onto a busy road. All sorts of people coming home from dinner or whatnot. Scores of wretches saw the body, or what was left of it. Can you imagine? That's a picture you're not going to get out of your head in a hurry. The local papers covered it at the time.'

'I read your report,' Iris said. 'You didn't express any doubts about the suicide verdict.'

'I didn't have any,' the old man said simply. 'The boy jumped. There was nothing to indicate otherwise.'

'But he'd been happy in the days leading up to his death,' said Iris. 'Multiple sources attest to that. And according to the police report, he'd been heard laughing and joking with a woman literally moments before he fell.'

The coroner sighed. 'That's very common, I'm afraid. When you've dealt with as many suicides as I have, you come to know the patterns. People are often incredibly upbeat, on a real high, in fact, right before they do the deed. According to the psychologists, it's to do with the fact that they've made the decision. They know they're going to do it, they know the pain's going to end, and a sort of euphoria sets in. Strange but true, I assure you.'

He took a contemplative bite of his own biscuit before continuing.

'I do remember the business about the woman. The police would be able to tell you more, but I think the chap's flatmate or neighbour or something believed there was somebody actually *in the flat* when it happened. Or right before it happened – I don't remember which. In any case, no one ever came forward, and there was nothing at the scene, no signs of struggle or anything, to indicate foul play.'

'Did the police have any insight as to motive? Why he did it? Might he have been having legal troubles?' Iris fished. 'I'm hoping to track down a lawyer I think Marcus spoke to in the weeks before he died.'

Rolf Carnaby smiled. 'You don't need a motive for suicide, Miss Grey. Only for murder. Suicides, by and large, are depressed. Now, Feeney certainly had antidepressants in his bloodstream. Which suggests that whatever happiness he was expressing prior to his death was probably a relatively new emotion for him. Probably brought on, as I say, by the decision he had made to end his life.'

Iris finished her tea. She liked Rolf Carnaby and she trusted him, but his confidence unnerved her. The ex-coroner seemed to view things in black and white, things that to Iris felt deeply grey.

'So you're sure, then? You're certain that Marcus Feeney killed himself?' she asked him.

The question made the old man chuckle.

'It was never my job to be sure about what *happened*, Miss Grey. I'm not God, after all. I wasn't there. All I needed to be sure about was my *verdict*. Because a coroner's verdict is based not on omnipotence but on evidence. In this case, the evidence overwhelmingly suggested suicide. Of that I am certain.'

Iris left the old people's home feeling strangely depressed. Carnaby had been sharp and informative and helpful and clear, but everything he'd told her reinforced a picture that felt wrong to her.

Somewhere, in the cracks between Dom's diary entries and the letter from Marcus and Rolf Carnaby's 'overwhelming evidence' of suicide, the truth had fallen.

With a sinking heart, Iris realised where she had to go to look for it.

CHAPTER TWENTY-EIGHT

St Aldate's Police Station was the exact architectural opposite of the city's coroner's office. A handsome Georgian building built in mellow Cotswold stone, it blended into the historic old city like cream into coffee: olde worlde, inviting and positively bursting with chocolate-box charm.

Inside, however, Iris was greeted by the kind of surly, unhelpful jobsworth of a desk sergeant she'd come to know and loathe in Hampshire.

'We don't keep records here, ma'am.'

'We can't comment on individual cases, ma'am.'

'Unless you're here to report a crime, ma'am, I must ask you to move aside.'

Two hours later, after a strong cup of coffee and a Caffè Nero chocolate panettone to keep her spirits up, followed by a brief research session online at her hotel, Iris found what she needed herself: both the name of the officer in charge of the Marcus Feeney investigation (Philip Steckenberger, an unusual one, thank God) and his address, or at least the last one he'd registered on the electoral roll.

The door at 29 Damson Street was answered by a white-haired

woman in curlers and slippers who seemed neither surprised by Iris's presence on her doorstep nor curious about it.

'If you want my Phil, he'll be where he always is on a Thursday. The golf club. At the bar, mind you. Don't go wasting your time looking for him on the green. I don't think he's swung a club up there in twenty years, the lazy sod.'

Despite this gloomy pronouncement, Mrs Steckenberger was happy enough to provide Iris with directions and also offered to take her name and number and any message she might want to leave 'just in case'.

The former DS Steckenberger was indeed at the golf club's bar, enjoying a gin and lemon with a small gaggle of like-minded pals, just as his wife predicted. And like his wife, he seemed to be cut from a far more cheerful and less misanthropic cloth than his modern-day counterpart down at St Aldate's.

'Now, you tell me why I *wouldn't* want to help a beautiful young lady who's come asking me questions? What are you drinking, my darling?'

Philip Steckenberger had been a relatively young man himself, just a few years older than Marcus Feeney, when he was charged with the grisly task of determining exactly what had gone on that awful night.

'Some kind of genius, he was, I remember. Doing his PhD at Oxford. And then – *boom* – it's all over, his skull smashed like an egg, all those brilliant brains spilling out onto the road like—' He stopped, registering Iris's horrified expression. 'Sorry, love. Maybe I shouldn't be so graphic. Did you know him?'

'No,' said Iris. 'I knew his brother.'

She explained, briefly, her connection to Graham Feeney, and how he'd confessed to murdering Dom Wetherby as an act of revenge, blaming him for Marcus's suicide.

'Feeney!' Phil gasped. 'Well, I'll be blowed. I never put two and two together. That it was his brother. My jumper's brother? Jesus Christ. Small bloody world, ain't it? What a dreadful story.'

Iris agreed that it was, accepting a vodka and tonic in the hopes that Phil would keep drinking and talking.

He did.

'There was no note or anything,' he told Iris. 'But he'd been on pills for over a year, according to his GP. I remember his doctor saying that Feeney suffered from "feelings of failure". A good-looking, charming young bloke with a first from bloody Oxford! I mean, I ask you. What does that make the rest of us?'

'I suppose it's all relative,' said Iris.

'It's these clever blokes,' the old policeman opined. 'All they do is worry. I wouldn't want a mind like that for a million quid.'

Iris asked him about the woman mentioned in the police report. 'Someone heard laughter coming from Marcus's flat, right before it happened. Can you tell me anything about that?'

Steckenberger rolled his eyes. 'Oh yeah. That was the hippy. Matthew something. He lived across the hall from Feeney. I say "hippy", but he was worse than that, really. He was a sad addict, and he wanted his fifteen minutes of fame, or at least attention. He was there when I arrived at the scene. Told me he heard Feeney with a woman, talking and laughing. He goes to take a shower, and when he comes out, people are screaming and Feeney's all over the . . . Well, you know,' he checked himself.

'You didn't believe him?' asked Iris.

'Well, he kept changing his story, didn't he? So first he said he *heard* a woman. And then later he comes by the station and says he *saw* someone leaving Feeney's flat, after. Running down the stairwell. He gave a detailed description. But why wouldn't he have mentioned that before? When I met him at the scene, he was all over the place, high as a kite and hysterical. Then again, it was pretty gruesome.'

'Did anyone else see this woman?'

'Nope.' Phil shook his head. 'This Matthew made the whole thing up.'

'I don't suppose you remember his description?'

'Not all of it.' The old man frowned, trying to dredge up long-buried memories. 'Young. Pretty. Blonde. Fancily dressed, you know. A date.' He shrugged. 'You'd have to read the report to get the full picture. But I wouldn't waste your time, love. There was no woman.'

Iris finished her drink and thanked him. 'If you remember anything else, I'll be at the Randolph till tomorrow night,' she said. 'My last name is Grey.'

'Sorry not to be of more help.' Phil helped her down from the bar stool, enjoying the admiring glances of his friends a few tables away. 'Ooh, I do remember one thing,' he said, as Iris headed for the door. 'Again, you should take everything Matthew said with a pinch of salt. But according to him, this mystery woman had a tattoo on her arm, like a bracelet. God knows why that stuck with me.'

Iris froze, searching her own memory banks. When she spoke, her voice sounded high and strange, even to herself. 'What was the design?'

Phil Steckenberger smiled, proud to have remembered such a tiny detail.

'Roses. It was roses and thorns.'

CHAPTER TWENTY-NINE

Ariadne Wetherby set the heavy basket of cut flowers down on the kitchen table next to a large Doulton jug she'd just filled with water. Slowly and methodically she began to separate and sort through the stems, trimming leaves here and there as she worked. It was so thoughtful of Harry to have brought her flowers, albeit in his usual embarrassed, half-apologetic way.

'You'd be doing me a favour by taking them,' the piano teacher had insisted, blushing, handing over the laden wicker trug on Mill House's doorstep. 'My garden's suddenly exploded with this hot weather. It's like *The Day of the Triffids* at my cottage.'

Ariadne was grateful for Harry's kindness and gratified by his attention, although she found his mealy-mouthed obsequiousness cringe-making at times. The truth was, a man like Harry Masters could never hope to fill the void left by Dom. Ariadne still felt Dom's absence every day. Her strong, masculine, alpha husband. More than she missed Dom himself, she missed being able to see *herself* through his eyes. It was Dom's strength that had made Ariadne feel soft and gentle, his masculinity that had transformed her into the ultimate woman. Mother. Wife. Helpmeet. Forgiver.

Ariadne had been saint to Dom's sinner. Without him she felt . . . not empty exactly. But different. *Less.*

Life would always be less, thanks to that snake Graham Feeney. May he rot in jail, and then in hell.

'Careful.'

Billy's voice startled her. She hadn't heard him come in.

'You'll crush them if you squeeze like that.' Cautiously, he removed a gladioli stem from her hand, cupping it tenderly in his own before sliding it into the jug. Then he turned to look at her with that queer mixture of detachment and an odd sort of forced affection that had become his 'resting face' since emerging from rehab. Certainly this 'new Billy' was a lot more pleasant to be around than the old version. And yet the old version had at least felt authentic. There was something disconcertingly artificial about the adult son who hovered about her now, Ariadne thought, all tact and deference. It was as if he'd been emotionally embalmed.

'Thank you, darling.' Ariadne smiled, resuming her own 'resting face' of calm femininity. 'I'm afraid I was miles away. What have you been up to this morning?'

'Oh, nothing much.' Billy arranged the flowers one by one in the jug as his mother handed them to him. 'Writing a little. Doing my breathing exercises. I'm going out this afternoon.' He avoided her eye as he threw in this last part. 'There's a job going at the bookshop in the village. I thought I might apply. I need . . . something to do.'

Ariadne looked at him, closing her hand over his.

'Oh, darling!' she said tenderly.

Hope, and something close to real happiness lit up in Billy's eyes.

'But are you sure that's wise?' said Ariadne, her expression unwavering. 'I mean, do you think you're ready?'

Like a switch flicking off, the hope died.

'Well, I . . . I . . .'

'I'd hate to see you set back, emotionally,' Ariadne continued, her eyes still fixed on Billy's, and the blank stare that had replaced his momentary happiness. 'After all your hard work.'

'You're right.' He exhaled, finishing the flowers and moving the jug to one side. 'It was a silly idea.'

Upstairs in one of the spare bedrooms, Jenna paced the room uncomfortably. It felt wrong and frightening, spying on her mother-in-law like this. If Marcus were to walk in and find her, watching Ariadne on the baby's video monitor, she could kiss her marriage goodbye. She felt a knot of tension like an iron ball in the pit of her stomach.

What the hell am I doing?

The irony was that it was Jenna who'd suggested the plan. After Iris called her from Oxford and told her her theory, Jenna had instantly thought of Oscar's baby monitor.

'I could set it up in the kitchen the night before, or early in the morning. It's not the kind of thing Ariadne would notice. There's a "record" button I can press from upstairs, on my iPad.'

It had all seemed so feasible on the telephone, so rational. But now that it was actually happening, it felt awful, deceitful and terrifying. Iris wasn't right about Ariadne. She couldn't be.

On the other hand, the interaction Jenna had just witnessed had turned her already-churning stomach. Poor Billy! Watching him reach out for a shred of encouragement and support, only to be slapped down so cruelly. And all the while that saintly smile fixed on Ariadne's face, as if everything she was saying were for his own good. Part of Jenna wished Marcus had been here to see that. But another part knew that, even if he had, he'd have found a way to interpret it differently.

Love sees what it wants to see.

Hatred, too.

'Iris! What a lovely surprise.'

Ariadne's voice jolted Jenna out of her reverie. She stopped pacing and sat down on the bed, the iPad propped on the pillow beside her. It was an effort to breathe. She watched Iris smile and hug Ariadne, accepting an offer of tea, the two women's grey forms like ghosts on the black-and-white monitor feed.

Let her be wrong, she found herself praying. *For Marcus's sake. For mine.*

Ariadne was pouring the tea through a strainer into two pretty bone-china cups. With Billy's jug of flowers beside them and sunshine streaming through the kitchen windows, it was an idyllic scene in the Mill kitchen. The perfect place to bid goodbye to Iris Grey and end another chapter in one of the most tumultuous times in her life.

'You're off on Friday, then? Are you packed?'

'Yes.' Iris sipped her tea. 'It's strange to think that this time next week I'll be up in the wilds of Scotland. But I'm ready for the change. It's time.'

'And your divorce? I don't like to ask, but is that all . . .?'

'It's done,' said Iris.

'So a fresh start in every way, then?' Ariadne asked, smiling.

Iris smiled back. 'That's right.'

It was as good a time as any. Ariadne was relaxed and unsuspecting. Casually extending a hand, Iris touched the scar on her wrist.

'When did you get the roses removed?'

Ariadne hesitated, a flicker of a frown crossing her face. 'How did you know about that?'

'Dom told me, at one of our early sittings,' said Iris. 'I couldn't imagine you as the tattooed type.'

Ariadne laughed. 'Oh, I wasn't really! It was a teenage thing, the summer after sixth form. A moment of madness. Dom always *hated* it. He thought tattoos on women were terribly common. I'm afraid he could be a dreadful snob when he wanted to be.'

Iris noticed the way her face still lit up talking about him.

'So you had it removed for him?'

Ariadne nodded. 'I think I did everything for him back in those days,' she sighed.

'Including killing Marcus Feeney?' Iris said it so quietly and calmly her words took a moment to register. When they did, Ariadne responded in kind, setting down her teacup softly and looking at Iris with an expression more curious than anything else.

'You didn't get rid of the tattoo for Dom,' Iris continued, filling the silence. 'You got rid of it because Marcus's neighbour saw you leave his flat. After you pushed him to his death.'

Ariadne said nothing. Instead, reaching for the teapot, she calmly refilled both her own cup and Iris's.

'You knew the tattoo was a distinguishing feature,' said Iris, 'so you erased it. The way you erased all the parts of your past you wanted to forget.'

Upstairs, Jenna watched, spellbound, her heart in her mouth.

'Of course, I can't prove any of this,' Iris said, sipping her own tea companionably.

'Of course not,' said Ariadne. They were the first words she'd spoken since Iris began, and she delivered them in a chillingly relaxed fashion. 'If you could, you'd have gone to the police, I imagine.'

'Quite,' said Iris. 'And of course, you don't have to talk to me about it. But I'm curious.'

'You really are, aren't you?' Ariadne sounded almost admiring. 'It's been quite astonishing, watching you squirrel away clue after clue following Dom's murder. I daresay you never believed the trail would end with Graham.'

'No,' said Iris. 'I didn't.'

'Nor did I,' said Ariadne truthfully. 'He fooled us all. When I think of the way Dom befriended him, took him under his wing. Bastard.' For the first time bitterness and a flash of rage forced their way through the smooth façade.

'Did Dom know?' Iris asked. 'About Marcus, and what really happened?'

Ariadne shook her head. 'Never.'

Upstairs, Jenna held her breath.

'My husband was an incredible man,' Ariadne told Iris. 'A wonderful man, in many ways. But he did suffer from a profound need to be liked. By everyone. Friends, family, colleagues, strangers. He could be selfish, of course, and he made mistakes. But Dom could never bear to be the bad guy. That was always somebody else's job.'

'Yours?' asked Iris.

'Sometimes. When it came to Marcus Feeney, yes. I had to step in. Feeney was threatening to ruin Dom. To destroy his reputation, to sue for God knows how much money. To take this house.' She quivered with anger at the memory. 'Dom wrote that book, Iris, make no mistake. It might have been "their" idea, but it was Dom who made it reality. Dom's work, his words, his voice. It was Dom who got the publishing deal, not Marcus bloody Feeney. And then when the whole thing took off, against everyone's expectations, including Dom's . . . well' – she sneered – 'Feeney decided he wanted his pound of flesh. And Dom was this close to letting him have it!' She held up a thumb and forefinger indignantly. 'Marcus was sending threatening letters to Dom about calling in lawyers. Dom tried to reason with him, but to no avail. He was too greedy, you see. Parasite. Anyway, I went up to Oxford myself to try to talk him out of it.'

'And did you?' Iris asked.

Ariadne laughed. 'You could say that! Oh, Feeney was happy enough to drop the lawsuit. He told me that over lunch at the Blue Boar. Just as long as we sold the Mill, wrote him a cheque for half and then kept on paying out. Indefinitely. He wanted fifty per cent – fifty! – of all Dom's future Grimshaw earnings. These would be books, stories that Dom hadn't even come up with yet, mind you! Marcus felt that Dom should do all the work, in return for which *he* would graciously agree to remain in the shadows – "unsung", as he put it, while Dom had all the glory – and that we should pay him through the nose for the rest of our lives.

'Of course, it was outrageous.' Ariadne's fury was building, lost in the moment and the memory. 'But I could see right away that there would be no reasoning with him. I knew from that moment that the only way out was to get rid of him.

'So yes, we came to an "agreement" on his terms. And I laughed and smiled and said that this had all been terribly silly and unnecessary, that of course Dom would be happy to cut him in, that he had always meant to, blah, blah, blah. Clearly I was quite convincing as Marcus invited me over to his flat that evening to celebrate. I went, naturally, dressed to the nines, as befitting a celebration of this magnitude. I even wore evening gloves, an elegant pair of kids that had belonged to my mother.' Ariadne cast a sidelong glance of triumph at Iris, delighted by her own cleverness. 'I remember Marcus complimented me on them.'

'No prints,' muttered Iris.

'Indeed.' Ariadne drained her tea. 'Marcus opened champagne. Before he got the glasses out, I asked to go onto the terrace. To look out over the spires of the city, where we'd all been so happy. The city where Grimshaw was conceived, where Dom and I met, and where Marcus dreamed of spending the rest of his life. You could say I made his dreams come true.' The spite in her voice was unmistakable.

Upstairs, glued to the screen, Jenna began to shake.

'I had my hand on his back and he was leaning forward,' Ariadne continued, 'pointing out some church or other, telling a story about Dom and one of the pranks they'd got up to together there. And I just . . . pushed.'

Extending a finger, she nudged the sugar bowl gently towards Iris.

'It was so easy. Instant. The wrought-iron barriers on those balconies were so low. He lost his balance and tipped over in an instant. I don't even remember him screaming. He was in the middle of a sentence and then – *poof* – gone!'

'So what did you do?' Iris asked, somehow managing to conceal her own feelings of horror. The conceit of the 'friendly chat' was what seemed to have enabled Ariadne to open up and tell the truth thus far. It was vital to maintain it.

'Nothing,' Ariadne said brightly. 'I left.'

'You just left?'

'Yes. I made my way out of the building by the fire stairs and back to my rooms on St Aldate's, where I packed, and caught the last train home to Hampshire. Of course, by then people were screaming and running all over the shop, commuters on their way home, students, tourists. It was easy to slip away in all the commotion. I do remember the neighbour seeing me, but I wasn't unduly worried. I was in the hallway, taking off my gloves and preparing to leave, when suddenly there he was, mooning around awkwardly. But I didn't think much of it. I knew I'd left no trace in the flat, and besides, he was one of those long-haired, greasy, drug-addict types that police never consider reliable.

'But even so, I decided to have my tattoo removed, just in case. Imagine you noting that, Iris. You *are* clever.'

Upstairs, Jenna kept watching.

'When I got home, I told Dom that when I got to Marcus Feeney's apartment, there were already police everywhere. A bystander told me what had happened – that he'd jumped. I told Dom I panicked and came straight home. After all, there was nothing we could do to help Marcus now, and it made no sense to have our names linked with the tragedy, or to dredge up private disputes over Grimshaw that didn't matter anymore.'

'And he believed you?' Iris leaned back in her chair, revolted by Ariadne's self-righteousness and utter lack of remorse, yet at the same time fascinated by it, and by the myriad contradictions that made up this woman, at once hypnotically calm and violently angry.

'Why wouldn't he? Dom was the master at seeing only what he wanted to see. Besides, he trusted me. I can be very convincing when I need to be, Iris.' A shadow fell over Ariadne's face suddenly. 'I daresay you think I'm a monster. But I was only protecting my family. I did what needed to be done.'

'You weren't protecting your family. You were protecting your wealth and Dom's reputation,' said Iris scathingly.

'Isn't that the same thing?' Ariadne shot back.

'You *murdered* a man so you could keep this house!'

'I silenced a blackmailer.' Ariadne's voice hardened. 'I loved this house. I still love it. It was the first real home I ever had, the first place I felt safe. I wasn't going to let Feeney destroy that. My own childhood—' She stopped and shook her head, trying to rid herself of painful memories like a dog shaking water droplets out of its pelt. 'My father made home an unsafe place for me.'

'Yet you invite him round for Christmas? Why would you do that, if he really did hurt you as a child?'

Ariadne gave Iris her best, most saintly smile. 'Because I've forgiven him, of course. I'm terribly good at forgiving.' She positively radiated benevolence. 'People say that about me and it's true. But what my father did . . . well, forgiveness or not, things like that leave a mark, don't they? The pain gets passed on.'

'You're talking about Billy,' Iris said softly.

'I couldn't love him.' Picking up a tea towel, Ariadne twisted it round and round between her fingers. For the first time since they'd started talking, she sounded guilty. 'I adored Marcus when he was born, but as soon as I saw Billy, it was as if all the fear and anger and pain came rushing back. I wanted to hurt him right from the beginning. I fought those urges, of course. I did try. To be fair, to be maternal, to see what other people saw in him. Dom, especially. But sometimes I . . . slipped.' She looked up briefly, but failed to meet Iris's eye.

Upstairs, in front of the screen, Jenna wept silently. For her own misjudgement of Billy but also for poor Marcus. She would have to show him this footage eventually. Or the police would. How would he survive, knowing that he'd missed every sign, that nothing – nothing – he believed about his family was really true? All these years Billy had been telling the truth. Ariadne *had* hurt him.

'I think Billy told Dom at one point,' Ariadne continued to Iris, 'but I convinced Dom he was making it up. I had to!' she said miserably. 'He might have left me if he knew the truth. I couldn't have survived that.'

Upstairs, Jenna checked the monitor screen, ensuring its red 'record' light was still flashing in the top right-hand corner.

'There are many things I regret in my life, believe me,' Ariadne said, standing up and holding out a hand for Iris's empty teacup. 'But killing that greedy, grasping bully Marcus Feeney isn't one of them. So . . .' She carried the dirty tea things over to the sink. 'Now you know.'

'Now I know,' repeated Iris.

'You do realise that I'll deny every word of this if you go to the police?' Ariadne said casually, not in anger but merely as a statement of fact.

'I do,' Iris acknowledged, getting to her feet and glancing just for a second at the baby-monitor camera perched on the top shelf of the kitchen dresser. Please God let Jenna have recorded all this. 'I suppose this is goodbye, then?'

Ariadne turned round, drying her hands on a tea towel before extending them to Iris. 'Yes, I suppose it is. You'll be on a train to Scotland soon. Well, take care, Iris Grey. And thank you, for uncovering the truth about Graham. He wouldn't be locked up if it weren't for you.'

And he wouldn't have killed Dom in the first place if it weren't for you! Iris thought, incredulous that even now Ariadne didn't seem to have made this connection. Graham had killed Dom because he blamed him for his brother's suicide. But there *was* no suicide! The only person responsible for Marcus's death was standing in front of Iris now, smiling beatifically, looking for all the world like a kind, artistic country widow, pottering harmlessly around her kitchen, content to live out her days in this beautiful, lonely, secret-crammed house.

'Goodbye, Ariadne.' Iris shook her hand, then allowed herself to be pulled in for a kiss on the cheek. Like Judas.

Ariadne turned away, back to the dishes. 'Goodbye, Iris'.

Upstairs, Jenna hit 'stop' and then 'save file'. The footage was long and took up several megabytes of memory. While she waited for the file to upload, a creak behind her made her jump out of her skin.

'Marcus!'

The door swung open. Marcus stood on the threshold, staring at her. He had the strangest detached look in his eyes. Suddenly Jenna felt afraid.

'How long have you been there?' she asked, her heart hammering.

'Long enough,' said Marcus.

He moved towards her, walking slowly. Instinctively Jenna shielded the screen, her precious evidence. There was a *ding*, followed by a written message, 'Upload complete'.

Marcus extended his arms and then rushed at her in a frantic lunging movement. Jenna panicked and let out a small, frightened shriek.

'Marcus, no!'

But instead of grabbing at the iPad or trying to hurt her, he collapsed into her arms, knees buckling, as his entire body gave way to deep, soul-racking sobs. Crumpling under the weight of him, not to mention her own relief, Jenna also sank to the floor. For a long time they remained there, holding each other.

At last, cried out for the moment at least, Marcus asked her, 'What will you do? Will you give it to the police?'

His voice was heavy with loss and despair. But there was also acceptance there. Resignation. Defeat.

'I have to,' Jenna said, as kindly as she was able. '*We* have to.'

'I know,' Marcus agreed numbly.

He turned to his wife and gazed at her across the chasm of distrust and unhappiness that had somehow grown up between them since Dom died, willing it to disappear. Jenna gazed longingly back.

For the last few months they'd both bravely papered over the cracks. Now, there could be no more dissembling. Marcus's 'perfect family' had never existed. Instead, like a bright, shiny apple riddled with maggots, the Wetherbys, once cut, had proved themselves rotten to the core. And Marcus's beloved mother was the most rotten and spoiled of them all.

Marcus still loved Jenna and he needed her now more than ever.

Yet at the same time he knew he could never forgive her for being right all along.

CHAPTER THIRTY

Two months later

Iris sat in the comfort of her first-class seat, admiring the hazy beauty of the Northumberland landscape as the intercity train from London King's Cross thundered towards Edinburgh. A few steps away, in the luggage compartment that divided first class from the rest of the train, two tattered suitcases carried all that Iris had chosen to bring with her from her old life, besides her painting paraphernalia and treasured doll's house, which she'd had sent on ahead to Pitfeldy Castle, where her next commission awaited her.

She'd persuaded Jock Mackinnon, the laird who'd hired her to produce a portrait of his new young American wife, to delay the job until late August. After Ariadne Wetherby's spectacular arrest in May for the murder of Marcus Feeney, Iris had found herself plunged once again into the eye of a media firestorm, at the same time that life began imploding at the Mill. Somebody had leaked the story of Iris and Jenna's baby-monitor ploy to record Ariadne's confession and the papers had gone wild for the idea of two women 'sleuths' solving a decades-old crime and in Jenna's case turning in a member of her own family.

Poor Jenna! It was bad enough for Iris, being rung up by idiotic twenty-year-olds from *Glamour* magazine and asked how it felt to be a 'real-life super-detective', as if Dom's death were some sort of comic-book story. But for Jenna, who'd had to stand by and watch helplessly while a devastated Marcus put the Mill up for sale, as civil lawsuits from the extended Feeney family began pouring in, demanding their slice of the Grimshaw pie, the last two months had been a living nightmare.

She and Marcus were staying together. 'We have to,' a desolate Jenna had told Iris. 'We have two children and now Lorcan as well. He's barely spoken since they took Ariadne away. God, I hope we did the right thing. Do you think we did?'

'Absolutely,' Iris had assured her. Despite all the awful consequences, for Lorcan and Marcus and for poor Billy, who'd suffered a complete nervous breakdown after Ariadne finally admitted mistreating him and was now once again in residential care, going to the police was the only thing they could do. 'Even Marcus felt that, remember?' Iris reminded Jenna. 'An innocent, brilliant young man was murdered and *we* knew his killer. We knew the truth. We had to act, Jenna.'

'I suppose so,' Jenna had sighed sadly. 'I just wish it weren't so hard.'

Iris wished so, too. Then again, unlike Jenna, Iris knew how much harder it was to know the truth and *not* act. How the consequences of that inaction could ripple out for ever, in never-ending circles of pain and guilt and loss.

As the train rattled on, Iris let her mind drift back . . .

1988. The little house on Bigley Street.

The day she learned the truth about her sister, Thea.

The day she learned what 'evil' truly meant.

The day that changed everything.

'Tickets, please! Any new tickets.' The conductor's nasal Scottish voice cut through the peaceful atmosphere of the carriage like wire through cheese. He'd already seen Iris's ticket, so he passed her by, nodding an acknowledgement as he bustled over to some recently boarded passengers a few seats along.

With an effort, Iris dragged her thoughts out of the painful past and back to the present. Unearthing the truth about Dom's murder, and Marcus Feeney's, had brought pain enough of its own. Most of that had been borne by the family, by Lorcan and Marcus and Billy, and poor Jenna. But Iris had suffered, too.

Facing the truth about Graham had not been easy.

Blindsided by the news of Ariadne's confession to his brother's murder, Graham had intensified his letter-writing campaign to Iris, begging her to come and visit him – just once – and to tell him exactly what she knew.

'You were there. I wasn't. Please, Iris. Give me this peace at least. I need the whole truth.'

Perhaps foolishly, Iris had given in, hiring a car for the day to drive out to the grim East Anglian prison very early one Sunday morning to ensure she made visiting hour.

It was, without doubt, one of the worst hours of her life. Graham looked old and gaunt, his eyes deeply sunken and his skin a sickly, cigarette-ash grey. Grasping Iris's hands across the scratched Formica table, he fired questions at her almost manically.

What had Ariadne said, exactly? Had she planned to murder his brother or acted on the spur of the moment? How had she covered her tracks? Why hadn't the police ever questioned her, or followed up on Matthew the neighbour's evidence? Was she remorseful?

And most of all, again and again and again, Graham asked Iris whether she thought Dom knew.

'Ariadne said he didn't. That she acted alone and never told Dom afterwards.'

'That can't be right, though, can it?' Graham shook his head and scratched compulsively at a patch of skin below his left ear, which Iris noticed he had worn red and raw. 'I mean, she *must* have said something! In all those years. Even if Dom didn't put her up to it in the first place, which let's face it, he probably *did*, there's no way she could keep a secret that big for that long without confiding in someone. They were in it together.' He nodded, desperately trying to convince himself that this assertion was a fact. 'They conspired together to keep the Grimshaw money and they killed Marcus to shut him up. Don't you think?'

'I don't know, Graham.' Iris shook her head sadly. She wanted to offer him the comfort he craved, to give the reassurance he was asking for. She wanted to be able to tell him that he hadn't drugged and drowned an innocent man for a crime he didn't commit. That Dom had been guilty, too, on some level, complicit in Marcus's death to a degree that made what Graham had done justified, at least in his own mind and by his own warped, eye-for-an-eye criteria. Because if he *wasn't* – if it was all Ariadne's doing – then that made Graham a monster. It meant that everything Graham had sacrificed – his freedom, his future, Iris – had been for nothing. But Iris couldn't give him that comfort.

The truth was, she would never know what Dom Wetherby had or had not known about Marcus Feeney's death. Maybe nothing. Maybe everything. Maybe he had his suspicions but was too afraid to dig deeper.

'If he hadn't cut Marcus out of Grimshaw in the first place . . .' Releasing Iris's hands, Graham rocked back and forth on his plastic chair. 'If he hadn't been so greedy, and fame-hungry, if he weren't such a goddamn liar, none of this would ever have happened. Marcus would still be alive. *Dom* would still be alive. I wouldn't be stuck in here. I wouldn't have lost you.'

Graham looked at Iris then with such haunted, desperate eyes, it was just unbearable. 'You killed a man, Graham,' Iris said quietly. 'You murdered him in cold blood. That's why you're here. For something *you* did, not for something Dom Wetherby did. Until you accept that, I don't think you'll find any peace.'

Graham shook his head vehemently. 'No. No, that's not right. You can't take it out of context. And besides, I don't want peace. I want justice. I want justice for Marcus!'

Iris stopped trying to reason with him after that. She listened for another twenty minutes to his self-justifying ramblings, the tortured questions coming in an endless, awful loop. And when the buzzer finally rang to signify the end of visiting time, she kissed him on the cheek and said goodbye, and bolted out of there and into the car park, sobbing for a full ten minutes before she had the strength to get into her car and drive away.

She was crying for Graham and the terrible thing he'd done that he couldn't face.

She was crying for the man she'd thought he was. The man he could have been, had life taken a different turn.

She was crying for the future she'd hoped they might have. And crying also with shame. Because for all the intimacy she thought they'd established, the truth was that Iris hadn't really known Graham Feeney at all. The Graham Iris had fallen in love with was an invention, a fictional character she'd moulded out of her own needs, her own loneliness, her own longing for a fresh start.

Talk about a cliché.

The trip to the prison was a low point. But it was in the past now, over and done, and in the days that followed a new lightness came over Iris, a sort of lifting, which had stayed with her and intensified as the job up north drew nearer. It was time, at last, to leave behind other people's secrets and sadnesses and to step into her own life, her own future.

Before her lay a blank page, and it was beautifully, dazzlingly white.

'Any refreshments, madam?'

A chirpy little man with a broad Geordie accent pushed a trolley laden with drinks and biscuits through Iris's mostly empty carriage. He had an old-fashioned face, Iris thought, like an old-time music-hall performer. A sort of cheeky-chappy, George Formby persona that would have been fascinating to try to paint.

That was something else she'd noticed since saying goodbye to Graham and leaving the Mill for good: her 'eye' was starting to come back to her, the desire and instinct to paint, and especially to paint people. To see faces the way that she used to. It felt good.

'No, thank you.' She smiled at the man. 'How long till Edinburgh?'

'Oh, not long now, ma'am,' he said cheerfully. 'A little over an hour.'

Iris turned back to the window, and the picturesque scene outside. It felt good to be travelling light, physically as well as metaphorically. Apart from the two cases she'd brought on the train, and the few things she'd sent ahead to the castle, all her other possessions – furniture, books and paintings from Clapham, mountains of clothes she never wore – were safely stashed in a storage facility somewhere outside the M25, until she figured out what she wanted to do with them.

'I'd sell the lot if I were you,' Iris's agent, Greta, had told her firmly. 'Storing clothes is the world's biggest waste of money – you'll never wear them again.'

For a woman whose life was art, Greta could be disturbingly practical sometimes. Iris thought wryly of her agent's own enormous London house, stuffed to the rafters with books, pictures and knickknacks of all kinds, but decided not to point this out. Because Greta was right, at least when it came to Iris. A grand decluttering of her life, mind and soul was exactly what she needed.

If travelling light was a novelty, so was travelling first class, and one Iris felt she could easily get used to. Ironically, after such a nightmare year, Iris now found herself if not 'rich' exactly, then at least much more comfortable than she'd ever expected to be, now that the divorce settlement had gone through. She already had a new commission lined up, as well as gallerists and collectors beating down her door, thanks to all the publicity surrounding Dom Wetherby's portrait.

'Your commission rate's doubled and your existing work is selling like hot cakes,' Greta told Iris excitedly. 'I know all your subjects can't come to grisly ends,' she added wryly, 'but it's awfully good for business when they do.'

Even Ian had made hay out of the Wetherby/Feeney tragedy. 'I've sold a play on spec based on the story. I wanted to call it *Betrayal*, but the publishers like *Murder at the Mill*,' he told Iris. 'Bloody philistines.'

Part of her wanted to protest about the moral murkiness of Ian profiting from Dom's death and his inside track on the story.

But then she remembered how Dom himself would have been the first to do the same and make a quick buck out of tragedy in the name of 'art' and she decided to let it go. Ian needed some good luck. They all did.

Iris looked at her watch. Soon they'd be in Edinburgh, where she'd have a forty-five-minute wait until her connecting train to Aberdeen. From there it should be another hour in a taxi out to Pitfeldy. Iris had agreed with Jock and Kathy Mackinnon to stay as their guest up at the castle for the first three days, getting to know Kathy, her soon-to-be subject, and the rest of the family before moving into a courtyard house in the heart of the village for the rest of her stay in Scotland. She had the particulars for Heather House in her handbag, dog-eared from weeks of thumbing by Iris, excited at the prospect of a new home, albeit a temporary one.

Looking again at the slightly kitsch tartan interiors, she felt a familiar tingle of anticipation. New places, new people, new paintings, new possibilities. Iris was ready for it all, already intrigued at what the next eight weeks might bring.

She smiled softly to herself as the train rattled on.

ACKNOWLEDGEMENTS

My heartfelt thanks are due to the entire team at Trapeze and Orion for their talent, dedication and hard work on this book. Especially my inspired editor, Sam Eades, without whom *Murder at the Mill* would never have been started, let alone finished; but also Debbie Holmes in design, Claire Keep in production, Jo Carpenter and the rest of the brilliant sales team, Claire Sivell in text design, Lauren Woosey in publicity, Jennifer Breslin in marketing, and the world's most thorough and on-the-ball copyeditor, Laura Collins. Thank you all so much. Every novel is a team effort, but *Murder at the Mill* was something totally new for me as a writer, and I could not have done it without so much support and energy from all of you.

My thanks also to my fabulous agents, Hellie Ogden in London (who introduced me to Sam and inspired me to try something new) and the lovely Luke Janklow in New York. Also to my family for putting up with me, especially my husband Robin and our children, Sefi, Zac, Theo and Summer. I love you all more than words can say.

Murder at the Mill is dedicated to my friend Fred Kahane in Los Angeles, a kind and wise man who has listened to me moan about this and countless other books over the last fifteen years, and never fails to put things in perspective. Fred, thank you for everything. I hope you enjoy the book.

T.B. 2017

AUTHOR Q & A WITH M.B. SHAW

Why did you decide to feature a portrait painter as your main character?

About ten years ago both my parents had their portraits painted by a hugely talented artist who lives close to them in Sussex. I was blown away by how accurately this woman was able to capture them, or at least a certain side to both of their characters. A few years later she did another portrait, of my sister and daughter together, that is truly haunting. I love it, and have it hanging in the room where I write in the Cotswolds. But many members of my family find it hard to look at, because it focuses on a certain sadness and wariness in both the girls. More than anything it was this picture that started me wondering about the process of painting a portrait, the things that you choose to include and the things you choose to leave out. To me at least there is something fascinating, and quasi-magical, about that process. I create and describe characters for a living, with words, but I can't draw or paint to save my life. So I loved the idea of a 'detective' figure who sees human emotion and motivation with an artist's eye. There is an innate mystery to that that I wanted to explore, and that's how Iris came to be.

How does the setting – The Mill and the surrounding Hampshire countryside – shape the story? What is your own relationship with that part of the world?

What I hope to do in the 'Portrait of a Murder' series is have Iris solve mysteries all over England, as her various commissions take her around the country. I live between Los Angeles and England (mostly in the Cotswolds) and am often hugely homesick whilst in America. So I enjoy writing about bucolic, rural England, partly as an outlet for my own longing. I also feel that the majority of detective series tend to be rooted in only one place or setting. I didn't want to write another 'gritty northern' or 'quaint Cotswold' series, but rather to try something with a bigger canvas, celebrating the whole of our incredibly diverse and beautiful country. I chose Hampshire as the setting for this first book having recently visited Winchester, and the countryside around it, for the first time. I was blown away by the beauty of the landscape, and especially struck by some of the grand Georgian houses I saw there. As for the Mill itself, my cottage in Gloucestershire is about a hundred yards away from a working water mill that I have always found both beautiful and oddly melancholy. So lots of different factors came together with the setting of this novel.

What drew you to the crime genre? Did you find the writing experience different from your previous novels? Were there more rules to follow?

Well that's a lot of questions! I have always loved reading crime, and recently re-read the Miss Marple short stories, which are so well plotted and brilliant, I suppose that might have been one of the triggers. In the last few years I have also started writing thrillers for Sidney Sheldon's literary estate, so I do have some background in crime writing of a sort. These Iris Grey books are quite different though, in that they combine the very plot-driven elements of my Sheldon books with the much more character-driven novels I have written in my own name over the years. As for 'rules to follow', I am sure there are plenty and I have probably broken them all! The only real rule for me is to keep your readers guessing and gripped, and to try to keep your characters true to themselves. I hope I have managed both in *Murder at the Mill*, but that will be for the readers to decide.

Cosy crime remains popular with readers. Why are we drawn back to these Golden Age mysteries?

I think there are many different reasons this genre is making a comeback, the most compelling one being that the best of these books are just such cracking stories. There is a reason that Agatha Christie has remained consistently popular for almost a hundred years. Beyond that, clearly there is also a nostalgic element, a very British longing for a (probably imaginary) idyllic past. *Downton Abbey* obviously tapped into this, and in many ways television has led the charge with series like *Foyle's War* or the adaptations of novels into series like *Vera* and *Shetland*. But this is clearly a growing trend amongst readers as well, looking for something escapist and bucolic, but also dark.

The book is filled with twists and turns. Did you know how the story was going to end? Or did it surprise you?

I knew! I am sure there are writers who can 'wing' this sort of novel, but for me getting the plotting right is a thoughtful and intricate process. I couldn't do it without a plan.

**You leave a few questions unanswered at the end of the novel.
Will Iris return?**
Oh yes, absolutely! She will return. She has discovered a new and
exciting sense of purpose in *Murder at the Mill*, and she is just
getting started. Watch this space. . .